The Fourth Haunting

F G COTTAM

2023

A Selection of Titles by F G COTTAM

Novels:

The Lucifer Chord

The Memory of Trees

Dark Echo

The Waiting Room

The Colony Series

The Colony

Dark Resurrection

Harvest of Scorn

The Fourth Haunting

Chapter 1

Pete Davidson was executive producing. Which meant that he was going to have to conjure from somewhere the finance for the project. Money men are in my experience prone to a higher than average level of scepticism. But with or without that, he had every right to ask any question of me he wanted to. And I knew that some of those questions would be bluntly uncompromising. That was okay. I had been the subject of low-level derision for the best part of three decades. It goes with the territory when you earn your living as what the tabloids insist on labelling a ghost hunter.

'You've narrowed it down?'

I said, 'Is that a budget-dependent question?'

He smiled tightly. 'I'd rather not send a location crew to Haiti on open-ended visas.'

'You'd prefer I find a location somewhere like Blackpool or Morecambe. A mini-van, a full petrol tank and a hand-held videocam.'

Another of his carefully rationed smiles. 'You know what I mean, Tom.'

'Well,' I said, 'Haiti is out. No voodoo. No blundering undead.'

'Relieved to hear it. So where?'

'Furthest afield, Chicago,' I said. 'Derelict Riverdale building with a history going back to when Capone and the mob ran the city. At various times a brothel, speakeasy and nightclub.'

Davidson twisted on his chair to look out of the window, though I don't think he was seeing the view. 'So far, so atmospheric,' he said.

'Seedy and dilapidated,' I said. 'And haunted.'

'Allegedly haunted,' Davidson said. 'What are the other locations?'

'A place at the foot of the Dolomites in Italy. Abandoned orphanage. Pretty remote, but no climbing involved.'

'Again, relieved to hear it.' He was thinking insurance.

'A house in rural Ireland. Strictly speaking, a cottage, out in the peaty wilderness of County Clare. And a place off the East Coast of Scotland. The Darkling Rock Lighthouse.'

Davidson still had his eyes on the window and his mind very much on the TV series we were discussing. He said, 'Why nowhere in London?'

'Because ghosts don't haunt to order?'

'London would be beneficial.'

Budget again. I said, 'You'd prefer the crew could get about using Oyster Cards?'

'London has history,' he said. 'Unrivalled, turbulent, bloody history. Cobbles, mansion blocks. Abandoned underground stations. Buildings that were once asylums housing the criminally insane. It's a ready-made film set and home to nine million people, a fair proportion of them eager to believe in at least some kind of afterlife.'

'London is a cliché, Pete, where this subject is concerned.'

'You're going for originality?'

'I'm going for authenticity,' I said.

'Chicago,' he said. 'In the Roaring Twenties.'

'Not expecting any roaring, Pete. Physical disturbance is likelier.'

'Seriously?'

'Seriously. The past, resonating uninvited into the present.'

He frowned. 'You really believe these four locations are haunted?'

'The evidence seems to me to be both consistent and compelling. It's an investigation and I'm at a very preliminary research stage of that investigation. But I think it's fair to say I'm hopeful.'

Pete Davidson opened a desk drawer and took something out and slid it onto the blotter in front of him. I recognised the voice-activated recording device he only ever used when he was being serious. He ran the flat of a hand a bit wearily over his face and then steepled his fingers in a show of apparent concentration. He stared for a moment at his little machine and then raised his eyes to meet mine.

'Chapter and verse,' he said. 'Though the verse doesn't need to rhyme.'

And I began the sales pitch I'd been rehearsing through a pretty much sleepless night.

****

Where did it begin? I can tell you when as well as where. I was 11 years old and living where I was born, in a town on the Lancashire coast. I had an uncle who worked in demolition; a magpie uncle who would gather lead and copper on the job to be sold as scrap. Who would go through the abandoned cupboards and left-behind wardrobes in venerable buildings shortly to be reduced to dusty hills of rubble. Owned a cocktail cabinet shaped like the prow of a ship. It was full of his hoarded booty. Pewter tankards, pairs of cufflinks, a silver hipflask, an onyx cigarette lighter, wristwatches in various states of disrepair. A powerfully built man who could swing a sledgehammer with impossible finesse.

One day, when I was 11 and my brother nine, our uncle turned up because his lorry was in the vicinity and he knew our mother would brew him a mug of tea. I opened the door to a familiar figure in lathe-caked blue overalls and steel toe-capped boots. The unusual detail was the top hat he wore that early afternoon, perched improbably on his head.

He took off the hat and held it out for me to examine. The label sewn against the purple silk lining told me that this item had originated in Liverpool. There was no date on the label, but I knew it was probably Victorian or Edwardian, because looking at photos of how people used to dress was just one aspect of my burgeoning interest in history. It was obviously old. The smell of it, as well as the style of the label, told me that. But it was very sleek and stiff. This particular topper hadn't seen a great deal of wear. Only a tiny smear of hair oil on the leather of the liner in a strip under the purple silk said that the hat had ever been worn.

'You can have it, Tom,' my uncle said, 'If you want it. Maybe one day you'll get to wear it at Aintree on Grand National Day. That's a few years off, but it's not a very practical item otherwise.'

I shared a bedroom then with my brother. I put the hat on top of the wardrobe we also shared, there at the foot of our beds, to the left of the bedroom door. And where over the coming days and weeks it seemed to insinuate its own character. Its still, silent blackness claimed the eye. It began to dominate my sightline as I lay dozing at night. I could see my brother too drawn to it in furtive glimpses. It brooded and impended and even seemed, unmoving and silent up there, to become somehow reproachful.

There came the day, or more probably the night, when both of us wanted to get rid of the hat. But by that time, neither of us dared touch it. We didn't even need discuss that shared, singular fear. That growing distaste for this antique item of dress. A glance between us and as much was mutually understood.

What happened next, still came as a shock, as things that are inexplicable tend to be – a harsh lesson in life for an 11-year-old to learn.

My brother was asleep. It was around nine o'clock on an early summer evening and dusk was creeping across the room in crepuscular shadows. In the limited light, the top hat had a matt, velvety dullness to it, a fusty absence of life and stubborn unfamiliarity disturbingly at odds with everything else my eyes could inventory. Posters of popstars. Model aeroplanes sharing shelf space with the Dinky replica of James Bond's Aston Martin car. A solitary, straight-backed, painted chair.

And then I heard it. A single bark of high, shrill, sardonic laughter pierced the silence and thrust a shard of ice through my heart. It was human, and adult, and scornful. And it came from within that small, confined space, where there was emphatically no one there to be responsible for it.

It awoke my startled brother. He shifted his back up into a sitting position, raising his counterpane like a barrier against his chest.

'We have to get rid of it, Tom.'

'I know. I know we do.'

I got it down. It was light and loathsome in the grip of my right hand. I knew that taking it to the end of our back garden and leaving it there as darkness gathered would be an ordeal. But I thought if we left it where it was, its dead owner might rouse and confront us in the small hours. That bark of laughter had been a good trick. But I thought it might just be a taster for something more substantial later in the night. Neither of us were imagining that brooding, impending mood the hat had imposed over the weeks in the refuge where we slept. And it was strengthening, wasn't it? It was making our bedroom a place of hazard and nightmare.

Towards the bottom of the garden, I lost my nerve. I threw the hat and it careened in darkness across night blackened grass on its brim, until coming to a stop against our garden hedge. In moonlight, it lay at a jaunty angle, as though being raised in greeting.

I fled back to the house with my hands clamped over my ears. To this day I don't think that would have hindered the sound of laughter had any repetition occurred, but it didn't, and the next morning I took the top hat in an empty coal sack to the local tip and climbed to the top of one of the long hills of household rubbish there and tossed it into one of the ravines made by old tin cans and torn mattresses and items of junked upholstery and television sets with smashed screens. Recycling was very much a remote thing of the future back then. And the tip up there on The Moss at the edge of Southport teemed with rats. But rats did not bother me. It was laughing phantoms, did that.

I tried to forget about the top hat. I tried to forget to the point that I never again mentioned it to my brother. Though to be honest, it had never exactly been what you would call a conversation piece. Neither of us had ever discussed it beyond expressing the urgent need for it to go.

Then one Saturday afternoon, I switched from World of Sport to BBC 2 and an ancient black and white film starring Fred Astaire. Probably directed by Busby Berkley, though I would not have known that then. Fred looked characteristically dapper in white tie and tails, his gifted feet in polished tap shoes performing seemingly effortless steps. But then he appeared in a scene wearing a top hat and rather than fall for his glittery, escapist charm, I sat aghast, shivering despite the July heat coming through sun-bathed windows into our living room.

Demolition then was a six day a week job and mobile phones had not yet been invented. My uncle didn't own a landline and neither, in those days, did we. So giving him time for a lie in, I went around to his house at 10am on Sunday. Where he was on the street outside doing something mechanical to his van that had covered his hands to his wrists in black and viscous oil. He had the bonnet up and was peering knowledgeably at the pipes and cylinders and electrical wiring of the engine. It seemed to me back then there wasn't anything he couldn't do.

'Uncle Terry?'

'Uncle Tom.'

He always called me that.

'What do you know about that top hat you gave me?'

He frowned and dipped his fingers into a tin of Swarfega balanced on the van's wing and rubbed them together and started to clean his hands with a rag.

'You've walked two miles on a Sunday morning to ask me that? My dog's got more sense.'

'Do you know anything about it?'

'Found it in a wardrobe in one of those big Victorian Houses on Weld Road. Council doesn't like to see them demolished, but this one had been derelict for twenty years. Half the slates missing, rotten roof joists, floorboards riddled with woodworm, damp in all but two or three of the rooms. Wonder the topper wasn't rotted, or at least mildewed, but that room was dry.'

'Who lived there?'

'Someone a bigwig in shipping in Liverpool. Miserable bugger apparently. Lived there alone. A recluse, like. The boss would likely know a bit more.'

'Can I come around tomorrow night?'

'I'll pop in to see you and your brother about six.'

He walked to the back of his van. I knew what was coming next. He took a bottle of Woodpecker Cider out of the van and unscrewed the stone stopper. He said, 'Wet your whistle with a mouthful of that for the walk back. Hot day already.'

My Uncle Terry. A man of few words, kind gestures and family jokes. I knew instinctively there had been no malice in his giving me the top hat. Events had just taken their own queer turn for a reason neither of us knew. I decided I wouldn't burden him with what had happened. I would tell nobody, never discuss its morbid detail with anyone. The cider was warm and sharp tasting, a refreshing couple of swigs welcomed by my parched throat. It made me feel quite light-headed on the familiar walk home. Which at the age I was, is not really all that surprising.

The route home took me along Cemetery Road, which explains itself, the cemetery large and spectacular, huge tombs and monuments and mausoleums from Victorian times, granite and veined marble weather-pitted, blemished by lichen and moss, celebrations of life – and death – carved out of reluctant stone.

I know words now I did not know, back then. But the feelings evoked by that great necropolis were usually no different from how they would be today. Names and dates etched and fading. Bible quotations and snatches of verse. Perished blooms on stems warping through the metal grilles of small vases. Quarried slabs canted to odd angles. The subsidence caused by marshy soil and the imperious weight it was never fit to anchor. Splendour and grief, slipping and lurching over time into folly and under it all the indifferent dead, rotting to dust in wormy boxes fashioned once from expensive wood with burnished brass handles for the coffin bearers to grasp.

Sometimes, more often than not, I'd cross the cemetery on a diagonal as a short-cut. It meant climbing a wall at the far end, with a long drop onto a grassy field on the other side of it. And I was agile enough for the jump. But on this occasion, something was different. I did not feel like being in such close proximity to death as to have to pick a route between the graves. Not even in daylight. Not even in the bright sunshine probably just then reaching its zenith. Even slightly giddy from the cider, I didn't at all fancy it. I could still hear the echo of that bark of night laughter, still shiver at its tone of scornful contempt. And its impossibility.

I opened our front door to my uncle just after six o'clock the following evening. I didn't wear a wristwatch back then, but my mother had our TV constantly switched on and the early evening news had just started. Uncle Terry's open face, with its pale blue eyes, wore an expression more complex than I could remember having seen on it before. Somewhere between embarrassment and guilt, I thought. A bit shameful. He would have been around thirty-seven years old and was not destined for a long life. But on this occasion, he looked childlike.

'Uncle Terry.'

'Evening, Uncle Tom.'

There were pubs out towards Ormskirk on a route very rural still, back then. They were proper country pubs. The term-child friendly had not yet been thought of. It was more a case of landlords being indifferent to your age if you were accompanied by an adult with the legal entitlement to buy their wares. I sat in the passenger seat of my uncle's battered Austin A40 as he drove, wordlessly. My thoughts were an anticipatory jumble. But I do remember thinking that whatever mechanical alchemy he'd performed the previous morning, it was working a treat. The engine had a throaty purr and when he pressed his foot on the accelerator, the car surged forward, rocking on its suspension, narrow tyres lightly adhered to the cooling tarmac.

He got us drinks and we took a table in the pub garden, scantly populated so early on a Monday evening. I sipped at my half of bitter. He cradled his pint of mild in the bludgeoning fist of his hand. The silence stretched out. My uncle studied the sky, so I did the same. An unsullied blue. Far fewer vapour trails back in those days.

Eventually, and quietly, he said, 'I've learned a bit about the original owner of the top hat I gave you. It's made me regret doing so, to be honest with you.'

'Go on.'

He looked at me, blinked slowly and then spoke again. 'Not everyone in the world is good. You're a bright lad, so that penny will have dropped with you by now.'

I nodded. Most of the bad pennies I had encountered had been on the screen, in films. But I knew what he meant.

He might have read my mind. He said, 'Real life isn't like the films, Tom.'

'I know that.'

'What I mean is, the baddies in real life don't always get what should be coming their way.'

'I've heard about police corruption on the news,' I said. 'They're doing a big investigation into the Flying Squad.'

He smiled. He said, 'It can be a lot more subtle than bribing a copper.'

'Meaning?'

My uncle hesitated. Then he said, 'The gentleman who owned the top hat was a shipping broker named Edward Swarbrick. He was the son of a shipping broker, someone born with a silver spoon in his mouth. He went to Merchant Taylor's School and then to Oxford University.'

I shrugged, 'Isn't that what rich people do?' I took a sip of bitter. I didn't really like the taste of bitter. It was what adults called an acquired taste and I had not yet acquired it.

'He was expelled from university in his first year. They call it being sent down. Some scandal that was hushed up and then he went to work for his dad and by the time he was forty he was very successful and bought that big Weld Road house we demolished not so long ago.'

'Where you found the top hat.'

'Aye, where I found Swarbrick's topper.'

'Go on.'

My uncle paused. Then he said, 'There were rumours Edward Swarbrick interfered with kids.'

'Little girls?'

'Little boys too. But rumours are not facts. And the police tend to regard the testimony of a child as unreliable. Especially when the finger is being pointed at someone of Swarbrick's stature.'

'He got away with it?'

'The police knew he was a recluse. And a cold fish. But they thought the stories swirling around him no more than malicious gossip stoked by envy.'

'Why would children tell lies about him?'

'Children might be egged on to do it by jealous parents. The feeling was it was the parents encouraging lies about a prosperous man whose only real crime was being a loner.'

Something ominous was coming. I could just tell it was, by my uncle's sombre tone and the expression in his eyes. Usually, they had this blue, amused sparkle. Like their owner could always see the bright side of life. Just then they had a dead aspect to them. There was a moment of silence, then, that was not really silence at all. Birds were singing loudly in the trees in a ragged chorus. I heard a high-pitched giggle, disembodied, from inside the pub's open door. The sound made by a young woman, tickled by something someone had just said to her. Normal background noises that in this strange interlude I was undergoing, did not seem normal at all.

'What happened, Uncle Terry?'

He sipped mild, black in his glass under its creamy white head, and let out a long breath. 'A child disappeared,' he said. 'Swarbrick got cocky, or he got careless, or maybe his luck ran out, picking the wrong little girl to take.'

'Go on.'

'She was the daughter of the headmaster of a local school. For once, there was a proper investigation. Two witnesses saw the victim on the sandhills at Birkdale Beach on the afternoon of her disappearance. She had got separated from the friends she'd gone there with. This in the summer holidays.'

'Birkdale Beach is close to Weld Road.'

More than that, Weld Road was the main approach to Birkdale Beach.

'And the witnesses saw a man that afternoon on the dunes. A distinctively dressed man with distinctive features. He answered Edward Swarbrick's description very closely. Under pressure from the headmaster, someone respected in the community, West Lancs Police hauled Swarbrick in for questioning.'

'And then?'

'My uncle grinned, mirthlessly. 'Swarbrick seems to have known the game was up. He was found hanged, from a coat hook, in a tall wardrobe in the master bedroom of his house. No note.'

I thought about this. 'Maybe he was murdered. The parents of some of his victims would have believed their children. The headmaster wouldn't have done it, with his daughter still missing. But someone might have. Did the little girl ever turn up?'

Uncle Terry shook his head. 'No, she didn't. And Edward Swarbrick's death was suicide. I hope a lonely and painful death, but he definitely killed himself.'

'How can you be sure?'

'He'd laid out his mourning apparel, as though he'd be attending his own funeral. A black suit and cravat, polished black boots with grey spats to button over them. A silver-topped mahogany walking stick. A silver-clasped black cloak, the short sort toffs used to wear attending concerts. And I suppose the better class of burial. Even the monocle he sometimes affected to wear. The clothing was folded into a neat pile, apparently, that bloody hat I gave you precisely placed on top of it all. Gruesome, Tom. I'm sorry.'

'You didn't know. How were you to know? When you gave it to me, the topper must just have seemed like a bit of fun.'

That bark of laughter. Because two boys had put his top hat in our bedroom? The thought shuddered through me.

'Something's happened, hasn't it?' My uncle said.

'No real harm done. I got rid of it, Uncle Terry. Took it to the tip.'

'Good.'

'Do you believe in ghosts?'

My uncle smiled, again without much mirth. 'Do you remember the Lodge?'

The Lodge had been a long, two-storey building on Boundary Road, where he lived. It had been a refuge for the homeless men of the town. Most of them were shell-shocked veterans of the Great War, invalided out gassed, or just unmanned by the artillery bombardments as they had cowered in trenches. They used to sit, many of them, sunning themselves on straight-backed chairs during the summer months, chatting quietly. Sometimes music would stir among these old soldiers from accordions or harmonicas. Marching songs and laments from the brief, glorious past that damned them.

My abiding recollection was of the prosthetic limbs, pewter coloured and punctiliously rivetted and buckled to stumps with leather straps where an arm or a leg ought to be. The Lodge was no more. But that kind of thing makes quite an impression on a six or seven-year -old. As did the smell; of elderly men not properly washed, attired in clothing they either couldn't afford, or didn't have the wit, to keep clean.

'I remember The Lodge,' I said to my uncle.

'And a few years ago, I was on the demo crew that razed the place to rubble. They left some souvenirs behind, Tom, I can tell you. If walls could talk, those there would have wept. So yes, I believe in ghosts.'

'So do I, now,' I said.

****

After my meeting with Pete Davidson concluded, I walked the short distance to the discreetly pricy Soho members' club to which I had forked out far too much money for a membership. I found an otherwise unoccupied booth and made some notes of my own, the old-fashioned way, with a rollerball pen and Moleskine notebook small enough to tuck into a jacket pocket.

He'd green-lit the Italian project, which I would shoot as a pilot. It was the prevailing way of the world, in these perennially uncertain times. Commitment had become the new C-word, far less acceptable than its earthy predecessor. If the derelict orphanage at the foot of the Dolomites worked out, he would commit to the following three episodes I'd proposed.

'Remember water-cooler conversation?' He had asked with a wink.

'Only as something that dates from the Jurassic Period,' I said.

'Social media, then. There'll always be ways to gain traction.'

'Nothing like word of mouth,' I said, trying to sound as though I shared his populist zeal. Which I didn't.

''I get you, Tom,' he said. 'You're one of those esoteric seekers after truth. But the real game has always been about bums on seats.'

'Ratings.'

'Always. The Baftas? They're the icing on the cake.'

Bums on seats. Icing on cake. Pete Davidson was prone to cliché. But you can't be fastidious about things like that when you're carrying a begging bowl. He'd sketched out four speculative second-series episodes to think about strategically if Series One successfully panned-out.

'What do you know about Anne Askew?'

I groaned inwardly. The Tower of London. 'Protestant martyr,' I said. 'Tortured so badly on the rack, she couldn't stand when they took her to Smithfield and the stake. She was chained to it seated in a chair and burned that way.'

'Abused religious fanatic meets hideous death. At twenty-three. Wouldn't she fit your resonance theory?'

'To my knowledge, no one has reported any sightings of the ghost of Anne Askew. Either in the Tower, or anywhere else.'

Davidson drummed his fingers on his blotter in a damped, restless tattoo. 'Anne was very easy one the eye, by all accounts. A Tudor babe. I'm thinking reconstruction.'

I thought, but didn't say, you're not thinking at all.

'And Alcatraz might be worth a shout, since you're going there anyway.'

'I'm going to Chicago, Pete, provisionally. A trip wholly dependent on how the pilot is received. Alcatraz is in San Francisco Bay.'

He shrugged. 'That's your creative weakness, Tom. You've never been able to think out of the box.'

I nodded, wondering how Pete had heard about Anne Askew. Maybe the burned Tudor babe had been the subject of a pub quiz question down his Crouch End local.

****

I thought I had finished with Edward Swarbrick after my pub garden conversation with my Uncle Terry. I also thought that Edward Swarbrick had finished with me. And that was the case, until the Spring, five years later, when I was revising for O-levels and manning an ice-cream kiosk on Southport's promenade, near the entrance to the pier, at weekends. I was 16 and had a hectic schedule, determined as I was to acquire the grades to do the A-levels that would make me the first person from my family to get into university.

I'd almost forgotten about Swarbrick's top hat. Teenagers are resilient and tend to lead eventful lives. Puberty derails you, or at least diverts you. Sex becomes a preoccupation. Normal sex, I mean; teen crushes often handicapped by crippling insecurity.

Conventional stuff. Not the nightmare stuff Edward Swarbrick inflicted upon the world.

It was raining and quiet in the kiosk on one grey and gusty Saturday and in those pre-internet, pre-smartphone days you took your entertainment where you could. So while the soft ice-cream maker slopped and churned and chilled its contents beside me, and the chest-freezer hummed to my rear, I leant with both elbows on the counter-top, pouring over the pages of our local newspaper, The strangely misspelled Southport Visiter.

One story in particular caught my eye. It was buried on an inside page, just before I got to the classified ads. It was about the financial woes endured by a local property developer facing a bankruptcy hearing at the next sitting of the County Court. He had invested heavily in building a luxury flat block on Weld Road in the upmarket district of Birkdale.

The block was handsome and modern looking, with its marble, Deco-style main entrance and slabbed granite façade and generously sized panes of tinted glass. Even in a heavily pixilated, smudged black and white newsprint picture, all that was apparent to see. As was the fact that the block occupied the site where the Swarbrick house had stood before the intervention of my uncle and his mates on a demolition crew.

I tended to avoid Weld Road. But after what I'd heard as an 11-year-old, I'd gone there to look at the flattened remnants of Swarbrick's neo-gothic pile; the mansion-sized dwelling reduced to strewn and splintered joists and lathe fragments and brick rubble and shattered terracotta tiles that had once shaped turrets pointing narrowly at the sky. I'd pedalled there on the bike I used for my paper round. I didn't even know why, really. There was only ruin to see and nothing at all to feel. But I'd gone there. And I'd lingered over my handlebars for a while and five years on, recognised the spot from what I could see in the newspaper photo of the buildings flanking the newly constructed block.

The developer facing bankruptcy, owned the property outright, the story said. He retained the freehold. The people who had bought there, were leaseholders. Except that he was having trouble with his leaseholders. Nobody wanted to live there. And of the few residents who had gone to live there, no one wanted to stay.

I didn't know what a leaseholder was. We lived in a council house and at 16, property ownership was a subject of which I was ignorant. But a couple of paragraphs in I got the gist. The leaseholders had bought their leases with a view to renting out to private tenants. Except that these private tenants would stay only a few weeks – in one case days – before cancelling their private tenancies and leaving. They did this despite the cost of lost deposits. And the leaseholders, without their rental income, were reneging on their mortgages.

'I can't afford to take private court action against mortgage defaulters,' the developer said. 'I spent the bulk of my working capital on a prestigious project, a luxury development. I'm between a rock and a hard place.'

I hadn't come across that expression before. It sounded American, incongruous in a story in the pages of the Visitor. But an unfamiliar expression wasn't the most interesting detail it included. The journalist had discovered that the developer had moved into the block himself, furnishing its penthouse for him and his girlfriend with the paint barely dry, only days after the building's topping-out ceremony. They had lasted there less than a month.

'Why didn't you stay? It's a well-appointed property in a prestigious location,' the writer of the story asked him.

'No comment,' was the developer's terse, two-word reply.

I had watched the weather forecast on Granada Reports the previous evening, which it paid to do if you were destined to spend your weekend manning an ice-cream kiosk. I'd known it was going to be both chilly and damp and therefore destined to be a quiet Saturday. So I didn't just have the Visitor as a distraction. I'd bought my History textbook and a notebook in which to write down anything worth remembering about the French Revolution or the repeal of the English Corn Laws. Just then, I thought the name of the Visiter journalist who had written that property story worth remembering. Because the story was by-lined. It was the work of a reporter named Joey Delancey.

I recorded the name in my notebook and then looked through the paper to see what else had taken Delancey's attention. It became obvious after a few minutes of study that Birkdale was his beat. He also featured on the arts page, where he had written a review of the new album by the Eagles. That didn't sound very local to me, but regional reporters had to be all-rounders and I suppose the paper was trying to be cosmopolitan. Anyway, he'd been impressed by the harmonies. I'd been impressed by his tenacious reporting of the story of the Weld Road developer's woes. He had even door-stepped a couple of past tenants. But they had been as tight-lipped as the developer was.

My ambition at 16 was to become a journalist myself. In truth it was more dream than ambition. My grandfather had been a boilermaker and my father a merchant seaman. There wasn't a man in my ancestry who hadn't worked with their hands. I aspired to be the first. I looked up from what I was doing then, because my first customers of the day were making a tentative approach. The wind had strengthened, scattering rain across the flagstones. A dad and what were obviously his two young sons. They looked miserable. How many days of their holiday would they have to write off to weather like this? I very much hoped only the one.

'Look at the plus-points,' I said to them, smiling. 'There's no queue. And it could always brighten up.'

The dad said something I didn't catch in a thick Scots accent and fished for change in a trouser pocket. His boys just stared at me.

The fact was, I'd brightened up. I had decided I would get in touch with Joey Delancey, Birkdale correspondent of the Southport Visiter. Unlikely authority on the West Coast American country rock scene. He might well tell a cheeky 16-year-old to stop wasting his valuable time and piss off. But I was intrigued enough by that developer's financial crisis, by the strange ill-fortune of the luxury flat block he'd built, to be willing to chance my arm.

****

I wasn't thinking about all that, in the here and now, decades on from it in Soho. I was thinking about the orphanage at the foot of the Dolomites a rational man had claimed was haunted.

To its considerable benefit, the story was both recent and not widely circulated. I'd got it from my brother, who'd got it directly from the person who'd endured the experience, a Spanish banker based in London who climbed recreationally to a standard that put him in the exceptional international clique of climbers to which my brother Andrew also belonged.

Both had been berthed at a Cairngorms hostel the previous summer. Both had been climbing solo. Over a cordial pint in a pub, they decided to team up to tackle a peak neither had attempted before and both considered too dangerously ambitious to try to conquer alone. They hadn't met prior to this but were aware of one another's reputations and accomplishments. It seemed a bit strange to me, when Andy told me about it, to agree to put your life in the hands of a stranger the following day over an early evening drink, but apparently, it's quite common practice among the climbing elite.

'If he'd have been an arsehole, I'd have heard about it,' Andy explained. 'And if he'd been careless, or taken unnecessary risks, given some of his more demanding climbs, he'd have been dead.'

Pragmatic people, climbers. Dreamers in terms of their lofty ambitions on the face, but unflustered, clear thinking and methodical, which is really a description of my brother's character. The last time I remembered seen him lose composure, was when something impossible stirred him from sleep in the bedroom we'd shared as children.

My brother and his climbing companion Phillipe Suarez reached the peak of their Cairngorm challenge at 2.30 in the afternoon. The language of climbing is understated, but this particular route was described in the handbooks as 'Difficult.' Straightforward enough when they were ascending in bright sunshine, impossible when a sudden and vicious storm set in when they were coming back down, no more than 30 carefully accomplished metres from the summit.

'We had no choice but to bivouac and sit it out,' Andy told me. And with wind shuddering the microfibre membrane of their shelter, with the gale making its titanium struts squeal, they crouched within, anchored to a four-foot ledge and discussed family and jobs and past climbs and future climbing aspirations, improvising a meal, sipping at soup heated on a camping stove, waiting for the let-up in the tempest that wouldn't come, until the moment came when they knew they would be spending the night up there. And that was when Phillipe told my brother about his strange experience of the previous week.

He got 28 days' holiday a year. A fortnight of that allowance was spent at a resort, usually a Mark Warner, with his wife and young sons. The other block was devoted to climbing.

Mostly, Phillipe climbed solo. In the Dolomites, on this particular day the week before meeting my brother, he'd climbed high to reach a demanding pitch, one the manuals described as, 'Severe.' He thought it probably the most testing experience of his climbing life, almost technically beyond him, a pitch that stretched him to the very limit of what he was capable. His descent afterwards a numb lurch of spent adrenaline during which he lost his bearings completely.

At the base of the mountain, he found himself in a densely wooded area, littered here and there with boulders he assumed the consequence of past avalanches, though there were no careening paths of crushed conifers to confirm this. He was exhausted and hungry and the light was beginning to go. Cloud was thickening above, the temperature had plunged and he thought he was experiencing the first symptoms of exposure; a condition that could prove fatal if he didn't find somewhere to shelter in which he could climb dry into his sleeping bag for the night.

Rain was starting to fall when he came across a building. It was unlit, clearly derelict, rectangular, two-storied and substantial. Something like half of its narrow and uniform windows on the ground-floor had broken panes, he thought likelier the consequence of severe weather than vandalism. The building existed in a state of isolation so profound, Phillipe thought it not just strange, but almost shocking. The only sounds were the strengthening rain hissing through pine needles and his own audible breathing as his mitted hands and booted feet numbed, a consequence of his now sluggish blood circulation. He had to get inside. That was now the most urgent of imperatives. Shelter was a simple matter by then, of life and death.

The man entrance to the building was huge; a studded oak door fit for a great church, even for a cathedral. And Phillipe's heart sank, because he knew a battering ram wouldn't breach that door and knew too that the windows were too narrow in their implacable stone berths for him to be able to squirm through any of them.

He studied the door. On the thick lintel above it there was carved the words of an inscription in Latin Phillipe's dull brain was far beyond trying to translate. Almost forlornly, he reached for the thick iron ring that would release the door's catch if it wasn't locked. Turning it seemed to require all his remaining strength, but turn it did, the mechanism obliging his effort with a loud and rusty sigh as the door creaked inward on what seemed to him like years, perhaps decades, of abandonment and secrecy.

He unclipped the torch from his belt. Of necessity, it was a light and tiny climbing tool, its beam intensely bright, but narrow, designed for the study of fissures and handholds, not large and lightless interiors. He saw he was in a high-ceilinged reception room. His torch beam lit on a desk and single chair, an ancient book he thought from its size might be a ledger, but he didn't linger because the place was of little use to him. Its bare stone floor would be too cold. Beyond that was a longer room, devoid of furniture, featureless but for a blackboard set into the far wall at about chest height. His torch beam picked out chalked words rendered a runic scrawl by time and neglect.

There were doors at the far end of the room, to the right and left of the blackboard. But Phillipe didn't examine them, because he'd noticed something his first sweep had missed. On the right side of the room, a ladder rose to a square aperture in the ceiling. Maybe the warmth of floorboards to sleep on, he thought through the blur of fatigue. If there's a God in heaven, maybe an ancient sofa or even a bed.

He had seen no religious symbolism, no font or alter or pew or wall-mounted crucifix. But he thought the building had about it the smell of prayer and piety; the stubborn and enduring atmosphere of faith.

Phillipe climbed the ladder. Its wooden rungs creaked under his feet with a noise that sounded shockingly loud. But they were firm as he steadily ascended, aware of the weakness of his legs and the weight on his back of the pack storing what he needed to survive. His torch illuminated the ladder, gripped between his teeth. Beckoning him, he was aware of the black maw of the opening above. Then he had reached it, and he saw two rows of the kind of cots soldiers slept on in war-films; iron frames, brass bedheads, and miraculously, each with a grey blanket folded neatly at its foot. Except that these beds were smaller than that, subtly diminished, big enough if you curled into a foetal ball, but child sized.

'An orphanage,' he heard himself say. 'This has to be an orphanage.'

He stepped from the ladder into the body of the room over a sturdy oak safety barrier about a metre high. He unbuckled his pack. He sniffed. There was a slight mustiness to the room that wasn't quite the smell of damp and he knew wouldn't bother him in the slightest. He drank thirstily from his water bottle, chewed down a protein bar and fumbled out and got into his sleeping bag still fully dressed. Warmth enveloped him in its narcotic embrace and a second after he switched off his torch, Phillipe Suarez was in the grip of a deep and blissful sleep.

The sound of a human voice awoke him. And something else, a mushy, repetitious slap that had a ragged sort of rhythm. He lay there for a moment trying to remember where he was. Then he did remember. He listened carefully, with an accelerating heart, to the sound coming from the classroom below. It was a woman's voice, broken by the occasional sob, and it seemed to be some kind of incantation, or prayer. She was speaking urgently between those wet, punctuating slaps and the only word he could make out coherently was her repeated use of the Italian, Fascisti.

Phillipe's eyes adjusted to the grey, enfeebled pre-dawn light now fingering its cautious way through the building's narrow windows. A floorboard creak would betray his presence. But he was rested now and a naturally agile man with the feline tread of someone born to climb. And he had taken off his boots before bedding down for the night.

Below, the words were increasing in volume as the beseeching seemed to be reaching some sort of crescendo. That damp, flailing hiss of noise was getting more and more frenetic. Phillipe shrugged himself out of his bag and stole across and took a cautious peak. He could see only what looked like a trickle of blood. But it was more than a trickle, wasn't it? It was more like a rivulet, black and creeping along the gaps between the flagstones down there in the miserly dawn light.

He eased around the barrier to where he judged he might have a view of the source of what he was seeing. And from this new vantage point he saw that it was human figure, a woman, wearing the white and grey habit and head-dress of a nun, kneeling on the bare floor. He watched. And he saw that as she prayed and sobbed, she flagellated herself with a leather whip, the strokes having stripped the fabric of her habit there and reduced the flesh beneath to a pulpy, bloody mess.

She paused, mid-word, mid-stroke, and Phillipe knew she must have sensed his presence there. She turned her head suddenly and framed by her white wimple, he saw her face.

Or he saw what there was of it to see.

She had no eyes, was featureless, except for the mouth, stretched open in a dark O of shock, or outrage. The mouth emitted a scream. And like someone walking into a dense fog, the kneeling figure vanished from view.

'What happened to the blood?' My brother Andy, ever one for the practicalities, put that question to Phillipe Suarez on the tiny ledge they shared the following week, close to a Cairngorm Peak, bivouacked in a raging tempest.

He shrugged, recollecting. 'Like her, it vanished. I cannot explain it. It seemed to evaporate.'

'Nothing remained?'

'Nothing physical remained.'

'What does that mean?'

'The anguish remained,' Phillipe said. 'I was left there alone, with the memory of pain. He hesitated. 'With the residue,' he said, 'of torment.'

My brother told me that story only at a family get-together at Christmas. Nevertheless, I'd had six months in which to research it. At the outset of that research, I had got Andy to cajole Phillipe Suarez into talking to me. That had not been too difficult because the two men had bonded in the Cairngorms and become firm friends since.

Phillipe would not go public on what he had seen, he said, because doing so would undermine his credibility in the banking world. Taking on hard climbing pitches was fine with his colleagues and contacts. Seeing self-lacerating phantoms, however, was beyond the bounds of what was acceptable.

'Did it seem fetishistic, a nun whipping herself?'

'No, it didn't. Not remotely. But that's another interpretation that would do me career damage.'

I took his point. I guaranteed him confidentiality. In return, he spoke to me at length. Subsequently, I was able to locate the building in which he'd spent the night, with the help of Google-Earth. There it sat, just as he'd said it did, in the Dolomite foothills, remote in a wilderness of thick pine forest and strewn boulders.

And only as an enigmatic rectangle of rust-coloured roof tiles on my computer screen.

My researcher was a woman named Daisy Chain. Her birth name was Polly, but her older male siblings thought calling her Daisy a hilarious joke and she was good-natured about it enough for it to stick into adulthood. Now, from my booth in my Soho club, with Freya Ridings' lovely contralto voice low on the sound system, I called her.

'Anything on the orphanage?'

'Congratulations.'

'What for?'

'I take it Davidson's green-lit the blue touch-paper.'

I smiled. Daisy Chain didn't work for me full-time. I had her on retainer. I did so because she was the best at her job I had ever come across. But she only mixed her metaphors in one-liners like that one when she was stalling.

'Nothing?'

'Sod-all. The Dolomite nun's prayer seems to have had some connection to fascism. Maybe the Mussolini regime had done something damaging to her order. Or maybe it was about to. There was a considerable amount of friction, and conflict, between

Church and State in Italy back then. As you probably know, since you took your degree in History.'

'Mussolini was only a child when I took my degree.'

But Daisy ignored the joke. She said, 'A lot of public and police records were destroyed. Some of the post-war reprisals were barbaric. If you'd committed some outrage against the Church or children or both, you'd want it kept quiet. There may have been no official account of what occurred in what we're still only assuming was an orphanage. If there was, it has certainly been destroyed.'

'How can you be sure?'

'Because, Tom, if it still existed, I'd have bloody well found it.'

I nodded. A stupid gesture in a phone conversation, but like a lot of stupid gestures, one to which I was prone.

Daisy said, 'I know I've aired this possibility before, and I don't wish to sound like the Harry Houdini of escape clauses. But Phillipe Suarez was physically exhausted and mentally traumatised by his Dolomites ordeal. He could even have been in shock. What if he just hallucinated the whole thing?'

'My brother thinks he was telling the truth.'

'Your brother isn't a detective,' Daisy said. 'Or a psychiatrist.'

'No, Daisy. Andy is a solicitor who specialises in fraud cases. Also, the most no-nonsense person I've ever met. Andy was someone wise to Santa Claus by the age of four. And he thinks, if anything, Phillipe played the episode down.'

'Then I'm sorry I haven't been of more use, Tom.'

'A brick wall?'

'At the end of a sodding cul-de-sac,' she said. 'A big fat zero on a one-way trip to nowhere.'

'There's one possibility we haven't explored,' I said. 'And I think you should have a look at it.'

There was a silence during which I could almost hear her thinking. 'Ah,' she said. 'Really?'

'It's an avenue,' I said.

'A full-blown bleeding boulevard if he'd been born in Rome, or Milan, or Verona. But he wasn't. He was born in Barcelona. Which makes what you're suggesting a fool's errand.'

'Not a wild goose chase?'

'Too obvious, Tom,' she said.

'It's what I pay you for, Daisy,' I said. 'Just do it.'

'Nike,' she said.

'They haven't used that slogan since the early nineties.'

'Older than I look,' she said.

I know, I know. Maybe it was the background music as I sat in that plush and softly lighted members-only booth, mellowing me out. But sometimes, you had to indulge her. She really was the best at what she did.

Chapter 2

We lived in Haig Avenue, opposite the main stand of Southport Football Club's ground, back then playing under manager Billy Bingham, having reached the heady heights of the old Third Division. Haig Avenue's public phone box was sited a hundred yards to the left as you faced the main entrance to the ground, outside Haig Avenue's modest parade of shops. I used it to call the Visiter's press section, rather than their classifieds, at 10 o'clock on Monday morning. Strictly speaking, I should have been at school. But O-level revision had given me and my fellow pupils some leeway in that regard. They had even stopped taking the register.

A bit to my own surprise, I got through to him.

'Delancey,' he said, 'Birkdale beat. And arts page.'

So, a bit of a wanker.

'I'd like to talk to you about your Weld Road property story. I'd like to do it face to face.'

I heard him scratch a match against the rough side of a matchbox to light a cigarette. I heard him inhale and then exhale slowly before he said anything else. Then he said, 'You in a position to add to that story?'

'Not exactly.'

There was a silence. I fumbled out another coin. Your ten pence didn't buy a lot of time on a public phone between 9am and 5pm on weekdays. Peak hours, they called it.

'How old are you?'

'I'm sixteen.'

'You're a kid. And a timewaster. On a Monday morning. Jesus.' And with that he hung up on me.

The Visiter's office building was mock-Tudor, double-fronted and sited on Tulketh Street in the town centre. Home to Millets and the herb shop, Tulketh Street wasn't exactly glamorous, and it never teemed with eager shoppers. So I felt quite isolated, standing there in the summer rain at 5 o'clock on Monday afternoon. I knew I should have been revising the lead-up to the American War of Independence, or the causes and effects of galloping inflation. Or the precise meaning of terminal moraine. But I wasn't. Instead, I was waiting to identify someone of whose appearance I was entirely ignorant. Someone who might be elsewhere, doing an on-the-spot piece, say, in Victoria Park, on the upcoming Southport Flower Show.

They filed out in ones and twos, mostly middle-aged men, quite formally attired, and women raising brollies or under those transparent plastic headscarves worn to protect hair-does from the rain. I was pretty sure the paper's Eagles album reviewer hadn't been a middle-aged man wearing a Dunn & Company suit. And he definitely wasn't a woman.

Suddenly, someone quite different appeared. Someone young, slender, tall; a belted trench-coat, a low-pulled trilby hat and a cigarette slouched to one side of his mouth. He looked like a crime reporter in Los Angeles or San Francisco in a Hollywood film set in about 1940. I couldn't really understand how you could get away with dressing like that in Southport in the late '70s without someone duffing you up. On the other hand, I was reasonably sure I was looking at Birkdale specialist and self-styled Eagles authority, Joey Delancey.

'Mister Delancey?'

He turned, tugged at the brim of his hat, plucked the cigarette from his lips and said, 'Who wants to know?'

'Nobody important,' I said. 'Just me.'

He pointed a finger and grinned. 'You're that time-wasting little twat who called me this morning. I recognise your voice.'

'Because you're good at your job.'

'Flattery won't get you anywhere,' he said. He made a show of lifting his raincoat sleeve and frowning at his wristwatch. 'I've places to go and people to see.'

'I'll buy you a pint.'

'Junior goes for the bribery ploy. The corrupt world we live in.'

But I could see he was curious. I'd read that curiosity in a journalist was an even bigger imperative than literacy. A much bigger imperative, it was the sub-editors who needed to be literate.

'We could go to the Ship,' I said. 'Or the Guest House?'

Delancey surveilled the street with a glance and shook his head. 'The Cheshire Lines,' he said. 'Safer.'

I nodded, with no idea of what he meant. The rough pubs in Southport's town centre were the Houghton and the Volunteer. But the Cheshire Lines was fine by me. Lax when it came to estimating the age of the customers it served. We all knew the soft pubs, me and my classmates. The Bedford, which was the nearest pub to the school. The Portland. The bar at the end of the pier, which would probably in those days have served a toddler up a drink.

I never fiddled the till, but my job in the ice-cream kiosk was reasonably well paid and beer was cheap back in those days in the North-West of England. And I was genuinely curious to know if there was more to the Weld Road story than Joey Delancey had been permitted by his editor to commit to print.

He looked to be in his early 20s. He drank Guinness, which should in theory have put a few pounds on his slender frame. He also chain-smoked, though, and I'd read that tobacco supressed your appetite. It was the reason models smoked, according to this article in Cosmopolitan I'd read in a dentist's waiting room. So maybe he didn't eat very much.

'What's this about?' he said. 'Level with me.'

'Have you heard of Edward Swarbrick?'

Delancey frowned at that. 'Sure,' he said. 'Guy owned a neo-gothic pile, on the site that property speculating loser Paul Wright turned into white elephant apartments. Unsavoury character. Under suspicion over a missing girl. Called it quits at the end of a rope.'

'You heard that from whom?'

Delancey grinned, showing yellow teeth, and sipped stout. 'Excellent grammar, kid,' he said. 'I'm almost impressed.'

So I repeated the question: 'You heard that from whom?'

'Know what the most important part of my job is?'

'No.'

'Contacts,' he said. 'You cultivate contacts. Your contacts book is your bible. Police contacts are the most important. They know secrets and do a job so high pressured that some of them find talking about it helps. Almost as good as therapy. Cheaper, too. But even those coppers that don't talk write things down. Second most important part of my job?'

'I've no idea.'

'Access. Access to files, minutes, logs, witness statements, diaries, ledgers, company accounts. You get my drift?'

'I'm starting to.'

Delancey stared at his now empty glass with a grief-stricken look. I took the hint and went to fetch him another drink. After I'd sat back down, he said, 'Swarbrick was never convicted. He was never even formally charged. But he was a bad man and the penny dropped late with the boys in blue that he'd been doing bad things for a very long time.'

'You've really researched this.'

'I've read the file, is all. It went further than the local constabulary. A little girl was snatched on the sandhills and two witnesses put a man answering Swarbrick's description in the frame. They seconded a guy from Liverpool CID, a Detective-Inspector with a shit-hot conviction rate. DI Billy Perry, a copper who'd cut it teeth busting the dockside razor gangs.'

'Blimey.'

'And for Perry, it was personal. He was in the same Orange Lodge as Swarbrick and the same Masonic Temple and resented the potentially catastrophic publicity a child killer could do to both. He'd have had Swarbrick swinging, if the old pervert hadn't beaten him to it. A job for Albert Pierrepoint.'

'Who's he?'

'Britain's last hangman. Stretched five-hundred necks, successfully. Lives right here in Southport. I've tried to get an interview but he's Yorkshireman by birth and so obviously wants paying.'

'Are Yorkshiremen mean?'

'They know the value of a pound note.'

I nodded.

Delancey said, 'The last hangings in England, two of them, were carried out on a single day in August of nineteen-sixty-four. Swarbrick topped himself early in sixty-two. Pathologist reckoned the body went undiscovered for about three weeks, but there wasn't much decomposition because the weather was cold and the house unheated. Born in January of nineteen-hundred. He was the same age as the century.'

I took a sip of my bitter. Keg bitter, Southport in the late '70s. Swarbrick's house had lain empty for close to two decades, before its demolition.

'What's your interest in this?' Delancey asked.

'Personal.'

He mashed out the stub of his spent cigarette in the ashtray on our table and immediately lit another. Through a cloud of tobacco smoke, he said, 'Not good enough.'

'It's going to sound stupid.'

'I'll let you know when you've finished, whether or not it sounds stupid. In the meantime, you have my full attention. Spill, Junior.'

So I told him. I didn't feel I really had a choice. Not if I wanted to get the detail I was sure he had and wasn't yet sharing with me.

He was silent when I'd finished. He picked at a hangnail and smoked, and his gaze had turned somehow furtive as he looked around the early evening pub he'd single-handedly made hazy.

'No comment?' I said, 'Isn't that out of character?'

He just shrugged.

'Your turn,' I said.

What does that mean, Junior?'

'It's a quid pro quo.'

'And you're too bright for your own fucking good. It's going to get you into trouble.'

'You didn't laugh at my top hat story.'

'Which I might have, as recently as a week ago,' he said.

'So your turn, Mister Delancey. Spill,' I said.

'Can't believe I'm telling this to a kid.'

'A bright kid, mind,' I said.

'Paul Wright had a girlfriend.'

'Past tense?'

'They were still together when I filed my Weld Road piece. The grapevine says they split up a couple of days ago.'

'The grapevine?'

'Jennifer Purdy is a looker. And she has the personality to match. She drinks some lunchtimes in the Arts Centre bar, which is close to her office. The bar manager is one of my contacts. And stop interrupting.'

'Sorry.'

'Jennifer runs her own estate agency. Probably how she and Paul met, parallel lines, a common interest, reasonable supposition, but not vitally important. Or not significant, anyway.'

Delancey took a sip of stout and continued. 'When Wright brushed me off with a no comment, I wasn't having it. Something had gone on at that flat complex and was still going on and whatever it was had forced him and his then girlfriend out before they'd got the cellophane wrapping off the sofas I'd bet money they bought from that swanky Swedish furniture shop in the Wayfarers Arcade.

'I had a hunch the first she'd know about me was when the piece appeared in the paper. Wright struck me as a close to his chest type. Not the sort of wheeler-dealer who pillow talks his business activities. Some guys compartmentalise their lives. He wouldn't have told her I was sniffing around about the ongoing problems with Weld Road. Meant I could come at her from a different angle.

'I cold-called her and introduced myself, telling her I was doing a lifestyle feature on prominent businesswomen in the region. Told her it might be syndicated and would be good exposure for her and I was right, she had never heard of me. And she was very amenable to an interview. Squeezed some expenses money out of my editor and booked a discreet table at a nice Lord Street restaurant for lunch. I can be charming, when I'm not sitting opposite a precociously nosy sixteen-year-old boy. Particularly in the company of a woman so easy on the eye. Charm did the preliminaries. Champagne cocktails did the rest. She ended up in tears.'

Joey Delancey paused, then, possibly for dramatic effect. Or he might just have been remembering a beautiful, stylishly dressed woman, dabbing away with the Kleenex at eyes running with mascara.

'She was vulnerable,' he said, 'no exaggeration to say traumatised. I think that's really what compelled her to tell me stuff I could never put in print and will always feel guilty about teasing out of her.

'They moved into that penthouse as excited as a couple of infatuated newlyweds. But every morning, in the small hours, they'd be awoken, sleep interrupted, by the same inexplicable sound.'

'What was it?' I asked, quietly.

'I said no interruptions, Junior.'

'I'm sorry.'

'So am I,' Delancey said. 'And so was she. What's your name?'

'Tom Carter.'

'The sound that awoke them, Tom, was a child crying. Inconsolably. When they both knew there was no child there to cry.'

****

The day after my audience with Pete Davidson was a Saturday. In other circumstances I would have been buoyant, energised by the Italian assignment, intrigued by its mystery, speculating on its possibilities, mapping a schedule in my head for the filming, thinking about a tentative outline script. Preparing a provisional budget for me and Davidson to debate, over an expansive lunch at Joe Allen's or the Ivy.

But on Saturday afternoon I was to drive the 60 miles to Hove to see my daughter. I hit the gym at 8am and stretched and pounded the treadmill and lifted heavy metal for an hour. None of which helped remotely. When I opened my locker to retrieve my clothes, I saw that Daisy Chain had messaged me to check my email. It meant she'd done the background on Phillipe Suarez already. So much is in the public domain these days that it's relatively easy for an experienced researcher to find out about people in considerable detail without doing anything unlawful. But it was still impressively quick. It meant she must have worked into the previous night.

Apart from junk, I had three unread emails. The first was an auto-send reminder about my visit to see my daughter Claire, as though it was something that might slip my mind. The second was from Pete Davidson. It was three voice-samples from actors he thought might be right to narrate the Italy pilot. And it was evidence of his enthusiasm for a project exciting him more that he'd been prepared to let on. The third email was from Daisy and I opened it.

When not risking his life on a regular basis mountain climbing, Phillipe Suarez is your run-of-the-mill city high-flier. He excelled at maths. the sciences and languages at school in Barcelona. He studied for his first degree at university in Madrid. He did a PHD at the London School of Economics before enrolling in the graduate entrance scheme at Lazard's Bank. Since then his progress has been steadily and lucratively upward. He lives with the wife he met at university in Madrid in a house they own outright in North London's Belsize Park. An educated guess says he bought that with a bonus. The couple have two young sons and holiday each year at Mark Warner resorts, usually on the Greek Islands. He has his Anderson and Shepherd suits hand-stitched in Savile Row. He wears a Rolex Explorer wristwatch, which might just be a City thing, but might be a nod to Sherpa Tenzing, who wore that model when he partnered Edmund Hilary on the first successful ascent of Everest. He drives a Tesla, so better green credentials than his wife Marianne, who drives a Range Rover Evoke.

Climbers can be very hedonistic people. Some of them are heavily into drink and drugs. They justify the excess as living all the way up, done for the same thrill-seeking reason they climb. But Suarez is a fitness freak, in the gym for an hour every day before work. He doesn't smoke and drinks only moderately. The climbing might seem paradoxical, or contradictory in a man so otherwise risk averse (he never gambles, for example). But his reputation among the climbing community is that of someone measured, methodical and highly skilled. He takes risks in the sense that they all do, but his professionalism minimises that.

He was raised a Catholic conventionally enough in a still Catholic country. He was never taught by nuns. Nuns seem to have played no significant part in his life and his faith must have lapsed, because neither he nor his wife are regular church goers. That said, they were married at a church service and both of their boys have been baptised. What I'm really saying here is that Phillipe hasn't had a bad or upsetting experience with organised religion. It can't be ruled out completely, but it seems extremely unlikely.

Mental health is monitored discreetly but quite seriously in the upper echelons of the banking world. People with the business success rate of Phillipe Suarez are assets far too valuable to neglect. In short, this is not a candidate for the funny farm.

I stopped reading for a moment. I'd thought Daisy too diplomatic to use a phrase like that communicating with me. I felt disappointed she wasn't. I rubbed the blear from my eyes and read on.

On balance, I'd say this particular subject is well-balanced. Your brother has known him for what? A year? Over that time, they must have shared some challenges together, some tight spots. As you intimated, Andy is a shrewd judge of character. Still a brick wall at the end of sodding cul-de-sac, Tom. Sorry I haven't been able to come up with more.

Driving rain slowed me on the route to Hove, but it made me concentrate on surface water and the blinding spray from lorry tyres, occupying at least the conscious part of my mind.

I found a place to park and then walked to Brighton and back along the seafront just to get salt air in my lungs and the tension of the drive out of my limbs. The sea itself was grey and turgid, the pennants limp and ragged on their flagpoles on a day defeated by the weather. I was in a part of the world that needed sunshine to come alive and craved the drink I wouldn't have because to do so would signal cowardice. Then I walked to what they euphemistically called the Retreat. *The funny farm,* in Daisy Chain's cruelly unthinking phrase.

I was on time for my appointment with Dr Pettifer. I would see Claire only after speaking to her. I was confident my daughter would wait. She was a captive audience.

Julia Pettifer was a good-looking woman who hid her attractiveness behind heavily framed spectacles and under a haircut unnecessarily severe. Maybe she just thought the styling gave her gravitas. I wondered, not for the first time, whether she had ever analysed herself. I thanked the orderly who had guided me to her office with a nod and closed the heavy door with a clunk of finality. Then I took the single chair in front of the doctor's desk. She hadn't risen to greet me, and she hadn't smiled either. We seemed to be beyond those sorts of courtesies.

'Any progress?'

'You can't reduce your daughter's condition to simplistic terms. It isn't helpful.'

'Oh? Isn't curing people what doctors do?'

'Only where possible,' she said.

I looked out of her window, which overlooked the promenade and then the sea, reminded that today, the view wasn't cooperating.

'What do you want, Mr Carter?'

'This is basically a place of incarceration. A sort of up-market prison. I want my daughter to be not serving a life sentence when she's committed no crime.'

'Your daughter isn't equipped for the world, Tom.'

That was a first. I couldn't remember her using my Christian name before.

'Not yet,' I said.

She opened the file in front of her. Claire's file. My daughter's loose-bound life. She said, 'Claire seems to be more responsive to the counselling sessions. There's marginally more dialogue than there was. And the hypnosis is encouraging. The self-harming has almost completely stopped.'

'She isn't exposed to sharp objects?'

'Of course she isn't. But we can't do much about the biting.'

I sniffed and made an effort to steady my voice, saying, 'Tell me about the hypnosis.'

'A chap who comes from Chichester once a week. Probably the most gifted practitioner I've seen. Gentle, patient, probing. And Claire is very suggestible.'

'That sounds optimistic.'

Pettifer tilted her head to one side. 'Your daughter's treatment record demonstrates that with her, it can be one step forward and two steps back. I'm cautiously optimistic.'

I stood. I said, 'I'd like to see her now.'

'Of course.'

In her room, Claire was at her desk, absorbed in completing a charcoal sketch. She was talented at drawing but couldn't be trusted with a pencil or pen without one-on-one supervision. She'd sketched a solitary winter tree, the bark skilfully rendered, the grass surrounding it rippling away as though stroked by wind.

'Beautiful,' I said.

She smiled. 'Me, or the drawing?'

'Both,' I said.

She stood and held out her arms and I hugged her. A touch day. Some were with my daughter. Others very much were not. It was something.

She was dressed in a white tailored shirt and a short black skirt, grey tights. Her entire wardrobe was monochrome. Not the regime here, her personal choice. She was deprived of the choices most 16-year-olds got. My life at 16 had been a riot of competing possibilities. Claire got to choose only whether or not to hug.

She looked at her window. High, barred. 'What's happening out there?'

I told her about the Dolomite orphanage and what Phillipe Suarez had experienced within its walls, leaving some of the choicer details out. The paranormal, the possibility of ghosts and magic, fascinated Claire. It was a common enough enthusiasm among girls of her age and didn't strike me as unhealthy. It was a distraction.

She talked about what she'd been reading and the films she'd recently been permitted to download onto her laptop. She talked about two new friends she had made in the conversation group regularly staged at the Retreat on three evenings of the week. She was learning macramé and had made the vase occupying pride of place at the centre of her bookshelf in pottery classes.

'I'll send you some flowers for it,' I said.

'That would be nice.'

There were charcoal sketches Blu-Tacked to her walls. Blu-Tack couldn't do the damage brass tacks could. Unless it was toxic if you swallowed it. There was a superb representation of Stonehenge under a full moon. A sailing ship that looked about to be overwhelmed by the huge waves of a storm. A curled cat sleeping before the flames of a cosy hearth. The ruins of a castle that looked medieval. A nun in an old-fashioned habit and wimple, her facial features hidden by a raised prayer book.

I gestured at this latter image. 'Where did that come from?'

But she only shrugged, giving it the briefest of glances. 'Where does anything come from?'

We were both silent for a moment.

Then she asked, 'How long have I been here?'

'Too long,' I said, carelessly.

And so the tears welled and the sobbing broke and I held her again, her breath hot and her eyes wet against my shirtfront. She held the cotton fabric covering my upper arms in the grip of her tight little fists. 'I want you to take me home, Daddy. I want you to look after me.'

It was what I wanted too, more than anything in the world. But it would have been weak and cruel, I knew, to tell her so. Not a kindness. Only the worst sort of self-indulgence. I kissed her cheek and stroked her hair and fought hard to retain composure. My daughter was grieving for the life she had never lived, and I could offer no shred of consolation. Sometimes the guilt I felt at that was almost overwhelming. But her predicament was far worse.

Claire had brightened by the time I left, just over an hour later. I did so without saying goodbye to Julia Pettifer. There was some dispute about whether my visits to that place did more harm than good, and it remained unresolved. Before leaving, at the reception desk, I asked would it be possible to meet the hypnotist treating my daughter. I knew hypnotherapy could work. I had used it myself to overcome a fear of public speaking that threatened at one time to cripple my own career.

They said it needed to be organised through the Retreat manager, who only worked weekdays. But that there should be no problem in principle in organising it. The man who came from Chichester was named James Balfour. I said I was more than happy to go to him. I was hoping for more than just the reassurance that he was well-meaning and properly qualified to do what he did. I was hoping for insights into my daughter's condition and a prognosis Julia Pettifer was altogether too tight-lipped and cautious to provide. Clutching at straws, maybe. But when straws are all you've got, believe me, you'll clutch at them.

The Retreat didn't come cheap. I'd had to re-mortgage my home to provide for Claire's ongoing care there. The sacrifice had not, though, been one I'd pondered on. There had been no decision to make. Nothing and no one on earth came anywhere near to meaning as much to me as she did.

I had left my phone in the car, quite deliberately. Distractions were never what I needed, on those visits to Hove. I'd missed a call from Daisy Chain, whose real name was Polly. Maybe she had found something out about Phillipe Suarez that altered the existing perspective on his orphanage account. She was punctilious, thorough. I returned the call.

'I'm so sorry, Tom. So very, very sorry. Utterly thoughtless of me to use that callous phrase. Can you forgive me?'

The funny farm.

Mental illness is better understood than it was. Recent events in all our lives have seen to that. People are generally much more sympathetic. And Daisy wasn't callous, not really, not generally.

'Forget it,' I said.

'You must have been offended.'

My phone pinged with an incoming text. In front of me, rain beaded on the windscreen, dribbling in haphazard paths down the exterior slope of the glass. I closed my eyes. I could not remember having felt more tired. Melancholy is an emotion we're ill-equipped to cope with. It exhausts us. Maybe it's a question of resilience. Certainly, it exhausted me.

'I've forgotten it, Daisy,' I said, hoping she could take comfort in the lie.

'Come over this evening, Tom. I'm having a barbeque. I'd like to invite you.'

'It's raining,' I said.

'Not here, it's not.'

She was in London, of course.

'I don't even know your address,' I said.

'It's in your phone. Texted just now. Swiss Cottage? Seven-ish?'

'Not really in the mood for partying,' I said.

'Just a couple of people, I promise.'

'Okay.'

Choices. Those of us who get to are privileged to make them. Apart from the occasional flat-white in the nearest branch of Costa after a meeting, I'd never really socialised with Daisy Chain. Probably to the detriment of my career, I'd become quite a solitary person after the divorce. People become an obstacle, but to what? It's very easy for privacy to slip into secrecy. What did I have to hide? Claire, I thought, I'm hiding Claire from the world. Out of embarrassment? Out of shame? I'd thought I was protecting her. But I might have been wrong about that.

Swiss Cottage. A transient part of the city, but far from cheap and a barbeque suggested outside space. A property there with a garden seemed unlikely on what a researcher would earn. But I knew nothing about Daisy's private life because she had never volunteered the information. And I had never bothered to ask.

****

Close-to-his-chest property developer Paul Wright had a caretaker or handyman at the Weld Road address he had endowed with the grand name, Kelmscott Court. Joey Delancey, who had a few contrived pretensions of his own, told me that before we parted outside the Cheshire Lines pub. I'd noticed that Joey's wristwatch was a Bulova Accutron, the space-age job kept accurate by a tuning fork. His cigarettes were Gauloises. And his trench coat looked very like the Burberry Humphrey Bogart wore in the film, *Casablanca*. Nothing to do with his provincial newspaper reporter's salary. Just a middle-class Southport boy living out his fantasies at his parents' expense. It was a common enough tendency in my affluent hometown.

The Kelmscott caretaker wasn't called that. He was called a concierge. And in theory he was a busy man, because the building to which he was concierge housed 24 flats over five spacious floors with lots of what was called exterior space. A handsome vestibule. Airy lobbies. A set of lifts. There was even a roof garden. Wright apparently insisted on calling the flats apartments and the lifts elevators. These pretensions hadn't made the place any more popular with actual or potential tenants, though. The concierge was probably twiddling his thumbs behind his large desk with its phone, telex machine and redundant intercom system.

He was a former lecturer from Southport Technical College who had taken early retirement. The Tech was where people went to take their A-Levels if they wanted to spend their lunchtimes in town and use the term 'guy' to describe other blokes without having the piss taken out of them. O-level grades permitting, I was content to stay on for my A-levels in the sixth form at Christ the King School. And the only Guy I referenced was the bloke named Fawkes who tried to blow up parliament and then shopped his fellow conspirators after some time spent being tortured.

'Concierge is named Tony Causley,' Delancey told me outside the Cheshire, sniffing the air. It felt like rain impended. I was quite surprised someone who smoked so much still had a sense of smell.

'Left the Tech under a bit of a cloud. Maybe had a breakdown.'

'Really?'

'More common than you might think in the teaching profession. Though why you'd think anything at your age, Junior, is something of a mystery. And whether he'd even speak to a jumped-up little twat…'

I said, 'Then why are you even telling me this?'

'Because the game is all about contacts,' he said. 'Because I have a hunch you might have something about you. And because in the context of what's happened since, I believe you about the top hat.'

'Really?'

He nodded as the first raindrops of the gathering shower pattered onto the shoulders of his trench coat. 'I had that lunch with Wright's ex-squeeze, Jennifer Purdy. A sassy, successful, independent woman. And she'd been half scared to death.'

I went to Birkdale, and Weld Road, and Kelmscott Court, at 11am the following morning. It was a nice, sunny day, the temperature in the mid-70s and the air freshened by an onshore breeze. The skies in Southport are huge and on days like this one was, spectacularly clear. And I had a stroke of luck, in that the fine weather had coaxed Tony Causley from behind his desk. At least, I assumed it was him. A man of about 60 was in the landscaped frontage of the block, next to its long gravel drive, clearing weeds from around a cluster of white-painted ornamental rocks, with a hoe.

I paused outside the exterior wall and said good morning. Despite Joey Delancey's constantly calling me a little shit/twat I wasn't exactly a midget. I was 5ft 10 at 16 and would grow another inch (and another shoe size) before I was finished. I could comfortably see over the wall and Tony Causley, if it was him, had a decent enough view of me.

People talk to strangers in the North-West of England. To this day, they do that, though I think it was an even more common and general custom when I was a boy. I nodded to the building at the hoe man's rear. 'What do they go for?'

He smiled. 'You couldn't do it on pocket money, son,' he said. 'And far more than you'd get for a paper-round.'

'I could win the pools. I could win Spot the Ball.'

'And pigs might fly.'

'I could be asking for my parents.'

He leant on the hoe. He said, 'I used to be a teacher. So I know you're not asking for your parents. And I suspect you should be at home, boning up for your O-levels.'

He was Tony Causley, then. I took a chance. I said, 'I've heard a rumour this place is haunted.'

His expression didn't alter. He had blue eyes, so pale, they looked diluted. He had a ragged swatch of grey hair that looked like it had never seen a comb. The stubble suggested he hadn't shaved since maybe the previous Friday. I'd expected a blazer, polished shoes, trousers with a knife-edge crease. He was wearing faded corduroys and a checked shirt with fraying cuffs. He wasn't even pretending the building had sitting tenants.

'Rumours aren't facts,' he said.

'I've an interest in the paranormal.'

That made him laugh. 'Big word,' he said, 'for a little boy.'

'I'm not that little.'

'And I'm not going to talk to you about this building. Not at all in my interest to do so. I can't get by on the pension my past life provided me with. I'm not going to gossip my way out of a job just to pass the time of day.'

He'd reminded me he'd been a teacher. I said, 'Don't you think curiosity is a worthwhile quality, in young people?'

He narrowed his pale eyes and then twisted to glance at the building behind him. Then he put down the hoe and walked towards me, to the other side of the wall that now stood between us. And when he spoke, he did so in a lowered voice. It was odd, almost as though he thought Kelmscott Court might be eavesdropping on what we said.

'You want to know what I think, so I'll tell you, my lad. But first you tell me: what's the biggest building on Weld Road?'

That was an easy one. The convent of Notre Dame, where the teaching order of nuns resided, was a huge, pale, gothic pile of a building. There was nothing remotely the same size to compete with it. Its façade stretched the length of an entire block.

'The convent,' I said.

'The convent indeed,' Causley said. 'But that wasn't always the case. Far from it.' He nodded in the direction of the seashore. 'There was a hotel, you see, before your time. The Birkdale Palace Hotel. A place so enormous it had its own railhead. Its own airstrip. And when it was being demolished, the workmen complained that its lifts were still running. Unmanned, without power.'

'You're saying the Birkdale Palace Hotel was haunted?'

'Spiritual conflict, my lad. The tension between good and evil. The Palace was a palace of corruption, a few hundred yards from a temple to piety. To use the terminology of my few friends in the Lancs Constabulary, Weld Road has a bit of form.'

At that, Tony Causley winked, and went back to his hoeing. But I knew what he said had stirred something in me. That in a sense, I would never see the world in quite the same way again.

Insanely, rather than go home and revise, I went straight to the Atkinson Public Library in the town centre. Birkdale had its own library and that was much nearer, but I needed a reference section. Films had taught me that swanky hotels could be decadent places. But evil? Really?

I discovered that the Birkdale Palace had been constructed in 1866 and demolished in 1969. All that remained of it was the old gatehouse. Now the Fisherman's Rest pub. Frank Sinatra had stayed there, probably I thought so he could play golf at the great links course, Royal Birkdale. The hotel had been the scene of a murder and at least three suicides. It had been opulent, but for all the amenities it boasted, never actually profitable. Guests stayed there in pampered luxury, but there were never truly enough of them. And after World War Two, it gained the unwanted reputation of being the most haunted hotel in Britain.

I learned all this wishing bitterly that the Birkdale Palace was on my O-level history syllabus. If it had been, I wouldn't have been completely wasting my time.

Then I came across an interesting photograph. It was in an elderly copy of the Visiter, at the centre of a broadsheet page of photos taken during the summer season in 1927, when Southport had been, the photos suggested, both a posh and fashionable resort. Three men in black tie, against a panelled wooden wall with carved reliefs, under a huge crystal chandelier. Each held a large cigar casually between the fingers of his right hand. The man on the left was corpulent and shorter than his companions. The other two shared the same spare, alert, limber build. All three wore smiles. None of the smiles struck me as at all pleasant. *The Birkdale Palace Hotel,* the caption read. *Guests Mr Klaus Fischer, Mr Harry Spalding and Mr Edward Swarbrick in attendance at the Jericho Ball.*

The man on the right of the picture had a strong jaw, chiselled cheekbones and his teeth were dazzlingly white in the camera flash. He wore his thick black hair combed straight back off his forehead and his square shoulders were broad.

You don't expect child molesters to be handsome men. Or stylish. Much less child killers. This was Swarbrick young, obviously, and not notably yet reclusive. But it wasn't hard to see how this prosperous society figure had got away with his furtive crimes for as long as he had. And he had friends, or at least, knew people with whom he had things in common. Status, the picture made plain, was one of those things. And secrets, I thought, studying their smiles again.

I remembered then that Swarbrick had been the same age as the century. In that photo, he was in his youthful prime. Confident, even arrogant, flashing that smile, flourishing that cigar.

He had died by his own hand early in 1962, a prominent Liverpool business figure who'd made his mark in the shipping industry before the dredgers finally lost their battle against the Mersey River's silt. There would be an obituary; probably in the Visiter archive, almost certainly in the archive of the Liverpool Daily Post. Both were broadsheets, both with daunting quantities of space to fill. So detailed obituaries. With a guilty sigh, I began to search for them.

****

I got to Daisy Chain's Swiss Cottage address at 7.15 in the evening. It was a tall, narrow, three-storey Georgian house I assumed she had inherited, unless she'd just married someone comfortably off. I didn't know. She was good at exposing the detail concerning other people's lives but pretty-tight lipped about her own. I rang the bell and after a pause she opened the door, bright-eyed with wine. Not drunk or even tipsy, I thought. Probably just the one disinhibiting glass.

She walked me through the house to a small walled garden flushed with early evening sunshine. Elderly orange brick, deck chairs on a manicured lawn. A small circular stove on a tripod giving off radiant heat from within its closed lid.

'Beer?' Daisy asked me. 'Wine?'

'I'm the first to arrive,' I said. 'How desperate is that?'

She smiled and blinked. 'I said a couple of people, Tom. We're the couple of people. Your hostess and my solitary guest. And no, this isn't a clumsy seduction bid.'

She had tied back her thick blonde hair and was wearing a knee length black dress made of some clingy fabric that emphasised her shape. I couldn't remember having seen her in lipstick before. The red was an attractive counterpoint to the green lustre of her eyes. Nothing about her struck me as clumsy. Nothing ever had.

'A beer would be lovely,' I said.

She went inside and came back out carrying her wine glass and a frosted bottle of Becks. We sat in opposing chairs. I said, 'This is very kind of you.'

She smiled and bit her lower lip. 'Like an act of charity?'

'More an unexpected treat.'

She raised her glass in a toast. 'To sunny days,' she said.

'I heard about a hypnotist today. He's very good, apparently. I'm going to meet him. I may even consult with him.'

Daisy hesitated. Then she said, 'Hypnotism doesn't work on depression, Tom.'

'And barbeques do?'

'They don't make it worse. And talking can help.'

'This is pretty left-field, Daisy.'

'It was studying Phillipe Suarez, a happy and contented man. And then it was all that talk about brick walls and cul-de-sacs. And I had a chat with your brother, Andy. There are people who care about you, Tom. About your wellbeing. You've been depressed since your divorce.'

'You spoke to my brother about my mental health?'

'I spoke to him about Phillipe, as you suggested I should. I got his number from you, remember? I didn't mention your state of mind. He brought it up.'

'I've been despondent since my divorce. Nobody celebrates failure. I'll be fine now I've got this four-parter to focus on. I'll bounce out of it.'

Daisy just frowned at that.

'Can I ask you're a personal question?'

'Don't ask, you don't get, Tom. Fire away.'

'How did you afford this place?'

'My inheritance,' she said. 'My late and rather wonderful father was a psychiatrist. Post-Freudian. Very eminent.'

'Ah.'

'Someone who understood the distinction between depression and despondency. Between grief for a dead marriage and a clinical condition. Denial is a route to nowhere. Acceptance the first step.'

I smiled at her. I had to. 'Who exactly is employing who, here?'

Those startling green eyes had narrowed. 'Pretty sure it's rooted in your childhood.'

And I had to laugh. 'Isn't everything?'

'How old were you, Tom, when you first experienced something paranormal?'

'I was eleven.'

'A vulnerable age,' she said.

'No argument there. And I need to ask you another personal question.'

She sipped wine. She said, 'I'm not above lying if the questioning gets too intrusive.'

'How on earth are you single?'

'You don't know I'm single.'

'I've got eyes, Daisy. I just walked through your house. Furnishings, pictures, décor, no hint of compromise. No male mementoes on that row of hooks in your hallway.'

'I might be gay.'

'But you aren't.'

'I'm just exceptionally choosy,' she said. 'What were you doing when we spoke on the phone earlier?'

So I told her about Hove and my visit to see Claire, whom she knew about only vaguely, unless she'd subjected me to the same scrutiny she had Phillipe Suarez. Which I doubted.

'That hypnotist you mentioned treating your daughter?'

'Yes. They say with some success.'

'Good news.'

What did I know about Daisy Chain? I knew that she drove an Audi TT. A convertible I'd been reminded of, seeing it parked at the kerb outside. I knew that she had a degree in Media Studies attained at the University of Kent. She spoke fluent French, having done some kind of post-graduate course in Paris. She played tennis recreationally and judging by her easy athleticism, I assumed to a high standard. I remembered that she enjoyed detective fiction, particularly the novels of P.D. James and Ian Rankin. No siblings. None at least that she had ever spoken about.

I didn't know, but now suspected, that she found men wanting because she measured them against her father. And she was kind. The earlier joke she'd made about an act of charity didn't cover it. She was compassionate, caring.

'I'm minded to make you sing for your supper,' she said.

'I don't know any songs, Daisy.'

'What happened to you at the age of eleven to make you believe in ghosts?'

I hadn't told anyone about that since telling Joey Delancey over a drink in the Cheshire Lines pub in Southport at the age of 16. Joey Delancey, who had died of throat cancer in 1989 without reaching the age of 40. He had risen by then to the status of a roving reporter on the nightly TV news programme, Granada Reports. Regional telly, but prestigious enough. He'd even been shortlisted for a couple of industry awards. That trench coat – increasingly shabby down the years – had become first a trademark and then almost a badge of office. It had been stolen once and they had launched a successful TV appeal for its anonymous return.

I didn't mind sharing the story of Edward Swarbrick's top hat with Daisy. I thought that telling the tale while sipping a second beer might give me the appetite for charred meat I didn't just then possess.

It hadn't occurred to me that I might be suffering from something more lingering than sadness related to something specific in my recent past. Sometimes it takes a stranger to point out the obvious. Daisy hadn't been quite a stranger, but in the last quarter of an hour she'd become a great deal more to me than she had before I'd sat down. She had always been clever, always outspoken, always attractive. Now though, she had a new significance. At Least, to me, she did. She was an acquaintance quite quickly evolving into a friend. So I talked, and she listened, never taking her eyes from mine until I'd finished.

'Edward Swarbrick's ghost inveigled its way into the bedroom of two small boys,' Daisy said, a moment after I'd stopped speaking. 'Which suggests what?'

'That he died unrepentant.'

'And that his carnal appetites didn't quite die with him.' She shivered, though it was still warm in her suntrap of a garden.

I told her about Paul Wright and Kelmscott Court and the story I read about it before meeting the reporter who wrote it, five years after parting company at Town Lane Tip with Edward Swarbrick's topper.

'You were tenacious even then,' she said.

'I had a cousin, Hangy Todd.'

'Hangy?'

'A nickname he got from wearing his big brother's hand-me-down jumpers on a skinny frame. The point about Hangy was that he had this knack with locks. Doors, windows, he could get through anything.'

'And you wanted him to get you into Kelmscott Court.'

I nodded. 'I did when I found out the concierge knocked off at 6pm. He was interesting, the concierge. Thought it was about more than just the site of Edward Swarbrick's demolished home. Thought there was tension in the area, an ongoing battle between good and bad. Have you heard of the Birkdale Palace Hotel?'

'Of course I have,' Daisy said. 'Glamour, debauchery, murder. Rumoured to be haunted. Marlene Dietrich was a guest there. Frank Sinatra. Though I don't imagine together.'

'Until it was razed in nineteen-sixty-nine, that was just down the road.'

Daisy was thinking about something.

'What?'

'You were a lot bolder at sixteen than you were at eleven.'

'Isn't everyone? Anyway, the ghost of a little girl, crying, isn't the spectre of a dead pervert, laughing at you.'

My second beer bottle stood empty at my feet. Daisy drained her glass and bent to pick it up and went to fetch us fresh drinks. She was a solicitous hostess, as well as excellent company. She made me realise how lonely I had allowed myself to become. Even Andy had noticed it.

She came back and handed me another Becks and I thanked her. She went over to the barbeque and lifted the lid and said, 'This is ready to go.'

'Good.' To my own surprise, I now felt really hungry.

'Is this the moment when you go all hunter-gatherer on me, Tom, and insist on taking over?'

'I think you're more than capable,' I said.

'I'll cook, you talk,' she said.

'Talk about what?'

'About what happened when Hangy Todd got you into Kelmscott Court.'

Chapter 3

Hangy Todd's bunch of keys were legendary. They had been steadily amassed, mostly at the car scrapyard on the Moss where he had worked at weekends since the age of 14. So they were mostly car door and ignition keys that made no vehicle in Southport safe should the urge strike Hangy to go for a joyride, which it frequently did. He'd become an expert driver still in his teens, able to shake off police pursuit, usually by aiming for the statistically fatal Formby bypass, where the historic death-toll made the boys in blue understandably cautious. Hangy wasn't cautious, he was a lunatic at the wheel. Even at the age when you're confident you'll live forever, I would never have risked the front passenger seat riding shotgun next to Hangy.

There were other keys on that iron ring of them. A lot of Yales. Enough brass to fetch a fair price if you weighed it all in on the scales at a scrapyard. But Hangy would never have done that. His keys were a gateway to adventure. He didn't steal stuff from the locations to which they gained him access. He just liked to have a look around. That struck me as a bit creepy, but fairly harmless compared to the havoc he could have wreaked. And he never sold on the cars he stole. He'd cruise in them and then put them back, around the corner from where he'd taken them, lighter on fuel, but undamaged. I imagine some of the owners were completely unsuspecting, assuming they'd parked up too absent-mindedly to remember exactly where.

I think Hangy's lightbulb moment came when he read about Harry Houdini one day in my copy of the weekly comic, Valiant. There was a story in it every week about the fictional Victorian escapologist Janus Stark, a rubber-boned character who could squeeze through any gap. But the real-life escapologist Harry Houdini used keys. Yes, he could dislocate his own shoulders to shrug free of the mailbags he was sometimes confined in, to twist himself free of straightjackets. But he secreted keys secured by wax to the soles of his feet, the article said. And to other locations it only hinted coyly at. Which sounded a bit unnecessary. That was how he shrugged off handcuffs and freed himself from safes and strong-boxes and prison cells.

'Keys are the key,' said Hangy, pondering over the Houdini piece, open-mouthed. Maybe with a bit of drool hanging from his lower lip. My cousin wasn't, in truth, much of a reader. But he came to be able to look at a lock and sort the relevant key, sometimes taking out the nailfile he carried for the purpose and calibrating the most minor of adjustments before slipping it snugly into the slot and turning it.

My week had begun with Monday's meeting with the picturesque Joey Delancey. Tuesday had delivered that elliptical exchange in Weld Road with Kelmscott Court concierge Tony Causley.

After that I'd gone to the town's reference library to learn what I could about the life of Edward Swarbrick. Though only the public aspect of that life had been available, the celebrated, successful, prosperous side. Neither of the obituaries I'd discovered there had mentioned the manner of his death. Neither had even hinted at his squalid, secret crimes. I was sure that Liverpool detective and stalwart of the Orange Lodge, Billy Perry, could have provided a choice epitaph. But he had not been invited to do so. Swarbrick had died respectable, if un-mourned.

Wednesday, Thursday and Friday I devoted to dogged and overdue O-level revision. Saturday, I spent busy in my ice-cream kiosk, the queue long and unrelenting because the day was hot and the sky a translucent blue. Until I locked it at six o'clock, cashed-up and then rode my bike out of town, along Scarisbrick New Road and out towards the Moss, where I knew my cousin Hangy would be working until around eight in the evening, when his boss, Indian Joe, would take him for a post-shift pint to the Richmond pub.

The thing that distinguished the lads who worked for Indian Joe – and to be fair, Indian Joe himself – was their almost surreal dirtiness. They subjected themselves to levels of used engine oil that were impossible to remove from the human body. No amount of Swarfega could get the stains out of their fingers and faces. The stuff was inked into them and their overalls were filthy, spectacular with what looked like decades of grime.

They were a cheerful bunch. Indian Joe was a genial and generous employer and there were perks. The cars, piled in precarious heaps, sometimes a dozen or so high, were packed with saleable spares. Anything without scrap value, Indian Joe would let the lads take. And there was a flourishing trade in second-hand speedos, tyres, brake pads, car seats, windscreens, lights.

Indian Joe gave me a wave of recognition. A couple of the lads shouted a hello. And Hangy ambled over to see what it was I wanted. Our mums were sisters, we were first-cousins, but very different characters. Hangy stole cars. I couldn't even drive one. But he seemed pleased to see me. His smile was a brilliant ivory flash against his oil ingrained complexion. He was manipulating a filthy rag between the fingers of both hands. Getting off the rough, they called it. As though they didn't have to worry about the smooth. This against the familiar soundtrack of a revving engine, metallic hammer blows, Bowie on a transistor radio somewhere belting out *Drive-in Saturday*.

'What's up, Clever Clogs?'

It was what my cousins called me when they weren't calling me Bookworm. Or Bamber, after University Challenge host Bamber Gascoigne. I didn't mind. I was used to it. I'd been called worse, recently, by Joey Delancey.

'I need you to get me into somewhere, Hangy.'

'Burglary?' He asked, frowning.

I shook my head. 'Trespass, at a push. Vacant flat block. There's a concierge, but not at night.'

'If there's a concierge, there'll likely be master keys to all the flats behind his desk. Numbered, on a wall panel. What do you need me for?'

'To get me through the back door and into the block itself.'

Hangy appeared to ponder on this, like someone struggling with the concept of a back door to anywhere as an obstacle to entry. I should add that he'd taught himself to pick locks, with tools of his own devising. Recently, he'd started repairing wristwatches for people. He did that for fun, rather than profit. He was just uncannily good at seeing mechanical things in three dimensions in his mind.

He said, 'Getting you in is straightforward. When you go to get out again, will you want to be able to lock the door behind you?'

'Ideally,' I said.

'Then I'll have to kit you out with a key. And I'll want it back, Bamber. You'd better not lose one of my keys.'

'I won't.'

'When do you want to do this?'

'Monday night. About eight o'clock.'

'Okay.'

Hangy hadn't asked me why I wanted access to an empty flat block. I was unsurprised by this. The truth was, he thought me studious to the point of being boring. We were family and he'd do me a favour, but he wasn't really interested in what I got up to in my spare time and on this occasion, I thought that to be to my advantage.

Monday brought rain, a persistent summer drizzle from a severely overcast sky that I thought gratefully would limit pedestrian traffic and thin the cars using Weld Road in the early evening to a trickle. Hangy turned up at five-to-eight by the level-crossing outside Birkdale Station and we walked the short distance to Kelmscott Court. He didn't speak, just whistled softly, tunefully enough, but a tune I didn't recognise. And then we were there, crunching softly over gravel to the rear entrance of the building, no one in sight, the windows unlit and blankly uniform.

Hangy took his huge bunch of keys from his raincoat pocket. He didn't look like Harry Houdini. He looked instead, for a moment as he studied, like the world's most industrious gaoler.

'Mortise,' he said, under his breath. 'And a piece of piss.'

He selected a key from the bunch and pried it off the ring and handed it to me. He didn't even try it in the lock. He just winked and tapped his nose with an oil-imbued finger and walked away. I looked at the key in my hand like someone who didn't know what to do with it. Then I fumbled it into the lock and twisted it and it turned smoothly and the door opened, stiff on its hinges with newness and lack of use.

I locked it behind me. I could feel thick carpet under my feet and waited for my eyes to adjust because I couldn't switch on a light. The building smelled of air freshener and furniture polish; Brasso and beeswax, mingling with something sweetly floral. It was completely quiet and entirely still. I walked past a row of lifts to the building's vestibule. Hangy had been right, there was a bank of keys behind the concierge's impressively large desk. I'd assumed the penthouse was number 24 but hadn't needed to assume anything. There was a key on a hook with the word 'Penthouse' etched in gold-leaf on the varnished wood right above it.

There were two passenger lifts and one that said 'Service.' Was taking the lift a risk? Probably not, but I decided anyway to take the stairs, located behind a door helpfully labelled 'Stairs.' Fortunately, the stairwell was situated against an exterior wall and lit by pools of natural light entering through a series of porthole windows. Eight short flights. I wasn't even breathing hard when I reached the plush corridor that led only to number 24.

It was still light. The windows in the block were abundant. It had been built, I thought probably at great cost, to give its residents an impression of expensive airiness. I turned the key in the lock and entered the biggest and most well-appointed of what Paul Wright insisted on terming its apartments.

It was still fully furnished. Wright and his then girlfriend Jennifer Purdy had fled leaving the place intact. They had got the cellophane off the two large leather-bound sofas in the huge sitting room, Joey Delancey had been wrong about that. But he had been right, I thought, that they came from that swish Swedish furniture shop in the Wayfarers Arcade on Lord Street. I'd seen the style before, occupying pride of place, behind their display window.

A Bang and Olufsen hi fi system. A huge lava-lamp. A tropical fish-tank that remained unfilled and unoccupied. In one corner, the biggest television set I had ever seen. An open drinks cabinet shaped like a globe of the earth and detailed in relief with continents and countries over its shiny exterior. I thought about putting the TV on, there was something heavy and impending about the silence in there, but I couldn't risk it and thought anyway that doing so would surely defeat the object.

To deflect myself from my own growing nervousness, I studied the framed pictures lining the walls. The frames themselves were made from thin wood painted gold. Their height and size were uniform, and they were all pencil studies of ships done almost with an architectural precision. They were bloodless and precise and sort of cold. I had the impression that Jennifer Purdy hadn't had much of a hand in the apartment's décor.

In the kitchen, the fridge was still well-stocked with food and fruit juices and exotically branded cans of beer and bottles of champagne. Wooden spice-racks and a gleaming hostess trolley. A wall mounted telephone and a jumbo-sized hourglass for timing breakfast eggs. Extravagantly fitted out in a manner now made melancholy. And they'd left the master bedroom in a rush, by the look of things, the bed unmade, a continental quilt tumbling from the mattress to the gleaming oiled wood of the bare bedroom floor. I'd seen similar patterns covering bedspreads in ads in the Sunday supplements of the papers I delivered. Liberty, or Laura Ashley. That at least, Jennifer's choice.

The light was growing incrementally dimmer. I told myself that the silence wasn't either as fraught or threatening as it seemed. It was just the consequence of sparse, rain-afflicted traffic on the road outside and expensive double-glazing. It was the very opposite of unnatural, I insisted to myself, though it didn't honestly feel that way.

Did I need to be in the bedroom? There was something voyeuristic about being in a bedroom occupied by two people who would never again share one. Something morbid, as well as invasive of their privacy. I could recline on one of the sofas in the sitting room, relax amid the fashionably vibrant scatter cushions nursing a large Scotch whisky in a crystal tumbler, fantasising that I belonged here, encouraging the brief illusion that this was all mine: this unwanted mausoleum of petrified movement and deathly hush.

I thought of Edward Swarbrick then. His turreted and spired domestic kingdom had squatted on this very spot. A baleful place of sin and squalor occupied by a man of unremitting evil. Triumphantly corrupt, I thought, remembering the previous Tuesday and that picture of him in his pomp with his cigar flourishing friends taken in 1927 at the Birkdale Palace Hotel. The Jericho Ball. What had that celebration signified? It was a strange name. Biblical. And over 50 years ago. Was there anyone left alive to know? It was certainly possible.

I smelled something then, something that wasn't the aroma of newness on freshly unwrapped furnishings. Something that wasn't the remembered bouquet of Jennifer Purdy's expensive Parisian scent. It was the sharp, sour secretion of fear. And it signalled to me that I wouldn't have to wait until the small hours to receive my visitation. The sobbing child was with me now, in this room, which had grown chill, and charged and thick with an almost tangible feeling of dread.

The open globe rocked and canted and then crashed to the floor, spirits bottles rolling drunkenly across thick shagpile until they stopped, and silence descended again. Until the abrupt sound of music spilling forth from the hi fi speakers. Something jazzy and frenetic and appallingly loud, the vinyl under the needle on the turntable sounding scratchy and uneven. I went to turn it off. But I saw that the system wasn't switched on. So I pulled the power plug from the wall and listened to the music fade. It did so only slowly and with what seemed like a churlish sort of reluctance.

'Help me,' I heard a child's voice say, no more than a foot away from where I stood. The sound was a whimper, full of wretchedness and loss. It was fully dark now, muted, shadowy. But there was no one else in the room with me. I felt the cold pinch then of a small hand on my bare forearm and heard the words again, fearful, desperate.

'Help me.'

The hand was clammy as well as cold. The pads of its small fingers brushed against my own skin, raising the hairs. Had her hand properly gripped my arm, encircled it, I think I would have screamed. But it hadn't, in life, possessed the span to do that. She must have been only a little thing. I heard the rustle of her dress and then a frond of unseen hair brushed against the back of my own hand and I dropped the key I'd been holding since my arrival there, the penthouse key, which I needed to lock the penthouse door behind me. Hangy's key was in the pocket of my jeans.

I did not stoop to retrieve the Yale I'd dropped. My body felt clumsy and unresponsive with terror. I lurched rather than walked to the door and out of it and along the corridor, stumbling and groping my way down the eight seemingly endless flights of stairs, in full darkness now, the stairwell's porthole windows black and sightless, to the ground floor and the rear exit.

I did lock that behind me, the gravel under my feet dull sounding, as though more remembered than heard, as something closer to human coordination returned to my tingling limbs. I had to remember to breathe. Breathing had by then become a conscious effort for lungs tightened in shock.

Terror wasn't all I felt. As I walked along Weld Road, it fought in me with shame and pity for ascendancy. What should I have done?

What could I have done? I was 16 and my world had careened into an unimaginable place.

I began to think about the chaos I had left behind; the delinquent hi fi system, the strewn spirits bottles and their toppled, globe shaped cabinet. The antic spirit desperate to avoid her own demise. It's pleading and panic. The key abandoned on the carpet and the open penthouse door. You didn't need to be Sherlock Holmes to know someone who shouldn't have, had been there, when daylight and sanity returned. You only needed to be a former teacher named Tony Causley, whose job it was now to keep Kelmscott Court in good order for its none-existent tenants.

I looked at my wristwatch, the last present ever given me by my womanising, itchy-footed, seafaring father before his final departure from my life. Though I did not yet know it had that special status then. It was half-past nine. I was approaching Birkdale village and a pub, the Old Ship, was lit like a galleon on the other side of the road. I had never risked the Old Ship, didn't know whether it was a soft, blind-eye pub or one of those with a shrewd landlord dubious about the age of his fresher-faced customers.

I decided to chance it. Going home just wasn't yet a realistic proposition, still reeling with the numbness of that impossible experience. I didn't have the composure for it. My mum would ask me where I'd been. Or my brother would. They were not conversations I could endure. They required a calmness I didn't just then nearly possess. So I crossed the road and went into the Old Ship and ordered a pint of bitter from a girl behind the bar who honestly looked no older than I did.

'See the rain's got worse,' she said, smiling. 'Strengthened, I mean.'

I realised I was soaked. I groped for change, finding only Hangy's key, at first, which I placed on the bar cloth in front of me. I counted out coins and paid for my drink, wondering whether my right hand would have the self-possession to pick up the glass without spilling most of its contents. So I picked it up between both hands and drank down half of it more or less in a single, shaking gulp.

The barmaid's eyes widened. 'Thirsty, as well as drenched,' she said.

I drank the rest of my drink standing there at the bar and ordered another, taking it to a table where I could sit alone. A song from the beginning of the decade was playing on the jukebox; Argent, *Hold Your Head Up*. Even though it was familiar to me, it was like hearing the tune for the first time.

The barmaid was blonde and pretty and friendly in a manner that on another night, would have flattered me. But on this singular evening, small talk was not really on the cards.

Small talk. I'd heard talk from a small person who wasn't actually there. Though she had been there in spirit, hadn't she, pleading, desperate. Abducted by the affluent and well-respected monster, Edward Swarbrick. Perished God knew how when still a child.

Tony Causley would know that his intruder had been me, of course. But I hadn't told him my name. And nothing had been taken or deliberately damaged. And my presence might not have even provoked the physical stuff. What if it had happened before? What if it was a regular occurrence at Kelmscott Court? Maybe damage limitation was in Tony Causley's job description. Patiently righting in the daylight hours, those bits and pieces in the penthouse wronged in the turbulent darkness of the night.

The barmaid came over to my table and sat down in the vacant chair opposite mine. The pub was quiet. Monday trade in an evening of heavy rain. She smiled. But the smile was quickly replaced by a frown.

'Landlord wants to see some I.D,' she said. 'Thinks you might be under-age.'

'I don't carry I.D,' I said. 'This is England. Nobody carries I.D.'

'Some people do.'

'I don't drive,' I said. 'I've never been abroad. No license, no passport. So where on earth would I get I.D?'

She grinned. 'Only pulling your leg,' she said. 'You're cute, sort of. Even with your hair plastered to your forehead, you're nice looking.'

'Thanks.'

'A bit pale, mind. Have you been given a fright?'

I said, 'Where do you go to school? You do go to school?'

'Greenbank,' she said.

'A posh girl, then.'

She pulled a face at that. I was only vaguely aware, still, of how pretty she was. But 16 is a resilient age and the beer was helping a bit. She said, 'You?'

'Christ the King.'

She raised her eyes to the ceiling. 'The opposite of posh.'

But that was no longer true. The Notre Dame Convent had ceased to function as a school a few years earlier and they'd been amalgamated with us. And some of those former Notre Dame girls were very posh indeed. Most of them had kept their brown uniforms as a sort of protest at being demoted from a grammar to a comprehensive. Our uniforms were black. The Convent of Notre Dame; that great grey gothic pile just down the road. The good against the bad in Tony Causley's weird equation.

The barmaid said, 'If I wanted to find you again, and it's a fairly big if, where would I be able to?'

'I work in an ice-cream kiosk at weekends,' I told her. 'It's on the Prom, just to the right as you face it of the entrance to the pier. And I knock off at six o'clock.'

She stood and went back to the bar, where a customer awaited. She left a cloud of her perfume behind to dissipate amid the beer fumes rising from the carpet and the stink of ashtrays and the thin drift of cigarette smoke. I recognised it because it was, just then, very popular among teenage girls. It was called Havoc, which seemed appropriate.

I'd put the big key Hangy had leant me on the tabletop when I sat down, to stop it digging into my groin in the front pocket of my jeans. It sat next to a big blue plastic ashtray with, *A Double-Diamond Works Wonders* etched in gold italics on its burn scarred rim. But it looked isolated there, antique, almost, tarnished by time and pitted with age. The key had the look about it of an untold story. Except I had learned part of the story, and it had not been at all a happy one.

The key would have to be returned. I certainly had no further use for it. My investigation into the dark life and sordid times of Edward Swarbrick had reached its fearful, incomplete conclusion. Bamber the amateur ghost-hunter was going to concentrate on revision; on O-levels, the necessary route to a future no one in my family had ever experienced before.

I still felt shame and pity, almost overwhelmed with sorrow for the fate of that little girl all those years ago, for her bereft parents and the way her killer had cheated justice. But my life had to return to normal. Physically at least, I was unscathed. And before I left the pub, I would ask the pretty barmaid her name, fairly certain she was the landlord's daughter filling in, rather than a paid employee. Fairly certain she was no older than I was.

Eyes on the key, my thoughts turned to Hangy Todd and his mates and Indian Joe at the scrapyard. Their endless tinkering and hauling and towing and jokey remarks. Their careful hoarding of used components they could clean up and refurbish and sell. Their clocked milometers and recharged batteries and sprayed panels and repaired windscreens and the oily summer odour of their overalls and skin. That was not my normality, but I envied it. Maybe I did so undergoing a kind of premonition about what my own future held; a sort of nostalgia for something that hadn't yet passed, I would despite that never be a part of.

Her name was Samantha. Sam for short, though I wouldn't ever call her that. And she was 16 too.

A resilient age, like I've already said. I walked home through the still teeming rain, listening to it gurgle along the gutters and into drains, as drenched by the time I reached Haig Avenue as though I'd immersed myself deliberately in a lake. Those two pints of beer wallowed a bit in my stomach. My shoes, Kickers, squelched with every footstep. But the streets were well-lit and I lived a good three miles away from Weld Road and Kelmscott Court and felt more secure for the distance.

Resilient, but not deluded. I didn't try to rationalise the experience I had earlier endured. That wasn't possible. And I didn't try either to deny to myself it had occurred. It had exhausted me. My mind wasn't up to speculative thought. I got home at a quarter to eleven at night, barely with the strength to climb the stairs and peel off my clothes and put them in the laundry hamper in the bathroom and pee and then climb into bed. Andy was already asleep.

I dreamed of waking the following morning. It was a very realistic dream. Andy snoring blithely on, early light slanting gauzily through the net curtain of our little window, the yeast of last night's beer on teeth I hadn't had the stamina the previous night to brush. And Edward Swarbrick's top hat, squatting with its sealskin sheen on top of the wardrobe, solicitously returned to us.

I think the dream might have shocked me into actually waking. And looking. And feeling a flood of relief that in the conscious world at least, there was no sign of Swarbrick's topper.

****

The orphanage at the foot of the Italian Dolomites was the first of my allegedly haunted locations because of its exclusivity. I had heard about it from a first-hand account given only to my rock-climbing brother. Neither I nor Daisy had been able to find anything about the spectral nun, or any other odd goings on, in the public domain. That gave the story a degree of originality that made investigating it the priority.

The lighthouse on the East Coast of Scotland was known about. It had been there for 150 years and manned until 1974, when its lamp had been converted to an automatic mechanism. The last senior lighthouse keeper had taken this decision a lot worse than his two subordinates. He had drunk himself penniless and then begged the bleak and solitary route, homeless, to drinking himself eventually to death.

Ged Ball had been 48 in 1974 and his redundancy package, for the period, had been reasonably generous. But it had been hard for a man of almost 50 to retrain to find other work after following such a singular occupation since signing on for his apprenticeship at the age of 14. And almost impossible to find a job that would enable him to stay in his remote and beloved location.

He grew increasingly bitter about his treatment as his money drained away. Bitter too about the principle of automation, which he said had destroyed his career and with it, his way of life.

Ball's liver finally surrendered to the whisky he drank in 2000, when he was aged 74. And it was only after his death that the beam from the lighthouse sometimes, inexplicably, started to falter and blink. In the two decades since Ball's death, four ships had foundered as a direct consequence of this mechanical failure. Eventually a pattern was noticed. The failures occurred in September, either on or very adjacent to the day Ball descended the steps to the base of his cherished beacon and handed over his keys for the last time.

There is such a thing as coincidence. And sophisticated electronic systems are never completely infallible. But rumour persisted and grew and then something happened that made the region's papers and became a story broadcast on the local radio stations.

Ball's lighthouse was sited on Darkling Rock, the largest and most prominent of a cluster of crags, reefs and sea stacks, potentially lethal shipping hazards a few miles from the mainland. An inlet had been built out of granite blocks to berth and shelter the supply boats sent with provisions in the days when the lighthouse had a human crew to sustain. On this particular September evening, a fisherman names Robert Alderman had anchored there, intent on night angling.

Alderman was a sober, stolid character not generally given to flights of imaginative fancy. One minute he saw a passing tanker, picked out brilliantly in a strong and steady beam of brightness, 'Like a ghost ship,' he later said. The next, the seascape was cast into a black void. Behind him, in that moment of blind silence, he heard the sound of a heavy wooden door slam shut. He got up and followed the sound, his eyes adjusting all the while until he could make out the contours of the rock, the bulk of the lighthouse base and a retreating figure headed for the inlet.

'Except he never got there,' Alderman said. 'He just faded from view, like a photograph will fade in strong sunlight over a few hours. Except that this happened suddenly, all at once.'

Haunted lighthouses are probably every bit as cliched as haunted prisons and I was mindful of my own scorn when Pete Davidson suggested Alcatraz might be worth a bit of paranormal exploration. But I liked the human element to the Jed Ball story. And the idea of a ghost's embittered tinkering causing death and destruction on a ruinous scale was a compelling one.

The segment would have atmosphere and isolation and unless we were very unlucky, stormy weather too. It worked as social history. And audiences like nautical tales. Even if their only experience of the sea is the pack of fish fingers they routinely serve up their kids, they like a briny story spun out on television.

Then there was the technical side of matters. Why did the light persist in failing when it was a piece of relatively modern technology scrupulously maintained? That was a mystery no one had solved. Perhaps we would solve it. But even if nothing other-worldly manifested, people like enigmas, whether there is an explanation of them or not.

The Irish cottage in its wilderness of peat bog seemed just as mysterious in its way. It was benign enough in daylight, but shunned at night, the entire vicinity avoided. It had neither power nor running water. It had been unoccupied for a century and as a consequence of that neglect, was not in the best of repair. Clare winters could be harsh, though the basic structure of the building was said to be sound enough.

Its last occupant was rumoured to have been an IRA assassin, working for Michael Collins as he rose to prominence in the Independence struggle at the end of WW1. Nobody – including Daisy Chain – had been able to establish this as fact. Collins had played his rebel cards extremely close to his chest. And 100 years after the fact, no one was around anymore either to confirm or deny anything conclusively.

Benign by day, as I have said. But after dusk, lights were seen to flicker in the cottage and music was heard to play. And not a local delinquent equipped with a beat box and a disposable lighter. Instead, the yellow flicker of oil lamps and the acoustic strains of old folk songs, weirdly distorted as they travelled over distance through the night air.

A persistent rumour had grown up concerning these spectral musical events. They were the gunman's victims, it was said, hosting their own wakes.

Only on one known occasion had anyone been bold or drunk enough to investigate. A burly farmer's son named Seamus Conner, a 21-year-old with a brawler's reputation in the local bars had mustered the nerve to go one night and take a personal look.

'Probably a party worth gate-crashing, that one,' he'd said. 'Sure, the ghosts are having a grand old time of it.'

He'd been discovered the next morning, stumbling around in shock in one of his father's stubble fields, snot caked, crying like a baby.

Seamus Connor would offer not a word concerning what he'd seen and heard at the cottage. Though people who knew him said he was now, ironically, a sort of phantom himself. A spectral shadow of the roaring boy he had previously been.

Ireland teems with folkloric tales. The leprechaun, in its traditional rather than tourist incarnation, is almost as sinister as the banshee. It is very bad news indeed to encounter either of these mythic creatures.

Much of the country's traditional music celebrates either ghosts or the supernatural generally. If I went in for the fraudulent stuff – and some of my rivals in the field persistently did - this was the one tailor made for a bit of embellishment. But I wouldn't be hiring a troupe of tight-lipped musicians to fake anything. And I wasn't really expecting a confrontation in Clare with any kind of spirit except maybe a bottle of Bushmills whiskey.

What I did think about doing was hire a detectorist. I thought the assassin story had the ring of authenticity about it. I thought the gunman hired by Collins might not only have known where the bodies were buried, but have buried them there himself. Peat is an excellent preservative of human remains. A few murder victim corpses, raised from death as fresh as the day they were concealed under the ground, would haunt the viewer with the potency of any ghost.

Ghoulish, obviously. But this is a sometimes ghoulish line of work. All ghost stories involve a necessary death. That's inescapable. And most ghosts have an axe to grind about the manner of their demise. It's why they're restless, according to tradition. Victims of earthly injustice in spiritual protest at the crime against fate they endured.

The fourth haunting offered a change of pace after the European enigma of the first and very Celtic character of those located on the Scottish coast and in the Irish rural wilderness. We're off to Chicago in the roaring 20s, the era of bootleggers, protection rackets, bought politicians, crooked cops and numbers running. A time when the Thompson sub-machine gun was the preferred method of settling business disputes and rival gangs had names a lot more entertaining than their aspirations tended to be.

Al Capone arrived in Chicago in 1919, after a youth spent among the criminal gangs in New York. He played semi-professional baseball for a couple of seasons but earned his corn as a bouncer in brothels and bars. Then he was taken on as an enforcer by the gangster John Torrio, who became Capone's mentor.

Scarface – a nickname he hated – is believed to have contracted syphilis in about 1923. It could have been cured by then, but apparently, he never sought treatment. He described himself as a businessman and throughout the remainder of that violent decade, his business certainly flourished. He had an appetite for women, cigars, sharp suits, jazz music and whisky. He enjoyed spells at the more prestigious and fashionable American resort locations, travelling to them with his entourage by train. He liked to gamble and to attend baseball games and boxing bouts. He was feted at their venues, the crowd applauding the character they thought of as their modern-day Robin Hood. He became wealthy, though he never opened a bank account. He did open a soup kitchen for the unemployed. And he hit women throughout his life, his first victim a teacher he punched in the face, resulting in his expulsion from school at the age of 14.

The building that had perked my interest seemed originally to have been a brothel. The brothel employed a talented pianist. The pianist came to Capone's attention and the gangster enabled him to recruit other Chicago-based musicians and form a band. The popularity of the band encouraged Capone to turn the brothel into a speakeasy with the band in residence, bootleg booze being more profitable in this era than prostitution. Their madame unceremoniously fired, the girls were put out on the street.

After Capone's conviction for tax evasion, the nightclub into which this place had evolved went into decline. With prohibition lifted, there was competition. Capone's preferred method of dealing with competing nightspots was to blow them up. But Capone was by now in prison serving a stretch of 11 years. The Great Depression began. What had been a brothel, a speakeasy selling bootleg booze and then a jazz club, suffered from terminal neglect. It became a cheap hotel. By the 1940s, it was a flop house and by the 1960s, it was derelict.

Chicago has had its economic blips over the last half century. There has been political graft, urban riots, simmering racial tension. But a building in one of its southern suburbs should have been ripe at some point for redevelopment. There has been boom as well as bust over that period in urban America.

Places can however gain an unsavoury reputation. This particular building was the scene of at least two mob-era murders. And then there are the girls. Three of the prostitutes employed there when it was a brothel met with a grisly end. One was found floating in the harbour. One was raped and strangled. A third was discovered in the basement of a boarding house apparently having starved to death while still in her thirties.

Bricks and mortar, timber and lathe. Old sofas spilling horsehair. Walls from which the plaster sags because they bleed damp even in the broiling summer months. Can a building be malevolent? Can it radiate despair, or just inflict bad luck? I thought the stories about this particular location perhaps far-fetched or unreliable. But it intrigued me.

I have always thought the 1920s, with that decade's mood of brittle hysteria and endless sensation seeking the most sinister of periods. It followed the Great War and the Spanish Flu' epidemic and was, I think, a reaction to those events. People were reckless and the mood a callous one. I hoped to find a sort of time capsule in that Chicago building, somewhere where the past might resonate shockingly into the present.

All a bit fanciful. All a bit speculative. But infra-red cameras in its empty rooms at four in the morning? Worth a few thousand pounds of Pete Davidson's precious investment cash.

The specific story I'd heard about the place had been told at a Manhattan cocktail party attended by someone I'd originally met at university. I'd got to know Sally Bruce quite well when we'd done a film course, The Language of the Cinema together, over the ten-week length of a summer term. You can get quite friendly with someone, discussing the Odessa Steps scene from Eisenstein's The Battleship Potemkin, at analytic length.

Quite friendly was all we ever got, but we'd stayed in touch and these days, emailed one another from time to time. Sally worked nowadays as a producer for Netflix. She specialised in fictional rather than factual, but she was familiar with my output.

The story was unusual not because it was about something apparently paranormal, but because it was self-deprecating. Americans, in my experience, don't do self-deprecation. But this property developer did, bemoaning his buying of a haunted address in Chicago.

'Like I wasn't warned,' he told his cocktail sipping audience of fellow guests in New York.

'Were you warned?' Someone asked.

'Several times,' he said ruefully. 'Place was a mob hang-out back in the bootleg liquor days. Fallen on hard times since. Pretty much derelict. Going for a song. Maybe should have listened more closely to the lyrics.'

'What happened?'

What had happened was he'd bought the property on spec and then asked the boss of a construction firm he'd used regularly before to check it out. The very busy, hard-pressed boss of a construction firm just then working insane hours. The man obliged his developer friend, but had a schedule that forced him to get up and go over there at 4am.

'Only he discovered he wasn't there alone,' the developer told the cluster of now silent fellow party guests in front of him. 'He walks into this empty room and he can barely see through the fog of tobacco smoke. But what he can see is women, in feather boas and fishnets and diamante and lipstick, smoking cigarettes through holders. And dancing. And he can hear stride piano like someone is playing it live and loud, right next door. And then one of the women turns slowly and sees my guy and her eyes bulge as though in terror and she screams. And the music stops. And the whole hen party just vanishes.'

'Hen party?' Someone asked.

'My description,' he said. 'My guy said they looked like hookers in a movie about the mob. They weren't from the present day. Fucking place really is haunted, excuse my French.'

'Tourist attraction,' someone said.

The developer shook his head. 'My guy's now on Diazepam. Dosage that would tranquilise an elephant. Can't stop dreaming about it. Wouldn't go back there for a million dollars.'

Do I believe this story? I believe the account of its telling given me by my old student colleague Sally Bruce. I believe the developer who told it believes it. And I believe his construction company boss thinks he saw what he saw. He might be particularly suggestible. Or he might have triggered something from his own subconscious, having heard about the place and its associations and then forgotten he'd done so. Or there might be something to it at an address worth checking out.

The experience doesn't make sense in naturalistic terms. Because if the piano was really being played that loudly, Construction Boss would have heard it before entering that room full of jazz-age hookers. He might even have heard it from the street. He approached a building characterised by abandonment and neglect, by dereliction. It was dark and it was still and it was silent. What happened inside it ambushed him. And shook him to his core and if what he says about his dreams is true, has haunted him.

What intrigues me most about the story is the reaction of that call-girl who saw him and then screamed in apparent terror. At that moment Construction Boss saw something from the past, did she glimpse an apparition from the future? It's an unanswerable question. You can't very well interview a ghost. But it's an interesting thought. And it resonated with me, because a long time ago and in another continent, I experienced something similar myself.

****

I returned my Cousin his key. I spent the summer holidays working in my ice-cream kiosk. I was there the day I got my O-level results. I got the grades I needed to carry on at Christ the King and study for the three A-levels I would require to get into university. And I began to date Samantha Dooley; to the general envy of my friends not only because she was a good-looking Greenbank girl but because her dad was a pub landlord. They all assumed that meant free beer, which it did, though not as often as they thought. Samantha's dad was of the doting variety. He was protective of his daughter and suspicious of me. Though the gainful seasonal employment and the good exam grades seemed to go down well.

Our dates were innocent enough. We'd go to the pictures, or to Pleasureland, which was Southport's permanent fairground. On my days off, we'd go to the open-air bathing pool, a deco masterpiece built in the 1920s that's now long gone. We'd sometimes snog in the back row of the cinema or on the sandhills on the beach. But matters didn't go further than that. We also played tennis some evenings after I'd cashed up. Samantha was a very good player. But then she'd been coached. I'd sometimes seen the Greenbank girls being coached during their PE lessons from an adjacent court on Victoria Park, which was handily sited only on the other side of the road from their school.

In August of that year, I read in the Visiter that property developer Paul Wright had finally been declared bankrupt. The headline over the story was, A Gamble Too Far and the by-line was Joey Delancey's. I never saw Delancey again, which isn't really all that surprising. His interest in the Weld Road address he'd written about was strictly in the present and mine was wholly in the past.

And in September of that year, he was talent-spotted by the producers of Granada Reports and relocated to Manchester. A story about the departure of their star journalist in the Visiter itself was how I found out about that. But I thought a misleading headline flawed the epitaph he wrote for Paul Wright's business career. The failure of Kelmscott Court to find anything other than temporary occupants had nothing to do with rolling the dice. It had been predetermined.

I didn't have any further uncanny experiences and wouldn't again until I got to university at the other end of the country two years later. I avoided Weld Road. Only obliquely, did I persist with researching the bleak life and dark times of Edward Swarbrick. My interest had been piqued by that photograph taken in 1927 at the Birkdale Palace Hotel's Jericho Ball.

I found out what I could about Klaus Fischer and Harry Spalding. The former was an industrialist of German origin, an inter-wars anglophile who bult a mansion on the Isle of Wight and liked to throw parties. He had influential friends and an interest in black magic fashionable in the period among decadent, wealthy people. The most interesting aspect of his life was that no one seemed to know what had happened to him. He disappeared without trace, just vanished. He might have been murdered, I suppose, the body weighted by concrete boots, resting at the bottom of the Solent. But wilful disappearance was much easier achieved back then and he might have been running away from someone. Or from something.

Harry Spalding too had a Wight connection. He sailed his racing schooner Dark Echo there every summer in the regattas. He was from a wealthy Boston banking family and had become a playboy socialite after the Great War. For a time, he lived among the bohemians of expatriate Paris. He blew out his brains in a New York hotel room in 1929 and did not leave behind a note. After America entered the war, Spalding had led a hand-picked special forces infantry unit. They were called the Jericho Crew. Jericho Crew, Jericho Ball; and far too much of a stretch to be coincidence.

Compulsory P.E. stopped at our school when I got into sixth form. I kept fit by boxing and fencing foil at the YMCA and by going for seafront runs. We stopped having to wear a school uniform. And we qualified for subsidised driving lessons which I didn't bother to take because an over-zealous teacher had told me fossil fuels would run out in a couple of years and by doing so render cars obsolete. And I foolishly believed him. I joined the debating society and experimented with fiction, writing a couple of very pedestrian short stories. I wasn't prepared to write about the interesting events that had occurred in my life. It would have felt too much like tempting fate.

Time slipped by, as time does, even at that age. Shaving became a daily routine. I grew that all important extra inch. I began to fill out physically, which might have been genetic, or might have been those rounds on the heavy bag I was doing three evenings a week.

My voice deepened, Mr Dooley suggested one day that I should call him Jack and Samantha and I grew quite serious about one another. Certainly, anyway, serious for 17-year-olds.

18 rolled around and the sobering one-shot-deal of A-levels. Lots of anguished night conversations about the fact that I was likeliest to go to Kent and Samantha to Oxford to study French – which meant not just a physical separation but for her, a year in France. How big a blow was that to romance? For someone not yet 20? Fatal, I thought, secretly and guiltily grateful my mum still hadn't had a phone installed. Those endless discussions were bad enough face-to-face.

I kept my seasonal kiosk job. I was there the day my A-level results told me that I really was going to Canterbury to study for a degree in History at the University of Kent. I was there the overcast, idle day in September, a fortnight before my departure from Southport, when Tony Causley strolled by in a fawn raincoat and recognised me and paused and looked and broke out a smile I couldn't read and came across.

'Still going on?' I asked him. 'That war being waged between good and evil?'

He shook his head, still smiling. 'No longer frequent that part of the world,' he said. 'So the truth is, I wouldn't know.'

I just nodded my head.

'It was you, wasn't it, made that mess that time in the penthouse.'

'You never experienced something similar?'

'I'm not a fool,' he said. 'Only ever worked there in daylight.'

'It was me,' I told him. 'But it wasn't me made the mess.'

His look was still unreadable. He turned away to go, but then hesitated and turned back again. He said, 'She had a name, you know. One you wouldn't easily forget. She was Arabella Pankhurst. And she was eight-years-old.'

Chapter 4

I invited Daisy Chain out to dinner a week after attending solo her impromptu Swiss Cottage barbeque. I told myself the invitation was reciprocal, an obligation owed to common courtesy. But that wasn't at all the truth. Truer to say that I was lonely and had thought her stimulating company. Her conversational style face-to-face was quite confrontational, but I liked that about her too. There was no contrivance with Daisy. If she felt like giving you both barrels, that was what you would get.

I could have emailed, or texted the invitation, but I chose to call her to offer it. The etiquette justification didn't even survive the opening exchange.

'Is this an attempt to lure me into bed, Tom?'

'I don't know,' I said. 'Possibly.'

She laughed at that. 'Lukewarm,' she said. 'Charming.'

'Is that a no?'

'Where are you planning on taking me?'

'The Ivy,' I said.

'Isn't the Ivy going very public?'

'Only if we canoodle.'

'Horrible thought.'

'Cheers,' I said.

'To be honest,' she said, 'I'd prefer somewhere a bit more relaxed.'

'Like where?'

'I like Cote,' she said. 'I like the atmosphere.'

'Atmosphere isn't what it was in the old days,' I said.

'It is if you can book one of the outside tables.'

'Any particular Cote?'

'The one on George Street in Richmond is pretty handy for you, isn't it?'

I said, 'But a fair old hike from Swiss Cottage.'

'You can treat me to a cab home,' Daisy said. 'An Uber, if you're feeling the pinch.'

'Or I could really push the boat out,' I said, 'and lend you my Oyster Card.'

'Classy, Tom,' she said. 'Classy.'

Then she told me she had uncovered a couple of things, researching. She had called Sally Bruce to try to find out the name of the Chicago construction company boss referenced at the New

York cocktail party Sally had attended. Sally had remembered it was a man named David Briggs. Briggs had a Facebook account. There were generous testimonials from contented clients concerning his all-round professionalism and expertise. From the personal stuff he posted, she gathered he was a vociferous voice for increased gun control. And he didn't much like far-right born-again Christian zealotry, either.

'He's black, self-educated, self-made, prosperous and completely no- nonsense. His chief hobby is iron man competitions. He's been married forever to his college sweetheart and has two kids. Favourite author, Hemingway. His son excels at college football. His daughter is studying to be a lawyer. He has an unblemished drivers' license and he files his tax returns on time,' Daisy said.

'Your conclusion being?'

'This is not a guy to make things up. And his four am visit to that derelict building wasn't the highlight of a bad acid trip. If he says he saw what he says he saw, that's only because he saw it.'

'Excellent.'

Her further background was far older. Al Capone had been a regular client at the brothel he later transformed into a speakeasy and then a nightclub.

'This was when he first arrived in Chicago, when information about him is scarce because he wasn't yet a major player. And because he was adept even then at concealing his activities. But his favourite girl was a Pole named Lisa Adamski. She was rumoured to be the woman that gave him the dose of the clap that led eventually to his derangement and death. Maybe she's one of the woman David Briggs saw.'

I was silent for a moment.

'What's going through what passes for your mind, Tom?'

'Just wondering whether David Briggs would do a piece to camera about what it was he saw in that derelict bordello.'

'Highly doubt it,' Daisy said. 'He wants to forget it, not relive the experience. He runs a construction firm and supports two kids at college. He's cement and steel girders and deals done on a meaty handshake. Bad business to come across as a crank.'

I said, 'He might find it cathartic.'

Daisy laughed. She said, 'Is that a flying pig I've just seen caper across the sky?'

We ended the conversation. She had agreed to have dinner with me the following Saturday. I called Cote and booked our table for 7pm. I had no real expectations of the evening. I was glad she had agreed to the invitation. Glad and, also, relieved. I was very rusty at romance and quite honestly felt flattered.

****

I said I did no further research, after the Kelmscott Court experience, into the life of Edward Swarbrick. And that's more or less true. But there was one incident that took place on the eve of my departure for Kent and university I think worth recounting.

We moved into the council house my mum was offered when I was 11 and my brother Andy nine. Prior to that, we lived in a rented terraced house with an outside loo and no bathroom. Water was cold, provided by a single kitchen tap. We had a zinc bath that depended from a hook on the whitewashed wash-house wall in our backyard, but since we didn't even have an electric kettle, that took forever to fill. It might seem odd now that people lived like this in England even in recent times, but I can tell you from personal experience that they did. That we did.

My mum belonged to the Union of Catholic Mothers' branch in our parish, St Theresa's. She wasn't particularly religious, didn't attend mass every Sunday. Though it wouldn't have been called that then, the UCM functioned principally as a sort of women's support group. Through it, my mum got to know and become firm friends with a woman of about her own age named Lucy. Lucy was married to a man named Tim and they lived in a nice house in

Birkdale. They had a son, George, who was away at a Lancashire seminary training to become a priest.

Lucy told mum Andy and I were welcome to go to their house for a bath on a Sunday evening. And so over the course of a few weeks, Sunday at their house became our regular Bath Night. And they became Auntie Lucy and Uncle Tim, a common custom in the north when mature friends of their parents take a kindly interest in the welfare of children.

Uncle Tim worked for the Cunard Shipping line in some senior catering capacity and judging by their house and furniture, he was impressively successful at this. But despite the existence of the absent George, he didn't seem to know a huge amount about children. Or about parenting them. He would greet us on bath night with bowls of cashew and pistachio nuts, when we'd regarded nuts as something people ate only at Christmas.

Then he'd say, 'Drink, boys?' And he'd serve up gin and tonics. And they were always large ones, brimming with ice. And he'd leave us to drink them, with a contented look.

In retrospect, I'm amazed neither of us drowned. And to this day I can't remember how we got home on Bath Night. And Bath Night ended when mum got our council house. But mum and Auntie Lucy always remained the best of friends. I even recuperated for a couple of weeks at their house, when a newly bought kitten triggered the allergic reaction of a severe asthma attack when I was 14.

We were about to celebrate Samantha's birthday. Since it was imminent, my mind was mostly on my days away departure for Canterbury. It was a Saturday, and I had walked the three miles from home to a fancy Birkdale Village delicatessen to buy my girlfriend a cheesecake. There was a queue to be served, which there always was in there on a Saturday. And I recognised the familiar figure of Uncle Tim at the head of it. He had bought a bag of coffee beans and was having them ground and the air was rich with the scent from the whirring grinder. He turned having paid and eyed me with surprise and said, 'Lovely to see you, Tom. Time for a G and T?'

They boxed my cheesecake and tied it with a black ribbon and I paid and followed Uncle Tim out of the shop and back to his house. It was a lovely, sunny autumnal day and we took our drinks out to the garden table at the centre of a lawn so immaculate, I'd always thought it would make a first-class bowling green. No weeds. No hint of despoiling moss, just perfectly mowed turf.

We talked about university. We talked about his son George, who had given up on the priesthood and was at Warwick, studying engineering and his father told me, amassing impressive runs opening the batting for the first-eleven at cricket. Uncle Tim had retired by this time, but then I remembered he had worked for the Cunard shipping line. Their name and logo embellished the ashtrays in the house he shared with Auntie Lucy. As a young man, he might have met Edward Swarbrick. Or if not, he might have known him by reputation. And so I took the opportunity to ask.

His glass jerked in his hand and made the melting ice chink audibly. He went pale.

'You knew him, didn't you, Uncle Tim?'

'I met him, Tom. There's a difference.'

'Just the once?'

He nodded. 'I was very young, only nineteen or twenty.'

'What was he like?'

'He looked like the undertaker with the staff who walks in front of the carriage hearse at a ceremonial funeral. Which was ironic.'

'Why was it?'

And so Uncle Tim told me the story.

It was on a Monday morning in the Docks Superintendent's office on Liverpool Harbour. Docks security was tight because pilfering was common. Stowaways on the liners plying the

Atlantic route were less common, but still a problem, with plenty of adventurous Scouse lads wanting to try their luck in America. Tim Ballard had just passed his probationary three-month period with the Cunard company and had thus qualified for his special pass.

Nowadays that would be laminated plastic on a lanyard, probably with a hologram to prevent forgery, certainly with a passport-style photograph and it would read Access All Areas. Back when Uncle Tim was a youngster, probably no more than a pasteboard rectangle bearing a smudged official stamp.

During the week before this chance encounter, the man who would become my Uncle Tim only in later life, told me he narrowly escaped a fatal accident. He was on the dock wall. A crane was unloading a pallet of whisky barrels. The load was forty feet above his head when it slipped, and the barrels tumbled freely through air and began to crash onto the cobbles around him.

'Only two of them burst open,' he told me, 'which even though they were iron-hooped, was pretty miraculous. More miraculous was the fact than none hit me, I would have been killed instantly. They were sixty-gallon barrels. And they weighed half a ton apiece.'

Tim Ballard's remarkable escape became the subject of a story in the previous Saturday's Liverpool Post newspaper and Swarbrick must have read it, because he commented on it, apparently recognising Tim from the photo illustrating the piece.

'What did he say?' I asked him.

'I said fate had smiled on me, something to that effect. Said I could have been a goner.'

'How did he reply?'

'Smiled a very unpleasant smile and told me not to make the mistake of thinking life ends in death. Far from it, he said. And to this day I don't think he was talking about the afterlife.'

'How did you know it was Swarbrick?'

'The clerk called out his name. His appointment was prior to mine. They must have been a bit behind, that morning. I was left cooling my heels for another half hour. But I've never forgotten that encounter. There was something unpleasant about Swarbrick, almost as though he gave off a corrupt smell. Something sinister.'

I nodded.

Uncle Tim drained his glass and looked at me and said, 'What's your interest in him?'

'I was doing a bit of research for my own entertainment into the Birkdale Palace Hotel,' I said. 'He was in a photo taken at a ball there.'

'The Birkdale Palace. Late and unlamented,' Uncle Tim said.

'Interesting, though.'

'You should leave all that stuff alone, Tom. Stirring ghosts can never end well.'

'The photo was taken in nineteen-twenty-seven. It's fifty-odd years ago. But there might be someone still alive who remembers those days.'

Uncle Tim lit a cigarette, a Dunhill King-Size, and slid his gold Ronson lighter onto the table where it glinted in sunlight. Next to the cream cardboard box containing the cheesecake I'd bought for Samantha. I needed really to take that home.

'People in the catering trade meet other people in the business at trade events,' Uncle Tim said. 'He's in his eighties and retired now, but I knew the head bar steward at the Birkdale Palace.'

'Think he'd speak to me?'

'He wouldn't have been head-man in that period. But he was there all his working life, so he'd likely remember nineteen-twenty-seven.'

'Where does he live?'

'Albert Hodge. Retired early after a big win on his Premium Bonds and bought a house on Rotten Row. We exchange

Christmas cards, so I know his address, but you can't very well doorstep an elderly man and drag him back to something he'd likely sooner forget.'

'You think he'd sooner forget it?'

Uncle Tim shrugged. He tapped ash onto the grass at his feet. He said, 'I don't know. That place had a bad reputation. On the other hand, he stayed put there. And he's always struck me as a genial man. So I don't honestly know.'

'Do you have his phone number?'

Uncle Tim looked reluctant. 'Might be able to dig it out,' he said. 'And old Albert might be happy to reminisce about the times he made highballs for Frank Sinatra. But if the rumours I've heard are true, Edward Swarbrick was a very nasty piece of work. You're better off leaving him alone.'

It was the second warning he'd given me in fewer than five minutes. But as I prepared to leave, he went inside and came back out again with a slip of paper with a Southport phone number written on it in black biro.

Have you heard of M.R. James, Tom?'

'No.'

'An excellent writer of short stories. Mostly, they concerned themselves with ghosts. He wrote one with the title, A Warning to the Curious. You could do worse than give it a read.'

I put the slip of paper in my pocket.

****

On the Thursday before my dinner date with Daisy Chain I drove to Chichester to meet the hypnotist, James Balfour, the man apparently making encouraging progress in his sessions with my daughter. He'd agreed to meet me. No real surprise, since we both knew that indirectly, I was paying his fee.

I hadn't looked him up and hadn't got Daisy to do it either. I wanted first-impressions unclouded by preconceptions. He was based professionally at a smart business premises just off the high street. There was a polished brass plaque on the street door with his name inscribed and some letters after it that suggested he was professionally qualified. Julia Pettifer, custodian of The Retreat, wouldn't have used anyone who wasn't. Neither would her insurers have allowed it. Amateurs couldn't roam through the minds of subjects who were a danger to themselves. Not when those subjects were as suggestible as my daughter was said to be.

He opened his consulting room door himself. Probably there would have been a receptionist once, but of course these days, a lot of that kind of expense has been dispensed with. All that stuff we used to consider necessary, when it wasn't really needed at all.

I was surprised at how young he was as he introduced himself, a tall, athletic looking, dark haired man surely no older, I thought, than his mid-twenties. He was softly spoken, friendly in demeaner. It was just after two in the afternoon.

He suggested a coffee shop or a bar. I chose bar, thinking likely more secluded, though because I was driving, I would only drink Diet Coke. He glanced at his wristwatch, a Heuer Monaco, the deliberate choice of someone who knows what they like and has a decent income. He wore a suit, over a black roll-neck sweater. The suit looked hand-tailored and the sweater looked like cashmere. I thought it interesting that he did not want to speak to me where he worked.

The bar to which he led me was dimly lit and spacious and it was easy to find a table at which we wouldn't be overheard. Leather armchairs. London Grammar at an ambient volume level through concealed speakers. Other patrons, designer clothed. Probably an expensive place, I thought, but didn't get to test that theory because James Balfour insisted on buying our drinks.

'I've seen you on television,' he said, when he sat back down. 'Julia didn't tell me, and I didn't make the connection through

Claire. I thought I was meeting a Tom Carter. Didn't know I was meeting *the* Tom Carter.'

'Does it make a difference?'

He shook his head, 'Not at all. Either way, your daughter is a remarkable young woman.'

'If damaged,' I said.

Speaking carefully, he said, 'I prefer to think of her as not quite intact.'

'Like a chipped vase?'

'Like a jigsaw puzzle with a couple of important pieces missing, Mr Carter.'

'I'd prefer you call me Tom.'

'Then please call me James.'

No surprise. The suit and watch didn't exactly add up to a Jimmy.

'She's highly intelligent,' he said. 'Almost off the scale.'

'Something not necessarily to her advantage, James.'

'Because she's bored?'

'Last week I told Julia Pettifer my daughter is like a prisoner, incarcerated without having committed a crime. It remains what I think.'

He said, 'If Claire were reconciled to what and to where she is, her position would be much bleaker. Her indignation gives us cause for optimism.'

'Us?'

'Me. That plural was a cop-out. I'm the one who is optimistic.'

'Even Doctor Pettifer thinks you've made progress.'

He hesitated. Then he said. 'The guilt is an obstacle. It stops her wanting to get well.'

But I knew that. I knew Claire blamed herself for her mother finally leaving me. I said, 'She isn't the reason the marriage failed. The catalyst, maybe. Not the reason.'

'Yet her mother never visits.'

'Not because she doesn't love Claire. Because she loves her too much.'

James Balfour didn't comment on that.

I said, 'You're thinking what I've just given you a slick, pat answer. It isn't. It's the truth.'

Quietly, he said, 'It doesn't help Claire.'

'What do you hope to achieve with her?'

He smiled. He said, 'I want to find the missing pieces.'

'You actually think you can?'

'I wouldn't be driving to Hove every week if I didn't. I wouldn't be wasting your daughter's time and taking your money.'

I pulled in a breath and fought for composure. The thought of my daughter completely well was an almost inconceivable hope. I said, 'Would more sessions be more effective? I'd happily pay.'

But he shook his head. 'Just now I said I want to find the missing pieces, Tom. But it's truer to say I need to help Claire find the missing pieces. They're where she'd hidden them. It's a process that takes patience and persistence and it can't be rushed.'

'I understand.'

'How long has she been like this?'

'We first began to suspect she was more than just unconventional when she was four or five. She might have changed. Or she might have always been that way and it took us time to notice. But that was when she began her long retreat from the world. She was eight when the self-harming began.'

'No single event, or cause?'

'I've answered all these questions for Dr Pettifer. School, diet, computer activity, friendship group, what she read – all of it. She was treated with love and kindness and consistently so. It was almost like she made a conscious decision to be strange.'

He said, 'Is there anything specific you want to ask me?'

'You've pretty much covered it,' I said. 'Except for one question I would like answered. Why are we sitting in a bar and not your consulting room?'

'That's where I perform,' he said. 'On one level that's what hypnotism is. It's performing. This isn't a performance, it's a private talk, a dialogue about a subject that has always been important to you and has more recently become important to me.'

Playing this conversation back to myself in the car on the drive home, I realised that some of what I had said was contradictory. If Claire had made a conscious decision to be strange, she couldn't have been born that way. If she had been born that way, it was the exact opposite of a conscious decision. What I'd said was really just a reflection of my own confusion. Claire had baffled Julia Pettifer and she was a trained analyst. But I was encouraged by James Balfour. I had liked him and more importantly, had the strong sense that he liked my daughter. He wanted to contribute what he could to the cause of making her well.

It did strike me that there was a degree of ambiguity in what Balfour had said about Claire. Was he young enough to have developed romantic feelings for her? It was possible. Despite the sober modesty of her dress, my daughter was quite stunning to look at. And she had an endearing innocence someone of his age might find beguiling.

A remarkable young woman.

Indeed.

How intimate a process was hypnotism? I realised guiltily that I didn't really know anything about it. I'd seen a hypnotherapist years earlier, who had given me some techniques to deal with the anxiety I suffered during the ordeal of public speaking. And they had been successful at the time. But I had never been lulled into a trance. Everything I knew about the subject came from TV shows I'd watched for their entertainment value rather than out of personal interest.

Discovering more would be straightforward enough. I'd do that and then when better informed, speak to James again about his own technique. Now that we'd met, broken the ice, I was fairly confident he would do that comfortably over the phone.

When I got into my car, I switched on my phone and saw that I had missed a call from my brother. I switched it off again. It was only then 3.30 in the afternoon. He might have a client sitting in front of him. He might be in court. I'd speak to him when he finished work, early that evening. A much more relaxed scenario. I'd tell him about my Saturday dinner date, since he was so concerned about my mood.

Home was in Teddington, which is why Daisy thought the Richmond Cote a good fit for me. It was only a pleasant walk away from where I lived. When I'd parked the car and switched the phone on again, I'd missed a second call from Andy. Two in a day from him was unusual. I called him back.

He didn't mince his words. His voice hoarse with emotion, he said, 'Phillipe Suarez was found dead this morning, at the foot of Beachy Head.'

I was incredulous. Even I knew that you didn't attempt to climb Beachy Head. The rock was soft, unstable.

'What on earth was he thinking,' I said.

And my brother grasped my train of thought. 'He wasn't climbing, Tom. No gear. He must have driven there before dawn. He jumped.'

****

Albert Hodge agreed to see me, but not at his home. The houses on Rotten Row stood behind a steeply grassed embankment and occupied one side of it, the east side, The west side, for its entire length, was occupied by Victoria Park. From the road, below them, the Rotten Row houses were invisible. You could not see either them or their front gardens and I had always been curious to discover what they were like.

'I'm interested in history,' I told him over the phone. 'I'm about to spend three years studying for a history degree.'

'Where?'

'Canterbury.'

'You sound like a local lad, a Sandgrounder.'

'I am.'

'Bloody long way from home.'

'I'm interested in the history of the Birkdale Palace, particularly in something that happened there in nineteen-twenty-seven.'

'Who put you on to me?'

Tim Ballard.'

Uncle Tim had said I could use his name.

Albert Hodge chuckled. 'You're a cheeky young bugger,' he said. 'Calling events that happened in my lifetime history. Wasn't always bar staff, either.'

'Really?'

'Did a bit of construction work, prior. Had a hand in the building of Stonehenge.'

I'd already reached two conclusions. Albert Hodge had all his marbles. And he was a bit of a wag. Barmen needed to be handy with the banter, even when they were the man in charge.

'Did you meet Frank Sinatra Mr Hodge?'

'Call me Al son, everyone does. And the answer is yes, though a lot later on than the time you're talking about. That was after World War Two. Generous tipper, Mr Sinatra. Very keen on his golf.'

'Can I come and speak to you?'

'You're in luck, son. The missus is at the Essoldo for the afternoon session. Know what that is?'

It was a bingo hall. My mum went there one night a week. 'Yes,' I said.

'Means she can't eavesdrop on this conversation. The wife doesn't like me reminiscing about the years before we met. Seems to think I should have known our marriage was written in the stars before we ever encountered one another. I was a bit of a lad, before, you see. Big hotels aren't exactly bereft of that sort of opportunity.'

I thought briefly of Joey Delancey. When it came to quotability, Al Hodge was pure gold.

'I take a constitutional every day on the pier. How are you fixed to meet me there at eleven o'clock tomorrow morning?'

I was in a Lord Street phone box. I shovelled in more coins. 'Are you about six-two, white-haired, a dapper dresser, straight as a guardsman?'

'That's me.'

'You used to pass my ice-cream kiosk. You never bought anything.'

'Nothing personal, son. Never had much of a sweet tooth.'

'I'll be there,' I said, 'at the end of the pier.'

'Only if it's fine, mind. If it's pissing rain, we'll rearrange. I know you wouldn't like the death of an elderly man through pneumonia on your conscience.'

'An elderly man who helped build an ancient monument,' I said.

'Cheeky bugger.'

It was the second time he'd called me that. I didn't mind in the slightest.

He liked to talk. You couldn't spend the whole of your working life in bar work if you didn't. But I was an 18-year-old he didn't know from Adam who had needed to use a payphone to contact him. I had the feeling he could remember those bachelor dalliances in the years before he met his wife quite vividly. And remember a lot more besides.

By this time, my own bachelor life had taken a significant turn. The Old Ship pub had undergone a refurb the previous month. Samantha's landlord dad had closed for a fortnight and taken her mum on holiday to Benidorm. With Oxford and her degree course so close, Samantha had opted not to go. And with dust sheets and step-ladders and the smell of paint on the ground floor, we'd climbed the stairs wordlessly hand in hand, and slept together for the first time. I had friends who had been sexually active for two or three years by then, but can honestly say it was worth the wait.

Over the time we'd been together, Samantha had become a more sophisticated person. I suppose in someone so intelligent, that was inevitable. She wore stylish clothes. Mary Quant's Havoc had been swapped for the Guerlain fragrance, Chamade. I'd bought her a bottle of that, along with the cheesecake, for her birthday. She smoked French cigarettes and had a Cosmopolitan magazine subscription and had 'adopted' a South-East Asian child to whom she sent some of the money she earned doing bar work every month. She read Sartre and Camus and Celine, none of them in translation. She listened a lot to Joni Mitchell.

Our separation loomed. We had adult conversations about it, talking with a detachment I didn't remotely feel about the sensible eventuality of calling it a day on our romance. And then we went and slept together, and I woke the following morning and stroked her hair as she slept, certain that I could never be without her.

But I was destined to be. She would be swept off her feet by a suave Frenchman with a taste for philosophy and a Citroen DS convertible car. He'd serve her coffee laced with cognac in his chic little Left Bank apartment. He'd wear Tabac cologne and look a bit like Alain Delon. He'd listen to the cool jazz of Miles Davis and play clay court tennis at weekends with the flair of a pro. A provincial English boy with no arse in his trousers (as my mother often reminded me), would be no competition for him.

I never told Samantha about Edward Swarbrick, or how his top hat had come briefly into my possession, or Kelmscott Court, my weird, ongoing obsession with the man and beyond him, more and more, with the paranormal generally. And I thought by then it *was* becoming an obsession, walking the wooden route to the pier head on a blowy September morning to meet a man I didn't doubt had served Swarbrick, in his pomp, his tipple of choice.

Albert Hodge stood ramrod-straight in a double-breasted camel coat with rows of leather buttons, looking out over the waves of the Irish Sea. For once, the tide was in, which it rarely seemed to be in Southport. The sea was a briny wallow and churn, under the iron pillars supporting the pier. It gave the impression of our being afloat.

He turned and looked at me. 'Professor Long-Hair,' he said. My student hair was admittedly then shoulder length, and unruly in the wind. He held out a hand for me to shake and I introduced myself and we went to sit down on a bench in one of the Edwardian shelters embellishing the pier.

'What do you know about the nineteen-twenties, Tom?'

'The Jazz Age,' I said. 'Al Capone. Prohibition. G-Men on the running boards of sedans firing Thompson guns.'

'There was a bit more to it than Bonnie and Clyde,' he said, chuckling.

'Enlighten me, Al. I mean, you were there.'

'A strange time,' he said. 'This town had a glamour that seems a bit far-fetched when you look back on it now. But it did. Lord Street was a shopping boulevard to rival anything in Europe. The open-air bathing pool opened. You could boat here on the biggest man-made lake in the world. Or water ski, which people also did.

There were casinos, there was the lure of our fabulous links course and there was the Birkdale Palace Hotel to put up the wealthy people who came here to misbehave in discreet luxury.'

'Did people misbehave?'

'And then some,' Albert Hodge said.

'Even more so than today?'

He scratched his cheek. We were facing south. It was one of those startlingly clear Southport days. Facing north, you'd see Blackpool Tower and beyond that, the rising hills of the Lake District. But Al was facing south, where the distant mountains of Snowdonia were clearly visible in Wales.

He said, 'We had the fourteen-eighteen war. Then we had the Spanish Flu'. A lot of people were left alive who'd thought quite reasonably that their number was up. It made them reckless. People think sensation-seeking was invented in the sixties. It wasn't. The nineteen-sixties were a sober time compared to then. The nineteen-twenties were a decade of madness.'

'I'm interested in the Jericho Ball, Al. It took place in 'twenty-seven. I don't know what date.'

'You don't need to,' he said, I thought gruffly, maybe even angrily.

'You were there?'

'For my sins.'

'Do you remember a guest named Edward Swarbrick?'

'No, I don't. But I remember the fellow who wrote the cheque that paid for it all. He was a guest at the hotel for the whole of that summer. A yank, Harry Spalding.'

'Tell me about the ball, Al.'

'Rum affair. Started off behind locked doors, none of the hotel staff permitted to go anywhere near them. Some sort of ceremonial. Took weeks afterwards to get the stink of incense out of the furniture upholstery and drapes. Then the fun began, we served up a banquet and then the drinking and dancing started and by midnight the mood was close to frenzied.'

'And that was that?'

'No, it wasn't. Some gate-crasher, sizeable bloke, confronted Spalding about an affair he thought Spalding was having with his wife. Spalding beat him half to death. Took five or six of us to drag Spalding off him. Inhumanly strong, he was. Covered in the other fellow's blood, grinning through the gore like a fiend.'

'Swarbrick was a friend of Spalding's,' I said.

Albert Hodge shook his head. 'No, he wasn't, son. Harry Spalding didn't have friends. Floozies, yes. And flunkeys. Crews for his boat. No friends. With the wisdom of hindsight, I'm pretty sure he was a psychopath. But he was rich and wealthy people could get away with a lot back then.'

'More than now?'

Al snorted, contemptuously. He said, 'Was the Russian revolution in 'seventeen that did it. The Bolshevik Menace. The Bolshies killed our king's cousin, the Tsar. Put the wind up the royal family good and proper. And the government, too. The authorities were terrified of revolution in the 'twenties, suspicious of the working class, maybe even afraid of us. That was especially true after the General Strike in 'twenty-six. If you were a toff in this country back then, you'd get away with murder.'

It was a bit disappointing that Albert Hodge didn't know more about Edward Swarbrick. But he had led me to believe that the Jericho Ball celebrated some kind of society. Maybe even a cult. Swarbrick had a proven appetite for those, having belonged to an Orange Lodge and been a Freemason too. A ceremony involving incense sounded pretty sinister, outside of a church. All underwritten by this character Harry Spalding, probably at enormous cost. Spalding, the feral American playboy I suspected was a friend of Swarbrick despite Al's scepticism about that.

'I've got a film,' he said, quietly.

'You've got a what?'

'A cine film of the Jericho Ball. Took it to spite them, really, all those rich, invulnerable bastards. Filmed them in secret. There's no sound, and it's black and white, obviously. But I've still got it, somewhere.'

'Could I see it?'

'We can probably arrange something. Quality isn't at all bad.'

A thought occurred to me. 'Did you go through your working life hating them, Al? Resenting your rich hotel guests?'

'Of course not. Don't be bloody silly. Miss Dietrich was always lovely, as well as being drop-dead gorgeous. Judy Garland could wobble, but she sang like a nightingale. Cary Grant held the patent on debonair. Mr Sinatra was an absolute gent. Most of the guests were charming people. But the nineteen-twenties? A funny time. And Harry Spalding was a cunt. You'll have to pardon my French.'

'Pardoned,' I said.

A film of the Jericho Ball. Footage of an event that had taken place in the summer of 1927 at the Birkdale Palace Hotel. At the age of 18, I was beginning for the first time in my life, to believe in fate. Then something else occurred to me. Albert Hodge hadn't risen to the status of the hotel's bar steward by then. He was just a lowly barman.

'How could you afford a cine camera?'

'I couldn't, son. It was the hotel's. And back then I was an employee of the hotel, not just the hotel's various bars. One of my occasional jobs was to film guests on the tennis courts or the driving range. You'd play back the film to them and their technique would improve. At least, that was the theory. I didn't own the camera. I borrowed it. I suppose if you were going to be pernickety you could say I stole the film.'

I tried to think did I know anyone who owned a projector.

'I know what you're thinking,' Al said. 'And the fact is, I do have a projector. Have a lot of things, since my boat came in on the Premium Bonds. Many of them I'll never use. Some that haven't even made it out of their boxes. Get to my age, buying things becomes a way of staying alive.' He shrugged, 'Or that's how it seems. That and keeping the missus contented. Anyway, I'd like to see that film myself. You've made me curious, after all this time, to have another look at it.'

****

I had a drink with Andy on Thursday evening. He was shaken by the Phillipe Suarez suicide. Suarez had been one of those men who compartmentalise their life. My brother was his climbing buddy and so had never met his wife or children. But he was sufficiently sensitive to appreciate the shock and grief they would be enduring in the immediate aftermath of his friend's violent demise.

He was also concerned for me. He thought there a connection between his unexpected death and what Phillipe had seen in the Dolomites.

'I know it haunted him,' he told me. 'I don't want it haunting you, with the same outcome. That sounds like a malevolent place. You're better off steering clear of it.'

My brother tended to be quite sceptical, but he'd heard that bark of laughter at the age of nine, when Edward Swarbrick's hat had resided on top of our bedroom wardrobe. And though we had never discussed the experience, I knew he hadn't forgotten it.

I didn't flag up the irony that it was Andy who had tipped me off about the Italian orphanage after hearing the story from Suarez himself. It wasn't the moment for point-scoring.

We were in the Flask in Hampstead, Andy's local, which was proof of his ongoing professional success. His handsome flat in a Grade-2 listed building was just around the corner.

He asked me, 'How's Claire?'

'Doing better,' I said.

He nodded. That's good news, at least.' He was her godfather as well as her uncle and I knew was extremely fond of her.

'She's undergoing hypnotism. I met her hypnotist today. I was impressed.'

'Why?

'His dedication. The ambition of what he wants to achieve with his subject. More accurately I think his patient.'

'If you ever need any help with that, Tom, you know where to come. I mean financially.'

'Thanks,' I said, 'appreciated, but I can manage.'

Which was true. But only true because of Pete Davidson's commission. No Dolomites pilot, no three-parter to follow, and in the immediate term, I would struggle.

I told him about my Saturday evening dinner date with Daisy. I wanted to put his mind at rest on that score too. He had enough to think about with the unexpected death of his climbing friend.

'She sounded lovely on the phone. I get the feeling she's very good at her job. Not at all like me to confide in a stranger about my concern for you.'

'Not like you to confide in me about it, Andy.'

That raised a smile. 'No,' he said. 'Always play them close to my chest. Always have.'

Except, I thought, where Claire was concerned. He didn't visit her, it wasn't permitted. Parents only until she reached 18. And no kind of electronic communication was allowed either. Instead, he wrote a letter every week, including illustrations, a talent they shared. He didn't write about the day-to-day routine of a lawyer specialising in fraud. He wrote about Hampstead Heath in its various seasons and moods. The illustrations were exquisite, and my daughter loved the letters, keeping them all; a treasured, growing collection in a special box.

I don't think my brother knew I knew about those letters. Claire had shown them to me only recently. I was surprised, she was good at secrecy. But she was also truly proud of the collection. I didn't and wouldn't mention them to Andy, for fear of embarrassing him.

And he didn't mention my ex-wife, perhaps for fear of embarrassing me. Instead, we talked trivia for an hour. Books, since in common with a minority of men, we both liked to read fiction. Malta, where he planned to go on holiday the following month, diving wrecks. Scuba diving was second only to climbing in what I thought of as my brother's short list of lethal pastimes. Or maybe just the compensations of an undemonstrative man;

right up there with parachuting and hang-gliding. And flying his bloody microlight.

We talked a bit about football, a bit about boxing, a bit about the best weekend and pizza binge Netflix watches currently available. I think I left him in a slightly better frame of mind than when we'd met, but knew he was still preoccupied by the unexpected death of someone in whose hands he'd probably routinely trusted his life on the rock.

I got an Uber home. I smiled to myself on the journey, recalling Daisy's joke about how she'd get back to Swiss Cottage from the Cote on Richmond's George Street. I shouldn't have been surprised at just how much I was looking forward to seeing her. I'd booked an outside table. And I'd been studying the weather forecast like a cricket fetishist on the eve of a tour deciding test match. So far, it looked likely to remain fine.

****

Albert Hodge wasn't hard to find in those mild autumnal days prior to my departure for Kent and three academic years that would determine my future life. His pier constitutional was a daily ritual you could set your watch by. If you owned one, which I didn't by then. Or at least not one that worked. The Timex my father had given me at 11 had long before stopped ticking.

Samantha had gone off to Oxford the day after we celebrated her birthday. Her term started earlier than mine, with some sort of induction. We'd tried to keep her departure, in the front passenger seat of her dad's Ford Cortina, as low key as possible. But the thought of all her things, all her precious possessions, packed into the boot of the car to be deposited somewhere I didn't know, more than 100 miles away, was a poignant one. I watched the car recede into the distance and then shrink to nothing with tears in my eyes. It was the end of something. Even if we endured as a couple, something had gone forever.

I got to see my house on Rotten Row a couple of days later, on a Tuesday evening.

'Wife belongs to a bridge club,' Al had explained to me, meeting up on the pier. 'One of the pretentions she's gone in for since the good ship Premium Bond sailed into harbour.'

I wondered was Albert Hodge's marriage altogether happy. And I'd developed a hunch about him, based on his age and bearing. I said, 'You fought in the Great War, didn't you, Al?'

'Did indeed, young man. Stupidly volunteered in October of 'fourteen. I was on the Salient. Do you know what that means?'

'Ypres,' I said.

'Aye, Wipers. Brass gave young Albert a gong. The pals I lost. Doesn't really bear thinking about.'

This late on Monday morning, Al sitting beside me ramrod-straight in his immaculate camel overcoat and highly polished toe-capped shoes. I just looked out at the distant whitecaps, serene in the late sunshine. There was nothing adequate I could say about his war.

'You're a good lad,' he said, 'Tommy Boy. I've an inkling you'll go far. Tomorrow night, seven-sharp. Don't dare be a minute early or a minute late.'

I got there on the dot. It seemed a large house for two people, but then Al had spent his working life domiciled in a large hotel. He must have got used to roaming spacious rooms. He had set up the projector in his library, or study, in the half hour since his wife's departure to make up a bridge four at an address in Ainsdale. The screen was large, pale, expectant.

'Drink?' He said.

He didn't wait for a reply. He took a bottle of Glenmorangie and two cut crystal whisky tumblers from a glass fronted cabinet and poured us what looked to me like triples. 'No mixers,' he said, handing me my drink. 'But then we're not expecting female company.' He chinked his glass against mine and winked and gestured for me to sit in one of the two straight-backed chairs positioned to the rear of the projector. Then he flicked a switch and in the early evening gloom of closed curtains and heady single malt, the projector whirred into life.

The bobbed hair and garish make-up of women wielding cigarettes in holders and bedecked in glittering sequins and draped in feathered shawls. There were diamond brooches embellishing the chests of sheath frocks hugging backsides and hips. These young women looked boyish, most of them and Albert Hodge must have read my mind.

'The fashion of the time,' he said. 'Girls trying to look more like pretty boys. Can't remember why. Maybe the influence of Hollywood. Maybe that actress, Louise Brooks. She was a sort, Miss Brooks, proper stunner.'

I had never heard of Louise Brooks.

The camera moved onto the men. At first, they looked to me like members of an orchestra denuded of their instruments, because they were uniform in white tie. But then the physical choreography established itself, the preening arrogance of their gestures, the gloating privilege of the expressions on their blandly handsome faces.

'Remind you of anything, son?'

'Reminds me of reading *The Great Gatsby*, I said.

'Saw the film a few years ago,' Al said. 'Robert Redford. But Gatsby was only a bootlegger. Trust me, this lot were worse.'

The camera pulled back to provide an overdue establishing shot. It revealed a huge ballroom, marble-walled, mature palm trees anchored in square wooded pots, a full-size locomotive sculpted from ice, glistening as it dribbled slowly into extinction.

'Heatwave,' Albert Hodge offered by way of explanation. 'An enterprising way of keeping the hotel guests from sweating.'

'Blimey.'

'We had an ice-house. We had everything. Ah,' he said.

The camera had moved on. A blond, tanned, sparely muscular man with skin that looked tautly stretched over facial bones. There was a kind of tension to him, he looked coiled, somehow. And he was Harry Spalding, I recognised him from the photo I had seen.

'He was here for the whole of the summer that year,' Al murmured beside me, sipping Scotch. 'Limped into Liverpool harbour in his storm damaged boat. It was being repaired in a dry dock there. A number of women disappeared that summer. The gossip put him in the frame. Spalding. Rented a house a few doors down from here.'

'Really?'

Another sip of Scotch. 'Reckon they should dig up the garden.'

'Bit late for that.'

'No time limit on the truth, son.'

The camera pulled back. Spalding was talking to a man I recognised as Edward Swarbrick. And he really did look like the head undertaker who walked with his ceremonial staff in front of the plumed horses pulling the carriage hearse at an old-fashioned funeral. He wore a monocle. There was a confidential character about his dialogue with the American, even in that crowded ballroom. The half smiles and winks and mutterings were somehow furtive.

'That Swarbrick?' Al asked me.

'That's him,' I said.

'Never a guest, I don't think. Don't recognise him as a bar regular, either. He was here specifically, for this occasion.'

'The Jericho Ball,' I said.

'And he knew that creepy yank. Pretty tight, the two of them, from the looks of it. I was wrong, Tommy Boy. Spalding did have a friend.'

Chapter 5

On the Friday before our dinner date, Daisy finally found out a few things about the Sacred Heart Orphanage; the first of those being that it had been called that. It had been established in 1921, as Church-run and staffed by nuns from the Notre Dame teaching order. The order was familiar to me. They had occupied the Weld Road Convent, since demolished, in my youth. One of them had taught me S-level English at school.

'In April of 'forty-two, an order was placed with a Bogolino carpenter for twenty-nine coffins. Bogolino is the nearest town to the orphanage. And the coffins were small. Half of them were no more than a metre long.'

'How did you find this out?'

'The phantom nun Suarez claimed to have seen said something about Fascists. Mussolini came to power well before Hitler did, but if you're looking for some sort of crime or atrocity, wartime is when it's likeliest to occur, because that's when it can be most easily covered up.'

'What was the clue?'

'The Vatican paid for the coffins. Then it was a question of finding the priest who officiated at the funeral. He had to be local.

And it would have been inconceivable that he would have kept quiet about it.'

I said, 'Nothing would have been reported in the press. Censorship in wartime Italy was strict.'

'I found the priest. He wrote a memoir, never published. But the archivist at the municipal library knew the whereabouts of the original copy. She read me the relevant section over the phone. The orphanage was for handicapped children. Some of them had what we now call Down Syndrome. Some of them suffered from what seems to have been autism. Others were physically impaired.'

'And they were what, Daisy? Euthanised?'

'Murdered,' Daisy said, 'If we're calling a spade a spade. The Mussolini regime didn't kill on the industrial scale of Nazi Germany, but they did have blood on their hands.'

'And the Suarez nun?'

'He seems to have seen her pleading for their lives. Or maybe warning of what was about to happen.'

'How did you find the priest?'

'Relevant dates, small rural population his ministry. Choice of two. And a stroke of luck, because the library archivist had heard the story from her grandmother.'

I said, 'I wonder why a massacre like that has never become public knowledge?'

Daisy said, 'Post-war, Italy was a country on its knees. The only industry in the Dolomites was tourism. Not exactly pragmatic to put off all those hikers, skiers and climbers with a gruesome tale of child slaughter. And shame was probably a part of it. Not only those who supported Il Duce but those who opposed him and despite that, did nothing to stop it.'

It seemed inappropriate to congratulate Daisy on what she had discovered. The orphanage had been closed by a horrible tragedy that was also a war crime. And a well-kept secret. I remembered the fact that Suarez had not explored the whole building in its entirety. I wondered would there be toys and clothes, callipers for polio afflicted limbs, shoes designed for club feet. Were the children slaughtered in the building, in front of their carers?

I asked Daisy did she know.

'In Germany they'd take them to a forest in a flatbed army truck,' she said, 'or a convoy of trucks. More efficient. No mess to clean up afterwards.'

'Barbaric,' I said.

Daisy was quiet at the other end of the line. Then she said, 'The people who did it may have seen them as mercy killings. None of those children were going to recover.'

'That's facile.'

'But one way of easing a guilty conscience.'

'It must have traumatised their carers,' I said.

'One of them in particular,' she said. 'The one Phillipe Suarez saw.'

There had been a story about the Suarez death in that morning's *Times*. He had made page 3. Two columns under a family snapshot with the faces of his wife and young children obscured. Saturnine good looks and a grin that said he hadn't a care in the world.

I thought the photo almost certainly taken before his visit to the orphanage. That wasn't, of course, mentioned in the story. It concentrated on the success of his career and the stunned disbelief of his colleagues at the manner of his death. And the story concluded with the number for the Samaritans.

I read an interview a couple of years ago given by a jumper who had survived the plunge into the water from the Golden Gate Bridge. One of the very few to survive it, the coastguard crew informed him after picking him up. Their job was usually fishing out corpses.

The jumper said he regretted doing it a fraction of a second after letting go of the guard rail. At the very moment, the drop became inevitable. And I wondered had Suarez felt the same way, in the long pause prior to impact from the top of Beachy Head.

I heard Daisy say, 'Are you still there, Tom?'

'You still okay for tomorrow?'

'This conversation has rather killed my appetite,' she said. 'But tomorrow is another day. And we can't do anything about events that took place seventy-odd years ago.'

We could sensationalise them, I thought. But I would be careful not to do that when we got to Italy.

'I'm looking forward to tomorrow evening,' Daisy said.

'Me too,' I said, which was true.

There were no details in the Suarez newspaper story about his funeral. I supposed it was too soon for the arrangements to have been made. I wondered would my brother attend. I thought he was probably a certainty to do so, to pay his last respects with complete sincerity.

My mind turned to those 29 coffins, some of them not much more than a metre long. Obviously they had not been buried in a cemetery. The priest would have conducted his service at some location kept secret by the authorities. A secluded burial ground that might show up from above, using a thermal imaging camera. A preserved body might. It depended on how substantial the coffins had been and the depth to which they had been buried.

****

I didn't see Samantha again until the end of the Michaelmas term. I didn't speak to her on the phone. We swapped postcards and wrote one another letters, but ten weeks is a long time in the turbulent life of an undergraduate new to everything happening to them. I moved into a shared house in Whitstable, where for the first time in my life, I was obliged to make my own bed. I met people more intelligent than I was. In some cases, much more intelligent. I got onto the university boxing team, having discovered that the resident coach was the veteran Commonwealth Games and Olympic coach who had tutored Alan Minter and John Conteh as amateurs. I ran along the seafront and through the Blean woods. And I made unlikely friends.

You change. That's inevitable. You think of it as growing, which isn't necessarily true. By the time I saw Samantha again in the Christmas vacation, I was somebody different and she was too. The history was still there. The physical attraction was still strong between us. Her mannerisms were familiar, and her speech pattern had not altered. I could still sometimes predict what it was she was about to say. But there were things about one another now, that neither of us knew, a fact that created a kind of tension. I think we both realised that we would have to work at not becoming strangers to one another. And we didn't have the time or the opportunity to put the effort in. Or the will, if I'm really honest. I became aware in those four weeks, back in my hometown, that apathy is a contagious condition in relationships which are meant to be, above all else, romantic.

We called it a day on the night before we both went back to resume our university lives and courses. No tears. Sad to say it, tears would have seemed melodramatic by that point. And then early in the New Year I endured a month-long bout of intense nostalgia for a simpler and less contingent life than the one I was now living. I turned 19. Affaires followed. This at the time when the pill was associated with sexual liberation rather than unpleasant side-effects. And commitment was neither fashionable nor realistic as a practicality.

Summer arrived, my first year ended and I went on what would be the last family holiday I would ever experience. And I learned a little more about the exclusive club to which Edward Swarbrick and Harry Spalding had belonged. And Klaus Fischer, their industrialist friend. I learned a bit more about him, because the caravan my mum had booked for a July week was on the Isle of Wight.

We were based for the week near Wootton Creek. It was a farmer's field, rather than an organised site. The nearest entertainment was a faux German Bier Keller complete with serving maids in bodices and oversized jugs brim-full of lager. I noticed the eye-catching woman, seated alone and smoking roll-ups on the first evening Andy and I went there. Her black clothes and white-blonde hair made her conspicuous. Vivid red lipstick against a winter-pale complexion. Black painted nails. She was strange, exotic and beautiful in a fragile sort of way that made her compelling to look at.

I approached her on the third night, only on an Andy dare. I wouldn't have done it otherwise and did it only expecting a cold rebuttal. She was unapproachable. Which I mean as a compliment. She had an intimidating glamour. 'Get lost,' was about the best I was hoping for.

Instead, she smiled, gestured for me to take the chair next to hers and said, 'You've taken your time.'

I said, 'I don't have any time.'

'Because you're only here for a week,' she said. 'And you're already three days in.'

'You're observant.'

'And you're on the picturesque side of handsome,' she said, 'So I haven't really needed to be.'

I'd bought her a drink and noticed the imperfections; the slightly tobacco-stained teeth, the split ends inflicted by peroxide bleach, before blundering badly by asking her how old she was.

'Older than I look,' she said. 'And that's an ungallant question, when you haven't even taken the trouble to ask me my name.'

'What is your name?'

But she didn't answer. She nodded towards the bar and said, 'You should re-join your brother before he stares so hard, he actually turns to stone.'

'Like with Medusa?'

She smiled. 'Exactly so.'

'How do you know he's my brother?'

'Because it's obvious.'

I stood.

'Wait.' She took out a slip of paper and scribbled on it and handed it to me. 'This is my address. If you can find it, find it tomorrow afternoon. I'll be in.'

She had scribbled her name. She was Helena. 'Tom,' I said, extending my hand.

'I know,' she said. And though I had no idea of how she knew, I was certain she was telling the truth.

Helena lived in a thatched cottage. Not the sort of building I'd ever been in before, though there was a bit of thatch in the oldest part of Southport, Churchtown, which was the first area settled back in the 18th century. When she opened her wooden front door, her age was no easier to determine in daylight than it had been in the smoky dimness of the Bier Keller the previous night. She could have been in her late 20s, but what she had said hinted that she might be ten years older than that. I gathered she lived alone, or she wouldn't have proffered such a casual invitation. She took me through to her back garden, where she invited me to sit on one of two rattan chairs pulled up to a small wooden table.

Her garden was carelessly overgrown. Thorn bushes in spikey tangles. Ivy climbing crumbly redbrick walls in untended swathes. Wild flowers and weeds in a colourful litter in the long grass around our feet. All of it emitting the powerful scent of summer.

There was a rolled cigarette on the table and Helena picked it up and lit it with a match. She blew out smoke to extinguish the match, the smoke vapid in strong sunlight. Then she said, 'I expect you'd like to go to bed with me.'

I said, 'I'd like that very much.'

'Of course you would. Boys your age want to go to bed with every woman on the planet under 40.'

'That might be a slight exaggeration.'

'Unless they're queer,' she said. 'You're not queer, are you, Tom?'

'No,' I said.

'It isn't going to happen,' she said. 'Not why you're here. Put it out of your mind.'

'I'll try.'

'I'm too old for you.'

'That's a matter of opinion.'

She frowned. 'Try harder.'

'Why am I here?'

She was silent, smoking. Then she said, 'What do you know about witchcraft?'

'Almost nothing,' I said, truthfully. 'Though I did notice a corn dolly on the kitchen wall coming through. And the tarot pack on the coffee table in your living room. And the bearded, grinning bloke with your door knocker between his teeth.'

'The Green Man.'

'Are they clues?'

'Very good,' she said.

She had on a cream-coloured smock-top. She was not wearing a bra. I could see her nipples budding through the thin, taut fabric.

'How old are you, Helena?'

'Since I'm not on your list of potential conquests, it doesn't matter, Tom. Stick to what's relevant.'

'Which is?'

'You've a sensitivity. If you haven't encountered a ghost, you're going to. But I believe you have.'

It was warm in that garden, a glorious, full-blooded, bird-chirping July day. And I felt myself go cold as well, I suspected, as pale. I was reminded of Edward Swarbrick and of his friend who'd had a mansion on Wight, on the edge of Brighstone Forest.

'Have you heard of a man named Klaus Fischer?'

And it was Helena's turn to grow pale. She said, 'It doesn't do to bandy that name about.'

'He had a house here. A mansion, actually. Louche reputation.'

Helena's eyes had taken on a vacant look, as though she were somewhere else. She reached to put a hand over mine, which rested on the tabletop. 'Promise me you won't go there,' she said.

The touch of her was intense, shocking. A wave of desire rippled through me. It shook my voice when I spoke. 'I promise,' I said.

She slid her hand away and her eyes found mine. She said, 'Fischer belonged to a secret order, or cult. They were called the Jericho Society. They enacted rituals. There was a rumour about human sacrifice. Then Fischer disappeared. What's your interest?'

'You were right. About my ghost? It was one of Fischer's friends.'

Helena said, 'Harry Spalding?'

'How do you know about him?'

'My grandfather sometimes crewed for him when he raced his schooner here. He was said to be a friend of Klaus Fischer.'

I told her about Edward Swarbrick and his top hat and about Kelmscott Court and poor Jennifer Purdy and my encounter with Arabella Pankhurst, whose relentless sobbing had awoken Jennifer and Paul Wright in their penthouse.

'Quite a story,' she said when I'd finished. 'And I don't think you've reached its conclusion. Do you have a girlfriend?'

I shook my head. 'Not since before last Christmas. What kind of witch are you, Helena?'

'I'm of the white variety,' she said, 'as pure as the driven.' She stood abruptly.

'Where are you going?'

'To the fridge in my kitchen. To fetch a bottle of chilled Chablis. Do you like white wine, Tom?'

'I do on a day as hot as this one is.'

'Good. We're going to drink that bottle of wine together. Share it. And then I'm taking you to bed.'

'But you said –'

'I know what I said. I also know it's a woman's prerogative to change her mind.'

We saw each other each afternoon until the day of the ferry taking me back to the mainland. Knowing there was no future in it telescoped our time together into something vivid with exaggerated life. I was right about the beauty, but wrong about the fragility. You need strength to be as honest about everything as Helena Donovan was. Never to deceive yourself or other people requires real stamina. And she did know things. She possessed a sixth sense much too strong to be described simply as intuition.

On our last afternoon she gave me a tarot reading. The frown that creased her forehead at the end of it struck me as disconcerting. 'What?' I asked her.

'What comes through strongest is how ambitious you are,' she said.

'I'm not ambitious at all,' I said.

'You're easy going now because you can be. I mean, you're a student, so being laid-back is part of the deal. When you graduate, you're in for a surprise about who and what you really are.'

'Are there obstacles?'

'Largely of your own devising.'

'What does that mean?'

'It means stay away from that derelict pile on the edge of Brighstone Forest.'

'I've already promised to do that.'

'Make it a promise you keep.'

'I'll miss you,' I said, without really meaning to, only giving voice to the thought that just then had entered my head.

'No you won't,' she said, smiling. 'I'm not a part of your real life. You'll slot back into your routine and forget all about me.'

But she was wrong about that. I thought about her often and think about her still. About her contradictions. Asking myself how was it possible for someone so brutally truthful to be at the same time such an enigma?

And Helena had provided me with a name. The Jericho Society. It made sense of the name given to Harry Spalding's crack unit of army assassins and to that long-ago celebration at the Birkdale Palace Hotel. A society so secret they could give their ball that name brazenly, confident that nobody would make the connection.

Bloody rituals. Rumours of human sacrifice. Had that been Arabella Pankhurst's fate at the hands of Edward Swarbrick? And did it matter? Exposing the wrongs of the past could neither undo nor reverse them. Nothing would bring Arabella back and her killer was beyond retribution.

Years later, I learned of Helena's age at the time I'd known her, shocked to stumble across her face at the head of a *Guardian* obituary. In the years after our encounter she had moved to America and written a successful book themed around fortune telling. I did the maths and worked out that she had been 41 years old at the time we met. More than twice my age. And not a day too old for me.

****

The fine weather held. I met Daisy Chain at the White Horse pub on Richmond Riverside at 6.45pm. The table at Cote was five minutes away and booked for 7.30. We could while away 40 congenial minutes watching the world go by over a cold drink, seated outside. It was a relaxed way to begin an evening over which I had no expectation at all. I knew Daisy was a first-rate researcher. I thought she was a decent human being. She was entertaining company, and I was beginning to think one of the most physically attractive women I had ever encountered.

I suppose my heightened awareness of that was one consequence of my changed perspective. She had always been a good-looking woman objectively. It's just that I had never been in her company as a single man, prior to the impromptu barbeque she'd hosted eight days earlier. And this was only the second time I had seen her socially.

She was on time. That was something else about her. She was always punctual. I asked, 'How did you get here?'

'Underground and then overground. Empty trains. Think they'll ever recover?'

'Not completely, no,' I said.

She'd worn her heavy dark-blonde hair loose. A pair of tortoiseshell Ray Bans had been pushed up into it. Locks of it splashed around the collar of the tailored white shirt she wore. A pencil-skirt the same dark blue as her strappy leather shoes. A fresh fragrance I thought probably Jo Malone. It had that summery exuberance. It suited her.

I rose to go inside to get us drinks as she sat at the wooden table between us and slid her bag onto it. She said, 'It's nice to see you smile, Tom. You don't do it enough.'

'You need something to smile about.'

'That's true.'

'Becks?'

'Anything cold and wet,' she said. 'I'm parched.'

When I got back outside, she said, 'What's your thinking on the orphanage?'

'We go in guerrilla style,' I said. 'Permissions would be tricky if there's an ongoing cover-up about what happened. The Vatican might be okay but the local legislature? Italy is notorious for red tape. The location is remote. We take full advantage of that and obviously we do it at night.'

'Personnel?'

'Team of three,' I said. 'One vehicle. Pete Davidson's budget will stretch to a hired four-wheel-drive.'

Daisy sipped beer from the bottle and said, 'Sometimes when I research these scenarios, I wish I could be at the sharp end when the camera starts to roll. Not on this occasion.'

'Back story couldn't be grimmer,' I said. 'But I'm going to concentrate on the nun apparition.'

'And name your witness?'

I shook my head. 'No,' I said. 'Unnecessary distress. Phillipe Suarez never told his wife, according to Andy. Not surprising. The state he was in when he took refuge there, she'd probably have banned him from climbing again for life.'

'Didn't help him,' Daisy said. 'And keeping your source anonymous makes the story a bit thin.'

'That depends on what happens, Daisy, in dead of night when we get there. And now I think we should talk about something else.'

She bit her lip and smiled. She said, 'Is this an actual date?'

'Well,' I said, 'It's probably a bit more than a virtual date. I mean, you're sitting there.'

'And you're sitting there,' she said. She sipped beer. She said, 'A toe in the water. Playing it by ear.'

'You only mix your metaphors when you're stalling, Daisy. What are you stalling about?'

She looked at me directly. She said, 'If we're going to get to know one another personally, I'd like to know some personal stuff. We could start with Claire.'

'Why Claire?'

'Because I have the sense that more than anything, you love your daughter. Yet you've never spoken about her.'

And so I told Daisy Chain about my daughter. About the eating disorder, the self-harming, the claims she'd made concerning psychic powers, the insecurity that evolved into outright paranoia, the breakdowns and the abrupt, final, disconnect from the world that put her into an institution.

'Final?' Daisy asked.

So I told her about James Balfour, about the Holy Grail of hypnotism, in which I realised, as I spoke, I was investing an awful lot of hope.

She took my hand when it was time for us to go and we walked the route to Cote. I think the gesture was spontaneous. The touch of her was a surprise that felt wonderful, her grip cool and firm in the dissipating evening heat. We got to the restaurant. We took our seats, and the waiter came out and we ordered. We sipped chilled wine and ate our starters, the hustle and bustle of George Street's pedestrian and road traffic almost restored to normal. I think that some of us erect barriers against the world. I knew I was in the company of a woman capable of dismantling them.

Then as we waited for our mains to arrive, I looked up and standing there on the pavement no further that five metres away, saw my former wife staring at us, wide-eyed, rigid in a cream Summer dress and floral silk shawl. Tanned, from what I thought must be a recent holiday. I couldn't read her expression. She looked indignant, but she also looked curiously satisfied. She walked over to where we sat in a few swift strides. I tried to remember had she ever met Daisy in my past life at some reception or industry event. I couldn't honestly recall.

'Tom and Daisy,' she said. 'As cosy as a nursery rhyme and so very picturesque.'

She looked at Daisy and said, 'Isn't he a little out of your league, darling?' Then she looked at me and said, 'Though way past your sell-by date.'

Our wine was in an aluminium bucket filled with ice on a stand next to our table. She reached for it with a careless backhand swipe. It toppled over, ice, wine and broken glass spraying across the flagstones.

'Bon appetit,' she said. 'Enjoy.' And she strode away in the direction of Richmond Bridge.

A waiter came out and began to clear up the mess with a brush and pan after righting the bucket's stand. I noticed the couple at the neighbouring table staring at us with astonished looks.

'I don't think you two ever met, did you?'

'No,' Daisy said. 'Quite an introduction.'

'How would she know your name?'

'Linked-in profile,' she said. 'Facebook, Twitter, a dozen ways. When you freelance, you need a public platform. Well, I do. You probably don't, being out of my league.'

'I'm so sorry that happened.'

'Not really your fault. I suggested this place. I suppose she lives here?'

'She got the Richmond house.'

'And you downsized to Teddington.'

'I'm so sorry.'

Our mains were served. I stared at my plate. Daisy said, 'Order another bottle of wine. We'll keep calm and carry on.'

'I don't know why she did that.'

Daisy laughed. She said, 'Proof, Tom.'

'Of what?'

'Proof that there's more than one way of being haunted.'

Our evening ended with a chaste kiss at the taxi rank opposite Richmond Station. It might have ended differently without the roadside cabaret of an hour earlier. I'll never know. My ex-wife's taunt about my sell-by date had hit home, to be perfectly honest. I knew Daisy's age, so I knew that there were 18 years between us. How much is too much? I vacillated over that one.

Before she climbed into the cab, I asked her, 'Can we do this again?'

She pulled a face and then smiled. 'Parts of it,' she said. 'Not all of it.'

I walked home through the late dusk as darkness incrementally fell, heavy hearted about my daughter. Talking about Claire had reminded me of the depth and complexity of the challenges she faced and that phrase I'd used, the Holy Grail of hypnotism, seemed both trite and absurdly optimistic.

' … there's more than one way of being haunted.'

That was probably true. I was supposed to be an authority on the paranormal, but sometimes the distinctions are blurred. Sometimes we're surprised, sometimes confounded and sometimes shocked. Certainties have a way of shifting. The world can be unpredictable, unexpected. It's characterised by much more ambiguity than we're comfortable believing.

I had been certain, really, of nothing in the world since something inexplicable endured at the age of 11. What did the darkness harbour now? I thought I was shortly to find that out at four locations at best dubious, at worst malevolent.

****

My breakthrough moment came at the age of 30, when I broke my promise to Helena Donovan and went to that derelict mansion built on the edge of Brighstone Forest on the Isle of Wight by the German industrialist Klaus Fischer. I did it because she had been right to say I was ambitious. Ambition superseded a pledge made in good faith never to go there.

I filmed over the course of a night, equipped with an infrared camera and a reel-to-reel tape machine. The camera picked up movement where there should have been none. Pulled curtains, slammed doors, windows opened and closed with shrieks of protest from warped wood. There were all sorts of sounds. The click of leather heels on parquet. The ivory clack of snooker balls colliding. A knowing smirk of mirth. The subdued tinkle of drinking glasses. It was not at all a reposeful place.

I edited the film down from 8 hours to the one-hour programme that's now had 7 million-plus hits on YouTube. When originally scheduled, the film drew a TV audience of 5 million viewers. It made my name partly because no two people seemed able to agree on exactly what it was, they were watching and hearing. Sepia phantoms in a faded ballroom? A bloated, grinning reflection? The glint of a ticking pocket watch? Some viewers claimed to have heard a jazz age melody played on a barrel-house piano. They just couldn't agree on the tune. Others, old shellac recordings, scratchy under a gramophone needle, operatic and faint.

A one-off cinema screening was organised. The venue was the Curzon in Richmond. Interested people attended. And a battalion of press sceptics. Altogether a full house. And that was where the real fun began. There were the sights that were strangely inconsistent, having only in common the power to disturb. But there were also scents, experienced by that sell-out audience. Cigar smoke, brilliantine, perfumes with an antique pungency. Some audience members sobbed. A few broke the ambient silence with sudden screams. Perhaps a dozen people left their seats, some clutching their faces, trying to cover their eyes or ears with their fingers.

That wasn't the end of it. There were, in the aftermath of the screening, what the newspapers euphemistically describe as sudden deaths. The wife of a film industry insider present at the viewing tried to sue me after he slit his wrists in his bathtub. The case got as far as the high court before being thrown out. The paradox of extreme stress and priceless publicity. But the suicides were a matter of such huge regret I thought about destroying the film. It would have been pointless. By then, there were a dozen pirate copies doing the rounds. It was a viral phenomenon before that phrase had been coined, beyond suppression.

Its uncertainty made the film all the more disconcerting. And led to its notoriety. And the tiresome accusations of trickery I've got bored since of having to deny. The truth is that when the world doesn't collude with us, when it doesn't cooperate, we're frightened. The Fischer House was a delinquent place. And some of the footage I shot through that endless night was so disturbing I had to censor it. I was unwilling to expose it to public view. I was sensitive to mental health and to how fragile that can be, long before my daughter's troubles began.

I was tired when I reached home. But before turning in, I checked my email on my laptop. In emergencies the Retreat people were supposed to phone me. But the definition of emergency could differ among the staff there. I always looked, last thing. Only by doing so was sleep possible.

Nothing from the Retreat. I decided I would visit the following day. Sundays were busy on the route to and from West London to

Hove and busy when you got there with summer visitors. The sunny weather looked likely to hold and if it did, and if it suited her mood, I could take Claire for a seafront stroll and an ice-cream or milkshake. She was allowed out chaperoned and would not be overwhelmed by the crowds in the company of her father.

An email from my brother. He had sent Phillipe's widow a letter of condolence. That was the sort of thoughtful thing my solicitous brother did. He had received a request to attend the funeral by reply. Slightly to his surprise, Marianne Suarez also requested to meet him over the week prior to the service. At his convenience, she said. A dilemma for him because he knew, and she did not, about what Phillipe had experienced in the Dolomites.

My phone rang. Daisy. A grasp the nettle sort of woman, I thought, resignedly. Calling to tell me that none of what we had experienced together that evening was in any way worthy of repetition.

'How are you, Tom?'

'Tired,' I said.

'It doesn't matter,' she said.

'What doesn't?'

'I saw your face when your ex made that crack about your age. You were hurt by it. When you walked me to my cab, it preoccupied you.'

'It did,' I said. My brother's words blurred on the screen in front of me. I closed my eyes. 'Eighteen years is a big gap.'

'I'm forty, Tom.'

'Which you don't look,'

'Nobody's going to mistake me for Lolita.'

That made me smile. I said, 'I'm glad you called.'

'Sweet dreams,' she said, and she broke the connection.

****

I got to Hove at 11am and met Claire where she was waiting for me at reception, rather than in her room, because I had called first thing to tell them to expect me. She had plaited her hair and secured the two plaits with red ribbons; red the one colour she permitted herself. I took this to be a good sign, a signal that she was in a buoyant, maybe even a confident mood. She stood to greet me. I put my arms around her slender shape and hugged her and she stiffened only very slightly in my embrace. I had bought her a bag of new books. I left them on the reception desk to take to her room later. Best to get her out without delay. Her moods could be mercurial.

Outside, she set off fast. My daughter was long-limbed, purposeful of stride. I laughed and said, 'Where exactly are we headed?'

'The pier, of course,' she said.

'It'll be packed on a Sunday, Claire.'

'Doesn't matter,' she said. 'I'm with you.'

Crowds made her anxious. Confined spaces had the same effect. But sometimes, with me, she would revert to how she had been when matters had more normality about them. Indifferent faces passed us belonging to blandly contented people. Some of them eating ice-lollies, always a reminder to me of my ice-cream kiosk days on the promenade in Southport. I had been 16 when I got that job. Just a few weeks older than my daughter was now.

'What are we going to do when we get to the pier?'

'Go to the amusement arcade at the end of it, of course. Play on the grabber machines.'

'Sea World would be cheaper. For me, I mean.'

'But staring at fish isn't fun. And they stare back at you, Daddy.'

Brighton was busier than Hove, more pedestrian traffic. And I think it was this that caused Claire to take my hand. I gave hers what I hoped was a comforting squeeze, mindful that whatever James Balfour was doing with her, it was working. Progress was being made.

'What are you thinking?'

'I was thinking about your hypnosis. James Balfour says you're an ideal subject.'

'It's relaxing. Afterwards I mean. And James is nice.'

That was interesting. First-name terms with Balfour, but she called her psychiatrist Doctor Pettifer.

We got to the pier, to the sound of Wurlitzer music and the smell of frying onions from hotdog stalls and the cloying waft of raspberry flavoured candyfloss. My daughter looked pale and thin amid all the bustle and colour and she winced as a large and muscular dog pulling its owner on a chain lead brushed past her.

The owner turned and looked at me. And I thought, what kind of moron takes a Rottweiler dog to the beach? And I gave him a look back that said, *if that bites her, I'll fucking well bite you.* I never stopped with the boxing training. It became a lifetime's routine. The rope, the speedball and the heavy bag. Regardless of sell-by date, I could punch. When people will resort to violence without compunction, their potential victims can usually tell. Dog Man got the message, I saw it in his eyes.

My daughter gave my hand a tug. 'Come on,' she said. 'I need to play the machines while I still can, before the luck drains away.'

I thought that a strange way to phrase it. I said, 'Does luck come and go?'

'Of course it does, Dad. Wouldn't be luck otherwise. It would be something else altogether.' Sometimes Dad, sometimes Daddy. I had never been able to work out what provoked the switch.

Claire's luck was certainly in. She won three cuddly toys from various Disney franchises I didn't recognise. She won a rubber skull and crossbones keyring. She won a plastic, three-draw telescope. We were entertained for over an hour and the experience couldn't have cost me more than about £35.

I'm joking. It was a novelty to swap notes for coins; not to any longer have to treat cash as something contagious. And my daughter was carefree for an hour. I could see it in her expression. And that was priceless. I got a plastic bag for our booty and took her for fish and chips and she ate like someone who had never had a problem with that. More points for James Balfour.

Walking back, her pace didn't relent. The only clue that she was fatigued was that she spoke less. The excitement, the anticipation, had gone. She got very hyped-up on those grabber machines. She played with total concentration. From being a five-year-old, that had never changed about her. It wasn't the prizes. She had probably already forgotten about the contents of the carrier bag held in my right fist. It was the process, the challenge. The grabber's grip was weak, the opportunity fleeting, the odds stacked, the technique required precise.

I picked up the bookbag at reception and we went to her room. To the right of the faceless nun, I saw that Claire had sketched another picture. It was an accomplished piece of work and it made me stare and swallow in shock. It depicted a man, prone and broken-bodied at the bottom of a cliff-face. My daughter saw me staring at it.

'They're a pair,' she said. 'I mean, different subjects, obviously. But they sort of belong together?' Upspeak. She did it when she was anxious. I didn't want her to be anxious but couldn't drag my eyes away from the picture. As levelly as I could, I asked her, 'Where did you get the idea?'

'Sometimes in dreams,' she said. 'Sometimes just in daydreams.'

'Did you see him fall?'

'I think he jumped. But no, I didn't see that part.'

Something occurred to me. 'Does the drawing have a name?'

'I don't know why, because he's wearing normal clothes. But I call it, The Climber.'

At ten o'clock the following morning, I called Julia Pettifer. I explained, without mentioning the name of Phillipe Suarez, the link to my work of the two charcoal sketches stuck to the wall of my daughter's room.

'Doesn't sound like coincidence,' she said.

'No. And not a consequence of anything I've said to her.'

Pettifer was silent. Then she said, 'You're aware that Claire has claimed a degree of psychic sensitivity.'

'Of course I am.'

'Consistently claimed it. Almost indignantly.'

'You don't buy that. You're a psychiatrist.'

She cleared her throat. She said, 'I'm not a total stranger to your TV work, Tom.'

It was the second time she had used my Christian name. Only the second time. Coming from someone so cold, it jarred.

'Meaning?'

'When some of your subjects have discussed atmospheres, presences, they've sounded sincere. Plausible. Even convincing.

We know little, really, about the workings of the human mind. I mean about its capabilities. Its potential, if you will.'

'You think my daughter might really be psychic?'

Another, longer silence. Then she said, 'James Balfour says Claire knows details about him that he hasn't told her and that aren't in the public domain.'

'Significant things?'

'Not ominous. And not intrusive. Playground stuff. Favourite meal. Favourite film. Favourite novel.'

'Stuff you could guess?'

'I doubt it.'

'Psychic sensitivity is a complication my daughter doesn't need.'

'And those sketches are quite ghoulish. Beautifully accomplished, but morbid.'

'So you've seen them?'

'Of course I have.'

I ended the conversation. It had achieved nothing. No conversation with Julia Pettifer ever seemed to. She had just demonstrated once again her reluctance to commit to any black and white conclusions. About anything. About Claire. Her hypnotist's favourite novel was one thing. A broken-bodied suicide careening through her mind was another entirely.

I thought about James Balfour. I didn't think calling him would achieve anything. Then I thought hard about Claire's demeaner discussing the sketch she had entitled The Climber the previous afternoon. She had been matter-of-fact about it, not traumatised by it, not remotely disturbed. If she started to produce images connected to the four hauntings I was investigating, I would have to reconsider the project, maybe even pull the plug.

Was she reading my mind? I hoped not. If she was, she would know what a preoccupation Daisy Chain had become to her father. If she did know about that, would she have mentioned it? In her mischievous Sunday mood, I thought probably she would have.

Feeling the frustration of my somewhat elliptical conversation with Doctor Pettifer, I went to the gym and worked out for an hour, eye on the clock because I had a lunch scheduled with Pete Davidson. I knew he would want something more substantial than he'd had so far to justify his production budget. He didn't know about the Phillipe Suarez orphanage connection and wouldn't get that from me. The only people who knew about it, so far as I was aware, were me, my brother and Daisy. And Daisy was almost as good at discretion as Andy was.

Anyway, Pete didn't need to know about Suarez. There was a grisly child massacre to brief him on. If that didn't qualify as a paranormal provocation, I couldn't imagine what would. Some places are repositories of grief and anguish. If you're sceptical about that claim, try touring a derelict hospital building or somewhere that was once in its history a lunatic asylum. And if those experiences don't do it, take a risk with your health cancer-wise and visit Chernobyl.

Years ago, I travelled back to Southport to interview one of the demolition crew responsible for reducing the Birkdale Palace Hotel to rubble back in 1969. He was a decade into retirement by then and living in a Scarisbrick care home. He was suffering from dementia, but I was assured could remember events from decades ago quite vividly. It was the recent past he had problems with, his son told me, when I sought permission to speak to his father. The man's mind was on the way to being destroyed, but was still then only at the frayed stage.

What I recall most about the interview couldn't be articulated in words. It was the look of empty dread on my subject's face when I brought him back to the Birkdale Palace.

'Was it true. About the lifts?' I asked him.

'Aye, it were true,' he said. 'Clanking away, without any juice to power them.'

'Must have been disconcerting,' I said.

He gripped my arm with a still powerful hand. 'It wasn't the worst,' he said.

'What was worse?'

'The rooms that wouldn't stay empty. The guests who wouldn't leave that none of us could see. The stir and babble of them.'

I met Pete at the Ivy at a quarter to one. As always, the place was full, teeming with prosperous energy and the gloating sheen of success. He looked tanned and brimming after a weekend, he told me, spent sailing on the Solent. I sat facing him and the wall behind him. He sat where he could play the room by waving and blowing air kisses at industry players he knew. Which from his restless gesticulation, seemed to be most of them.

'Didn't know you sailed,' I said.

'Question of spending my money on something more wholesome than buying you a pricey lunch. Learned as a boy in Sea Scouts. Great to get out of town, even better when you are on the water.'

'And it's put you in buoyant mood.'

'Which terrible puns like that could rapidly sabotage,' he said. 'Or should I say sink.'

'You must be quite good,' I said. 'The Solent is a busy stretch of water.'

'Anything I'm only quite good at I don't bother with,' he said.

I grinned. 'Didn't figure you for a quitter, Pete.'

'It isn't a simple matter of capitulation,' he said. 'It's more a philosophical standpoint.'

I pretended to ponder on this. Then I said, 'And presumably the reason you're still single.'

'Don't push your luck, Tommy Boy. The furlough scheme wrapped up a long time ago. And you wouldn't have qualified anyway.'

The ritual verbal jousting completed, I told him about what Daisy Chain had discovered about the history of the Dolomites orphanage. He brightened even further, contemplating the specifics of the story.

'You really think there might be relics? School exercise books, threadbare cuddly toys, child prosthetics fashioned by Italian craftsmen eighty years ago? That would colour the narrative wonderfully. All that added poignancy.'

'It's possible,' I said. 'But unconfirmed until we get there.'

He looked at me. He said, 'We could always get creative with the props this side, have you take a bunch of stuff.'

I shook my head. 'I'm not that man, Pete. You know I'm not.'

'But you are ambitious.'

Which seemed a strange observation. 'What does that mean?'

'Saturday evening, Tom. Berthed on the Island. Ventnor Harbour. Nearest pub for a stiffener and ran into an old flame of yours. Pure coincidence. Got chatting to her because she was on her lonesome and so easy on the eye, in a widow's weeds, boho sort of way. Somewhere between a Goth and a fallen angel. But you know that.'

My mouth had gone too dry for me to respond. He continued.

'Asked me what I did, and I happened to mention our project, and you, and she smiled a knowing smile. Told me you were ambitious. And not really to be trusted. Only a brief chat, mind. She had to dash.' He looked at the ceiling. 'Small world. I'll have her name in a second.'

But I didn't require a second. Because I knew that Pete Davidson was talking about Helena Donovan. Just as I knew that Helena had died in 1995. In September of that year, at a San Francisco hospice. I still recalled the shock of seeing her smiling, beguilingly pretty face above her Guardian obituary. A detail I would spare Pete. He didn't need to know. And in all fairness, she had only spoken the truth in discussing me with him.

Chapter 6

Samantha found her Frenchman. She settled down to domestic life not in Paris, as I'd gloomily predicted she would, but in the south of the country, on the coast, in Toulon. I learned this from her father. I was 22 and single and on a visit to Southport from London, where I was working then as a regional newspaper reporter. My first real career break was about to occur, though of course, I didn't know that. I was about to change course, but at that age, was largely clueless about which way. My sense of direction has never been my most impressive asset.

It was Christmas. The carol singers were out, under their paper lanterns, in their coats and gloves and scarves. It was cold enough for snow, which is rare on the coast and therefore picturesquely welcome when it falls. I'd run into an old school friend outside the deli in Birkdale Village where I'd gone to buy mince pies. He suggested a drink and the nearest pub was the Old Ship. I was a bit trepidatious, not knowing whether Samantha's father was still the landlord there, not knowing whether I'd qualify for a seasonally frosty welcome. But since I hadn't actually been barred, and it was three years on from the break-up, I decided to risk it.

Her dad was manning the bar. He looked exactly the same. I didn't, having had my hair cut fashionably short in preparation for a working life and having kept it that way since. I'd spruced up my wardrobe too. But the expression on his face said that he recognised me straight away. To my surprise, he seemed pleased to see me. To my astonishment, he stood us our drinks. Then after a few minutes he came over to our table and mentioned Samantha. My schoolfriend, sensing something, drained his glass and made his excuses and left.

Jack Dooley said, 'You look like you've prospered, son.'

'I wouldn't say that. Suits are the fashion, is all,' I said. 'You knew me when I was scruffy.' Then, inevitably, 'How is Samantha?'

And he told me about her new life in the South of France. I think he was aiming at neutrality, but he sounded quite despondent about it. Seeing beneath the surface was, just then, one of the new journalistic skills I was trying to develop. It might have been simply that he missed his daughter. It might have been something more. He'd bought a half of lager to the table. For a moment, we sat there and drank in silence.

Then he said, 'I'm sorry it didn't work out, between you and Sam. Genuinely sorry.'

'I'm flattered you say that, Jack, but some things just aren't meant to be.'

He raised an eyebrow. He said, 'Wasn't that, in my view. It was that you met too bloody young. Sixteen is no age to start becoming serious. And you two were serious from the start. It's no wonder the romance ran out of steam.'

I didn't know how to reply to what he had said, so I just nodded and sipped at the drink he'd bought me.

'Remember the night you came in here,' he said, 'that first time. Drowned, you were. And pale as a ghost.'

'I didn't see you.'

'You'd seen something, though. I knew you were underage. Let Sam serve you because you looked so bloody terrified. And the rain was torrential that night. Couldn't show you the door without a bit of fortification. Always wondered what had been going on, before you came through the door. Whether you'd murdered someone, or someone had tried to murder you. Meant to ask, from time to time. Never seemed like the right moment.'

'Murder was involved,' I said, to my own surprise. 'But I wasn't. Not directly, anyway.'

'Why don't you tell me about it.'

And so I told him about the events of six years earlier concerning my interest in Edward Swarbrick. And Kelmscott Court and what had happened to me there. About Arabella Pankhurst and the enigmatic concierge, Tony Causley. I told him all of it. His seasonal trade was brisk, but he had a couple of people, students by the look of them, working the bar. And he showed no interest in returning to it.

'Paul Wright used to come in here occasionally in the early evening when Kelmscott Court was being built,' he said after I'd finished telling the story. 'He'd have a cheese roll and a pint of lager and talk telephone numbers to anyone who'd listen.'

'Telephone numbers?'

'How much money he was speculating on property deals. Flash character. Once or twice had a right stunner on his arm.'

'Jennifer Purdy. Before she dumped him'

'He never introduced her.'

'You didn't laugh at my ghost story, Jack. I thought you would.'

'You're not the only one with a story about Kelmscott Court, Tommy Boy. And it's not the first time I've heard Edward Swarbrick's name.'

'Go on,' I said.

'I'm third generation in the licensed trade. Father and grandfather. Not always here. My granddad had the Black Boar in the town centre. Long demolished, a branch of Boot's the Chemist occupies the spot where the Black Boar stood. I suppose the story he told me goes back to the nineteen-thirties.'

'I'm all ears,' I said.

'Everyone smoked back then. No link between tobacco and cancer. Not just fags but cigars and pipes. My granddad profited particularly from the sale of cigars to his regular clientele. His source was a Liverpool importer who supplied domestic as well as trade clients. One of those, was Edward Swarbrick.'

Jack Dooley's glass was empty. So was mine. I went to the bar for fresh drinks and came back for the rest of the tale.

'This must have been after Swarbrick got reclusive, or he could have picked up his own smokes. Anyway, Cigar Man goes to his house in Weld Road. And they're in Swarbrick's study, while Swarbrick writes a cheque. And there's a phone call. And Swarbrick goes to take it, in the vestibule, where people in big houses in those days kept their phones in a sort of alcove with a chair and a shelf or a small table the phone sat on.

'He goes out the door. But that's not the only exit from the study. There's a separate doorway opposite with a heavy velvet floor length curtain. And Cigar Man, curious, takes a peak behind it.'

Jack paused to take a sip of his beer.

I said, 'You can't leave it there.'

He swallowed. 'And what do you think he sees?'

'I've no idea.'

'Only a bloody altar. Marble, elaborately carved, engraved with symbols. But not Christian, pagan, he said.'

'What kind of symbols?'

'Don't know, Tommy Boy. He was a cigar importer, not an expert on religion.'

'Shame.'

'Something else, though.'

'Go on.'

'He only got a glimpse. Didn't want to get caught out prying if the phone call was a short one. Swarbrick wasn't the sort generally to waste words, by all accounts. So only a quick look, but he saw something else. What he said looked like a ceremonial dagger in a scabbard mounted on the wall.'

'Blimey.'

'Rum sort, Edward Swarbrick,' Jack Dooley said. 'Up to no good, was the general view. And we've all heard the story of Arabella Pankhurst, even though it's only today I learned her name from you. That's why I didn't laugh at what you've told me. And you have to remember I saw the expression on your face when you came in here afterwards.'

I thought about that evening. About being shocked and rain-drenched, about the well-lighted refuge this pub had seemed from the other side of the road. About how my hands had shaken fumbling for change with Hangy Todd's key in front of me on the bar. About seeing Samantha Dooley's lovely face for the first time. Six years and a lifetime ago.

'What's up, Tom? You look sad.'

'You're right, Jack,' I said. 'I met your daughter too soon. She'll always be the one that got away.'

'That she did, son. All the way to the South of France.'

****

Two days after my chat with Samantha's father, I learned of Al Hodge's death when I saw his Visiter obituary. He'd made it to the venerable age of 88, but I was still shocked. Cancer though, sadly, is no respecter of dapper dress and good deportment. Or a still sharp mind. Or a healthy bank account. The obit said he bore his final illness with unfailing courage and good humour. That did not surprise me in the slightest.

He 'd told me they'd given him a gong at the time he was losing pals on the Ypres Salient in the Great War. The Military Cross was awarded for an action in which he single-handedly captured a German machine gun. The MC Bar was for rescuing a wounded comrade from no man's land, carrying him over his shoulder back to the relative safety of a British trench and then after a short rest, on to a dressing station as one half of a volunteer stretcher party.

He'd played down the heroism with me. What he hadn't played down was his later contempt for the toffs who attended the Jericho Ball. I wondered if he had known more about their circle than he'd been prepared to let on to an 18-year-old boy. Debauchery wasn't something someone like Al Hodge would have been comfortable discussing with a callow teenager.

It was a full year before I later learned that I had been a beneficiary of the will Albert Hodge had left behind. It took that long for the legal people to track me down. But the legal profession is scrupulous and dogged about that sort of thing. And the package reached me, recorded delivery, after they called me at the offices of the Gazette to confirm that I was indeed me. Some sharp-eyed legal eagle must have seen my by-line on a syndicated story.

He'd left me the film taken surreptitiously at the Birkdale Palace Hotel in the summer of 1927. It was a unique piece of social history that to my knowledge, only two people, one of them dead, had ever previously viewed. And six months after I received it, that film was the clincher when the BBC enabled my first televised foray into the paranormal when they commissioned my hour-long documentary about the hotel, it's glittering array of famous guests, the crimes committed there and its sustained reputation as somewhere haunted.

'*Son,*' the note accompanying the film began, *sometimes it's possible to give someone deserving a leg-up in life. If you're reading this, then I've gone to my grave, reasonably contented after a fair innings. I know, because Tim Ballard told me, that you're making your way in the world of journalism. This film, in its black and white way, is a world exclusive. Be sure that you use it shrewdly.*

A word of warning though, before I say goodbye. There were rumours during the season Harry Spalding spent as a guest at the Birkdale Palace. And not just concerning those young women who disappeared. There was talk of some kind of cabal, of the practice of black magic. I think that some kind of ritual was enacted before the ball began. I remember telling you about the stink of incense afterwards in the fabric of the furnishings.

Showing the film is harmless enough. All the people in it will likely be dead and buried. By all means discuss the hotel in general terms. You're a bright lad. You might by now have found out things for yourself. And by things, I mean secrets. Don't speculate publicly about a secret cult. I think it's still around, still secret, guards its privacy jealously and is extremely dangerous. Remember that some things are best left unsaid.

I hope this missive finds you well, Tommy Boy. I hope to God you've by now had a sensible haircut. Remember that if you keep your trousers sharply pressed and your shoes shined, you won't go too far wrong.

Raise a glass to me if you would,

Your Old Friend,

Al.

I finished reading his note with tears stinging my eyes. I read it in the editorial office and saw that a couple of the other reporters were looking at me curiously. I folded the note and put it into my pocket. When I got home, I would burn it. I'd been right about the Birkdale Park's old bar steward. He'd known a great deal more than he'd let on to me and he thought that knowledge dangerous. When I left the office, the film secure in my bag, I stopped off at an off-license and bought a quarter bottle of Grant's whisky to raise that parting glass.

Jericho Crew. Jericho Ball. Jericho Society. I knew about their secret cult and had since meeting Helena Donovan on Wight. I had already been warned by her that they were dangerous. My pub conversation of almost a year earlier with Jack Dooley had revealed the presence of a pagan altar in the long-demolished home of Edward Swarbrick on Weld Road in Southport. Altars were for rituals. Daggers were sometimes used for sacrifice. The evidence was circumstantial, but still compelling. Spalding, Fischer and Swarbrick had been members of the same secret, pagan brotherhood.

My burgeoning interest, though, was less in old and blasphemous crimes than it was in matters ghostly. That much acknowledged, I did not though really want to provoke another visitation from the spectre of Edward Swarbrick. One, endured as an 11-year-old, had been quite enough. He had plainly been a bad man. But I was content to leave him and his reputation alone, in peace. I had been born in a country with a long and colourful history. It had a rich architectural legacy, some of it intact, some of it preserved as atmospheric ruins. You didn't need to delve into black magic and criminality when folklore abounded. There was much I could investigate, leaving the Jericho Society alone.

And that is what I did, after my BBC breakthrough. Concentrating on investigating spiritualists and seances, on haunted castles and abbeys and churches, on poltergeist activity and omens and curses. I became a well-known and often consulted talking head on television, on the subject of the occult. I wrote in newspapers about the plausibility of reincarnation. I did documentaries and became a sometimes paid consultant on feature films aimed at scaring people subtly, without haemorrhaging gore.

But after almost a decade of doing this, it all plateaued. Partly this was a consequence of my own fastidiousness. There were competitors less scrupulous than I was, coming up with spectacle and scariness on a regular basis. Not necessarily authentic, but entertaining despite that. My material seemed a bit timid and cliched by comparison. Hackneyed and tame.

I needed something spectacular, a reboot, something sensational. And I remembered Klaus Fischer's derelict mansion on the edge of Brighstone Forest on the Island. And Helena Donovan's grave warning about the place. By this time, Helena was enjoying some success as an author, living in New England, six thousand miles across the Atlantic Ocean. Though I was unaware of that, then.

Nor did I know what that ruin harboured. Maybe nothing more than dust and woodworm. Maybe only shellac and brilliantined memories of the frenzied decade of its partying pomp. If walls could speak, the saying goes, but they tend to remain, overwhelmingly, silent. They call them the Roaring Twenties. I couldn't guarantee that the twenties would roar in an empty island dwelling.

What did I have to lose? Most obviously, my name as a keeper of faithfully made promises. Beyond that, the price of a return ferry ticket. A single night's sleep. A couple of days of my time.

And it got to the point where it seemed not just worthwhile but necessary, even essential. If you're in the business of exploiting some rare mineral, and you discover a rich seam of the stuff, you mine it. To do otherwise is simply foolish. I believed that the Fischer House was a place of enduring malevolence. I could exploit that possibility without ever mentioning the cult to which I believed Klaus Fischer had in life belonged. Anything subsequently broadcast would put me on the radar of the Jericho Society, if indeed they still existed. But I had no reason to think it would make me their target.

There is one significant detail I have not yet disclosed about the showing of my Birkdale Palace Hotel film on BBC TV. And it is this. The programme was viewed by the granddaughter of Billy Perry, the Detective Inspector from Liverpool CID seconded to investigate Edward Swarbrick after the disappearance of Arabella Pankhurst. She knew what her granddad's suspect looked like. She recognised him in the ballroom footage. And she wrote to me, telling me who she was, and informing me of who Swarbrick had been.

I knew very well, of course, who Swarbrick was, but he had not been the point of the film. That had been the hotel and its sinister reputation. I wrote back to Margaret Jones (nee Perry) telling her I knew about Swarbrick, explaining that I was Southport-born and interested in history as well as in phantoms. She had her grandfather's investigative notebooks, she subsequently revealed. She asked me would I like to see the notebook pertaining to the Swarbrick case.

Exposure encourages exposure. If that film had never been made and broadcast, I'd never have heard of, let alone from, Margaret Jones. Her correspondence made me realise how far I had come from being that kid in the Atkinson reference library, looking stuff up that wasn't to do with O-Level revision. How much easier matters become when you have the keys to unlocking doors adulthood and career, rather than Hangy Todd, can provide.

Margaret – we quickly established first-name terms – wanted the notebook back but was quite happy to post it to me to borrow for a couple of weeks. And I read through it the day it arrived, scouring Billy Perry's painstaking copperplate for information about the man, the case and his suspect.

I knew a bit about Perry already. I'd learned it in the Cheshire Lines pub all those years earlier from Joey Delancey. Perry had been born in Ulster and was a hard-line Unionist, thus his membership of the Orange Lodge in Liverpool. He had joined a tank battalion and landed in Normandy on D-Day and fought his way through occupied France. He had come across as a dogged sort of man, Delancey said. He hadn't, like Al Hodge in a previous conflict, been given a gong.

He did though, earn citations throughout an impressively successful police career. Even as a 16-year-old I'd known that some coppers were bent, that suspects were often beaten in the cells and that known criminals were fitted-up for offences they hadn't committed when they couldn't be nailed for those they had. A lot of bad apples in the police barrel, when I was a kid. It was the era of the George Davis is Innocent campaign. Which that old villain had been, of the particular offence for which he'd been convicted. Bribes were pocketed, blind eyes turned, examples of rough justice plain to see in the black-eyes and freshly broken noses of police mugshots. Billy Perry had not been like that, Joey Delancey had insisted. And the notebook Margaret Jones sent me confirmed it.

The notebook contained testimony from the two people who described a man answering Swarbrick's description on the Southport beach sandhills with Arabella Pankhurst on the day of her disappearance. They were both middle-aged men. One was a shrimp fisher, the other a birdwatcher. Their descriptions of the suspect were detailed and consistent. The girl, having become separated from her friends, was crying, they stated. Swarbrick offered her a linen handkerchief with which to dry her eyes.

Neither witness knew that Arabella had been with a group of friends. They assumed the well-dressed man comforting her to be related to her. They assumed he had taken her there. Probably each thought, her granddad. Though they were grotesquely wrong in this assumption.

So far, so predictable. But this was Perry's personal notebook, not an official document such as a witness statement. In it, he speculated about entering Swarbrick's home uninvited to search for hard evidence. He did not have enough to be granted a search warrant. Swarbrick was never exactly popular. But he was a relatively wealthy man with an unblemished record. He paid his taxes and his bills on time. He had no creditors. He had never bounced a cheque or since he didn't drive, committed an offence at the wheel. He was abstemious. Cigars seemed to be his only vice. And Winston Churchill, saviour of the nation, smoked cigars.

Towards the end of the notebook, Perry's tone became querulous. He hinted that the investigation into Swarbrick wasn't quite as straightforward as it should have been. A very senior officer he didn't name called him in for frequent briefings, which in today's terminology I thought would actually be described as debriefings. One of the brass in the Liverpool Constabulary seemed anxious to know what it was Perry had on his chief suspect. What the strength was of his evidence. What progress he was making.

This seemed anomalous to me. Arabella's disappearance was the Lancashire Constabulary's case. Billy Perry had been seconded, hand-picked, for his detection skills. But someone higher up than him in the Liverpool police hierarchy seemed bent on interfering with the conduct of the investigation. With what motive? I wondered.

It was both tempting and easy to see Edward Swarbrick as a man without friends. But he'd had friends back in 1927 and they had been influential friends, hadn't they? Klaus Fischer disappeared in the Autumn of that same year and in 1929, Harry Spalding ended his own life at the business end of a revolver in a New York hotel room. But the Jericho Society had not ended with them, had it? And maybe it looked after its own. And maybe it had tentacles that stretched to the upper echelons of the police service.

About three months before the discovery of his body, Perry documented work he had discovered was done at Swarbrick's house. He established that it was a job of removal and that it was overseen by a monumental mason. He questioned the mason, though neither under oath, nor under caution. And the man was uncooperative. He refused to say what it was that had been removed.

Perry assumed that the mason was tight-lipped because he'd been well paid for the job. He further speculated that the object removed could have been a crate or coffin containing the remains of Arabella Pankhurst. If so, however, why a monumental mason? Why not the anonymity of a couple of casual labourers and an unmarked van? A fly-tipped packing crate would be a hard object to trace, he speculated, gloomily. Impossible, if it had been drilled with holes and dumped to sink in the Mersey silt.

Here's where I had the advantage over Billy Perry. In tracking a cheque Swarbrick had signed from clearing bank back to the monumental mason, he had confronted only a puzzle. But I knew about the curtained-off room in Swarbrick's house containing an altar. My conclusion was that he had needed expert help in dispensing with that. He knew that Perry was closing in, that a prosecution was imminent. He had already decided to end his life. He needed to rid himself of damning evidence. And to protect the cult to which he had dedicated his seedy and destructive existence.

A passage towards the end of the notebook struck a particular chord.

My 18-year-old boy opened a birthday package this morning. It contained a dead bird, a finch, decapitated neatly, probably with secateurs. And my wife received another of the poison pen letters, anonymous, of course. The slashed car tyres are tedious, but the feeling of being followed is worse. It's done expertly. Haven't been able to pick up the tail thus far.

Even the rarest and most valuable variety of apple can be bad, wormy to its corrupt core. But the good outnumber the bad and the bad fucking know it. It's why there's no moniker on those letters the missus gets. They don't fucking dare.

I will not stop. I don't care who his connections are. I don't care how far they reach. Arabella Pankhurst was eight years old. I'll get him and then I'll go after them. Thou Shalt Not Kill. He'll burn in hell. But before he does, he'll dangle on the end of a rope. I'll nail that bastard if it's the last thing I do.

After reading that, I had to find out what had happened to Billy Perry after the closure of the case against Edward Swarbrick. By now, I had his granddaughter's phone number. And so I called Margaret Jones.

'It was tragic,' she said. 'You're reading the last words he ever wrote. He was killed a week after Swarbrick's burial. A hit and run, the culprit never caught. So obviously, I never had the chance to know Billy. Hard for my father, he was only eighteen when he lost his dad.'

****

With our departure for Italy only six days away, I booked a weekend on Wight on the presumption that Daisy liked surprises and would be free, as well as willing, to accompany me. Then there was the tricky assignment of phoning her to tell her I had done it and to ask her would she come.

'What's the weather forecast?'

'Variable,' I said.

'A variable outlook. Hmm.'

'Sunny periods are predicted,' I said. 'If not guaranteed.'

'Where are we supposed to be staying?'

'The Hambrough,' I said. 'I've booked us separate rooms.'

'Really?'

'Really.'

'Then you've wasted money.'

My heart sank. 'You won't come?'

'Not if you're exiling me to a separate room. What would be the point?'

I could have booked somewhere in Cornwall or on the Norfolk coast or in Cumbria. Since the staycation frenzy of a couple of years earlier, it had actually become possible to make those decisions again. It felt like a kind of luxury to once more have the choice. But the island was somewhere I loved that had been significant at different stages of my life. I was ambivalent at best, it's true, about Brighstone Forest and an abandoned building at its edge. But Ventnor was probably my favourite place in the world. I wanted to share its charms with someone quickly becoming important to me.

Before our departure, I called James Balfour and told him about the connection between Phillipe Suarez and the images my daughter had conjured from charcoal and paper. I did so without naming the dead man.

'The brain is a physical organism,' he said. 'It can be examined and weighed and dissected. None of that really tells us anything about the mind.'

'You sound like Julia Pettifer,' I said.

And he chuckled. 'Which I doubt is intended as a compliment. But it's true. I'll say this, Tom. Your daughter is extraordinarily sensitive. And quite seriously challenged in some significant ways. But she is as sane as you or I. And those sketches were not provoked by emotional disturbance. And they have not resulted in disturbing her. And I hope that reassures you.'

It did. It wasn't an answer, but some mysteries will always remain unsolved. Claire was proud of having produced those images. She was pleased with them. They wouldn't have been on display, otherwise.

Daisy insisted we take her car, because we were off on a summer weekend away and because she drove a convertible. She drove us to the ferry terminal at Portsmouth. We parked and climbed the metal stairs to the main deck and sailed past the Solent sea forts. And she looked surreal to me, impossible in her jeans and jean jacket, looking out over the blue sea, with the wind teasing the tresses of her dark blonde hair.

Then she turned and held my gaze. 'You should take me,' she said.

'I am taking you.'

She shook her head. 'Not to Wight. I mean next week. You should take me to Italy.'

'Too gruelling,' I said. 'Too harrowing. And possibly, too dangerous.'

'So it's boys only? Too scary for the girls to be included?'

'It's not that.'

'Sounds exactly like that.'

'It's fieldwork,' I said, sounding lame to my own ears.

'Which I never get to do,' Daisy said.

'Leave it, Daisy.'

'Do you know what the front-liners called the admin people in wartime, Tom?'

'No.'

'They called them desk jockeys. I'm tired of being one. Want to be at the sharp end for once.'

'It's a long trip to a remote and quite hostile location,' I said. 'Where I'm pretty much one-hundred per cent certain absolutely nothing will happen through a tedious hours-long vigil. We'll get establishing shots and some night-vision footage as atmospheric as we can make it. Bonus time if the props are there. Then home. A sombre voice-over scripted by me and recorded by an actor in a Soho studio. Nothing to see here, basically.'

'Pete Davidson isn't in the business of bankrolling nothing to see here,' Daisy said. 'And you trust your hunches.'

I shrugged. 'There might be a cold spot. You can't film a cold spot.'

She said, 'Breath, fogging, in Italy, in summer?'

I shrugged again.

Daisy had narrowed her eyes against sunlight. Her Ray Bans were hanging by an arm from the breast pocket of her jacket. She said, 'I'm going to work on you over the weekend, Tom Carter. I'm going to get my way.'

That evening we ate at the Spyglass Inn. The food was better at The Bistro, but I wanted to save The Bistro for the following night. We walked up the hill back to the hotel shortly after sunset. What happened when we got back to our room was what happens between consenting adults. It felt to me both completely normal and utterly wondrous. I lay in the bed on my back afterwards, aware that words just then were both inadequate and unnecessary. Daisy lay silently to my right. I could hear waves break on the shore at the edge of the night sea beneath us. I could hear her breathing, smell her scent.

Her hand reached for mine. She squeezed. 'So it begins,' she said.

'What was it you said? That you're exceptionally choosy.'

'Fishing for compliments, Mr Carter?'

'No. Just feeling exceptionally fortunate.'

She laughed. She said, 'You'll get no argument from me.' She twisted towards me and rested her weight on an elbow and said, 'It's here, isn't it? That place that put you on the map, all those years ago.'

'I don't know,' I said truthfully. 'It could have been demolished.'

'Would have been discussed if that had happened, Tom. On the internet forums dedicated to haunted buildings.'

'They put a fence around it. A twelve feet thickness of steel spikes and razor wire. It's a hazardous location.'

'In more ways than one?'

'I thought so.'

'I'd like to see it,' she said. 'Just from the outside, I mean. We could go there tomorrow.'

'There are things I'd rather do,' I said.

She stroked my chest. She said, 'There's a time for everything.'

'Is the time now?'

'If you want it to be.'

'I do,' I said.

We slept in understandably late. We awoke on what promised to be a fine day. The sea was emerald and glittery in mid-morning light. It seemed to stretch to infinity beyond the picturesque anchorage of harbour fishing boats. Daylight brought the decorum of separate showers. Then I watched her comb out her freshly washed hair, tawny limbed, clad in a satin dressing gown, unable to quite believe she was actually there and that I was with her. Once dressed, we walked down to a seafront café for breakfast. And over coffee and croissants she mentioned the Fischer House again, casually, as though visiting it would be routine.

'I can't go on calling you Daisy,' I said.

'Why not?'

'Flippant. Bogus. Not really who you are.'

'My birth name is Polly.'.

'Polly is perfect. Polly suits,' I said.

We drove to Brighstone Forest. You had to walk through the forest to get to where we were going. I noticed that Polly had laced on a pair of hiking boots. In common with the previous night, this had always been her plan. I knew that she was capable of spontaneity. She was also someone capable of scheming. She was too intelligent and wilful to be otherwise. I had begun to think that keeping her from coming on the Dolomites trip might be a struggle I would lose.

It was cool and dim under the forest canopy. Loamy soil, veined with exposed tree roots, pale in musty clusters with fungal growth. Tricky going, which I remembered it had been the first time, which was also the last time, 28 years and a lifetime ago, because I'd been a different person then, not married, not yet a parent. Not someone who could book a table easily somewhere people liked to be seen to eat. Not someone used to double-takes of public recognition taking a stroll through the West End's streets. Not yet the TV industry's favourite purveyor of things that go bump in the night. No one at all, really.

We were getting closer to our destination. I approached it uneasily aware that things can go bump in the day just as easily as they can in the hours of darkness. And I was aware of how quiet the forest had become all around us. No birds sang in the vicinity of the Fischer House. I remembered that now. The actuality of it, first experienced nearly 30 years ago. The conviction not only that no birds sang there, but that none ever had.

Polly, who had been Daisy, reached for my hand. And I had the irrational thought that I'd not just diminished her, but somehow killed her off. And she must have read my mind.

'It goes on being Daisy, Tom,' she said, her face set seriously, eyes searching mine. 'Ill omens aren't something you invite into your life. Not deliberately. Not carelessly.'

'Do you want to turn back, Daisy?'

She bit her lip. I want to press on,' she said.

The trees cleared suddenly, and we were there. The expansive sweep of moss blotched gravel. The gabled and turreted ambition of Klaus Fischer's overreaching home. Stained stone given a gaunt look by windows blackened by the darkness within. All this behind an encircling barrier of iron spikes and steel thorns rusted by years of rainfall. But still a formidable barrier. One you would need to carry specialist equipment to the spot to have any hope of successfully breaching. Though a word such as hope seemed unsuited to this particular location. Without gauntlets and a protective suit, you'd be looking at serious lacerations and the tedium of a tetanus jab in A&E somewhere. At best.

'First thoughts?'

'Isolation isn't always splendid,' Daisy said.

The house didn't look significantly different from how it had on my previous visit. The front door was still the same massive oak obstacle sunk into its granite frame. Perhaps the building had lost a few more rooftiles. Sometimes that can give a structure a toothless sort of look. Not here. The Fischer house looked ready to bite.

'How many rooms?' Daisy asked.

'There's a baronial hall on the ground floor, which is huge. There's a catacomb like cellar full of separate chambers. But the staircase to the upper floors was too rotten to trust. It might have perished entirely by now. So the honest answer is I don't know how many rooms.'

'You shot most of the footage in that hall, didn't you?'

I shook my head. 'The footage broadcast,' I said. 'There was some material unfit for the public domain.'

'I'd like to see it.'

'No, Daisy. You wouldn't.'

She was silent, staring, studying. Then she said, 'It's not a tranquil place, is it, Tom. It kind of … I don't know. It kind of broods.'

Her voice was a murmur. As was mine when I replied. 'Let's go, Daisy. There are a hundred places I'd rather be.'

She nodded and turned and then swiftly turned back again.

'What?'

She pointed to one of the high, remote, narrow windows on the uppermost floor. 'I saw movement,' she said. 'In there. A pale face. A person, watching us.'

I tugged her back towards the forest. 'Nothing any longer human,' I said.

'A tramp,' she said. 'A vagrant, taking shelter.'

I didn't reply. I just pulled her along after me back the way we had come. Back towards the sunlight and sanity on the other side of the forest gloom.

'The face looked small, like a child,' she said, when we reached the spot at which we'd parked the car.

I hadn't seen anything. That raised the question of Daisy's sensitivity to what some people saw, and others missed. I knew from viewers' varying reactions to my Fischer House film that levels of sensitivity were never the same in two separate individuals. My personal opinion was that Phillipe Suarez had been an extreme example and the fact had become impossible for him to bear. I doubted very much that the orphanage in the Dolomites had been his first encounter with something otherworldly. Though I sensed it was the most shocking up to that point, which was why he had needed to share it with someone, confiding in my brother.

What if his faceless, sobbing, self-flagellating nun had subsequently invited some of her charges into his life? Or just into his dreams, tormenting his sleep. How long would a man be able to tolerate that? He had managed to keep his gift, or affliction secret, because he had kept it under control. But he had returned from Italy and discovered it to be ungovernable. Would he have thought himself going mad? Would it have driven mad an otherwise intelligent, ordered, precise taker of calculated business risks? Was that how a man who lived by algorithms perished?

From the passenger seat beside me, Daisy Chain asked, 'What are you thinking about?'

'Dinner.'

'Liar.'

'What did the face at the window look like?'

'I only glimpsed it.'

'Concentrate,' I said. 'Visualise.'

She sighed. 'Lost,' she said. 'Do you think you know who it is?'

I thought momentarily about saying something trite, brushing her off with a pat answer. But I didn't want her actually thinking me a liar. So I told her the truth. I was discovering Daisy, or Polly as she really was, to be one of those women who compel the truth. I said, 'I think I know who it might once have been.'

My source was an investigative journalist named Paul Seaton, a Dubliner who had settled in England after graduation from Trinity College with a good degree in English. He'd had a girlfriend in the early 1980s on her way to a bad degree in fashion design because her dissertation hadn't been written. She was a genius at bias cutting, he told me, but remiss when it came to written work. Very remiss, it turned out. So much so that he offered to conjure the required 8, 000 words in a matter of a couple of weeks on her behalf.

I met Seaton because he wrote to me after my Fischer House programme was broadcast on TV. That showing opened a lot of doors. Paul's was one of them. The subject of his girlfriend's dissertation was a pioneering portrait and fashion photographer named Pandora Gibson-Hoare. Seaton, in his research, discovered a kind of diary Pandora had secretly kept over a period of weeks in 1927.

She had been a guest during the period at the Fischer House on the island. She described the sometimes uncanny events that had taken place there then. They included a duel during which the man who came off worse suffered a sword wound that should have proved fatal. Except that a fellow guest, the magician Aleister Crowley, performed some arcane rite that apparently stopped the bleeding and saved the man's life.

There were several well-known people present at the house among Fischer's guests. They enacted a series of nightly rituals, some of them descending, or deteriorating, into orgies. Black magic was fashionable among louchely wealthy people in the period. The 1920s was an era of sensation seeking. But Seaton said some of the occult claims made in the journal were only explicable if potent magic existed as a fact.

Gibson-Hoare came across as an adventurous woman, addicted to novelty, in over her head. She referred in her diary to someone she termed the sacrificial. To his horror, Seaton discovered that the sacrificial was a young boy from an impoverished background abducted from a Welsh village on behalf of Fischer's decadent, amoral clique of dabblers in the occult. Gibson-Hoare experienced a crisis of conscience and tried to save the boy. But the attempt was foiled. And he was murdered in a ritual enacted in the cellar of the house.

Paul Seaton was doggedly determined to discover the identity of the boy. And using his investigative skills, he succeeded in this. Their victim was Peter Morgan, a child prodigy in academic terms intent on a career in medicine. Seaton surmised that the potential for good in him had been what gave the sacrifice its potency. Or so at least, his slayers had believed. And I told Daisy all this, the whole story, made incredulous, I thought, by it being related at a sun-warmed wooden table outside the Spyglass Inn on a bright and gentle summer afternoon.

'You think I saw Peter Morgan at the Fischer House,' she said, tonelessly.

'The ghost of Peter Morgan,' I said. 'Fischer had a factotum, a minder really, an ex-bodyguard of Al Capone's. He was the boy's gaoler.'

'Still there, trapped in the place they took him to, to meet his death. God, Tom, what an awful thought.'

'They're not sensate, I don't think,' I said. 'They don't feel.'

'You don't know that.'

'No, I don't,' I said. 'But they're not there. Not really, they're not. They're seen only by those of us with the sensitivity to be aware of something that shouldn't be there at all. Something that defies reason and logic and physics. Someone, apparently, like you.'

'And like you?'

'Not really, Daisy. Not to the same extent, I don't think.'

I regularly used a jobbing cameraman, Jeff Potts. He was the calmest, most undemonstrative, least imaginative man I had ever encountered. And they were precisely the qualities that recommended him to me. Jeff had filmed for me in locations tangible with foreboding, places that had made my skin crawl with dread. And all he worried about was lighting and focus and whether to tripod-mount the camera or freestyle it on one of his burly shoulders. He saw nothing, ever, out of the ordinary. Daisy Chain wasn't like that. I suspected she had been gifted with a curse.

'Doesn't this morning make you think that going to that orphanage in the Dolomites might be a terrible idea, Daisy?'

She sipped chilled beer from the moisture-beaded bottle in front of her. With the forefinger of her free hand, she sketched the circle of condensation its base had left on the weathered wood. She smiled.

And so I pressed, 'It could be dangerous.'

'I don't believe ghosts can do me physical harm,' she said.

'I'm sure Phillipe Suarez would have said the same.'

She said, 'I'd have thought I'd have been something more to you now than a researcher on an arms-length retainer.'

'That's not fair.'

'It's completely fair,' she said. 'And I'm an adult.' She raised an eyebrow. 'A consenting adult.'

After that conversation had concluded, we climbed the hill to the hotel and sort of tumbled into bed together. It was lust and comfort combined, I think, and also a kind of abandonment, a sort of recklessness. I think we were making up for time we hadn't known was lost to both of us. And sex can be a sort of escape, too.

While we were in bed, I missed a phone call from my brother. I took my second shower of the day before going out to the balcony to call him back. He told me he'd spent the afternoon with the widow of Phillipe Suarez.

Her husband's behaviour had altered, after his experience in the Dolomites. Slowly at first, but incrementally, to the point where he seemed a different person. Marianne Suarez did not know the cause, but was able looking back, to determine the trip that had changed her husband's demeaner, character and religious convictions.

He slowly filled his study with religious artefacts. By the time of his death, it had more the appearance of a shrine than somewhere a studious man might work. It had hung crucifixes, plaster images of saints and religious depictions in oil paint mounted on its walls. There was a set of rosary beads on his desk. He kept bottles of holy water and prayed for an hour in a new habit that became a nightly vigil.

He refused to discuss these changes in his taste, habit, routine or faith. But he had begun to dream, or more accurately suffer from nightmares. They were so bad that they would wake him. But before they did that, they would provoke him into speaking aloud. And when he did this, the language he spoke in was always Italian.

It was not a language he had previously known. But Marianne knew some Italian and could discern the words and sentences he spoke. He was pleading with someone and his tone was anguished because the pleas weren't being listened to. The nightmares inflicted insomnia. The prayer sessions lengthened. Misjudgements, the consequence of fatigue or preoccupation, occurred at work, ugly stains on a hitherto unblemished business career. And this up to then most patient and loving of men began snapping at his children, unprovoked. And then the catastrophe of the cliff fall. Two bereft sons and an anguished widow and no note to explain why he had felt the need to escape his life.

'You told her, didn't you, Andy.'

It wasn't a question. I knew my brother.

'I didn't feel I had a choice, Tom. The woman was in limbo, emotionally. Telling her was a mercy. Telling her was all I could do.'

'She'd guessed he'd confided in you?'

'I saved Phillipe's life on our first climb together. That Cairngorms ascent? No one's mistake, equipment failure, a snapped rope. I've never told you that. I've never wanted you to know how dangerous climbing can be. But Phillipe told Marianne. She thought if he had subsequently confided a secret in anyone, it would be me.'

'Shrewd woman.'

'Not shrewd enough to prevent her husband's suicide,' Andy said.

'Think telling her brought her any comfort?'

'No. Too raw. Maybe eventually. Where are you?'

'On the island.'

He was silent. Then he said, 'Looking up Helena Donovan? Didn't have old flames down as your thing, Tom.'

Helena Donovan was of course long dead. It wasn't something my brother needed to know. 'I'm here with Daisy,' I said, 'whose real name is Polly.'

'She told you that?'

'I already knew. But we're becoming close,' I said.

I looked through the balcony glass at Daisy asleep, her hair splayed lustrously against the white of her pillow, her lovely face reposeful. She had dropped off as I showered. It was a siesta, if it wasn't just a nap. She had only had the one lunchtime beer after our adventure of the morning. Or our ordeal of the morning, I thought, which was a more accurate word. I thought it had tired her.

'I'm glad, Tom,' Andy said. 'You've punished yourself enough.'

I nodded, though I could think of someone who might disagree with him.

'Claire sent me a charcoal sketch,' he said. 'Arrived in the post this morning. Beautifully done. Her draughtsmanship really is breath taking.'

I shivered and looked up to see that the sky wasn't quite unsullied. The sun was momentarily obscured by a small, pale cloud. I said, 'What was the subject?'

'Quite a coincidence, if I'm right,' he said. 'It looks like that baronial pile on the island where our most illustrious hunter of ghosts originally made his name.'

Chapter 7

Fair to call Samantha my childhood sweetheart? Corny, but true. We were 16 when we met and from the lofty heights of adulthood, 16 seems a long way short of maturity. The relationship didn't survive the physical separation of university, I often thought in retrospect mostly because neither of us really had the faith that it would. After graduation, she went back to Toulon, where she'd spent her year in France. And back into the welcoming arms of the Frenchman she had met there during that year. They lived in his rented flat, from what her father told me. For a couple of years, she worked teaching English as a foreign language to French businessmen at a school set up by the chamber of commerce in that vibrant port city.

Then came a change of direction I would never have anticipated. I had known Samantha was clever but had never thought her a particularly artistic person. We had toured galleries together, but only in that vapid way young people do when they don't have the money to fund more self-indulgent distractions. I had never heard her voice a strong opinion concerning art.

She became a ceramicist. She began making objects out of clay. They weren't implements, either. They were figures, or figurines; clowns, tramps, ballerinas, opera divas, acrobats, soldiers, musicians. They were immediately successful, both domestically and internationally. She staged exhibitions in Toulon and Paris. Her work became hugely sought after in Japan. Shrewdly, she added a Samurai warrior to her repertoire that became a best-seller. Music industry people and film stars in Hollywood collected her work. Disney did an animated series inspired by her most popular clown figure. The deal struck over that was very lucrative for Samantha.

I learned all this from a story in the Southport Visiter carefully clipped out of the paper and sent me by my mum. At the time I got it, the contrast in our fortunes could not really have been greater. I was renting a shitty Lambeth flat and scraping a living freelancing for magazines. My finances were horribly precarious. I felt like someone about to fall from a tightrope. It occurred to me, reading the piece, that a tightrope walker might be a popular figure to add to Samantha's profitable roster of little clay imaginary people.

Reading that Visiter feature on my ex-girlfriend might have been what made me decide to break my promise to Helena Donovan and not just visit the island and the Fischer House, but rent a videocam, splurge my scant savings on a ferry ticket, and spend the night filming there. If it wasn't the reason for doing it, it was certainly the catalyst. I swapped tightrope walking for a throw of the dice. And in a sense, the die settled on two sixes.

****

I met Samantha again only by accident. I was on the treadmill at the expensive gym on Millbank my new-found prosperity had enabled me to join. One of the staff members came in suited and booted, showing someone the facilities. The someone was Samantha Dooley. She looked different. Her hair was stylishly bobbed and her fawn wool coat and cashmere scarf obviously expensive. The diamonds set in her earrings glittered in a way that said they were real. Her face was lightly made-up and the fine lines at the corners of her eyes seemed to make them sparkle and gave her a character she had not possessed years earlier, in our time together.

She recognized me, though I must have looked different too. I hopped off the machine and we exchanged a few words, awkwardly, me slightly breathlessly, mopping sweat away from my face with my towel. Why was she being given the tour of a central London gym? It could only have been because she had relocated. Unless her success was so great that she could divide her time between France and England, with a showroom or gallery in each country.

'We ought to catch up, Tom,' she said. 'Does this place have a coffee shop?'

I shook my head. It didn't. There was a pool and a steam room and an aerobics studio, but nowhere there to socialise.

'There's a place right around the corner,' I said. 'On Horseferry Road.'

She smiled brightly. She said, 'Half an hour?'

'Perfect,' I heard myself say. Which was my honest impression of how she looked. She resumed her tour leaving a cloud of expensive perfume in her wake. I recovered my breath, did a few warm-down stretches on one of the mats and went to shower.

It was October, and unseasonably cold. The place to which I had sent Samantha was drably Italian in a street grown shabby since its 1960s heyday. The café was double-fronted, and condensation dribbled down glass that was steamed up to the point where it couldn't be seen through. The customers inside were just blurs in the dim interior light. I opened the door absolutely sure that Samantha wouldn't be there, resolutely certain that she wouldn't join my gym for fear of running into me again.

She was seated at a table towards the rear of the café. She had ordered herself a coffee and was smoking a cigarette. I pulled out the chair opposite hers and sat down and she smiled, French tobacco and her perfume competing with the regular café smells. A waitress came over and I ordered a Diet Coke. My workout had left me thirsty.

'Full disclosure,' she said. 'It's the only way to avoid all that verbal tiptoeing around we'll both do otherwise.'

I nodded. I thought, success does this to people. Makes them confident. She had outgrown the pub landlord's daughter from our hometown she'd been. The diamond earrings suited her. I noticed there was a Rolex on her left wrist with a face made of mother of pearl.

'I met him too young,' she said, 'which seems to be the story of my life. He runs a scuba school. When I started earning more than him, he became uncomfortable. When I started earning ten times what he was, he became impossible. The final straw came a month ago. It wasn't the only thing that broke. He took the key to my studio, went there drunk and used a hammer to smash every figurine he could find.'

I said, 'So the move here is permanent?'

'I've rented in Victoria,' she said. Her face darkened and then brightened again. 'I'm looking to buy in Pimlico. What about you?'

'Getting by,' I said.

'The nation's favourite ghost hunter,' she said. 'My dad sent me that programme you did on cassette.'

'Which programme?'

She exhaled smoke towards the ceiling and scrabbled out her cigarette in the foil ashtray on the Formica topped table between us. 'The really frightening one,' she said. 'The one you did in that derelict mansion on the Isle of Wight. How you stayed an entire night in that place I'll never know.'

'What did you see?'

'It's what I heard,' she said. 'The music, the sardonic laughter. That child's screams. I had to switch it off.'

'Do you actually know anyone in London?'

She shrugged. 'The gallerist who represents me. A few acquaintances from Oxford days. But no, not really.'

'It can be a lonely place.'

'Is that a dinner invitation?'

'I'd prefer we were friends,' I said.

'It has to be London,' she said. 'Career-wise, I mean. It's just the logical choice.'

The best advice, the only advice, is never to go back. But sometimes going back seems the easiest of alternatives. We walked through the freezing rain of the early dusk along Horseferry Road towards Victoria and the mansion block Samantha was living at and I kissed her chastely on the cheek as she gripped my shoulders in her familiar, forgotten way and we said our goodbyes. But we did so having swapped phone numbers with a commitment to keeping in touch. I hefted my gym bag and turned for my own home, by then in Clerkenwell, stirred inside in a way I hadn't been in years. It wasn't anything so simple as nostalgia. I felt suddenly more complete. And far more fully alive.

At first, it was a friendship. We would try to have a drink or dinner once a week. But that arrangement was relegated to once a fortnight, once Samantha settled into London life. She was as popular personally as her work had proven to be. She got invited to a lot of exhibition openings and had the confidence not to require an escort. A role I would anyway have felt uncomfortable occupying.

Nothing significant happened for almost a year. Then Jack Dooley suffered the fatal heart attack all too common in the licensed trade. And since he was a widower and Samantha his only daughter, it fell to her to make the arrangements for his funeral. She left London for Southport. I met her at the Pimlico home she was living in by then and we took a taxi to Euston and the Liverpool bound train. Her eyes were raw with grief. Before she got aboard, she asked me would I attend her father's funeral. I think mingled with the grief was remorse that she had moved so far away from him for the last decade of his life.

'Of course I'll come,' I said. 'I'll drive up and then bring you back here in the car.'

'That would be nice,' she said. And then, I think impulsively, she leant forward and kissed me on the mouth.

She had more composure by the day of the service and the burial. The wake was boisterous, her dad had been a popular man. I'd been fond of him myself, and I think him of me. Samantha could have hired a plusher venue, even at relatively short notice, but her father had loved his pub and had imbued it with his character and it seemed the most fitting place to have his friends remember him and celebrate a life lived convivially.

It was after midnight before the last guest stumbled out of the door. We locked up together. Then we sat at a table in the lounge bar and shared a nightcap. Samantha, I had observed, had drunk only very sparingly up until then. She had taken her obligations as hostess seriously.

'The brewery takes back the keys in a couple of days,' she said. 'There will be a refurbishment, a new landlord with fresh ideas. My first home, the place I grew up in, made alien to me.'

'Does that seem strange?'

She was staring. 'I met you here,' she said.

'I remember,' I said. It was not something I would ever forget. The pub that night like a lit-up galleon in the pouring rain from the other side of the road. The fear, the being drenched, the welcoming warmth of Samantha's lovely smile.

She swallowed back the remaining wine in her glass and smiled and stood and held out her hand. 'Come,' she said. And we climbed the stairs wordlessly to bed, I think both aware that some eventualities are well beyond discussion.

We moved in together the following Spring. I sold Clerkenwell, Samantha sold Pimlico and we bought a place together close to the river, in Southwark. The logic was that despite her hectic schedule, we would spend more time in one another's company than if we met for sporadic dinner dates, however romantic and intimate those dinner dates had become. And it worked. The house had a spacious studio in the garden to its rear for Samantha and her worktable and crafting tools and kiln. I'd become busier since the breakthrough film, but all freelancers have down time and she was the person I most wanted to spend it with.

We married the following Summer. I enjoyed some of the happiest and most contented years of my life. We travelled. I wrote a best-selling book about the supernatural that spawned a TV series sold to 28 countries. Samantha added to her roster of clay characters. Disney did a sequel to the clown film. And then Samantha fell pregnant with Claire, who had not been planned.

We were both delighted. And at first, we played happy families with our bouncing baby as happy families will. Looking back on it, Claire began to manifest behavioural difficulties from a quite tender age. We both did a lot of reading in an attempt to find a solution for ourselves. Only when we had failed in that, did we seek professional help. But none of the routines, the drills, the therapies, worked. We consulted a dietician, full of optimism. But that didn't help either. Claire was excluded from school at six. We employed a home-learning tutor who resigned after less than a month.

I door-stepped him indignant, he hadn't exactly come cheap.

'I couldn't stand the headaches,' he said.

'For Christ's sake, you could have taken an Aspirin.'

'Your daughter told me she was doing it. Triggering them deliberately.'

I laughed at that. I said, 'A malevolent spell, inflicted by girl who's only just turned seven?'

'Laugh all you like,' he said. 'All I know is that since I left, they're stopped.'

There was other, more mundane stuff. A spate of shoplifting. Temper tantrums. The boycott of her ballet class by the other girls attending. Phobias that seemed to change on a weekly basis. A refusal to speak. And then the refusal to eat.

There was a fire at the ballet school, a former Methodist chapel equipped with a sprung wooden floor and barre. The police knocked on our door, Claire having allegedly threatened this. But the fire had broken out in the small hours, the accident investigation people said. A time when our daughter was fast asleep in bed. She was exonerated by her alibi, so no charges were brought. But rumours followed. The close relative of accusations. And we all know, don't we, that mud is inclined to stick.

I should have noticed sooner the effect all this was having on Samantha. Clinical depression is sometimes hard to diagnose, but I should have seen the signs. She grew physically listless. The intervals between her bursts of creativity grew longer and the bursts themselves more manic in character. She became barely interested in food and seemingly too preoccupied for conversation. She lost all interest in sex. Having quit when she first fell pregnant, she started smoking again. Without telling me, she began to take medication. She hid the pills, but Claire found them and showed them to me with a gleam of triumph in her bright green eyes.

By the time she reached the age of 10, it was clear to both of us that Claire needed the full-time care we had neither of us the skills nor resources to provide her with at home. A friend recommended the Retreat. The friendship did not survive the recommendation, but we enrolled her there, to use the Retreat's own euphemism for commitment.

Sending our daughter away sounded the death knell for our marriage. To use another cliché, her absence left a chasm neither of us could bridge. We had failed jointly in the most important job our lives had given us to do. We divorced the following year.

By then we were living on Richmond Hill. Samantha got the house. I had enough money to buy my home in Teddington. But paying the Retreat's monthly fees was a duty that fell to me and within another year I was forced to re-mortgage to pay for my daughter's ongoing incarceration.

****

I wanted a tight team for what my cameraman Jeff Potts predictably insisted on calling The Italian Job. We needed to be able to occupy just a single vehicle. Convoys attract attention and we wanted none of that, just in for a night vigil and then out again. If nothing manifested – and it seldom did – then we had enough with location and back story for a compelling hour of television. Atmospheric lighting and soundtrack music can be very suggestive of ghostly goings-on.

I have written extensively on what makes a haunting and concluded that it's a kind of contagion. It's when a place is not just imbued by the traumatic events that took place there but contaminated by them. It invests the specific location with an unwanted energy people sense. It can be uncomfortable. And it can provoke emotions that chiefly manifest as fear or sadness. Some people speculate that cold spots indicate the presence of actual phantoms, unseen, lurking, exiled from a restful death. I disagree with this. Cold spots occur because the location is out of kilter with its surroundings. It exists as a perverse distortion of nature that doesn't comply with natural laws. It is delinquent, volatile. And some of us sense this abnormality very strongly.

That was one argument for taking Daisy Chain to the abandoned orphanage at the foot of the Dolomites. She had seen what I believed to be the ghost of Peter Morgan at a turret window at the Fischer House. Peter Morgan, who had died a strange and violent death on the island in 1927. I hadn't seen the face peering down through the narrow pane of glass. Something, her sixth sense, had compelled Daisy to raise her head and turn and look. It was evidence of a strong sensitivity.

Whether she saw anything or didn't at the orphanage, I wanted Daisy to do a piece to camera on location. If she saw and heard nothing out of the ordinary, she could still explain her discovery of the child massacre. Poignancy with a very pretty, photogenic face. I am sorry if that sounds callous or mercenary. But successful television programmes don't happen by accident. They are calculated creations. They are crafted by those of us with the ability to manipulate the emotions of the viewer. It's done in adverts for car insurance and gravy granules, for Christ's sake. Let alone the subject matter I dealt with.

Sound on a job like this is as important, if not more so, than the footage. I've already mentioned Jeff Potts, phlegmatic East End son of a scene shifter at the London Coliseum and grandson of a fairground rigger so in a sense, born into the business end of the business of entertaining people. Jeff liked to come across as the potty-mouthed barrel-boy cliché familiar to the industry. But he wasn't quite that. I'd been for dinner on a couple of occasions at the neat Docklands flat he shared with his husband, Barney, a chef at the Savoy.

I relied for sound on Lizzie Cox, whenever her busy schedule could squeeze me in a slot. A geeky, taciturn woman in her midthirties, Lizzie wasn't just good technically. Temperamentally, she was a perfectionist. She was in demand as a recording engineer at some of the most prestigious music studios both in England and on the other side of the Atlantic. She was a proud credit on the sleeves of successful albums; the sort with special editions in high grade vinyl cut for audiophiles. I knew zero about her private life. It wasn't a subject she discussed. But I trusted her professional skills absolutely.

Jeff and Lizzie together were good enough to wing it. Neither had time prior to our departure for an informal introduction to Daisy. But that was fine. Even if we were seated separately on the plane, we could get cosy on the longish drive from Venice Marco Polo Airport to our final destination, once I'd picked up the hire car. And I was confident that Daisy would get along with both of the other members of my tight little team. Nobody could be as successful at research as she was if they rubbed people up the wrong way. She had charmed my brother Andy on the phone into confessing his personal concern for my emotional welfare. Andy wasn't a natural confider in anyone.

We got out of the airport at two in the afternoon. I'd been advised to allow two-and-a-half hours for the 150K drive. But the weather as we descended and then landed, signalled that it might take longer than that. The landing was bumpy with a heavy crosswind and the aircraft portholes rain lashed from a lead coloured sky. And it was no better when we got out of the airport; though the situation improved when we took charge of our four-wheel-drive. Daisy had managed to arrange the hire of a Land Rover Defender. Not a huge amount of elbow room inside, but a five-speed manual shift gearbox, a petrol engine, a set of tyres that looked like rubber compound fortresses and enough luggage space to store our equipment and foul weather gear.

The rain strengthened on the route. The sky darkened like a freshly inflicted bruise. I found myself driving at a steady 50 with the headlamps on full beam.

'Look on the bright side, brother,' Jeff said from the seat behind mine. 'At least the wipers don't squeak.'

Lizzie occupied the front passenger seat. Putting Daisy there would have hinted at hierarchy and altered the balance of matters in a way I wanted to avoid. If either Lizzie or Jeff resented Daisy being there, it hadn't shown yet. I was the tense one, at the wheel. The other three, Lizzie included, were chatting amiably enough.

Everyone present knew about the fate of the orphanage's charges, about Suarez and the flagellating nun, about the man's subsequent suicide. But the practicalities of the job, its specific demands, occupied all our foremost thoughts on the way to our destination. Only when we left an increasing narrow and vague succession of country roads for open ground did I sense the mood shift to one of nervousness, to one of real apprehension.

The sky was still gloomy, but the rain had stopped. With no other moving objects to negotiate, I had switched off the headlamps. The area was remote, and I felt a strong sense of our isolation there, but the noise of the engine was a big enough indication of our presence, without putting our names up in lights. Lizzie was navigator, holding the hand-drawn map I had completed a few days earlier. Other than for the engine noise, we travelled in silence now.

The ground was grassed, bumpy, rock-strewn. Ponds to encircle, occasional streams to cross. A wilderness the thinning air signalled was at altitude. That, and the descending temperature. I drove carefully around boulders bigger than the car. Then I spotted a copse of stunted trees, more bushes, in reality, but substantial enough in which to hide our vehicle.

I asked Lizzie, 'How far?'

'About a quarter of a mile,' she said. 'Unless you want that in kilometres?'

'We walk from here,' I said. 'We can manage the gear.'

'Bleeding Hell,' Jeff said. 'No one said anything to me about hiking.'

But he said it good naturedly. He knew as well as I did, that we couldn't advertise our presence at the orphanage with a parked-up Land Rover. I looked at my watch. About two hours of light left in the day. Plenty of time to get there and set up before darkness fell. What snags would we face? The terrain between here and there was demanding on foot. But not impossible. Suarez had found the main door of the building unlocked. What if that was no longer the case? The was a short but brutal looking crowbar in my travel bag.

I smiled, thinking momentarily of Hangy Todd and his medieval ring of keys. Hangy, who had died of asbestosis in a Southport hospice back at the start of the noughties.

Conifers, boulders, rising ground, an increasing chill, distant crags and the whisper of rain as the skies opened again.

'Not tourist weather,' Daisy said.

'We're not tourists,' Lizzie said. She had pulled on a Barbour jacket and a waxed cotton jockey cap. She had my map in one hand and a small compass in the other. Her sound recording gear was carried in a shoulder bag I knew to be lined with polystyrene. She looked business-like but also slightly strained. Even tetchy.

She must have read the expression on my face. 'There's remote and there's remote, Tom,' she said. 'This landscape is creeping me out.'

'Let's get where we're going,' Jeff said. 'I'm personally gagging for a brew. Anyone object to me lighting up?'

There was no one around to smell his tobacco smoke. No one else, I mean. I thought of the boys and girls, innocently flawed from birth, being driven in an army lorry off to be shot in the wilderness. Would they have known their fate? I thought those only physically impaired would have guessed. They would have seen the distress of those nuns whose vocation it had been to take care of them.

A quarter of a mile is a distance determined really in its length by topography. The incline was gentle but relentless. The ground, more sodden by the moment, was slippery underfoot. And there were objects to have to skirt around and nothing resembling a path to follow.

Eventually the building that was our destination came into view. Walls of uniform, grey, rain-streaked stone. Windows not much wider than arrow slits. Two storeys. A front door, as the late Phillipe Suarez had told my brother, fit for a cathedral's main entrance. We paused for a moment and studied the exterior of the Orphanage of the Sacred Heart in the gentle hiss of the rain.

Standing next to me, to my left, Daisy murmured something. 'It's like the Fischer House,' she said.

I frowned. 'Architecturally, it's completely different,' I said. 'It has more the look about it of a church.'

'I meant the mood of it,' she said. 'The mood it evokes.'

'Yes. It does have that.'

'Stop mumbling, you two, and let's get inside, Jeff said. 'Better once we're in the dry and we've got a brew on.'

'Wish I had your faith in tea,' Lizzie said. 'Lonely sort of place. Probably great acoustics, though.'

'If there's anything to hear,' I said.

The building, when we got to it, was bigger than it looked from distance. Its uniformity enabled that trick of perspective. The absence of interior life, its sense of emptiness, also somehow emphasised its size. I tried the door with a tentative hand and on balanced hinges, it groaned inward. There was still an hour of light left to us theoretically, but the vestibule was cast into darkness by the dullness of the day and cake of dust on the interior of its miserly windows.

We were all four of us equipped with powerful Maglite torches. But as our group stood in the vestibule and I closed the door behind us, I thought it better to wait for our eyes to adjust to the gloom than to risk what inquisitive attention the anomaly of torch beams seen flashing in an abandoned building might bring.

I walked through the second door into the schoolroom Suarez had described, which was slightly, though not much, brighter. It was whatever lay beyond that, that I was curious to see. The rooms the late merchant banker had not explored. There was a door to either side of the blackboard sufficiently far apart to make me think the building divided beyond the wall I was facing. I walked to the door on my left, my trio of companions wordlessly following me, and tried the tarnished metal handle above the lock. It moved freely in my fingers. And I had the sudden intuition that the nuns had not been allowed to lock these doors. A higher authority had forbidden that provocation to its rule.

I pushed the door wide. And the first thing I saw was what was hung on the far wall. Vintage tennis racquets, their shafts sawn down to accommodate a child's abbreviated swing. Each hanging by a nail pushed through the catgut strings. I glanced to my left. The rolled canvas and neatly bundled wooden staves of old-fashioned frame tents. I looked to my right. On the floor, a rocking horse which looked handmade. Someone had improvised a mane from the strings of a mophead. A four-wheeled metal pedal-cart that looked to be fashioned out of beaten tin. Wall-mounted above those items, three rows of open sided wooden cubicles containing building blocks, model trains, boxes of Meccano, puppets, dolls, spinning tops, sagging leather footballs and four threadbare teddy bears.

Behind me, I heard Jeff let out a whistle. 'Jackpot time, Tommy Boy,' he said. 'There won't be a dry eye in the house when this lot hits the screen. Pete Davidson will cream his pants.'

The remark made me feel uneasy. It seemed not just tasteless, but somehow provocative. I glanced at Daisy and saw from her expression that she felt the same way I did about what Jeff had just said. Besides, my eyes weren't entirely free of tears at that moment.

My own daughter was resident at an institution, dependent on the kindness of the staff, beneficiary I hoped of their tact and expertise. I wasn't standing in a roomful of stage props. These punctiliously assembled items were tangible proof of what the nuns had tried to do for their damaged charges. There had been games and camping trips. Fresh air and a kind of freedom. A concerted attempt to make childhoods enjoyable, involved, immersive. That last one was not a word, even in translation, they would have used 70-odd years ago to describe their approach to care. But I thought it accurate.

We pressed on, walking into a music room. There was an upright piano and there was a semi-circle of stands designed to hold scores or lyric sheets. A closer look told me that the last recital had been duel-purpose. Both choral and a lesson in English. They had been singing, *10 Green Bottles*.

There was a wall-mounted cupboard full of neatly stored away instruments. Triangles, recorders, tambourines. The triangles had tarnished over time. The other instruments though looked like they could have been played yesterday. Seeing musical instruments in repose brought home to me how profound the silence was in that building. Other than our breathing and the scrape of four sets of feet on dusty floorboards, there was no sound in there at all.

Floorboards. That hinted at a cellar, didn't it? I didn't like cellars, hadn't since my vow breaking visit to the Fischer House all those years ago. And once again, Daisy Chain read my thoughts.

'I think there's a basement,' she said.

'The gift that keeps on giving,' Jeff said.

The rest of the ground floor, the rooms we explored behind their classroom, were fairly routine, institutional fare. There was a large kitchen with a spacious pantry and a dining room in which three long bench tables sat parallel. There was a tiny chapel, too small for general use.

'This must have been exclusively for the nuns,' Daisy said. 'So where would the children have attended mass?'

'Probably in their classroom,' I said. 'The priest would have come on a Sunday. He wouldn't have needed pomp and ceremony to perform the sacrament for so humble a congregation.'

'This is getting to you, isn't it, Tom?' Lizzie said. 'The fate of those kids.'

And it was. It was to do I think partly with my daughter. But mostly it was the young lives so mercilessly taken in so premeditated and methodical a way. That roomful of toys had made it somehow tangible. The home-made horse, rocking on unridden. The jigsaw puzzles that would have lain there, incomplete.

I just nodded back at her.

'We need to see the basement,' Jeff said. 'Then we need to get cracking, setting up. I'll give you a bit of notice before your cameo, Daisy, love. You can pull a brush through the barnet and freshen up the slap. Until then you're the lucky punter on tea-making duty.'

We switched on the Maglites, unobtrusive in the basement. It looked innocuous enough in the anaemic, battery-powered light. Just one cavernous space, the stone walls mossy in places with damp. An earth floor. Odd pieces of stored furniture littered here and there and a pervasive smell of staleness.

On the upper floor, the dormitory in which Phillipe Suarez had taken refuge for his broken night of sleep. And off that, a room he hadn't explored. A smaller dorm that must have been the sleeping quarters of the nuns. Full-sized beds with thin, hard mattresses designed for women for whom sleep would presumably have been a kind of penance.

'No rest for the wicked,' Lizzie said.

'They weren't wicked,' Daisy said. 'They were good and kind,'

'Catholicism,' Lizzie said. 'Predicated on the belief that everyone is wicked.'

'Theology,' Jeff said. 'Give me strength.'

But I sensed from the strain in his voice that the levity was forced. I had never seen or heard Jeff Potts discomforted. But he was that way now. It was fully dark. Darkness had crept up on us. And in darkness the place we were in came fully into its own.

Jeff and Lizzie went to work with establishing shots and a stubbornly silent soundtrack. He hadn't filmed the exterior of the building on arrival because he reckoned the structure would better suit dawn light in the morning to come. With luck, we'd have the clear sky then denied us on our arrival. The sky had partially cleared, we were no longer blanketed by complete darkness. Starlight and flits of moonlight illuminated our surroundings in a starved, monochromatic sort of way. Jeff was shooting with the infrared camera. It picked out detail in the most portentous, atmospheric manner possible without something actually manifesting for his lens to focus on.

When they had finished, we clustered child-sized chairs in the classroom where the Suarez nun had whipped her back to pulp and waited. Nobody really spoke. I sensed Jeff's craving for nicotine, but he didn't ask could he light up a cigarette.

Eventually, Lizzie said, 'Hear that?'

'Hear what?' I asked.

'A ticking clock,' Daisy said. 'Or maybe the swing of a pendulum.'

'There is no fucking clock,' Jeff said. 'We'd have seen it.'

'There must have been, once,' Daisy said.

And it grew louder and more insistent, and at once we could all hear it, ticking away invisibly in that very room, probably looted casually by one of the soldiers come to kill the children. Their commanding officer, perhaps, taking the solitary valuable object in a place overseen by women governed by a vow of poverty.

'You'd need a clock, for the timing of lessons,' Daisy said.

'Shut up,' Lizzie said.

I said, 'Try to be civil, Lizzie.'

'When your squeeze is stating the bloody obvious?'

She was every bit as rattled as Jeff. The ticking clock grew in volume, as loud as a rebuke. It was true what Daisy had said before we'd even entered the building. The place impended. It had that in common with the Fischer House. It promised dread. And I remain convinced that all four of us were sure, in our private ways that before the morning and the sanity of daylight came, it would deliver.

The singing began some time after midnight. A ragged chorus of *10 Green Bottles*, seeping out of the music room, trickling into our ears. Jeff had his camera resting on his lap. He stood and shouldered it.

'Showtime,' he said, with a bravado I was certain he didn't feel.

We stood. The singing, like the ticking of the clock earlier, was growing in strength, as though the orphanage itself was summoning strengthening memories of its past, recalling what it had been and who had lived there when it had been somewhere with a purpose. With a life. With lives.

In the absence of light, my little crew looked as pale as corpses. I probably looked no different. The impossible song plodded on. Lost voices, sound snatched from almost 80 years ago and dumped raggedly in the present. What sight would we see? We shuffled together in the direction of the music room, through the toy store where the items were now a heaped, jumbled, floor-bound litter of obstacles, the cart canted on its side, the horse rocking on its runners, the footballs fully inflated and only waiting for the joyous kick at them that would never come.

There was nothing to see in the music room. The singing sounded no less disembodied in there than it had before we entered. We were hearing nothing more than a memory. Relentless, repetitious, unending. And the loudness of it was growing intolerable.

'Oh Jesus, look,' Daisy said, pointing all around her.

But you didn't need to look, not really. The coppery odour flooded through the room. Lizzie Cox screamed. All around us, the walls were dripping blood.

We retreated to the schoolroom. The blood didn't trickle after us. Eventually, the singing faded and then stopped altogether. The ticking clock ceased to mark its phantom hour. We waited, shallow breathed, shock assaulted, fearful. But no further madness occurred that night and eventually, dawn broke. And I felt sufficient sanity return to find my voice.

'Think we've got something?'

'I should fucking say so,' Jeff said. Lizzie only nodded.

'Up to doing your piece?' I asked Daisy. She nodded too.

We returned to the room full of toys. We found them as precisely stored away as when we'd arrived. Daisy did her cameo to the backdrop of the open wooden cubicles, boxed jigsaw puzzles and model boats and pressed tin steam engines bright behind her. She spoke fluently and I didn't see her blink. In the circumstances, it was a remarkably assured performance. Then we heated water on the primus stove we'd bought, breakfasted on a mug of tea apiece and left.

'Nothing you couldn't fake,' Jeff said, lighting up gratefully on the walk back to where we had hidden the Land Rover.

'Bravado fully restored, Jeff,' I said. 'You've got your mojo back. But you properly lost it, didn't you?'

'No camera shake, guv,' he said. 'When you employ me, you're paying a pro.'

I stopped walking, so he did too. I said, 'What do you really think? No bullshit.'

He squinted into low sunlight. He said, 'What I really think is that I wouldn't spend another night in that place for a million quid. I might come out of it. But I wouldn't trust myself to come out of it sane.' He pointed with the hand holding his cigarette back in the direction from which we'd come. 'That's a nightmare, Tommy Boy. One you might never wake up from.'

I swallowed. 'I don't feel much like driving,' I said. Anyone else fancy the job?'

'I'll drive,' Daisy said. But there was something in the expression on her face and in the tone of her voice that told me she might have seen more at the orphanage than the rest of us had.

We went for a drink in Swiss Cottage two evenings later and I asked her. 'Women in habits weeping in corners,' she said. 'I saw uniformed men, swaggering, wolfish grins. Guns in buttoned holsters on their hips. And the children.' She heaved a sob. 'Callipers, club feet, a little girl holding a horn at her ear to amplify sound. It was terrible.' There were tears coursing from her eyes down her face.

'I'm so sorry,' I said. 'I should never have taken you.'

She shook her head, vehemently, and sniffed. 'I asked to go. I practically threatened you.'

I didn't know how to reply to that.

She gripped my arm. 'You'll stay the night?'

'I'll stay every night,' I said. It was a reflex. I said it really without thinking. But as soon as the words were out of my mouth, I knew it was what I wanted. I couldn't think of anything I wanted more, other than for my daughter to be lulled back gently into some kind of sanity.

Pete Davidson called me a couple of days after I'd biked him a rough cut of the film. He said, 'I'm pulling the plug on the bogey in the bog. And on Captain Birdseye by the sea, our Scottish lighthouse sulker.'

'Why?'

'Impact. Old World, New World. Ying and Yang. The Italian Dolomites and the windy city of Chicago. There's mileage in those locations. Unless the Italians demolish the place after we broadcast.'

'They won't,' I said. 'Though they might put in a turnstile and a ticket office.'

'Sometimes, and only sometimes,' he said, 'I think you might actually get the world we live in.'

'Thanks.'

'You're basically the twilight zone's last living inhabitant.'

Then his tone changed. 'How's Claire?'

'Better.'

'Good. I'm right on this, Tommy Boy. Mileage in Italy and Chicago. We're miners hitting the black seam. Prospectors, onto the vein of gold.'

'Maybe we are,' I said.

He was silent. Then he said, 'Tom, did you and Potts and Cox fake this shit?'

I closed my eyes. 'We didn't need to,' I said.

'Jesus.'

'Don't think he had a lot of involvement.'

'And where have you been hiding Daisy Chain? She belongs in front of camera, not googling behind a laptop screen.'

'Agreed.'

Another pause. 'The film's really genuine?'

Ten Green Bottles.

'I swear it.'

'Then some of us might be joining you.'

'What does that mean?'

'I mean in the twilight zone.'

I drove to Hove to see Claire. When I entered her room, it smelled both fresh and fragrant. A huge bouquet of flowers rose colourfully from an expensive looking frosted glass vase on her desk. There was a bowl of fruit there too. White grapes, glossy purple plums, cherries, bananas. Nothing you would need a knife to eat. The bowl heaped high with all this bounty had the rich polish of rosewood.

'Your mother's been to see you,' I said, redundantly.

'Yesterday,' Claire said. 'She cried.'

'Was it good to see her?'

'It wasn't good to see her cry, but yes.'

'Any other news?'

'A lady came to see me in the night. She wore clothes like in the picture I drew. She told me you had been to the Orphanage of the Sacred Heart. She spoke English with an accent but was easy to understand.'

'Were you frightened, Claire?'

'Why would I be frightened?'

I shrugged. I said, 'I don't know.'

'She told me that what you're doing is the right thing. She said it needed to be exposed. That the secret has been kept for too long. She was nice. But she made me feel sad.'

'Did you dream her?'

Claire raised her eyes like someone dealing with a slow-witted child. 'I didn't need to dream her, Dad. She was as real as you are.'

I gestured at the table. 'Will you eat the fruit?'

'Everything except the bananas. You can have those if you want.'

'I don't think your mother would approve.'

Claire smiled. She said, 'Then that can be our secret.'

I wasn't as shocked as I might have been. I suppose the pictures she'd drawn had prepared me for something like her casual revelation. The Fischer House drawing she'd sent my brother had half convinced me that there was some psychic link between me and my daughter. I thought she had dreamt it, but the dream had been so convincingly natural that she had confused it with actuality. She was only 16, after all. It can be a confused and confusing age in girls with far less sensitivity than my daughter possessed.

I was more surprised in all honesty by Samantha's visit. It must have been an ordeal, emotionally. I wasn't surprised by the tears. And it would be easier the next time. And I thought there would be a next time and a time after that, because there had been no ice in my daughter's heart for her absentee mother to have to break. Only love. And forgiveness. An also perhaps, understanding.

'Have you been seeing James Balfour?'

Claire pulled a face at that. She said, 'I'm kind of going off him?'

Upspeak.

'Why?'

'Too many questions.'

'It's probably his job to ask questions, darling,' I said.

'But I don't know the answers to questions about you and your childhood. You've never talked about it. You've never mentioned Edward Swarbrick to me.'

I sat down, hard, on the straight-backed chair in front of her desk.

'Doesn't he tell you to forget about the questions? Before he brings you out of the trance?'

Claire grinned at that. She said, 'I'm not as suggestible as he thinks I am. And he's not as good at hypnotism as he thinks he is.'

'You've been playing him along?'

'Not always, but sometimes. He's cute looking. You must have noticed that.'

'Not my type,' I said. And my daughter laughed. And a shaft of sunlight suddenly cleaved the room, bright, busy with dust motes. I said, 'Fancy a walk to the pier?'

'Really? Right now?'

'Right now, Claire. I've an urge to spend money I don't really have.'

And she laughed again. And despite what she'd told me, that was a beautiful sound to my ears.

Later, before leaving the Retreat, I requested and got an audience with Doctor Julia Pettifer. We swapped the usual, slightly formal greeting.

'How did you find Claire?'

'Buoyant. A two-hug day. I think that seeing her mother has done her the world of good.'

'I'd agree. What can I do for you, Tom?'

'A question,' I said. 'How did you find James Balfour?'

She blushed slightly. She said, 'It was actually more a case of him finding us. He wrote to me suggesting hypnotism might help those Retreat residents with self-harm issues or eating disorders. I thought what he said made perfect sense. Made me wish I had thought of it myself, sooner. He was conveniently Sussex based, was able to furnish excellent references and when I checked him out personally, was highly qualified.'

I nodded.

She cleared her throat with a cough and said, 'Can I ask why you ask?'

'Natural curiosity,' I said. 'I started out in working life as a journalist. It's the first requirement.'

She smiled. She said, 'It's the first requirement in anyone intelligent.'

My turn to smile. 'Is that a compliment, Julia?'

'I suppose it is, rather,' she said.

It's said to be a life of surprises. But I'd had enough of them for one afternoon.

On something a lot stronger than a whim, I drove to Chichester. It wasn't all that far away a place to take a punt on. I arrived at 5 o'clock in the afternoon optimistic that James Balfour would still be in his clinic, or studio, or consulting rooms or whatever else he called his place of work. I waited at a reasonably discreet distance for him to emerge. Which he did, just after 5.15. He punctiliously locked his street door and then set off for home, or for where he presumably parked his car. I followed him. Looked around. Few people about, no CCTV cameras, birds chirping. The odd, somnambulant summer passing car. I really didn't, by that point, honestly give a fuck. Claire, my daughter. My only child. I shortened the distance between us to a single stride. I tapped him twice on the shoulder and he turned around.

The headbutt hit him where I'd intended it to on the bridge of his nose and caused him to reel back, bleeding. I rearranged his posture with short hook to the liver that took him crumpling to the pavement.

'I'm not scared of you,' he said. So I stamped on his crotch to encourage him to think harder about that premature conclusion.

He groaned. I looked around. Still no witnesses. He said, 'You don't know what you're dealing with.'

'Edward Swarbrick? I think I do,' I said. 'Jericho Society. Long arms, deep pockets, bad news.'

'You'd better believe it.'

I gave him a kick in the ribs. He was all bluff, his nose gushing in crimson spurts with his accelerated heartbeat. Ruining the white shirt under his designer suit. Seeping into a tie I thought probably Paul Smith. He didn't look cute now. I still felt like damaging him further. Disfiguring him.

'It goes well beyond me,' he said.

I got down on my haunches. I said, 'Go anywhere near my daughter again and I'll kill you. I don't give a shit about the consequences. I really don't.'

He giggled then and spat blood and snot, the high-pitched sound weirdly hysterical. 'You love her more than life,' he said.

'And you've just had the crap beaten out of you by an old man. You think you're invulnerable? A sad illusion. Give that some serious thought.'

Poor kids get bullied. You haven't got the right shoes, the right football boots, the blazer, the expensive hardback books. A cheap pen. Never a decent haircut. You don't go on that summer trip to Spain they organise, or the skiing holiday. You don't even have a seat on the coach for the day excursions. Your family don't own a phone or even a fridge. You open your front door on Christmas Eve and there has been a charity collection for the poor of the parish. And the people proffering the resulting hamper are your own classmates.

It draws unwelcome attention. You are on the sonar of every kid in the playground with sadistic instincts or just a mean streak. That was me. That was my childhood. And you know what? You sink or swim. The boxing had never been enthusiasm for sport. For the noble art. It had been a survival mechanism. I would not honestly recommend an upbringing like mine. But it had endowed me with a certain discipline and had taught me useful things about myself. And I remembered them, and they had never changed.

The air-kissing with fragrant PR women intent only on flattery. The gushing reviews and profiles in the press. The champagne flooded receptions and dinners at restaurants with coveted tables. The industry accolades and first-class air travel and occasional limousines and recognition in the street. None of this was who I really was. I was who I had been born. And in sometimes significant ways, my talent for violence had stood me in good stead all my life.

I did not underestimate the Jericho Society. I appreciated fully that attracting their attention was dangerous. I had not done that deliberately. Probably I knew more about them than was safe. And that was why they were trying to establish the extent of what I had learned.

Anger and the desire to protect my daughter had been my motivation in threatening James Balfour, if that was even his real name. I did not think giving him a beating had put me in greater jeopardy than I was in already. But it had illustrated my weakness, which was my attachment to Claire. Harming her was the most effective way of hurting me and they would know that now. I had proven it to them. I had given them a public demonstration of that fact.

Chapter 8

Pete Davidson's logic was not unassailable. I thought there was still mileage in the Irish and Scots stories I had proposed him at the outset. But what they were not, was time sensitive. They could wait for future investigation. For the present, I was content to focus on the Italian material we had and the Chicago story that would follow it further down the road.

Pete's instincts as a producer tended to be sound. And the Dolomites orphanage was no longer the proposed subject of an hour-long paranormal one-off. It was to be a three-parter Pete would lobby the network to show on consecutive evenings.

Part one was to be nothing more really than an elaborate teaser. It would include the history of the Orphanage of the Sacred Heart and its climax would be a dramatization of what Phillipe Suarez claimed to have seen there. We would not mention his name, but we would allude to the manner of his subsequent death. And my brother had agreed to relate his hearing of the tale anonymously, to camera, but filmed in silhouette. And to describe beforehand the dramatic circumstances in which he learned the detail of the event.

Part two was to be a reconstruction of the war crime that effectively put an end to the orphanage. Pete said it would be staged tastefully. That it would not be exploitative. I did not see how that would be possible. But at the same time, I agreed with my daughter's nocturnal visitor from the past. The secret had been kept for too long. Exposure was not justice, but it was what the victims of that child massacre deserved.

Part three was the payoff. The footage of the interior of the building, with particular attention to the toys. And then the music room and that ragged rendition of *10 Green Bottles* and the walls leaking blood. And an interview with Jeff Potts already in the can and one to come too from Lizzie Cox. Jeff was as gruff, straight-talking and salt-of-the-earth on film as he was in life. Lizzie I was sure would be equally convincing. These were superlative technicians, consummate professionals, the interviews would imply. They are not the sort of people to collude in making stuff up. Doing that would only compromise their hard-earned status in the industry.

Happy with the format, Pete was also bullish about the ratings he expected the short series to achieve. So much so that Chicago was already green-lit. Again, he saw it as a three-part project. It meant that I was getting six episodes of broadcast time as opposed to the original four. Probably the reason I was philosophical about the Irish and Scots proposals. They could and would wait. If Pete were right about the potential of what had originally been the fourth haunting, my Celtic connections would surely follow.

And a massive stroke of good fortune. My Netflix friend Sally Bruce had got in touch with David Briggs, the phlegmatic builder and Hemingway fan who had seen and heard something redolent of the Jazz Age at the derelict former brothel and speakeasy once owned by Al Capone. She had suggested to him that his uncanny experience had the potential to inspire a drama. Briggs had been hesitant. Then, though, he had mentioned the approach to his wife. And she had told him in no uncertain terms that with two kids to put through college, they had to take every possible opportunity to maximise their income.

Briggs worked out for himself that the best way to legitimise his experience was to go on the record with the story. And the most effective way to do that was by featuring as a witness to a paranormal event in the factual programme Sally told him I was putting together.

I had already called Briggs to finalise matters and found him even over a transatlantic phone line to be drily articulate and extremely convincing. He asked me what my personal take was on hauntings.

'I think they're sometimes real,' I told him.

'No shit, Sherlock. I took in a couple of the shows you've written and fronted.'

'Really?'

'Not a difficult thing to do, Mr Carter. They're sold on Amazon.'

'I think the past gate-crashes the present sometimes, Mr Briggs. But only in places contaminated by deep emotional trauma. It's a kind of reverberation. And different people see and hear and even smell different things. And some people are aware of nothing at all. Depends on your psychic sensitivity.'

He laughed. 'That mean I'm sensitive?'

'Evidently.'

He was silent. Then he said, 'It wasn't an experience I'd be happy to repeat.'

'I don't think it ever is.'

'Yet you court it.'

'I'm a ghosthunter. It comes with the job description. The paradox being that I'm not particularly sensitive myself. So I'm not as traumatised as some.'

'What was that crazy place on that island off the British coast?'

'The Fischer House.'

'Man, you wouldn't get me within a mile of it.'

It occurred to me that David Briggs was the kind of person who would see a face at the window. Maybe several of them. I said, 'It's a place wisest avoided.'

'That empty joint full of hookers in fancy dress?'

'Yes?'

'I'm not going back in there, Mr Carter.'

'And you don't have to, Mr Briggs. You can do your piece to camera from the comfort of your favourite armchair.'

'Which is in my study.'

'There you go.'

I planned to colourise some newsreel footage of Chicago in the period of the brothel/speakeasy's pomp. More natural to see things that way, more immediacy. Dave Briggs hadn't seen what he'd seen, after all, in monochrome. The precise format of the three consecutive episodes, in common with the Italian Job, would only be decided on the basis of our experience when we got to our location.

And we weren't going to be the same tight-knit team. Lizzie Cox had quit on me. *10 Green Bottles,* she texted me to say, had been for her the last haunting. She was happier dealing with petulant rock stars. She didn't have recurrent nightmares about them. And the dead ones she had worked with in the past, stayed that way. They didn't insist on echo-drenched comebacks. They didn't bleed through walls.

Pete Davidson suggested I ask Sally Bruce to recommend someone in situ from the Netflix roster of sound recordists, no doubt thinking of the saving on air fare. But when things start seriously bumping in your night, I knew from experience a cool head was the only route to a safe pair of hands.

My brother Andy recommended someone over a beer. Again, a woman, someone who had recorded interviews and confessions for the Met Police when the stakes were too high to leave the job to amateurs. She had also done court and surveillance recording. The fact that she had never been involved with fiction appealed to me. She was a technician, a seeker after clarity rather than drama. Her name was Susan Masters. She was 34. She was someone unlikely to collude in doctoring a film, or even being suspected of doing that. Her record exuded accuracy and integrity. She sounded ideal.

Andy called Susan and explained the job, which she told him intrigued her. She was willing to at least have the conversation.

I met her a couple of days later at my Soho members' club. She had alert brown eyes and looked younger than her age. Elfin figure, no hint about her of the terrible things she must have heard confessed in rooms with secure steel doors and bars on their windows. Absolute composure and the most enigmatic of smiles. She sipped at a double espresso while I told her what Andy had not.

'Barrelhouse piano,' she said. 'That would play havoc with my sound levels.'

'We might hear nothing at all,' I said.

'Or get the full Dave Briggs experience,' she said.

I wondered how she would gel with Jeff Potts. It occurred to me that Jeff could probably recommend someone. But I already liked Susan Masters. She was confident, friendly and expert.

'Do you believe in ghosts, Susan?'

She shrugged. 'I've an open mind. I've never seen one. So if I see one in Chicago, it'll be a first.'

We agreed a rate for the job. We discussed timings, schedule. Finally, we shook hands on a deal. Her grip was firm. I wasn't at all surprised.

The Italian Job – we had all taken to calling it that by now – came together in the edit suite. And it was gruelling. Though not as gruelling as it had been for Daisy Chain in life. Or as gruelling as it had been for the children of the orphanage in death. The footage of the toys was almost unbearably poignant. But Lizzie Cox was right, *10 Green Bottles* was a sinister ordeal to listen to. It sounded disembodied, only because it was. It had about it the lifelessness of reverberated sound. Except that it seemed to go on forever.

After working on the series until late one evening, I thought I was followed home from the train station. I told myself I had been spooked by the sight I'd that evening witnessed on the screen of blood seeping through stone, blackly, through the infra-red camera lens. Then I remembered what I had done to the hypnotist James Balfour in broad daylight on a Chichester Street. That too had involved blood. And then I remembered the fearful look on Helena Donavan's youthful face in her summer garden on the island when she had spoken to me about the Jericho Society.

The footfalls behind mine were steady and light. They sounded confident, deliberate. They got no closer and when I stopped, they did too. I did not surrender to the temptation of turning around to look. It was fully dark, moonless, and the Teddington streetlights were suburban and scant and expert tails, I knew from my brother, were adept at staying in the shadows.

I was not being followed by someone eager to learn where I lived. That sort of information is laughably easy to come by without having to get out from behind a computer screen. I was not in Swiss Cottage only because Daisy was in Scotland for a couple of days, doing a job for someone else in Edinburgh. Would someone wait outside the station, every evening, just on the off chance?

And the off chance of what? Intimidating me? Reminding me of how far their tentacles stretched? I did not even know what it was specifically that had provoked their interest in my younger life. The Fischer House had made my early reputation, but I had made no mention of Klaus Fischer's connection to them. Yet they had set up the whole elaborate scam of Balfour to try to learn something specific about me. It was mystifying.

I was half a block from my front door when the footsteps behind mine faded away to nothing. I turned my key in the lock of my front door and opened it and entered my home. And I was aware of a very faint scent, for all the world the smell of cigar smoke. Except that cigar smoke was never faint. It was an always pungent aroma. And I had never smoked anything in my life. And there were no open windows for the night drift of an odour from outside. The windows were all not just closed but locked.

I shook my head. My imagination was overwrought, was all. And then my phone rang in my jacket pocket and I pulled it out and it was Julia Pettifer's number at 11.30 at night, so I fumbled through the call.

'Sorry to call you so late, Tom, but I felt it necessary.'

'Is it Claire?'

'Only in a manner of speaking.' Her voice sounded uncharacteristically strained. 'We employ an accountant who works sometimes unconventional hours. He called me fifteen minutes ago. He was looking at our payments to people like him, people on our freelance payroll. He found an irregularity with a National Insurance number. The number belongs to James Balfour. Bluntly, it doesn't look as though our hypnotist is who he says he is.'

Relief surged through me. 'Do you know who he is?'

'Far too early to say. We will alert the police in the morning. Impersonation of that sort isn't just unethical. It's illegal. Our procedures in this instance were obviously flawed. Which is why I'm phoning personally to apologise. I'm where the buck stops on this one.'

No harm had been done to my daughter. I felt that I could be magnanimous. But I also felt I could get something back from this situation than might prove useful to me.

'Orchestrated deception is hard to spot when you can't see an obvious motive,' I said. 'You made an understandable mistake for the right reasons.'

She said, 'I'm grateful to you for seeing it that way.'

'If the police discover Balfour's real identity, will they reveal it to you, Julia?'

She laughed, shortly. 'I'm the victim of a crime, so yes, I expect they will.'

'If they do, I'd be obliged if you would reveal it to me?'

'Curiosity again, Tom?'

'That's the one,' I said.

I didn't want to get embroiled in a dangerous game played against deadly people. But little is more hazardous than a position of ignorance. I wanted to know why the man who had called himself James Balfour was so interested in my earlier life. I needed all the clues I could accrue.

The situation wasn't without a certain irony. Balfour had tried to exploit my daughter. In fooling him, Claire had clearly given herself something she could feel proud of. He had unwittingly bolstered her sometimes fragile self-esteem. Without it being his intention, he had evidently done my daughter a lot of good.

Who did I know who smoked cigars? I lay in bed awaiting sleep and thought about that. I was sure Jeff Potts would enjoy the occasional panatela, probably at Christmas with a Harvey's Bristol Cream. And Pete Davidson smoked the odd celebratory Havana in his more ostentatious moments. But it had fallen out of fashion since its revival of the 1990s, when Cigar Aficionado had been a prestigious monthly magazine dedicated to the habit.

Then I remembered Jack Dooley and the curious story told by the importer who'd sold Jack's landlord grandfather his cigar stock at the Black Boar pub in Southport. The man who had caught a glimpse of the altar in the home of Edward Swarbrick in a room with a dagger mounted on one of its walls. He had been there to sell Swarbrick his cigars, hadn't he? Was Swarbrick coming back to haunt me? Had he started to do so already? I was too tired to contemplate that ghoulish eventuality. I closed my eyes and drifted off to sleep and *10 Green Bottles* on a loop tape in my head.

****

Daisy learned something about the brothel-based pianist around whom Al Capone had built a jazz band in Chicago in the 1920s. He was of Creole heritage and had been born in New Orleans in 1890. He was the grandson of Slaves, both of whom had picked cotton on a plantation in the anti-bellum South. His father was one of the Union Army's Buffalo Soldiers in the American Civil War. He'd fought at Shiloh and Gettysburg before his 20th birthday. Perhaps that was why Levon Laporte named his own son Ulysses. Perhaps in honour of the American General Grant.

Ulysses Laporte learned his jazz trade in the city of his birth, which had possibly the richest musical tradition of anywhere in

America. Though by the end of World War One, Chicago was rivalling New Orleans for inventiveness and virtuoso players on its own vibrant jazz scene.

Ulysses seems to have relocated for pragmatic reasons. There was some sort of scandal surrounding his mother and involving the practice of folk medicine. At the age of 27, the pianist with the growing reputation found that his family had come to the attention of the police. It was unwelcome attention and it impacted on his ability to get booked at venues that considered themselves respectable.

'What did his mother do?' I asked Daisy.

'Impossible to say for sure,' Daisy said. 'Could have been anything from brewing bootleg liquor to abortions. Could have been voodoo, which was widely practiced in the rural parishes around the city Ulysses grew up in. But New Orleans became too hot for him and he rode freight to the Windy City armed, I suspect, only with whatever dollars he had saved and his piano playing talent.'

'He must have been good,' I said. 'Capone knew his music.'

'I was coming to that,' Daisy said. 'He was good. He died of tuberculosis in Baltimore in the Autumn of nineteen-forty-one at the age of fifty. But he cut several records and you can listen to a couple of them on YouTube. Seventy-eights, so comparatively primitive recordings. But you can hear the quality of his playing quite clearly.'

'And if we can find out about copyright, maybe use them on the soundtrack,' I said. 'What's your gut feeling on the mother?'

'I'm still on the hunt,' Daisy said, 'no stone unturned.'

'Mixed metaphors,' I said.

'They're my curse,' she said. 'When I'd far rather have a blessing. My gut feeling is involvement with voodoo.'

'Tell me about his band.'

'A quintet. Piano, drums, upright bass, trumpet and tenor sax. They could go from a frenetic rag to something languorous and bluesy. They could make that switch in the space of a beat.

'You needed instinctive rhythm and the ability to improvise was essential. The standard was arguably higher than it is now, just because there were so many more venues and players. You needed stamina for the marathon sets they used to play in those days. You needed to be loud enough to be heard without amplification. Blow-hard is a pejorative term now, it was an accolade back then. You had to be an all-rounder, you had to be able to do it live and the competition was ferocious.'

I asked, 'What was Ulysses Laporte like as a character?'

'If you were black in those days, it was only sensible to keep a low profile. But this is the son of a woman who may well have been a voodoo priestess. Someone who paid his jazz dues in New Orleans in the early twentieth century. And he was physically imposing. A good enough boxer to spar professionally with Harry Greb and Jack Dempsey. He liked loud suits, fast cars, loose women. But he was teetotal and doesn't appear to have indulged in drugs, which almost everyone on that scene did. Also had a cultured side. Composed music, which meant that he could read it. When he died, he bequeathed a personal collection of five hundred books to the Baltimore Public Library.'

'Anything else?'

'In nineteen-seventeen, he volunteered to fight in World War One. He probably did so in the wrong part of the country, he was still in Louisiana. He was rejected, I'm assuming on racial grounds. Not like he would have failed a physical. And he didn't have a sheet.'

'What does that mean?'

'Whoops, sorry Tom. American terminology. It means he did not have any criminal convictions. Never married. No children'

'Visuals?'

'Photos of both him on his own and with the quintet. Black and white, obviously. Some sepia, nothing in colour. He liked having his picture taken. There might be something on celluloid somewhere in a private collection, but nothing so far in the public domain. Stressing so far. I'm still on that.'

'Don't stress too much,' I said. 'You've already done brilliantly.'

We were having this conversation on the phone. We weren't spending every night together after all. Daisy was a naturally resilient woman and had tried to put her orphanage experience into some sort of perspective. Occasionally she had flashbacks to what she had witnessed there, but it did not impinge upon her daily life. I had suggested as tactfully as possible that sticking to the familiarity of routine was the best route to recovery from the shock of being confronted by something inexplicable in rational terms.

'Cold feet?' She had asked, ruefully.

But for me it was the opposite of that. I thought the way for this still-novel relationship to have the best chance of being successful was for it to evolve naturally. But I was thinking tentative, rather than cautious. Me moving all at once into her Swiss Cottage home did not leave a lot of room for spontaneity. I did not want to suffocate her. I thought it best she should continue with her tennis and book club and all-round domestic independence. And when we did see one another, I thought it best we did not discuss the project we were working on together. Best to keep the professional and the personal apart. Blurred lines are tedious. Thankfully, Daisy had also reached that conclusion. We had both endured, in common with everyone else, the life curtailed. It had taught both of us how precious leisure, choice and freedom really are.

So we had that conversation about Ulysses Laporte during an 11am phone call. And when I saw Daisy next, it was three evenings later and for dinner at Cote at a pavement table on George Street in Richmond. And I had by then asked Daisy to try to inventory the books he bequeathed to the Baltimore Public Library. I thought there might be volumes giving a clue as to whether his mother was involved in magical rites.

The voodoo tradition in Louisiana is sustained in two languages. And it is overwhelmingly an oral tradition. But I thought that inventory was an avenue worth exploring, even if it eventually wound up being one of Daisy's cul-de-sacs.

Julia Pettifer had called me with her revelation about the man who wasn't really named James Balfour late on Tuesday evening, the same evening I had thought I was being followed home from the station. The same evening on which I had been reminded of Jack Dooley's story about the Black Boar landlord and what a

Liverpool tobacco importer had only glimpsed through a shifted curtain at Edward Swarbrick's house on Weld Road in Southport.

I met Daisy for dinner at Cote, the following Friday. It was a sunny summer evening and there were, this time, no pavement pyrotechnics. No cameo appearance from my ex-wife, the mother of my child. A woman I felt I had known all my adult life, now estranged from me and angry. In other circumstances I would have welcomed an emollient meeting with Samantha and a serious discussion about her visit to see Claire and the implications of their rapprochement for our daughter's future. But there is a time and a place.

After dinner, we walked back to my place in Teddington, a relaxed stroll, me with no sense that we were being skilfully tailed by someone feathery on their feet, stealing along somewhere behind us. But I had only put the key in the lock and opened the door for Daisy to enter the house when she stopped dead in the hallway and said, 'Someone's been here.'

'Who?'

'I don't know.'

'When?'

'Can't you smell it, Tom?'

I sniffed at the air. Nothing. Maybe leather from the recliner beyond my open study door to the left of us. Maybe a floral hint of bleach from the loo at the top of the stairs on the floor above. But really, nothing.

'Do you smoke cigars, Tom?' Daisy was wide-eyed.

'No.'

'No. And you don't wear hair oil. Or cologne. And you don't starch your shirts.'

'I smelled cigar smoke here on Tuesday night. Or thought I did. It was very faint. I can't smell it now.'

'Vetiver.'

'What?'

'The cologne. A Guerlain fragrance popular in the early part of the last century. Still going. Peter Sellers wore it. You don't.'

I put my hands on her shoulders and squeezed. I remembered how much more sensitive she had been in the Dolomites than the rest of us. Four evenings earlier, in my nostrils, the cigar smoke had only been a hint I thought I was imagining. But someone had left their residue and Daisy sensed it powerfully.

'There's no one here,' I said.

'I know,' she said. 'I'd know if there was.'

'How do you know so much about perfume?'

'Researched it. It's what I do, remember? That cocktail of smells isn't from the present, Tom. Whoever came here, came here from the past.'

'What do you want me to do, Daisy? An Uber to yours?'

She shook her head. She said, 'Is it the kind of thing we can run away from?'

'I don't think so.'

She smiled then, I thought bravely. She said, 'Open all the windows. It's not like we'll exactly catch our deaths in July. Air the place. And then pour us a large drink. My own preference would be vodka.'

It was twenty minutes later, and I was nursing a large whisky and Daisy a tumbler full of vodka and tonic and ice when my phone signalled an incoming call and it was Doctor Pettifer. I put down my drink and stood to take the call. I always stood when it was the Retreat. A nervous reflex.

'Julia.'

'Tom.'

'Claire?'

'Only adjacently,' she said.

'What does that mean?'

'Police update. Someone answering the description of the man claiming to be James Balfour was treated in A&E for a broken nose. He went to hospital in the early evening of the last day you visited your daughter. I'd trust that was a coincidence.'

'He probably tripped up. I mean physically, as he also did metaphorically.'

'Claire tells me you used to box. Seriously, she says. Says you still do the training.'

'I'm only a few years off my free bus pass, Julia. Plus, I'm not a vigilante. Also, how would I have known?'

'You visited your daughter earlier the same day.'

'You've said that.'

'Your exceptionally bright daughter, Someone James Balfour probably underestimated.'

'Innocent until proven guilty,' I said. 'How is Claire?'

'Everything is relative. But she seems to be thriving.'

'Thank you.'

'Sweet dreams, Tom.'

Daisy sipped vodka and asked me about the context of the call. So I told her, honestly.

'Is that a civilized way of dealing with things, Tom? Beating people up? Didn't you just demean yourself, fighting in the street?'

'He inveigled his way into my daughter's room where she was unchaperoned masquerading as someone he wasn't. It was a deliberate deception and a betrayal of trust. And he tried to manipulate a vulnerable person not just under false pretences, but entirely to his own ends.'

'He disappointed you,' Daisy said. 'What did you call it, the Holy Grail of hypnotism? You were angry.'

'I am protective of my daughter. I have a duty of care.'

'And you were angry,' she said. 'And disappointed.'

'Yes, Daisy. I was.'

She was quiet for a while. Then she said, 'Ominous, this ongoing interest they have in you.'

'I don't know the reason for it,' I said. 'Not really.'

She pondered on that. She said, 'They're addicted to secrecy and they think you've got something on them. Something damaging you might one day expose. Exposing sinister cults isn't a million miles away from what you do. And your status in the industry makes you powerful.'

'I've got nothing on them. Nothing current.'

'It was you exposed the footage of the Jericho Ball. It was you made your name with what you filmed at the Fischer House. You're on their radar and they think you're just keeping your powder dry.'

'Mixing metaphors again, Daisy.'

She sighed and sipped from her drink. She said, 'It was Edward Swarbrick who came here, wasn't it, Tom? It was him.'

'Yes. I think it was.'

'He hasn't finished with you either.'

'Cheering thought.'

We lapsed into silence. A comfortable rather than an awkward silence, both left to our individual thoughts until I realized Daisy was humming, absently, *Ten Green Bottles*.

I thought it was time then for the happy distraction of bed.

****

The self-deprecating developer Sally Bruce had met at that New York cocktail party was named Jerry Barden. He was still the titular owner of the Chicago property that had once belonged to Al Capone, the place to which he had sent his regular contractor Dave Briggs to do an estimate on refurbishment. He had miscalculated with that particular acquisition, but his business record generally was seriously impressive. He owned a vast property portfolio.

I thought Barden might consider me an irritant or just a crank. But Sally had got to know him slightly since their first encounter and offered to pour on the oil before the water had time to get troubled.

Sally did me the favour of contacting him on my behalf and we had a brisk email correspondence. Then one afternoon shortly after, he called me. He did not stand on ceremony and by then we were on first-name terms.

'You really Britain's most famous ghosthunter, Tom?'

'Allegedly,' I said.

'Notoriety isn't exactly a selling point. Not where real estate is concerned. I'm doing this only as a favour for Dave Briggs. He's a solid guy.'

'There's no guarantee anything will manifest.'

'And if something does, I can sell the building to Disney and they can dismantle it and reconstruct in their theme park in Florida.'

'Unlikely to happen.'

'You're not looking at the big picture, my friend. Think of the merchandising opportunities. Fedoras. Buick Sedans. Correspondent shoes. Guns named after you,'

'What?'

'Tommy guns.'

'Ah.'

I could see why Jerry Barden got on as well as he apparently did with his chum Dave Briggs. They had a similarly mordant sense of humour.

'Seriously, you might run into complications. This isn't the Italian countryside.'

I had outlined briefly in an email what we had done in the Dolomites. And why we had done it.

'If local media get wind of what you're up to, it won't be a derelict flop-house with a colourful history. The place will be a zoo.'

'Only you and Dave Briggs know our schedule. I'm trusting you both to keep it to yourselves.'

'Okay with me,' he said. Then he laughed. 'Wouldn't want to spoil the party.'

I had thought about tipping off the Chicago Police Department. But doing that risked a pre-emptive leak to the press. And we weren't actually planning on doing anything illegal. We had the owner's permission, emailed in writing. We had the keys, still in the possession of David Briggs. We had work visas stating that our short visit to the States was for location filming. To use an American term, I thought we had all the bases covered.

Jerry had sent me some shots of the building, exterior and interior, taken by one of his minions in daylight. After speaking to him I examined them, for the fifth or sixth time. A narrow building on a neglected street comprising five floors. The ground-floor had a glass shopfront to the right of a wooden front door scabrous with peeling brown paint. The shopfront interior was dark, some trade or brand name too faded on the pane to be legible. The four floors above all looked identical, each with two rectangular windows shaped out of unembellished brick and equipped with tattered blinds the same brown at the brickwork. On the right of the building, a spindly iron fire-escape descending into an alley lined with trashcans.

The interior shots showed no improvement. Smaller rooms than would be fashionable today. All of them wallpapered a long time ago, judging by their tattered and fading look. Truckle beds stripped of mattresses. Bronze wall sconces canted at crazy angles, wires trailing out of them where the bulbs should have been.

Ceiling fans bereft of almost all their blades. Brown circular light switches protruding like Bakelite boils from the sides of doorframes. Bare wooden floors, the boards in places ruptured, or missing or split. What looked like a smashed ceramic washbowl and jug set. An antique typewriter, a Remington Standard according to the legend under the roller, dusty, rigid, silent, perched heavily on the baize of a card table. A single sheet of paper in the roller, age-yellowed and blank.

And one clue about the building's past, about the violence of the period that witnessed its prime. A line of bullet holes from a weapon that had fired automatically studding the plaster of one wall. I thought about the deafening loudness of that lethal burst of lead, about the exploding plaster fragments and wince-making ricochets.

****

Our Sacred Heart Orphanage series was scheduled to be broadcast at 9pm from Monday to Wednesday with our departure for Chicago scheduled for the Monday after. Pete Davidson figured two days enough for us to respond to what he hoped would be an avalanche of media and public reactions.

He did not want me over-exposed, prior to getting Chicago safely in the can. The longer we left it, the greater the chance that someone would gossip, and we would be beaten to the punch. He made Jeff Potts and Susan Masters sign confidentiality agreements. Then the suspicious bastard made me and Daisy Chain sign one too. As though she would blab. As though I was into self-sabotage. Jerry Barden and David Briggs, he had to take on trust. Though I don't think Pete really trusted anyone, possibly including himself.

In the fortnight prior to the showing of those first episodes, I tried to arrange a meeting with Samantha. I wanted to discuss the impact and importance of her renewed visits to see Claire. I asked Daisy did she think this was the right thing to do.

'Of course it's the right thing to do,' she said. 'If you hadn't suggested it, I would have tried to persuade you to do it. But don't push too hard.'

'I'm not a bull in a china shop.'

She smiled, her head to one side. She said, 'The bloke masquerading as James Balfour might take issue with that particular claim.'

Samantha stonewalled. She was icily polite in her reply to my email, but maddeningly non-committal. But over that fortnight before transmission – The Orphanage: Life, Death and Afterlife in the Dolomites, not my choice of title – I travelled to Hove to visit my daughter five times. And on the fourth occasion, Samantha was there, at the Retreat, in Claire's room with her.

I got no cautionary warning from the front desk. I don't suppose they knew much about my domestic circumstances beyond being Claire's father. Julia Pettifer did, knew of necessity the whole background to Claire's birth and upbringing. But she was presumably behind the blind obstacle of her closed office door. It was just after 2pm on a Thursday. I did what I always did, knocked softly twice and then entered. And they were standing together side by side, leaning against the edge of Claire's desk. That faced the window. They were facing me. And my second thought, after the shock of recognition, was how like her mother my daughter was coming to look.

Dumbstruck is a cliché. But like most clichés, it has endured because it describes a truth. I found myself incapable of uttering a word. Samantha just stared at me, her mouth slightly open, revealing her bottom row of teeth.

It was Claire who spoke. She said, 'Now, you're not going to have a scene. I remember those. I never liked them.'

Looking at me, Samantha said, 'You remember the scenes?'

'Christ, mum, I remember being ten. I might be a bit doolally. I'm not a moron.'

'Hello, you two,' I said. To my own ears, I sounded pitiful.

'Mum only just got here, Dad. So you two go and have a nice chat together and come back and see me in an hour or so. The Ginger Pig is supposed to be okay. And only around the corner. Coffee and cake, that kind of thing. A bar too, I think.'

We walked out of Claire's room and out of the Retreat to the indifferent glances of the women behind the reception desk. We walked out onto the street and turned for the corner and the Ginger Pig as we had been instructed to do, obediently. We found a table and ordered. Coffee for me, Earl Grey tea for Samantha. Neither of us spoke until our drinks were served. I inventoried my ex-wife. Silk floral dress, Cartier wristwatch, pearls that looked real. Her hair was artfully tinted and she hadn't allowed the tan to fade. I didn't recognise the scent, but she smelled expensive. Life was evidently being good to her.

She sipped at her tea before either of us spoke. Then she said, 'I can't believe how well she seems. Is it too much to hope that she one day might come home?'

Which home, I wondered. That had become a question now. I said, 'That's the dilemma, Samantha. Do it too early and she would have to go back. And she loses all hope and is crushed. But I don't want her locked up a moment longer than she has to be. They do seem to be doing well with her. Better, I mean.'

Samantha smiled. She said, 'We both know you're the reason she's getting better.'

'You look well,' I said.

'Finally met Mr Right two years ago. And working again. I want to share the cost of the Retreat until we can get Claire out. Happy to backdate it.'

'Quite a hefty sum.'

'If you can afford it, I can too.'

'That would be a help.'

'And I owe you an apology for that scene outside Cote.'

'No lasting harm done,' I said.

She looked at me frankly, her hands flat on the table to either side of her teacup, fingers spread. 'We met when we were sixteen.'

'I do remember.'

'And I'll never stop caring about you. I don't want you hurt, Tom. You can be naïve.'

'I don't think I'm naïve.'

She turned her head to look out of the window. The décor inside the Ginger Pig's restaurant was stylish and original. Idiosyncratic, very Hove. But the place didn't boast an interesting view. She turned back to look at me again.

'Remember when we reconnected, when I fled the South of France and ran into you at that Millbank Gym?'

'I was on a running machine. It was me practically ran in to you.'

She smiled and titled her head. 'Still think that was coincidence, Tom?'

'Wasn't it?'

'There was a profile in one of the Sunday supplements. You were becoming well known by then. Name-checked your gym. Said you worked out at midday during the week, instead of eating lunch.'

'Ah. You're thinking no fool like an old fool.'

'A harsh way of putting it,' she said. 'We both know you look nowhere near your calendar age. I just don't want you hurt.'

We finished our drinks. I paid the bill, and we went back. And we were there for two hours in a scenario that even a couple of weeks earlier, I would have thought impossible. It was natural, unforced, effortless, really. I watched our daughter blossoming with a contentment I had never dared hope for.

'I think you're coming home,' I whispered, embracing her on departure.

'When?' She asked.

'Soon,' I said.

Samantha hesitated on the pavement outside. I said, 'Where are you parked?'

'Aren't you shocked, Tom, by my Millbank revelation?'

I shrugged. 'Clever women are schemers. That's the price you pay, avoiding the tedium of being with someone stupid, or just unimaginative. Anyway, we had some happy years.'

'Yes. Yes, we did.'

'Where are you parked, Samantha?'

She smiled. 'Train, I'm afraid. Driving ban. Caught speeding through Richmond Park.'

'That was naughty.'

'And selfish. And anti-social. What can I say?'

'I'll give you a lift,' I said.

'That's kind of you, Tom.'

'I know the route. All the way to your front door.'

And she laughed.

An eventful Thursday. On Saturday morning I received an A-4 envelope in the post. It had a Brighton postmark and my name and address had been done in Claire's bold script. Inside were a rectangular sheet of cartridge paper and an accompanying note. She had sketched a face-on headshot of the man we had both known as James Balfour. The likeness was good. He was recognisable despite the two black eyes and the splinted plaster stretched across his nose. I read the note:

I'm glad you did this, Daddy. He tried to touch me. I told him to stop. I told him I would tell you. He said you wouldn't believe me. But he didn't try to touch me again.

I did not mention anything about this to Mum. Or anything about hypnotism. My situation upsets her. She has managed to stop crying but I can see the sadness in her eyes.

Our eyes are the most truthful part of us. I saw in your eyes that you were going to do this. But they don't see everything. This drawing is of something I saw only in my mind.

All My Love,

Claire x

She rarely sent me artwork. On those occasions when she did, they were attached with Blu-Tack to the walls of my study. This one was straight away taken screwed up to a street bin at the end of the road.

****

Daisy discovered more about Ulysses Laporte. His mother was a Creole woman named Adele Berouet. She married the pianist's father at the age of 15 in 1870, when her husband was 23. She was still alive when her son died in 1940. She was 85 years old and long a widow by then but still apparently vigorous. He had been her only child. She had his body brought back by train to New Orleans to be interred.

'Which is where things get a bit weird,' Daisy told me. 'Because there is no record of a funeral service. No record of a burial. No headstone, no marked grave. Her home was in St Charles Parish. She was comparatively prosperous. That might have been on account of her son's generosity. Or it might have been the consequence of what she was paid as a healer.'

'She was a practitioner of folk medicine?'

'Depends on which account you believe,' Daisy said. 'People were grateful when she cured them of rheumatic fever or the pox. But she was reputed to be a voodoo priestess and she doesn't seem to have denied it.'

'Why didn't she treat her son?'

'His condition went undiagnosed and his decline was rapid. Not surprising when you think of the decades of passive-smoking he would have done in the jazz clubs where he played.

'There's something else that's odd. After his death, two people claimed to have seen him walking the roads of St Charles Parish at night.'

'I doubt those roads were street-lit,' I said.

Daisy said, 'He was a distinctive figure. You've seen the photographs.'

I had and he was.

'Maybe he didn't die at all,' I said.

'He died all right, Tom. In a bed at Baltimore General. They keep an archive and I've seen the death certificate.'

It was odd and anomalous, and the voodoo connection was intriguing in its way. But the real point of Ulysses Laporte in our narrative was that he was the catalyst that saw Al Capone's Chicago brothel become first a speakeasy and then a music venue with the house band he led. Horrible pun, but he was instrumental in that transformation. Our focus was on the prostitutes Dave Briggs had seen partying with their punters. The cast-off call girls who had met bleak destinies when they were no longer seen as the most profitable use of the building. Casualties of greed and callousness who seemed disinclined to be restful in their graves.

Ulysses Laporte, I wanted more on the soundtrack than featuring in the story. Though as someone with an interest in boxing, I was impressed he had been good enough to trade blows in the gym with a fighter who hit as hard as Jack Dempsey had. And share the practice ring with a man with the skills of Harry Greb, who some knowledgeable people still claim was the greatest middleweight ever to lace on a glove.

Daisy had trawled through that list of books the pianist donated to the Baltimore Public Library. They included, unsurprisingly, Gene Tunney's scientific volume on the noble art. Equally unsurprisingly, the list numbered books about the war in which his father had fought with such courage and distinction. There was a book about the virtuoso cornet player, King Oliver, whom Ulysses could conceivably have played with. Another on the peerless trumpeter, Louis Armstrong. Did Ulysses jam with Satchmo? Both men, like him, had been Louisiana born.

A Harry Houdini biography. Reference to the great escapologist brought to mind, with a smile, my own dead cousin Hangy Todd. A couple of books about spiritualism. And a solitary volume entitled, *An Unauthorised History of the Practice of Voodoo Magic*. No author was credited on the title page. The book had been published anonymously. How close had Ulysses Laporte been to his mother? He had moved a long way from his Louisiana roots geographically. On the other hand, he had been an only child.

Chapter 9

Monday's part 1 audience was eight million. By Tuesday's second instalment that figure had grown to ten million. And on Wednesday evening an estimated fourteen million people tuned in to see the climax; to see walls bleed and hear *Ten Green Bottles* sung by the lost chorus of children who perished more than 70 years ago in a murderous war crime kept secret since then.

The reaction on Thursday morning, both from press and public, was unprecedented in my personal and professional experience. Condemnation of what had occurred at the Sacred Heart Orphanage came swiftly from the Italian Embassy in London and from the Vatican in Rome. The Italian government pledged a full and immediate investigation into the massacre. And those responses had the immediate psychological effect of legitimising our trilogy of films.

The negative reaction though was almost equally swift. A hatchet piece on me and my programme making record in Friday's Daily Mail. A statement from the Archbishop of Canterbury intimating that belief in ghosts represented a kind of blasphemy. A film special effects veteran who explained exactly how we had faked everything on the national news on Friday evening.

And then something completely unexpected. On Saturday, The Telegraph carried a full-page interview with Marianne Suarez in which she detailed the experience her husband had endured in the Dolomites. She described the effect it had had on his character, behaviour and ability to do his job. She could not have given the interview without knowing what my brother had told her about Phillipe's mountainside confession to him. She actually went so far as to namecheck Andy in the piece. Said she owed him her thanks for solving a mystery that had tortured her. Said the knowledge of what her husband had witnessed was helping her slowly process the grief she felt.

I rang my brother.

'Of course I told her she could reveal my identity,' he said. 'It won't impact as much on me professionally as having you for a sibling does. And I thought going public on the reason for her husband's death might prove cathartic.'

'Have you spoken to her since it came out?'

'This morning. As soon as she'd read it. She was tearful, but she thanked me again. She will keep the article and when they're old enough, show it to her boys. She says the future owes them an explanation for their father's death and that now she can provide that.'

'You're a much nicer man than you pretend to be, Andy.'

'Do me a favour, Tom. Keep that frankly libellous opinion to yourself.'

'Is being related to me really a hindrance?'

'I was joking. Contrary to popular belief, lawyers are capable of humour. When it's suggested from time to time that you and I might be related, I just deny it.'

The Marianne Suarez piece further legitimised what we had shot and recorded at the orphanage. On Saturday afternoon I did a long interview for the Sunday Times, knowing that the only place they could position it if they wanted to use it in the following day's edition was the main news section, the most widely read part of the paper.

I sat there in front of a microphone and one of their highest-profile staffers airing afresh my long-held theories about how malevolent places provoke the past into the present in volatile and sometimes dangerous ways.

'Can an encounter with a ghost be fatal?' I was asked. It was a serious question and so I gave it a serious answer.

'I don't know,' I said. 'I hope never to find out.'

It seemed slightly insane, sitting there pontificating in my study on Saturday afternoon when on Monday I was flying to Chicago to start the process all over again. But we were working to the insane schedule insisted upon by Pete Davidson. And he was really the architect of what we had so far achieved in terms of overall impact. To put it another way, he was pulling the strings. And as a puppet master, it was futile to fault his skill.

Sunday's Mail picked over the bones of what their sister title had said about me with the fresh revelation that I was the father of a daughter receiving institutional treatment for mental illness. They did not name Claire and even if they had been able to obtain a photograph, since she was only 16, they could not have printed it. But they linked her problems to my, 'long and controversial history of paranormal investigation.' My dark dabbling had taken, 'an inevitable toll,' on my daughter's health. It had destroyed my 'blissful' marriage. I was self-absorbed, driven to the point of fanaticism, rumoured to be dating a woman half my age. My character had been shaped, one nameless 'source' said, by an impoverished upbringing.

You have to try to retain some perspective. Nobody reads yesterday's papers. I was 24 hours away from flying to Chicago on another quest to discover further evidence of how little we know about the world we think we shape. Claire would not see the story. It couldn't hurt her. I did wonder whether someone close to me had been that anonymous 'source.' But it boiled down to three candidates. My brother, Samantha or Daisy herself. Realistically, it was none of them.

Then I remembered Jeff Potts and Lizzie Cox on the Dolomites trip and Lizzie concluding that Daisy was my 'squeeze.' She was the likeliest suspect. Except that if she had spoken to the paper, they would have named Daisy and sourced a picture. It didn't matter. Yesterday's papers. Pete Davidson held to the mantra that all publicity is good, regardless. God help me, I thought. I'll ride this out, trying for once to think like him. Which felt a bit like being possessed. And I don't mean in a good way.

Sunday afternoon delivered a more welcome surprise. I got a call from the Retreat, and rose to my feet, as always, to take it.

'Hi, Daddy.'

'Claire?'

'Don't worry, I haven't gone rogue. One of the orderlies is with me.'

'They're allowing you to make calls?'

'Only to you and Mum. As of yesterday. Part of what Doctor Pettifer is calling my rehabilitation.'

I felt my heart rip itself free of its moorings and take off in my chest. 'That's great,' I said.

'I just wanted to wish you luck in America. In Chicago, I mean. I hope it goes well.'

'Thank you, darling.'

'But you need to be careful. It's a dangerous place.'

'You mean street crime?'

'No. I don't mean street crime. I don't mean street crime at all.'

'I'll be careful,' I said. 'I promise.'

'Good.'

'Rehabilitation,' I said. 'That's fantastic news.'

She was silent. Then she said, 'Is the world a kinder place, now?'

I thought about this. She deserved the truth. 'It's not necessarily always kinder,' I said. 'But we live now in a world that takes less for granted than it did. I'd say it's a humbler world.'

'Less judgemental?'

'I think so, darling.'

'Be very careful in Chicago, Daddy. I need you to come back in one piece. So does Daisy.'

I swallowed. 'I haven't told you about Daisy.'

'There are things you don't need to tell me,' Claire said. 'I've drawn her picture. She's pretty.'

'Can you read my mind?'

'There's no need,' she said. 'It's all in your eyes.'

'Maybe I should invest in a pair of sunglasses.'

'You wouldn't, though. You're not that kind of person.'

'I'm so pleased,' I said. 'About the rehabilitation. Nothing could mean more.'

'I know, Daddy, and I love you too. Come back safe.'

****

Jeff Potts wasn't the same man. Unless it was just too soon after the orphanage. He looked like someone enduring battle fatigue. He had aged a decade, his movements had a swimming in gravy ponderousness. And he wore an expression of permanent preoccupation. All this was obvious as soon as the three of us met at the airport, before we shuffled through to the departure lounge. The Jeff I knew, despite being gay, would ordinarily have flirted with a woman as attractive as the elfin Susan Masters. It was just part of his barrow-boy persona to do that, almost a compulsion with him. But a big part of him was missing. I had said he had got his mojo back when we had finally exited that baleful building in Italy. I had been wrong.

And Susan noticed. She had never previously laid eyes on Jeff, much less spoken to him. But there was a cautious look in those alert brown eyes as she sipped an espresso from a vending machine. And when he went for a pre-flight pee, she took her opportunity to comment.

'You know he's on medication?'

'How can you be certain of that?' I asked.

'His pupils,' she said. 'I know the signs. My brother had a problem a few years ago.'

'I'm sorry,' I said.

She shrugged. 'And we checked in together. He had to declare the Diazepam in his hand luggage. Do you think he's up to this?'

They were calling our flight. My turn to shrug. Nonsensically, I wished suddenly Daisy were there, to calm matters. To make everything okay. Maybe just to hold my hand in hers. At my age.

I had never experienced what you might call a premonition. I think I came closer than ever before to having one then. I had a duty of care to Jeff and to Susan. They were grown-ups and there of their own volition. They had both been comprehensively briefed. They were being generously paid. Susan had earlier said that she was even looking forward to the experience. But if Jeff had enjoyed a single night of uninterrupted sleep since our experience in the Dolomites, it didn't show in his haggard expression. I'd lost the cold and taciturn brilliance of Lizzie Cox because *Ten Green Bottles* played on a loop tape in her now tortured mind.

Jeff returned from the lavatory and we boarded. We were the three of us flying business class, Pete Davidson provoked into largess by the ratings the Orphanage of the Sacred Heart had garnered over three nights of compulsive TV viewing. Ordinarily whenever I flew business, or first class, I thought of where I had come from, the zinc tub hung on the washhouse wall. How far I had progressed in life. But on this occasion, glancing at my two companions, I thought we looked like troops from the side losing the conflict on their fraught route to a war zone.

We were booked into the Four Seasons, another comfortable demonstration of the Davidson largess. And our schedule looked like this. Tuesday at 11am, Dave Briggs' Cicero home for the full and frank interview brokered by Sally Bruce. We would discuss the implications of that for our location shoot over dinner on Tuesday evening. Wednesday, the 16-mile drive to the former brothel in the run-down suburb of Riverdale to set up for our night vigil. Anything subsequent overnight, dependent on events. Pack up and leave at dawn. Back to the hotel for some fully deserved R&R. and an early flight out on Friday morning from Chicago O'Hare airport on a direct flight to Heathrow.

It was a timetable with a lot more slack than the Italian Job had provided. But we were in a sophisticated city rather than a wilderness and this was not a hit and run. We had all the necessary permissions.

Tensions dissipated somewhat when we reached the Four Seasons. Sumptuous surroundings can have that effect when someone other than yourself is underwriting all the luxury. I met Jeff and Susan in the bar at 7pm. None of us knew Chicago, so it seemed most sensible to eat dinner at the hotel. Then an earlyish night. Jet lag is always worse coming back, but as courteous and down to earth as he came across by reputation, I did not think Dave Briggs likely to be a man who suffered fools. Professionalism would get a better reaction from him on film than would fluffing the procedure as a consequence of tiredness.

Jeff seemed better after a couple of stiff whiskies. The colour returned to his cheeks and his language. It turned out that Susan's grandmother had been a dresser at the Coliseum back in its operatic boom years in the 1980s and beyond. She and Jeff's father would almost certainly have known one another and this thought seemed to cheer him up. Both Jeff and Susan had seen the Jonathan Miller production of Rigoletto on that celebrated stage, care of complimentary staff tickets, I supposed. And they had both loved it. Then came the moment when Susan went to powder her nose.

'I know what you're thinking, Guv,' he said, quietly.

'What would that be, Jeff?'

'That old Jeff has gone and lost his bottle.'

'Have you?'

'Ain't been sleeping brilliantly. And when I do sleep, I talk. That's freaked out Barney good and proper.'

Barney. His husband.

'I was shocked when I saw you arrive at Terminal Five, Jeff. You've aged, mate.'

'I know. A sight for sore eyes. But I can still do a job, Tommy Boy. Wouldn't have come if I couldn't.'

He sounded more as though he was trying to convince himself than he was me. Then Susan returned from the lavatory. And I thought about her experience recording police interviews with hardened criminals, listening to offenders confess in detail to the most heinous crimes. Her neat, precise, pretty appearance was totally at odds with some of the ordeals she must have endured sharing high security cells up close and personal with bad people. I thought that if Dave Briggs came out with a single inauthentic word the following morning, she would be the one of us to know.

He opened the door to us himself. He and his family lived in a large single-storey house on a spacious plot. There were two vehicles parked on the drive. One was a pricey looking Subaru saloon. The other was a Jeep with a crane mounted on its open back. The Jeep had 'Briggs' stencilled onto its side.

'We've come to the right place,' Jeff said, a moment after we climbed out of our taxi. A still slightly anaemic version of the old Jeff. The old Jeff, on any assignment, I missed.

Briggs was built like a heavyweight boxer. Maybe a retired heavyweight who still did gym sessions three or four times a week. Serious sessions. He was in the construction business but looked like someone who could tear down a building without the benefit of tools. Intelligent eyes and an immediate smile. The expression of a man who, when he commits to something, does not at all entertain self-doubt.

The day was already hot. He took us through to the kitchen and poured us each a glass of iced lemonade from a large carafe.

'I'm equally partial to a mint julep,' he said, sipping his own. 'But my wife would rightly say it's a little early in the day for that.' The lemonade tasted homemade and delicious.

The introductions done, he took us through to his study and his favourite chair. It was summer vacation time from college, but neither his children nor his wife seemed to be around. The chair was a battered leather Chesterfield. I had the intuition that it was an item of furniture probably inherited from his equally generously proportioned father.

We set up while he watched on, detached, maybe slightly amused, completely nerveless. When Jeff had positioned his camera on its tripod and adjusted lighting and focus, when Susan had a sound level she was satisfied with, I asked him to relate his story. He did so in a clear, deliberate tone, without pause or hesitation. He was a man who had relived the experience. Probably many times. And that had made him word perfect in describing it.

I asked him a series of questions, which he answered in his forthright way. I saved the trickiest for the end only because it was pragmatic to do so. 'Your favourite author is Hemingway. He lived through that period, set quite a bit of fiction in what we now call the Jazz Age.'

'And you think that makes me suggestible, Mr Carter?' He smiled. 'I like Scott Fitzgerald too, who did that a whole lot more in his stories. But this wasn't played out in my head, provoked by the building's age and atmosphere. It was real. Those girls and their johns were real. And that music being played next door? Fingers schooled in the Big Easy. Wasn't modern, no sir. Wasn't reproduction or nostalgia. I'm saying straight out of about nineteen-twenty-five. I was hearing piano played before the Wall Street Crash.'

Then I asked an impromptu question, one I had not scripted. 'You don't seem perturbed by it all. Aren't you?'

Anger flashed briefly through the geniality in his face. He raised a finger and said, 'The past doesn't belong in the present. Witnessing it break through is a physical assault, as you of all people should know. Unless you are faking, which I am not. A physical and a mental assault. An abomination, Sir. And it leaves its mark. I only came off medication a month ago.

'If I seem okay that's only because of a promise I made to myself never to go back there. An easy promise to keep, Mr Carter. Because I don't envy you people your visit to that place one little bit.'

He was subdued as we packed the gear away. My spoken assumption that he had recovered from his other-worldly experience had not just been a facile observation, but one that had rankled with him. I regretted saying it, even knowing that his indignant reaction would make compelling viewing. That is often the way. You often get the truest reaction only by being crass and insensitive.

He showed us to the door. I said, 'I didn't mean to insult or slight you, Mr Briggs. If I did, then I'm sorry.'

He waved away the apology. 'It's not you, man. You're probably a nice guy. In other circumstances, we could maybe crack a beer, chew over the ball game.'

'I'd be out of my depth, discussing the ball game,' I said.

He smiled. And his eyes travelled momentarily elsewhere. Then they came back to me and he said, 'Find yourself out of depth in that godless dive in Riverdale?'

'Yes?'

'Do yourselves a favour. Get the fuck out.'

Nobody spoke in the cab on the way back to the hotel. By the time we got there, it was two in the afternoon. I wanted to see and hear what we had, which we did at 3pm, facilitated by the hotel's screening room, something we'd set up by prior arrangement. We had just under an hour's raw material. Dave Briggs was a commanding presence on the screen. I wanted to ask Susan what she thought about his performance, but wanted to do that privately, out of Jeff's earshot. We had the three of us arranged to meet for a pre-dinner drink in the bar at seven. I rang her room and asked her to come down instead at a quarter to.

She let out a long breath and took a sip of the beer she had ordered. She said, 'He thinks he's telling the truth. And frankly, so do I. We were a necessary inconvenience.'

"There's a commercial angle,' I said. 'The event could form the basis of a televised drama. He's aware of that.'

Susan shook her head. 'I've seen this before. Confession is cathartic. He was driven to tell his story. It's a survival mechanism, Tom. It's how people prevent themselves from going mad.'

'So you're saying he saw what he saw?'

Her expression was serious, her complexion pale. In the bar's fashionably miserly light, her brown eyes appeared almost black. She said, 'That, and probably more.'

Then Jeff arrived.

The following morning, I received three significant phone calls. The first was from Pete Davidson. He had a Foreign Office contact, he said, someone with whom he went to school. I hadn't had Pete down as the public schoolboy type, but media people reinvent themselves in a needs-must sort of way and that was apparently what Pete had successfully done.

His old chum – from Eton or Harrow or wherever they had bonded – had some Dolomites related gossip. The Italian authorities had wasted no time in their investigation into the Sacred Heart Orphanage child massacre. They had identified the military unit responsible and further identified the five men guilty of the atrocity. Only two veterans remained alive of the company to which the five had belonged. And they had kept the secret for over 70 years out of a combination of loyalty and shame.

An uneasy combination. Confronted by an Italian police investigator, they had readily confessed to what they knew. Importantly, they had been approached independent of one another, so there had been no collusion. In naming the five, they were corroborating one another's stories.

I said to Pete, 'So none of the five are still living?'

'Three of them ate their pistol barrels in the weeks after Italy capitulated in 'forty-four. A fourth tried to body-check a Milan bound express train just outside Verona. You can imagine how well that went. The fifth and final culprit managed to survive until nineteen-forty-eight. He hanged himself in the forest where the Italian authorities now suspect the orphanage victims are buried in unmarked graves. They're digging there as we speak.'

By my calculation, those soldiers would all have been men in their 20s. Early 30s at the oldest. Five child-killers. Five suicides. It seemed improbable. And I said as much to Pete.

'Why would they kill themselves?'

'Remorse? Maybe they just got sick of listening to Ten Green Bottles.'

I thought he was joking. I also thought that successful attempts at humour always possessed a kernel of truth. Something unbearable had stayed with those men. Unless it had just visited them from time to time.

My second caller was Daisy.

'How's the five-star life, Mr C?'

'Tolerable,' I said.

'Had one of those hyper-realistic dreams last night,' she said. 'The kind that eventually force you awake?'

'Been there,' I said. 'Go on.'

'Ulysses Laporte on the stage. Playing solo, no accompaniment. Mine the only occupied seat in the auditorium. There was no sound when his fingers pressed the keys. And his movement was unnatural. Clumsy and slow. It seemed to frustrate him. Eventually he turned to his audience of one, I think in exasperation. And his face was rigid with lack of expression and his eyes were turned up in his skull.'

'Dreams are weird,' I said.

'He was dead, Tom. Dead and ambulatory. Do you know what that means?'

'I don't do zombies, Daisy. Got my hands full with ghosts.'

She was silent. Then she said, 'Tonight's the night, isn't it, Tom.'

'It is.'

'You need to take care.'

'I always take care.'

'A stupid request,' she said. 'Met with a lie. I honestly preferred the black and white world of certainty I knew and trusted before our trip to the Dolomites.'

I said, 'It's been a couple of years now since any of us enjoyed real certainty.'

'And I miss you,' she said.

I could have met that remark with something pat about it only having been a couple of days. But that would have been another lie, or at least an evasion. Because the truth was, I missed her. I was in the company of a woman with zero experience of what we might be about to confront and a man whose nerve was shot. We were hardly the Three Musketeers. And I was feeling more and more the sense of foreboding that comes when you are about to be confronted by something for which you have no coping techniques. I missed Daisy. I wanted to be with her, doing something trivial and fun, rather than in an alien city planning a night journey into the unknown.

I gave Daisy the assurances I didn't remotely feel and then said a reluctant goodbye.

My third call was from Samantha. She said, 'They want us to give Claire a phone as part of her rehabilitation. Some restrictions, obviously. But if you've no objection, I'm five minutes away from buying it.'

'Why didn't they raise this with me?'

'They know you're away because you gave them notice that you were going. And frankly, I just think Julia Pettifer finds me an easier person than you to deal with.'

'Makes sense,' I said. 'And I've no objection at all. To the phone, I mean.'

'Great. Fantastic.'

Our daughter was coming back to us and her mother could not keep the joy at that realisation out of her voice. It stirred feelings in me for my former wife I had thought long dead and buried. Well. I was the UK's favourite ghosthunter, when all was said and done.

Lunch with Jeff and Susan felt like that last meal the condemned prisoner gets before walking that shackled journey along the linoleum to the chair. Susan ate carefully and spoke little. Jeff ate almost nothing and said less. I made no attempt to jolly things up. I thought the law of averages meant that the evening to come would offer nothing but dereliction and tedium. Anti-climactic hours dragged out somewhere absent of home comforts. Until I remembered Daisy's weirdly silent dream and the feeling of foreboding speaking to her had inflicted upon me.

After lunch, I tried to read. Then I tried to watch some television. 80 channels and not a hint of anything worthy of attention. I got down on the floor and did press-ups until my arms could no longer support my weight. I took a shower. I wrote an email to Claire telling my daughter only truthfully how proud I was of her progress. How much I loved her. And eventually it became time to assemble in the lobby and climb into our waiting cab. I did so recalling the complex expression on the face of David Briggs as he'd handed over the building's keys the previous day.

Maybe you've been to Riverdale. It sounds pretty, which it isn't. We're decades on from when its rival gangs made the place notorious. And London had taught me in Hoxton and Clapham how unlikely neighbourhoods can come up in the world. But Riverdale had not. Too many of its buildings were empty shells. With its potholed streets and closed-down stores and walls of rusting corrugate, the place had a vacant look. Meagrely populated. Drearily down at heel. Pawn shops and liquor stores. Cars burned out or just abandoned on tyres no longer successfully taking their weight.

Our building, when we got to it, looked exactly as it had in the photos I'd studied taken by one of Jerry Barden's people. I'd emailed scans of those to Jeff for him to block out angles and rehearse lighting rigs in the run-up. But as our taxi drove away, he stood on the pavement smoking a last cigarette, studying the exterior, the bland brick façade of somewhere with secrets that were sordid and callous and cruel.

'Murders,' he muttered, under his breath. 'You can actually bloody feel it.'

I had never heard him speak like that before on a job. I looked at Susan, who was also studying the building, chewing gum. So slightly built, she almost looked childlike in her Puffa jacket and jeans and Timberland boots. She smiled, I thought ruefully.

'The only thing we're going to catch out here, is cold,' she said. And it was cold, unseasonably so. A chill wind blowing litter in hurried gusts along the alleyway lined with trashcans to our right. A black cat crept from behind one. It saw us and froze and arched its back as cats sometimes will. And it turned tail and fled.

We went inside. All the action Briggs had described had taken place on the third floor. It was reached only by a surprisingly narrow staircase. And with no power, there was no light provided other than from the torches with which each of us were equipped. When we got to the third floor, the first thing I did was open the exterior door connecting to the fire escape. But shadowy as the fading daylight cast in the alley was, I could see iron steps spindly with corrosion and splotches of orange rust on a withered handrail. It might at a push have supported Susan's weight, but I wouldn't have bet money on it.

'Nice gaff,' Jeff said, sniffing the air. It smelled of damp and desolation.

'A few dreams have died in here,' Susan said.

'And a few people,' Jeff said. He was studying the line of puncture wounds made in the plaster by bullets we had both seen in photos of the place. 'Head height,' he said, 'given that the average man was about five-foot-seven back then. I'm guessing they were made to face the wall and that St Valentine's Day didn't mark the only fatal event of its kind.'

Was he sounding slightly more himself? I thought he was. The shadows, though, were lengthening. I would film an introductory piece to camera, the bullet craters my backdrop. Then Jeff and Susan could set up for anything coming our way afterwards.

The building was a seemingly deliberate warren of rooms. More easily defended that way, I supposed, in an era of lethal turf wars. But the cramped size of each individual room inflicted a feeling of claustrophobia.

We walked into the room with the card table bearing the vintage Remington. Susan studied it. Then she turned to me and said,

'Probably a belated question at this stage, Tom, but how does this business actually work?'

'Ninety-nine times out of a hundred absolutely nothing happens. Something only ever happens when the witnesses to it have a degree of sensitivity. Not everyone gets the same experience. We had someone with us who saw far more in the Dolomites orphanage than showed up on the film.

'We might get a cold spot tonight. We could get zilch. But we have got the history of the building and some nicely colourised period newsreel footage. And we have got the Briggs testimony. The bullet holes in the wall of the room we just left tell a story.' I nodded at the Remington. 'That tells another.'

She said, 'We don't know what they are.'

'We can speculate,' I said. 'And when that row of bullet holes shows up on the screen, I'm going to get you to dub the sound of automatic gunfire hitting a plaster covered wall in sync with it.'

'Nice touch,' she said.

'The volume increasingly incrementally each time we show them.'

'You're good at this,' she said.

'Sometimes I've needed to be.'

'And sometimes not,' Jeff said.

We waited. We drank Four Seasons coffee we had requested be poured into vacuum flasks. Jeff twice risked the fire escape to smoke. I was familiar with the phrase, dying for a cigarette, but had never met anyone actually prepared to do so. Still, he got away with it. We waited. And nothing happened.

'What happened to the working girls?' Susan asked, eventually.

'We only know the fate of three of them,' I said. 'One was beaten to death. One was fished out of Lake Michigan. A third starved to death in a tenement slum not long after the Wall Street Crash.'

Susan shivered. 'The twenties didn't roar for them.'

'No. They didn't.'

'Not so much as a whisper,' Jeff said.

We waited. And nothing happened. Until a little after midnight, when the front door opened and slammed shut again and after a pause, we heard footsteps start to ascend the stairs.

'Didn't you lock that?' Jeff Potts, his voice a gravelly whisper. I glanced at him. He was positioned to my right. He had grown so pale his skin was translucent. A tiny, meandering vein beat blue at his temple and his voice was coming in shallow gasps. His camera, though, was steady on his shoulder.

I glanced to my left. The portable machine she used for location recording was slung over Susan's shoulder on the nylon strap attached to its case. She held a large foam damped microphone out in front of her. No extension rod screwed on. I had the giddy intuition that you could not anyway catch a virus from a ghost. They presented quite different hazards.

The steps got louder. They ground up the stairs. The wood creaked under their weight, or just the memory of weight. Hobnailed leather, I thought. Dear Christ, this is happening.

Then the singing began. An Irish ballad, *The Mountains of Mourne*. An unaccompanied voice, deep and distorted, swelling and fading, but getting unmistakeably closer as its owner ascended deliberately to the room where the three of us stood. And another sound, closer. Jeff trying to control his breathing and having by the hoarse, accelerating sound of it, little success in doing so. He was not far off hyperventilating. When he spoke, his voice was a shrill gasp.

'Okay till the Italian Job, Tom,' he said. 'Right as rain till then.'

The song swelled to something deafening and then faded to silence and we were hearing only the stolid trudge of booted feet. And then we saw him. The high peaked cap and double fronted tunic of an officer of the Chicago Police Department in the years immediately following the Great War. No belt, the tunic loose. A wooden night stick or billy club secured to his right hand by a thin leather strap at the wrist. It was possible to peer dimly through his torso, see the eruptions of lathe poking through old plaster on the wall behind him.

He did not enter the room. But he did turn, incuriously to face us. There was a luxuriant moustache over his black open maw of a mouth. And his eyes were no more than two deep and nocturnal sockets.

'Is there someone there?' Said his forgotten voice. The dutiful habit of a lifetime that must have ended well over half a century ago. We were silent, but for the faint struggle of Jeff's troubled breathing. And after a pause, almost reluctantly, the phantom moved on and we heard his booted feet grind their deliberate way to the floor above.

He didn't come back down. I had a vision of him sitting on one of those skeletal truckle beds up there, frozen in attitude and time. But I managed to put it out of my mind. I could have walked over to the window overlooking the street outside and opened the blind a chink. What would I see? Maybe the headlamps of vintage Packard and Model-T Fords driving sleekly by, their paintwork gleaming with a factory fresh newness in a lost age. Us, stranded there. Our clothing and equipment nothing more than further novelties in an era obsessed with them.

I did not dare do it. And besides, there were other distractions. A tinkle of girlish laughter. The aroma of cheap perfume lavishly applied. The rustle of silk or satin. A single feather from an unseen boa appearing suddenly out of nothing at chest height and sashaying to the floor. The staccato clip of steel-tipped high heeled shoes. A babble of voices that came and just as suddenly departed. I looked at my watch and saw with surprise that somehow, we had reached 3am. And then, in the adjacent room, the clack of typewriter keys from that vintage Remington as it returned to staccato life.

I walked into where it sat on the torn and faded green baize of the card table, the single item of furniture in there. There was no one operating the machine. The keys were depressing themselves, words appearing, faded, in my torch beam. The other two entered and flanked me, filming, recording. We all jumped when the words reached the end of their line and the carriage return flung up the page and began another one. And then it stopped. And I rolled out the page and read what had been written:

'Daddy, this is Claire. Don't ask me how. Just do what I say. You need to get out now. Piano Man is coming. He is all wrong and so dangerous. Get out immediately. Go as fast as you can.'

I heard it, then. It was a sound I had never heard before and it took me a moment to make sense of it. It was echoing around the trashcan lined alley to our left, a reverberating, repetitious, loudening clang and squeal. Corroded metal under protest. Someone or something was climbing through the darkness up the fire escape's spindly, rusted steps. Heavily. Determinedly.

Without warning, but with an emphatic thud, the single door that led to the wooden staircase and our exit from the place slammed shut. Only a fractional degree of play in the handle when I tried to turn it. It rattled in my hand but would not budge. Another clang outside on the fire escape steps. Ponderous, but getting closer.

'You have the keys,' Susan said, from behind me. 'Probably in your jacket pocket.' Her voice husky with quiet strain.

I reached for the small bunch with mutinous fingers. Keys slipped and slid through them on their ring. From outside, a weighted moan of metal fatigue and another grunting upward step. The doorknob was brass. The keyhole at its tarnished centre. I slipped in the one that fitted and turned it and the lock released and the door opened when I jerked it free of the jamb.

We fled. Or more accurately, I fled and the other two followed. We tumbled down the staircase and out of there, in the direction opposite the alleyway, aiming instinctively for light, bustle, people. Except that Riverdale lacked any of those comforting considerations. The street lit, but emptily. The only vehicles fugitive hints of orange taillight shrinking in the far distance. We stumbled along, in the middle of the road, away from the shadows, where it was brightest.

We had waited quite a while before following Dave Briggs' advice to get the fuck out of the place. We had more than enough material. Even if that patrolling police officer was no more than an indistinct smudge framed in a doorway, we had the sound of his ascent and the singing. Susan had seen the volume metres on her recording machine shift with the changes in volume and pitch.

We found an all-night diner. Brightness, indifference, living, breathing, chatting people from the present time. They sold beer. I felt like something stronger. Piano Man. The son never buried by his voodoo priestess mother. That was one performer and one encore I could happily live without.

'What was typed on that sheet of paper?' This from Susan.

'Gibberish,' I said.

And I could see that she did not believe me. It didn't matter. I would not show either of them my daughter's note, now folded into the back pocket of my jeans. It was a private communication and would have to remain so. I had suspected since she was four that my daughter would become capable of extraordinary things. Had known it, truthfully. Her claims over the years had been made too casually for them to be mere lies spun to impress. She could do things ordinary people couldn't. That was her normality, whether she liked it or not.

There was not much normality just then about my two companions. Susan looked pale and preoccupied, her facial skin taut over delicate bones. Jeff was ashen, haggard. I bought us a beer apiece. Had I known it was the last beer Jeff Potts would ever drink, I would have stood us a second round. Fifteen minutes later he suffered the heart attack that killed him in the back of the taxi the owner of the diner did us the favour of calling. We diverted to the nearest hospital, but Jeff was dead before he reached the emergency room.

Back at the Four Seasons, while an exhausted Susan Masters slept in her suite, I took Jeff's camera to the hotel's screening room and studied the highlights of what he had shot. He had of course filmed the typewriter's rogue antics, but in that light and at that distance, it was impossible to make out the words on the page. They were too feint and obscured by reflection from a torch beam. It was enough for our audience to see the keys depress themselves. I would stick with the gibberish claim. To the average viewer, that might seem scarier. There is something unsettling about chaos. Though to me, the truth was more disturbing.

I called Pete Davidson. 7am in London, and I caught him at the gym. He said his production company's insurers would cover the cost of returning Jeff's body to the UK. His office would handle the red tape and he personally would pay for the funeral when the time came. In the meantime, he offered to break the news to Jeff's husband. He suggested we return as scheduled on our early flight to Heathrow the following morning.

'Get something, Tom?'

'Enough to make people think.'

'Jeff's epitaph?'

'Not worthy of a death,' I said.

'Maybe it was just his time.'

'Tell that to Barney.'

Susan stirred at 2 o'clock on Thursday afternoon. By then, I had taken a nap myself. We viewed the raw footage together with the sound roughly synched. It might sound callous to be doing that so soon after the death of a colleague I was close to. It was different for Susan, who had not known him at all, really. But the fact was that I needed a distraction. I knew nothing at all about practical magic, nothing about psychic connections or telekinesis. But I thought the expenditure of energy in what Claire had accomplished probably colossal. And I wondered whether her having done it would hamper her general recovery.

At great cost, Susan and I realised that we had gathered some genuinely compelling material. The revenant beat officer neither looked nor sounded like a special effect. He was terrifying, even from the comfort of an armchair in the plush depths of a five-star hotel. Jeff had done a brilliantly atmospheric job with the exterior and interior establishing shots. My piece to camera worked. The Briggs interview, as we already knew, was sober, thought-provoking and manifestly sincere. The series would not have the pathos of the orphanage. But would have its own context and qualities. A worthy follow-up in its own distinctly original way. Jeff's epitaph, though I thought the Jeff I had known in truth already perished.

We had cleared passport control at Heathrow, before Susan again raised the subject of what had been typed on the piece of paper by a manual machine with a decades dried-out ribbon and nobody present to manipulate the keys.

She said, 'I'll email you the audio file as soon as I get home and I've uploaded it. And I'll see you in the edit suite, nine on the dot in the morning on Monday. I think you're a nice man, Tom. One who also happens to be a good man. And you pay top rate. But I won't work with you again when this job is wrapped up. Can't handle the subject matter.'

'You were very unlucky.'

'Or I was very lucky,' she said, 'depending on perspective. I was right about Briggs, at least. He was telling the truth.'

'He was.'

'It wasn't gibberish, was it, on that sheet of typing paper?'

'No, Susan. It was a warning.'

She nodded and hefted her recording machine on her shoulder on its strap. She hadn't even trusted to an overhead luggage compartment. It had spent the flight on her lap. 'I heard that thing, whatever it was, coming up the fire escape. You told me ghosts couldn't interfere with the living. But they interfered with Jeff Potts. They killed him.'

There was nothing to say to that.

Susan shook my hand, in that endearingly formal manner she had. 'Monday,' she said.

On Friday evening I saw Daisy. A Swiss Cottage gastropub was still a novelty after the long litany of restrictions everyone had endured. Spontaneity still felt almost like recklessness. The old ways were coming back only with reluctance and I did not believe would ever fully return. Worse for the young people who would never now experience a truly carefree life.

'You look terrible,' she said.

'Jetlag,' I said.

Jetlag did not honestly feel like the half of it. I had wanted to see her, hear her, hold her more than anything that night. But I felt drained, exhausted. She took my hand across the table between us and said, 'Tell me everything.'

And so I did, leaving nothing out, showing her the typed note I had folded into four and kept on me since its completion.

'What do you think, Daisy? I mean, which parts do you believe?'

'I was with you in the Dolomites. Frankly, I'm inclined to believe all of it. It was Ulysses Laporte climbing that fire escape. Whatever is left in the world of Ulysses Laporte. It sounds a lively location even without his guest appearance. I'm glad I wasn't there. And I'm very sorry about Jeff Potts. I liked him. You couldn't not.'

'He wasn't the same, Daisy. The orphanage had beaten him. Jesus, I'm tired.'

She squeezed the hand she still held. She said, 'I don't think you should worry too much about the toll this has taken on Claire. You're safe, that's all that will matter to her'

'But the effort?', I said.

'I think she used your energy. That would be the logical way to do it. I mean, if you could do it, if you were capable. Some kind of transference? Your energy because you were there. You've said you don't generally get jetlagged. Claire tapped into your strength. It's why you look and feel so beaten up.'

That made a kind of sense, as impossible as it was.

'You must be anxious to see her.'

'I should spend some time with you.'

'Spend the drive down with me tomorrow. Then spent the drive back'

'What will you do in the meantime?'

'I'll stroll on Brighton Beach,' she said. 'You can do that these days without risking a fine or being told to go home by a placard wielding local.'

'What fun times we live in.'

'They're better than they were,' Daisy said.

And so the following morning I called the Retreat ahead and we drove down for a visit to my daughter scheduled for noon. Claire was waiting in the reception area, pacing, wringing her hands as she sometimes did when anxious. She sprinted across the distance to our hug. And that very precisely marked the moment of my retirement from the job that had until then defined my adult life and what degree of worldly – and other worldly – success I had enjoyed.

We had originally scheduled Chicago as the fourth haunting. In the event, Pete Davidson had changed all that and Al Capone's brothel had become the second haunting after the Sacred Heart Orphanage. I would not bother debating its status. Except to say that as far as my hauntings were concerned, Chicago was emphatically the last.

Claire had on a pair of high-waisted vintage blue jeans and a red retro windcheater. Her feel were laced into green high-top sneakers with a black rubber trim. I had never seen my daughter in colour since she had started to choose her own clothes.

'Shopping trip with Mum,' she said, reminding me that she could easily read my mind.

'What happened to black and white?'

She raised her eyes to the ceiling. 'Monochrome is *so* yesterday,' she said.

We didn't do anything much with our two hours together that afternoon. We strolled to Waterstones, where Claire chose some books. Then we ambled back and just sat on a seafront bench in the sunshine. I persuaded my daughter that an ice cream cornet with a double flake and strawberry sauce was a good idea and went to fetch it for her. Returning to where she sat, I noticed that she looked younger brightly dressed. She had tied her hair with ribbons the same pale blue as her jeans. She had been in the open air this summer more than I could ever remember in the past and the sun had encouraged a light spread of freckles across her nose. She looked altogether lovely.

When she had finished eating her ice-cream she said, 'There's nothing left of him that's human.'

'Who?' But I knew who.

'Piano Man. He has no soul.'

I swallowed. 'Really?'

Claire burped. 'Taken from him when his mother wouldn't let him rest.'

'Does it bother you? Knowing that the monsters are sometimes real?'

'Not really, Daddy. It's something I've always known.'

'I'm giving it all up, Claire. Retiring.'

'You're too young to retire, Dad.'

'I'm not doing it anymore. What do you think of that?'

'I'm glad,' she said. 'The last time was so scary.'

But we none of us, do we, have a crystal ball. Not even my daughter had one of those.

Chapter 10

It's probably time to tell you about what I saw all those years ago, when I broke the vow made to Helena Donavan and visited the Fischer House on the Island. This in the days before the notoriety of my subsequent programme about it provoked the authorities into surrounding the place with a ring of spiteful steel.

I knew about the connection between Klaus Fischer and his dubious Birkdale Palace Hotel friends and the Jericho Society. I had learned that from Al Hodge, who had seen and secretly filmed their ball and bequeathed me the film. I'd had it confirmed by Helena herself in a summer conversation that had taken place in her wildly pretty cottage garden.

After the programme aired, Paul Seaton contacted me. Seaton the investigative journalist who had sourced the account clandestinely kept by Pandora Gibson-Hoare as Fischer's guest on the island in 1927. When she had alluded to their sacrificial, an abducted boy from an impoverished Welsh home.

Persistent and talented at what he did, Seaton had succeeded in identifying the boy. His name was Peter Morgan. He came from a village called Penhelig and he was an intellectual prodigy intent on a career in medicine. Their sacrifice gained in power, Seaton surmised, from the prevented good Peter would have done in the adult life denied him. From the surgical procedure he would have pioneered, the vaccine he would have developed or just the life-saving operation successfully performed on one of the great statesmen of the age.

I thought Paul Seaton's speculations, some of them at least, a bit fanciful. But then I broke my promise to Helena and went to the Fischer House to try to film my way into climbing higher than the career plateau I felt myself to be stranded on.

Ambition made me bold as well as dishonest. I ventured into that derelict mansion's fearful catacomb of cellars. I still think that the house required a human catalyst to trigger performances from its past. And that night I saw the most serious of their ceremonies. And the deadliest. I saw their sacrifice of Peter Morgan and with the dagger fatally plunged, Klaus Fischer, wielding it, raised his surprised face and saw me, filming what he was doing, what must have been by then decades after his own death. He saw me, just a momentary glimpse of someone from the future, before I stole back into the shadows of his house.

I could never have publicly shown that section of film. But neither could I find the will in me to destroy it. It resided in a Hatton Garden strongbox along with the Jericho Ball cine film Al Hodge saw fit to leave me in his will. I have never viewed it since editing it out of the programme eventually shown. There was enough delinquency in that blighted place without resorting to something obscene. Or even referencing it in my script. Al had warned me that the danger that cult represented was not a thing of the past. And I took the warning seriously.

What I later did to whoever James Balfour was, might seem to contradict that. But Balfour's elaborate deception proved I was already someone of interest to them. Even if I didn't yet know the reason why. If they had wanted only to kill me, they would not have approached my daughter for answers about my childhood. They could have done what they did to that resilient police detective Billy Perry all those years ago when his investigation into Edward Swarbrick's fatal role in the death of Arabella Pankhurst threatened them with exposure and scandal. Perry's stubborn courage did not save him from dying in a deliberate hit and run.

****

Pete Davidson was impatient to see what we had assembled after our return from Chicago. We did not yet have a final cut of any of the three episodes, but we knew where we were going. The first part concentrated on the history and mystery of the location itself. Organised crime in Chicago, prohibition, Al Capone's relentless rise and the role of Ulysses Laporte in changing the use and character of the building. And the casualties; the three prostitutes we knew had become collateral damage as direct consequence of Capone's aspirational ambitions.

Episode two was pretty much the David Briggs show. This included a dramatic recreation of what he claimed to have seen. Pete had seen that as an opportunity to shoehorn some glamour into the series. The sequence had been shot while I was in Chicago, by some veteran director who used to specialise in glossy rock videos. I assumed Pete had personally overseen the casting. It did look convincing, period perfect and to my eye much more sinister than salacious.

Three was me to camera to raise expectation and rack up tension and then a slickly put together edit of what we had shot and recorded during our night vigil in Riverdale. Pete bought the story that the typed message was random nonsense more easily than Susan Masters had and Susan, to her credit, kept shtum. When the disembodied staircase singing climaxed in the wraith police officer's appearance framed in the doorway, I think all three of us viewing it went cold.

'No camera shake,' Pete said. 'Not even a hint of it. Poor Jeff was a pro to the end.'

'How did Barney take it?' I asked.

'Badly. Maybe give him a call?'

'I will.'

'And we conclude episode three with a tribute. Something classy. White words on a black background. A few piano chords of Ragtime on the soundtrack, heavy on the echo and sustain. Slow fade. Kind of a dedication.'

'Good idea,' I said.

'Great work, you two,' Pete said. 'Fucking brilliant television.'

I had not yet broken it to him that this was my swansong. To use an expression popular in the industry, I did not want at that stage to rain on his parade. Not until after the series premiered. Which it would do from the following Monday on consecutive evenings after a weekend of teaser trailers. No point in changing a winning formula. Forward orders for the download and DVD editions of our orphanage series were already close to breaking industry records.

It seemed a perverse time in which to contemplate retirement, with anticipation over the second series approaching fever pitch. But I kept thinking of Piano Man, the man without a soul, and his determined trudge up that night fire escape towards a confrontation we had only narrowly eluded. The still ambulatory shell of someone who had traded blows in the practice ring with Jack Dempsey a century ago. You invite darkness into your life, and it comes willingly. I had reached the point of craving only light.

Pete wanted to call the Chicago trilogy, The Fourth Haunting. His counter-intuitive logic was that viewers would be frustrated at having missed out on the second and third. It would create anticipatory demand. He had already blocked out shooting schedules for the Irish and Scots stories I had originally pitched to him. He had even given them jokey working titles; Shocked Jock and Rebel Button Man. Hauntings two and three would thus follow four and be greeted by an audience already sold on the concept and format. Except I now had no interest at all in doing anything with either project.

I met Samantha for lunch at Bill's in Richmond. The significance of the venue was that it was somewhere we had never gone when living there together as a couple. It harboured no memories, fond or otherwise for either of us. She was tanned, toned, chic, immaculate. I would never have recognised her as the Greenbank girl who drew a frightened me a pint in her father's pub all those years ago. She had been only the same age then as our daughter was now.

'Claire tells me you're retiring.'

'It's true,' I said.

'We talk a lot, now she has use of a phone.'

'That's good,' I said, 'You're good for her.'

My ex-wife studied me. She said, 'You've done the hard yards, Tom. For years, you have. Then I come back into the picture. You're not resentful?'

'Why would I be? You make her happy. Happier, anyway.'

Samantha sipped her drink. She said, 'Claire told me about Piano Man.'

Only lunchtime, but she had ordered a large gin and tonic prior to our choosing our food. Now I knew why.

I said, 'She has unusual gifts. I don't want them used in that way. No more insights, dreams, no more of those sinister drawings referencing my work. I want all that to stop before it damages her.'

'How will you manage?'

'Okay, with you paying half the fees for the Retreat. And with any luck, even that won't be for very much longer.'

'The orphanage story was huge. It's still huge. Is Chicago on the same scale?'

'I think so,' I said. 'In a different way.'

She frowned. She said, 'Similar impact?'

'Pete Davidson thinks so.'

Samantha snorted and gulped gin and wiped her mouth with the back of her hand. 'Him,' she said.

I shrugged.

'Won't you miss it, Tom?'

'Miss what?'

'The attention,' she said.

I shook my head. 'No.'

'You've changed,' she said.

'We all change, Samantha. That's inevitable.'

'Pete Davidson being the exception that proves the rule.'

'Pete's a construct. There's someone decent underneath it all.'

'I'll take your word, Tom. But you've changed for the better.'

'So have you,' I said. 'Tell me about Mr Right.'

He was a Kingston University lecturer. His subject was architecture, so they had an aesthetic sensibility in common. Strong ideas about creativity and design. He painted and enjoyed gardening. He rowed. He toiled through Richmond Park, Lycra-clad, on a road bike. No doubt a high-end, hand-built road bike. My slightly sarcastic phraseology. But he sounded alright. Someone decent, solid, industrious. Safe.

'We don't live together,' she said. 'In case that's an issue when Claire gets out and wants to stay with me?'

'I like the new clothes you bought her. The retail therapy worked.'

Samantha bit her lip and swallowed gin. 'You think she's okay, Tom? About Piano Man?'

I said, 'I think she is. But I also think all that has to stop.'

Samantha was frowning again. I asked, 'What?'

'She said she goes inside your head because it's an interesting place.'

'It needs to be less interesting,' I said. 'I'm sure I can manage that.'

But Samantha was looking at me quizzically again. She said, 'I wonder how Daisy Chain will take your opting for the quiet life. When you're no longer provoking headlines, no longer a member of that magic club that never needs a table reservation at places booked out for weeks in advance to ordinary mortals. When you get to the closing stages of the London Marathon and Sophie Reyworth doesn't proffer her microphone for that congratulatory chat.'

'Because Sophie's forgotten who I am?'

She shrugged. 'People have short memories. Even for the nation's favourite ghosthunter.'

'I plan to write fiction,' I said.

She raised an eyebrow. 'Some would say you've been doing that for years. Wasn't Derek Acorah from Southport?'

'He just lived there, Samantha. He was born in Liverpool.'

'He was a charlatan.'

'Watch the Chicago trilogy. Then tell me *I'm* a charlatan.'

'Looking forward to it.'

But she had given me food for thought. It had been overcast, a brooding sky outside when we sat down to eat. When we left Bill's, it had begun to rain. I walked Samantha the short distance to what used to be our home holding her umbrella over her. We said a polite goodbye and I walked back to Richmond Bridge and then along the river towpath to Teddington Lock and the bridge taking me to the other side.

The rain strengthened. The route became gloomy, rain dripping from the leaves and dribbling down the bark of the summer trees. Rain danced busily on the surface of the river itself. And I thought about the change of direction to which I was committed. My daughter's mental health might not depend on me giving up paranormal investigation, but equally it might. The Piano Man event had made that a risk I was no longer prepared to subject her to.

Daisy would not be sorry to see me stop ghost hunting. She had proven herself far too sensitive in the Dolomites to continue with any personal involvement in the field. Her research into Ulysses Laporte had been scrupulous, even exhaustive. But when I had told her about the events of that night in Chicago, the look on her face had been one of disdain as much as dread. She thought we had been reckless with our lives. And one of us had lost their life in consequence. A fatal casualty rate slightly in excess of thirty per cent. And without Claire's intervention? Not good odds at all.

I had not written any fiction since those vapid stories done as a student. I had concluded then that they were weak because they side-stepped the subject that most really intrigued me. I was now probably as well equipped as anyone to write a paranormal thriller. Assuming, of course, that I was capable of dreaming up a decent plot.

A fair bit of income would be generated by the two series I had just made. Or it would if *The Fourth Haunting* went down as well as *Death and Afterlife in the Dolomites*. I would have a better idea about that after the first episode transmitted. Enough money for a year, maybe for a year and a half. If I failed to get a debut novel in front of a publisher in that timescale, I needed to be doing something else.

Stretches of the towpath had become surprisingly dark for a July afternoon. Trees in full leaf, the sheer density of the canopy in some places and the thickness of ungoverned undergrowth. It was difficult in parts to see the puddled, muddying ground. And it had grown quiet, no other people about, no one with my eccentric enthusiasm for a thorough drenching.

I stopped when I heard something disturb the foliage to my left. I turned to look, thinking it must have been something bigger than a squirrel or a pair of flapping wood pigeons. Something, or someone, much more substantial. But I saw nothing. I stood perfectly still. And on the damp air for just a moment sniffed a pungent hint of cigar smoke. Then it was gone. And I smiled. Because I knew that me giving up the ghosts, was not the same thing at all as the ghosts ever giving up on me.

****

Our Chicago trilogy didn't quite replicated the success of the orphanage either in the UK or throughout Continental Europe, though it did well in Italy, where Al Capone's ancestors had originated and where he was still considered to some extent to be a local story. In the United States and Canada, though, it was a sensational success. Dave Briggs was transformed overnight into a media star. He was asked to endorse a range of health supplements, I supposed because of his imposing physique. He was asked to become a brand ambassador for Jeep 4x4s and Tudor wristwatches. Talks opened with Netlfix and Amazon , both competing to turn his uncanny experience into a drama.

I think what probably pleased him most, was being guest of honour at a Chicago Red Sox game. I remembered that he liked his sport, preferably accompanied by a beer.

A few days after the final instalment transmitted over there, he called me. Curiously, he did so to apologise.

'I was terse with you people. Not welcoming,' he said.

'The lemonade was very welcome,' I said.

'Truth is, it was only out of concern for you folks. I knew when that hooker looked at me and screamed, that she had seen me *then*. I was in her time. And I wasn't at all confident I could ever get back to mine.'

'Did you enjoy the series, Mr Briggs?'

'Ceremony seems a bit silly, now, Mr Carter. I'm Dave. And I guess you'll be Tom?'

'You got it, Dave.'

'Most I enjoyed the story of the stride piano player, Laporte, and how his voodoo momma never buried him. Glad it wasn't that dude I ran into at four in the morning.'

'With you there,' I said.

Some family connections were established. The beat cop we'd filmed was identified as the great-uncle of a women sitting in the United States Senate. His name was Jacob Mahoney and he had been the recipient of several commendations during a distinguished police career. It occurred to me that he could have only been visiting that place alone and relaxed enough to be singing, to pick up the graft dollars Capone's people paid him for turning a blind eye to prostitution and the sale of banned liquor. Or was that me being cynical?

A couple of days after his earlier call, Dave Briggs called me again. It transpired that he too had a family connection with the former brothel in the suburb of Riverdale.

'My great-granddaddy was a boxer. Nothing special, just a club-fighter. And black fighters almost never got championship bouts back then. Turns out he supplemented his purse money right there. He worked as a whorehouse bouncer. Makes Capone an equal opportunities employer. Who knew?'

I wondered how well had Briggs' great-grandfather known Ulysses Laporte? They might have trained together at the same

South-Side gym. I also wondered whether the family connection had been what provoked Dave Briggs into seeing what he had seen there. Psychic sensitivity was an unpredictable attribute. Jeff Potts had only ever filmed in the direction I pointed at, seeing and hearing nothing until his visit to the Sacred Heart orphanage, where Daisy Chain had witnessed far more than me or Jeff or Lizzie Cox. You couldn't demand this stuff make rational sense. It did not conform to what we think of as normality.

One more detail about Chicago. There were two murders in Riverdale in the early hours of the night we were there. A nightwatchman and a delivery driver were both beaten to death. The detail that got the local press excited was a grisly one. Both corpses were partially consumed. No arrests were made. And no suspects named. Police speculation was that a bear scavenging for food in neighbourhood trashcans might have been responsible. My own theory differed from theirs.

Pete Davidson asked me to scout the locations for the second and third hauntings. I did not want to tell him yet that I had personally canned both projects. I had originally signed a contract to do the four. It had been his idea to get a total of six episodes out of only two of them. And we had done that with extremely successful results. But I did not have the legal expertise to know whether reneging on the original agreement could jeopardise my ongoing income stream from the orphanage and brothel series' and leave me in a position to be sued.

I wanted to consult my brother Andy on the legality of what I had signed. And I had a copy of the contract to show him. But he had taken a month's holiday and travelled to the States, to climb in the Rockies in Colorado and the Yosemite National Park in California. He wouldn't be back for a fortnight. I really didn't want to shell out on an expensive legal opinion when I had a sibling with the expertise to do it for free. That was assuming he survived his planned solo ascent of El Capitan, a climb he intended to tackle via a famously difficult route.

I decided I would treat it all as a jaunt. Travelling freely was still something of a novelty and there are worse summer locations to visit than the East Coast of Scotland and County Clare on the West Coast of Ireland. I had never before been to either place, so it would be a bit of an adventure. I had always wanted to see the Cliffs of Moher. And a lighthouse built in Victorian times would be an interesting building to explore. It was situated on a rock several miles from the mainland. Its isolation alone would be intriguing.

To my surprise and delight, Daisy said she wanted to come with me.

'Think there'll be fireworks, Tom?'

'Nope. I'm anticipating peat fires, single malts and folk singers in chunky sweaters who can only perform with a finger in one ear.'

'That's a thing?'

'Certainly it's a thing.'

'No ghosts?' She had done some preliminary research.

'Gremlins at the lighthouse. Of the electrical variety. The more sophisticated the setup, the more fallible it becomes. Lighthouses are magnets for lore and rumour and legend, but I expect the truth to be quite mundane.'

'Wasn't there a farmer boy traumatised by his visit to the cottage in Clare?'

'A brainless brawler who finally took too many on the chin in bar fights. Someone whose head met with a stone floor halfway through a pub lock-in, shitfaced. Or someone who makes that claim because rural life is tedious, and it gives him a point of interest no one else shares. Makes him special.'

'I hadn't had you down as a cynic.'

'Cynicism on this subject would not have survived the Dolomites, as you know. Nor would it have survived Chicago, as I'm relieved you'll never know. I had an instinct about both of those places. I don't anymore about these two. If I did, I don't think I would take you.'

'No reservations?'

'Apart from flying Ryanair?', 'No. Not a one.'

Before we left, I went to see my daughter. Samantha and I had worked out a rough sort of roster. I could visit on any day that was Monday, Wednesday, Friday or Sunday. She got Tuesday, Thursday or Saturday. She insisted I get the greater choice. She said my dedication over the years Claire had been at the Retreat gave me a deserved seniority. It didn't seem exactly tyrannical and I said if she ever got the urge to go on what was supposed to be my choice of day, I'd waive the privilege. No child has anything close to a substitute for a mother. I did not exempt myself from that judgement.

I went on Wednesday, because we planned to travel to Scotland on Friday. Before seeing Claire, I had requested some time with Dr Pettifer. Who had become Julia, quite suddenly, after all our years spent warily circling one another.

She told me that the self-harming had completely stopped. Claire was eating not just healthily but consistently and with relish for the food she was served. The manic episodes had died down completely. She was engaged socially rather than withdrawn. She took a lively interest in the exterior world. The periods of black depression that had left her not only speechless but bedbound, had ceased altogether. The improvement was remarkable.

'So she is now a normal sixteen-year-old girl,' I said.

'She will never be that, Tom. She is close to being ready to leave us. But we both know she will never be what conventional people call normal.'

'You might care to explain what you mean, Julia.'

'I saw the three-part series you did on the haunted Riverdale brothel. The place owned by Al Capone? Made for gripping television.'

'Thank you.'

'And Claire told me about Ulysses Laporte. About his attempt to return to the place and confront you. And how she warned you. It happened, didn't it?'

I kept that faded sheet of typing paper on my person. Almost as though it had some talismanic quality. That had quickly grown into a superstition with me. Now I took it out and unfolded it and slid it onto the psychiatrist's desk and she read the words typed there.

'Miraculous,' she said. And she smiled. 'If miracles are your thing. She described him to me, Piano Man. I think you had a lucky escape.'

I nodded.

'Almost ready to leave us, but your daughter will never be normal, Tom. I would say she is quite unique.'

Probably for the first time, I observed the items on Julia Pettifer's desk. The uniform blue of the pencils in their slender little white vase. The stapler and letter opener and pens in perfect alignment to the right of her immaculate cream blotter. The compact voice recorder, for the taking of memos, in perfect alignment to the blotter's left. The deep polish of the spotless wood supporting everything it did.

This was a woman whose job it was to try to impose rationality when mental chaos confronted her. She was someone who I sensed craved convention, predictability, what could easily be described as normal. My daughter flouted her values and challenged her perspective on the world. She could return to that, really, only after Claire's departure. She would not rush that, because she was as conscientious as she was professional. But I sensed she would be mightily relieved when it happened.

Now, she asked, 'Penny for them?'

I smiled and rose to go and said, 'At a penny, Julia, they'd be outrageously overpriced.'

The visit itself was uneventful. We walked to Sea World, where Claire no longer seemed to mind the fish looking back at us. We went for tea and scones at a promenade café. Claire was wearing a white and red floral dress, the most colourful garment I had ever seen her attired in. She was carrying a shiny green purse. On the route back to the Retreat, she unzipped it at one at one of the seafront shelters and took out a ten-pound note and handed it to a homeless man.

'They let you have money now?'

'Mum gives it to me. She asked permission.'

'But they don't let you out to spend it?'

'Not on my own.'

'That was thoughtful. Of your mother.'

'She's a thoughtful mum.'

'And she loves you.'

'I can see she does,' Claire said.

And I thought, just not in the way that other people see things.

We decided to drive to Scotland. It was a hell of a long way, but Daisy's Audi was a mile-eater of a car. It was still the safest way to travel. And we were spending Pete Davidson's expenses money on the fuel. And we were travelling light, no gear, unless you counted what our phones were capable of doing.

I told Daisy of my decision to quit at a motorway service station on a break, three hours into the drive as we sat at one of the faux wooden benches outside their Costa branch and drank coffee, grateful that the motorway coffee shops at least had survived events. Or maybe just endured them. The coffee was hot and so was the sun on my back as I said what I had to with no real feeling of trepidation.

'So this is your swansong,' she said.

'Not really. Because I don't expect anything to happen.'

'Tempting fate, saying that,' she said.

'How do you feel about my decision?'

'Relieved, if I'm honest, Tom. The Dolomites was horrible. And if anything, Chicago sounds even worse. Even if you come out of those experiences intact, and poor Jeff Potts didn't, they take their toll.'

'They haunt you,' I said, quietly. Because they did. And they had been doing it to me since I was eleven years old.

'I'd like to show you my hometown,' I said.

'Sunny Southport by the sea,' she said. 'I think I saw that written on a postcard as a child. Researched Les Dawson a few years ago for a TV documentary. He riffed about Southport beach in his stand-up routine. Said it was the only resort where they had camels instead of donkeys.'

I laughed. 'Bit unfair. A lot of sand before you get to the sea. But they do have donkeys. You can ride one.'

'Know how to spoil a girl, don't you, Tom.'

We could drive from Clare to Dublin and get the Holyhead ferry. That was 120 miles or so from Southport, so just over two hours. I could make reservations at the Vincent on Lord Street and we could stay just a couple of nights before returning to London. My hometown wasn't the place it had been in its prime, when factory fortnight had filled its tills and packed its guest houses every summer. And more recently the restrictions had bankrupted its flagship theatre there. Even my modest little ice-cream kiosk was long demolished.

I realised Daisy was staring at me. I wondered was she thinking about my diminished future status, no longer the subject of press profiles and ratings wars. Just someone who was once a media name, heading towards anonymity.

She said, 'Samantha is from Southport, isn't she?'

'Yes.'

'Is taking me there a kind of exorcism?'

'It's a way of sharing something with you I no longer want to be unique to me.'

'Then I should take it as a compliment?'

I blew out a breath and stared into the coffee grounds at the bottom of my empty mug. 'You're right,' I said. Why should you have any interest in ancient history.'

I was still gripping my mug in the fingers of my right hand. Daisy reached across the table and squeezed my wrist. 'It's your history,' she said. 'And I'm interested in you.'

We got to our Scottish destination at 7pm. It was remote, rugged, at the edge of a sea with no respect for the niceties of the season. It boiled and raged under the clifftop pub in which we were staying in what had looked on the internet like a cosy refuge from the elements. Unless the weather calmed overnight, the sea was too rough for the crossing. I had checked the forecast prior to our departure, but pointlessly, really. Weather in that part of the world I knew had an elemental unpredictability. I would hope it calmed and not mention my pessimism concerning the conditions to Daisy.

Our room smelled faintly of tar and brine. The two upper floors of the pub were constructed from wood and I thought must have been built using ship's timbers. We had a view north of a wilderness of water, sea stacks and reefs. Gulls, gannets, puffins in a shrieking sky. A brass-mounted telescope at the window through which to study it all. A wood burning fire. A good start.

By prior arrangement, by Pete Davidson's organisational alchemy, a key to the lighthouse was now in the possession of the local coastguard. We had permission to enter and tour the building, but only if chaperoned. Our guide would be the pilot who ferried us across in a coastguard vessel which I hoped would be a solid, seaworthy craft and not one of the RIBS they so often nowadays use.

I had never suffered from seasickness, since my father had seen to it that I spent much of my infancy on the Formby shrimpers and Mersey tugs aboard which he had, for the most part, earned his living. But I wasn't sure whether Daisy had her sea legs. No point her getting to where we were going green and bilious. This was supposed to be an enjoyable trip, a short tour best described as a holiday. It was important to me that she had a good time.

When I woke up on the first morning proper of our trip, Daisy was gone. After a desolate moment I swung out of bed and opened the wardrobe door and the things she had hung in there the previous night were still all present. I brewed coffee. Then I heard footsteps on the steep staircase outside and she came through the door carrying kindling she must have gathered for the fire bunched between both hands.

'Gorgeous day out there,' she said. She looked excited, face flushed, eyes bright, her hair windblown. Tresses of it cascaded from her head and curled around her jaw. I still hadn't opened the curtains over the window. I did so now, thinking gorgeous day, gorgeous woman. A few minutes earlier, I thought she had gone. I was slightly incredulous that she was actually there.

'I hope it's a RIB,' she said. 'For the crossing?'

'Why would you hope that?'

'They're fun.'

I studied the sea. 'There's a swell.'

She was setting the fire. It was still early. We wouldn't leave for a couple of hours and the room was chilly. She turned her head and smiled at me. She said, 'You're never too old.'

'For what?'

'For a white-knuckle ride.'

'How well do you play tennis?'

She struck a match and lit the fire. It took straight away, the briny scent in the room strengthening with the bright flicker of orange and yellow flames. She must have walked down the cliff path to the beach and the tideline and gathered her kindling there.

She blew out the match and said, 'County level.'

'I think I might have underestimated you.'

It was a boat rather than a RIB, a sturdy looking 20-footer we boarded at the small harbour sheltering fishing vessels a mile-long descent from the pub we were staying at to sea-level. Our skipper was sailing the craft solo and I was relieved to see it was equipped with sonar. He would know the underwater hazards of the region well enough I thought to recite them in his sleep. But a bit of insurance was comforting in such naturally challenging waters.

The day was clear enough for us to see Darkling Rock in the distance, its beacon rising as the only man-made feature in that vast and ragged vista. It looked closer than it was in the vivid morning light, but I knew the crossing would take about an hour.

The man piloting our boat was taciturn, grunting out a sort of greeting and saying nothing more to either of us, until he recognised me. And recognised Daisy too. He had seen the series on the Orphanage of the Sacred Heart. He was going to watch *The Fourth Haunting* on catch-up.

'Rum, that business in the Dolomites,' he said.

Which was one way of putting it.

He didn't know how Darkling Rock had got its name. But he knew Robert Alderman slightly, the man who claimed to have seen long-dead Jed Ball steal away from the lighthouse entrance door after its beam had been extinguished. And his father had known Jed Ball. He declared himself open-minded about what we had filmed and recorded at the orphanage. But he was sceptical about the alleged haunting on the rock.

'Took dedication, to be a lighthouse man,' he said. 'Months of being cooped up, usually with only two other men for company. You've got to be able to tolerate the solitary life while being at the same time tolerable company. Jed Ball was that, according to my dad. But the thing that marked him out, was his dedication to the light. That was total. Inviolable. I'm not dismissing the notion of ghosts. I'm just saying why should he be so different in death from the way he was in life?

Daisy said, 'And the night-angler, Robert Alderman?'

Our skipper shrugged. 'Obviously, he saw something.'

'Someone,' I said.

'The rock is uninhabited. But Bobby Alderman doesn't hold a patent on the place. You might use the anchorage to fix a problem aboard your boat and then decide to stretch your legs ashore before casting off again. You might, just out of interest, take a walk around the base of the tower. You might be curious to do that, particularly if you'd just seen the light extinguished.'

I said, 'Alderman isn't a fanciful character.'

'I can vouch for that personally,' our skipper said. 'But night fishing. How long had Bobby been without sleep? Eighteen hours? Twenty? Tired eyes tend to see what tired minds allow them to.'

Daisy laughed. She said to him, 'You're raining on our parade.'

'No, you're not,' I said. 'You're just confirming what I've come to suspect about this particular story.'

We were there. We tied up to mooring posts fore and aft in the little harbour that had been used by the boats supplying the men who had manned the lighthouse up to a fateful day in 1974. And it occurred to me only now I was on the verge of quitting these investigations, that I preferred my hauntings modern. I never really wanted to go back further than the early years of the 20th century. As though recent phantoms had more power and potency than those from a more remote time. Maybe ghosts, like the living, had a lifespan of their own. It struck me as an interesting thought.

We went through the heavy, weathered wooden door and were confronted by the set of steep iron steps rising to the first floor of the tower. And I shivered, reminded of the last time I'd looked at a set of those. But only briefly, because they were a continent away and these looked like they could comfortably take a man's weight.

'This climb will be the death of me,' our skipper said. But I think that was just his idea of humour. He looked fit enough.

Climb we did, though. Pausing only when we reached the sleeping quarters directly under the chamber housing the lamp. And I knew they always called it the lamp, regardless of its brightness, or how sophisticated was the way in which it was generated. This one was huge and looked state of the art. The anomaly to either side of it of two antique bronze bells going green with disuse and neglect. They would have been for when the lamp did fail, back when the lighthouse was manned and a bell tolling at sea signalled danger.

'Anything?' I asked Daisy.

She shook her head. 'The legend says he comes in September, during the month when he left this place for the last time. That's when he puts out the light. And we're here in July. But I think the only way Jed Ball came back here after he left was in his memory. And then he died. And nothing since.'

The clement weather held. We picnicked, the two of us, on the rock before the voyage back, while our skipper returned to the anchored boat and its galley for his own midday meal. The seagulls, wild creatures here, had not the tameness to harass us for scraps as we ate. Which reminded me of Brighton and Hove where they stole your seafront chips or pecked at your ice-cream. Which reminded me of my daughter, whom I hoped would soon be free.

'You're thinking of Claire,' Daisy said. 'Not the Irish Clare. The person.'

'How did you know?'

'This expression you wear on your face. Sort of sadness and tenderness at the same time. It's changing, though. I'd say less of the former and more of the latter, recently. You've burdened yourself with love and done it willingly. It's one of the things I've always liked most about you.'

'I never had a choice,' I said.

It was odd, really. There had been plenty of anti-climactic disappointments in my ghost hunting career. Lots of cul-de-sacs, damp squibs, blind alleys, false alarms, no-shows. You can apply the cliché of your choice, as I had, more often than not, been forced to do. But what I felt when the Darkling Rock lighthouse provided nothing worthy of further investigation, was only relief. Relief that I wouldn't be cheating the sometimes generous and sometimes professionally supportive Pete Davidson out of something of substance. Something with genuine feature-making potential.

I was more relieved though that Daisy had endured nothing other-worldly. She was a resilient person, but her foray into fieldwork had been a huge miscalculation on my part. The orphanage experience had exposed her to something someone as sensitive as she had proven to be should have been kept well away from. She had not really gone into the specifics about what she had seen and heard, but neither, I was sure, had she forgotten it.

She was with me because she had emphatically wanted to come. And so far, we were enjoying ourselves. I was reasonably confident that the Clare cottage, in the isolation of its peaty wilderness, would be benign. The Irish love a legend and overwhelmingly, they are without substance. But I was not quite so emphatically sure about the cottage as I had been about the lighthouse. The Irish Civil War had been a bloody event contested by ruthless people on both sides. The idea that a professional assassin had occupied the cottage in a season of bloodshed, was a plausible one. We would see.

We left for Ireland the following day, early in the morning. I drove us the 200-plus miles to the Holyhead ferry terminal. We disembarked at Dun Laoghaire and Daisy retook the wheel. Pub accommodation again, this time in the county town of Ennis. We got there tired after a day's travel, ate a traditional dinner of lamb stew and had a nightcap. Daisy's was a G&T and mine a glass of

Bushmills Black Label drunk potently and deliciously neat. I was asleep seconds after my head hit the pillow.

We had a rough timetable for the following day. Visit the Cliffs of Moher and then drive inland to our destination. We planned to leave there long before dark. Daisy's sensitivity meant that she could pick up the vibes in daylight. She had certainly done so in the Dolomites on her first exposure to somewhere authentically haunted. If she did feel anything, I might go back at night alone. Or I might not, that was a toss of a coin decision. What I did not want was Daisy anywhere the place in the night-time.

I barely noticed our surroundings prior to waking the following morning after a deep and easy sleep. This time, Daisy had gone on no dawn mission to gather firewood. She lay asleep beside me, breathing evenly, so beautiful I could barely believe my own good fortune. I kissed her lightly and got up to make coffee.

A garret room with beams. Rough plaster over stone buckled in places with age. Rugs scattered over a wood floor. An ornate, elderly bronze radiator. A shelf full of hardback books, most of them leatherbound. A nice, plain, simple room, its only modern touch a coffee machine I put on. I opened the curtains and saw that here, the weather had broken. A heavy veil of cloud lay seemingly not much above the level of the ground. I smiled to myself, thinking there's a reason Ireland is such a verdant country. We would still go to the Cliffs. There was always the chance it might brighten and if it didn't, we would see the Atlantic view through a Celtic mist.

The weather had not brightened when we got there. The air was pungent with salt and the grass slick under our feet. Before even seeing them, I could hear the waves break against stone 400 feet beneath us. Daisy reached for my hand as we risked the edge of that great rampart against the Atlantic Ocean and peered down. The sea raged and toiled against the rock in a mist drenched glimpse of how old the world we briefly inhabit truly is. It was a majestic, dizzying sight from which we retreated I thought, humbled.

Daisy looked along the gaunt and massive contours of the undulating face. 'No words,' she said, squeezing my hand.

'I'm so glad you came on this trip,' I said. I kissed her.

'Yes, well,' she said, smiling. 'It isn't over yet. We have a rural Irish property to visit. Charming location, colourful history, in need of some repair.'

'Or just a little love,' I said.

'That's the one.'

The drive took 40 minutes. The cart track leading to the cottage itself was too much for the Audi's clearance. We parked up and began the wet walk over the thistle and scrub and nettles erupting over the decades out of the thin spread of gravel. We had both worn boots. Gaiters would have been a good idea. My jeans were soaked to the knee in minutes.

'Could have done with our Italian Job Land Rover,' I said. But that unfortunate crack had the effect only of making Daisy shiver at the recollection.

The untended field around us was grassed over but undulant, ploughed in preparation for some crop, but then abandoned or just forgotten about. A place now only of memory and neglect. The air was still and damp and there were no birds in the air. The sky was featureless, uniform, blandly unconcerned with our progress. Until a light rain began to fall.

'Nowhere has rain like Ireland does,' Daisy said.

'You've been here before?'

'County Cork,' she said. 'Great for seafood. Prefer it to here.'

'I'll take that on trust,' I said.

'Can you feel it, Tom?'

'All I can feel is falling raindrops and wet denim clinging to my calves.'

'You will,' she said. 'You will soon enough.'

The cottage was sighted in a dip. It must have been, because the slate roof was the first part of it that came into view. Then its whitewashed walls. A window to either side of the red-painted front door. The paint full-blooded, not faded at all by time. A crimson exclamation mark defying the general dullness of the day.

Eventually we reached it. The place was curiously well-preserved. The small panes of the windows were intact. Only one or two slates had slipped over time from the roof. Up close, the whitewash was fissured like the skin of someone afflicted by old age, but the yellow stone underneath seemed sound and sturdy. We walked around the cottage. To its rear, the neglected remains of what had once been a kitchen garden. Its wicker fence was still intact in parts. There was an old-fashioned hand pump for drawing water, a hooped wooden pail still beneath it. And to our left a wooden shed with a torn felt roof that when we looked, was hung with an assemblage of rusting tools.

I asked Daisy, 'What do we know about the gunman?'

She shrugged. She said, 'It's all rumour and supposition. Collins was discreet about the men who worked for him. The men and the women. They were dangerous times. Look what happened to him.'

'Someone left here in a hurry.'

Daisy said, 'Let's go inside.'

A single room. A cloth-covered armchair disgorging horsehair, a truckle bed against one wall, a rectangular wooden table with two straight-backed chars pulled up to it, a shelf with a few items of crockery placed upon it. Stone flagged, with a small fireplace.

'No valuables,' I said.

'They would long have been stolen.'

'No keepsakes.'

'An unsentimental man,' she said.

'Think the place comes alive at night, Daisy?'

She was looking out of one of the windows flanking the cottage door. At its top left side was a dusty web with a large black spider quivering at its centre. She wasn't looking at that. Evidently spiders did not bother her. She was looking through the discoloured panes out over that undulant field.

'Nothing happens here at night,' she said. She nodded. 'They're out there, where he buried them, the dead.'

'At peace.'

'At rest,' she said. 'They don't celebrate their own demise, Tom. He did a thorough job.'

'I don't like this place.' Neither did I like large spiders. There was nothing more to see or say. We left.

We duly went to Southport. We had a good time. We enjoyed ourselves more than I had thought we would. It was great, right up until the moment on Wednesday morning when I got a call from Julia Pettifer. She phoned to break the news to me that my daughter had gone from her room. They did not know at what time during the night she had left. Her absence from the Retreat was only noticed there when breakfast was being served.

Chapter 11

I asked Julia to tell me everything she knew. She said that Claire had been present at lights out the previous evening. The reception desk had been vigilantly manned, as it always was, throughout the night. That was necessary because though the windows in the rooms were secured, the residents were permitted the limited freedom of an unlocked door. One staffer, but someone professional and experienced who said that she had seen no one enter or leave the building overnight through the main entrance.

The rear door was locked. The fire escape door could be unlocked manually from the inside to comply with fire regulations. But that was covered by CCTV, the monitor was on the front desk, and opening the fire door immediately triggered an alarm that had not been deactivated or tampered with in any way. After a thorough search of the Retreat building produced no results, Julia had done two things. She had informed the police and sent three staffers out to search for Claire in the surrounding area.

'We know she likes to go with you to play the grabber machines in the arcade at the end of Brighton Pier.'

'She wouldn't go there alone,' I said. 'She isn't comfortable with crowds. She wouldn't abscond in the first place. She is only weeks away from release and rehabilitation. She knows she is. She wouldn't blow that opportunity. She's waited too long. What did the police say?'

'They wait for twenty-four hours when someone is reported missing before they start to investigate. Claire has money of her own now, Tom. Her mother's suggestion. Foolishly, I agreed to it. She could have taken a train. Or a taxi. She could be aboard a coach going anywhere.'

'Except she isn't, Julia,' I said. 'Because she didn't leave of her own free will. She's been taken.'

Julia Pettifer was quiet. Then she said, 'How?'

'The man who called himself James Balfour. Your receptionist saw him, alright, she just can't remember it. That's one of his skills, remember? And he knows his way around the place. And though I don't quite know what it is, he has a motive.'

'Would Claire go with him without a fight?'

I closed my eyes. The phone was trembling in my fist. Daisy was pale, staring at me wide-eyed with realisation. All this on Lord Street. My heart lurching from beat to beat in dread and panic at the centre of an indifferent world.

I remembered Julia's question. 'Only if sedated,' I said. 'And you wouldn't need much. Claire is slightly built naturally and still probably slightly underweight.'

'Still a tricky proposition, Tom.'

'Not if he had help. A vehicle, an accomplice to drive it.'

'Oh, God.'

'Does Samantha know?'

'She's my next call. I had to tell you first.'

We were only a block from the Vincent. In twenty minutes, we were packed, had checked out of the hotel and were on the road. Brighton was 300 miles from Southport, but Daisy was a fast driver in a fast car. We stopped once, for fuel. Samantha called me as we left the outskirts of Ormskirk on the M6 approach. She was sobbing.

'I'm on my way to Brighton,' I said, 'I'll find her.'

'How long before you get there? I'm going now.'

'A few hours. Mid-afternoon. I'll find her, Samantha. I swear I will.'

After trying and failing to calm and reassure my former wife, I turned to Daisy and said, 'Head to Chichester first.'

We got to Chichester at two in the afternoon. Daisy had averaged 90 between the speed cameras and the traffic had been thankfully light, at least in the outside lane. Balfour's brass plaque had been unscrewed. Lacking one of my cousin Hangy's keys to get through it, I forced the street door with a shoulder. The inner doors weren't locked. Each opened on vacancy, abandonment. James Balfour no longer existed.

When I returned to the car, I broke down. 'He tried to touch her.' I told Daisy. 'I didn't tell you that detail. But Claire told it to me.'

In Brighton, just before 3pm, I walked into the main police station, explained who I was, and told a Detective Sergeant what I suspected had happened to my missing daughter. About the Balfour alias and the attempted sexual assault. Then I emailed the police half a dozen portrait shots of Claire from my phone. I did all this with Samantha seated beside me.

Daisy was by then on her way back to London having offered to look in the places there that Claire had liked to go. They were the Southbank, the Natural History Museum, Regents Park Zoo, Coram's Fields. I knew that she would be in none of those places. But Daisy wanted to help. And it seemed to offer some comfort to Samantha.

'What if we never find her?' Samantha said, sobbing once more when we left the police station. The eyes in her make-up free face were raw. Her hair was a dishevelled mess and her clothing rumpled. She looked distressed and somehow younger than she did when perfectly groomed. I hadn't seen her so helpless looking since the moment six years earlier when it hit us that we couldn't cope at home with Claire any longer.

I hugged her, hard, and she hugged me back. 'He hasn't taken her just to kill her,' I said. 'There's more to it. And as long as she's alive, there is hope.'

There were things I could not confide in my ex-wife. I could not tell her about the Jericho Society, the deadly clandestine cult I had first learned something about as a teenager. I could not tell her that the man masquerading as James Balfour was a member of a cabal of people who practised occult rituals and perhaps had for hundreds of years. Influential people. People in positions of power and authority. That Balfour was only a foot-soldier, perhaps acting on orders from above.

I could not tell Samantha that I suspected Claire's abduction somehow connected to me. I could not tell her, because there was no point, without knowing what the connection was. I needed to try to remain calm and to think about that. That connection could be the key to finding my daughter safe.

There was a third consideration I would not willingly discuss, though my ex wasn't stupid, and I knew it would occur to her independent of me. And that was the damage, even if we found her physically unharmed, that this experience would inflict on Claire's mind. She had been on the brink of being well enough to come home. As if abduction wasn't cruel enough, Balfour could not have chosen a more heart-breaking moment to take her.

We took adjacent rooms at the Ginger Pig. In a normal year, in a normal era, in the month of July, the place would have been fully booked. But events had made people distrustful of hotels and their inevitable characteristic of close proximity to strangers. There was no real logic to staying in Hove. I think it was a shared instinct. We were closer there than anywhere to our missing daughter.

We arranged a meeting on Thursday afternoon with Julia Pettifer. After a sleepless night I had run five miles that morning just to dissipate some pent-up energy. Eyes scouring the landscape in the desperate hope of recognising a pale and familiar figure, a young girl, someone colourfully clothed now, someone purposeful of stride. Over every inch of the route, I searched for her, vision blurred by my tears.

I wanted to know had the man using the alias of James Balfour got careless in conversation with the psychiatrist, offered any clues as to his roots, his family, his whereabouts. Maybe a favourite holiday destination or town familiar to him that wasn't Chichester. He had proven in his dealings with my daughter that he was a man capable of a slip-up. He had demonstrated to me the over-confidence that so often flaws arrogant people.

Julia looked as though she had not slept any better than had the parents of her missing charge.

'You didn't make a misjudgement over the money,' Samantha said. 'She left only under duress. Tom is right about this. Our daughter was abducted.'

'I wish only my misjudgement were to blame,' Julia said. 'I really do. I wish with all my heart Claire was off on some teenage jaunt somewhere. But I fear you're right. More pertinently, so do the police.'

'I know,' I said. 'We had a conference call with them this morning. It's an active missing persons investigation now headed up by a Detective Inspector. They're examining CCTV footage from the area around the Retreat. A painstaking process, but they might get something. A numberplate. A good shot of the accomplice I'm bloody sure that bastard had. Sorry for the language.'

'Don't be,' Julia said. 'Bastard doesn't come close.'

'The staffer on the desk still doesn't remember anything unusual occurring?'

Julia shook her head. 'Nothing. But she used an odd phrase describing it. She said it was a night like any other. As though she'd been programmed to think it routine. I know you think she was. I've come to believe that too. James Balfour put her under.'

'He isn't James Balfour,' I said. 'He's someone else and you might have a clue as to who. Think hard, Julia.'

She was thinking hard. The serious expression on her face said so. She said, 'He talked once about the bay. The something bay. The name of it sounded contradictory, I remember thinking. I can't remember the name of it, though.'

'But you will,' I said. 'It will come back to you. And when it does, you'll call me.'

'Of course I will,' she said.

We left, I think both of us a bit reluctantly. There was nowhere else to go, nothing else to do. No leads, no direction to follow. We stood in the strong sunshine on the pavement outside almost paralysed. Samantha's cheekbones looked more prominent than usual, sculpted, sharp. It occurred to me that she had probably not eaten since the morning of the previous day.

'We should examine her room,' she said.

'The police will have done that by now.'

'We should have done it yesterday. Bloody obvious thing to do. There might be clues.'

I thought that it might be taped off, a crime scene. But it wasn't and the Retreat people let us examine it without objection.

Everything seemed intact. Her drawings, except for that one of the Fischer House she had sent my brother. Her vivid collection of new clothes neatly folded in the draws of her dresser. Her box of treasured letters concerning Hampstead Heath from Andy. And under her pillow, that vivid green zippered purse full of the money her mother had been giving her.

'She didn't take a cab,' Samantha said, unzipping the purse, staring at its contents.

I sniffed the air, as though Balfour might have left some spoor we might follow. But the room smelled of nothing at all. The trail was cold.

I could feel panic rise in me. I prayed I was right, and that Claire was the lure and safe until at least they got whatever it was they wanted from me. It occurred to me that there might have been an approach by post, something particular to my daughter sent to my home address in a parcel as proof that they had her. They knew, after all, where I lived. I fumbled out my phone and called Daisy and asked her did she have time to go over there.

'I'll make time,' she said. She was on the Southbank as she spoke, no doubt looking out for Claire. Talk about clutching at straws. 'Only I don't have a key, Tom.'

'There's a spare under the flowerpot with the Basil growing in it in the front garden.'

'That's not very sensible.'

'Day to day, I agree with you,' I said. 'But right now, it's convenient. And don't put it back when you leave, if you disapprove. Hang onto it.'

Her number came up on my phone an hour later. She must have taken the train from Waterloo, I thought, to get there that quickly.

'There's an envelope addressed to you,' she said. 'Something stiff inside it.'

'Open it.'

The something stiff was a photograph.

'Describe it, Daisy.'

I thought it would be Claire, perhaps with her hands bound and a strip of duct tape stuck cruelly over her mouth. But it wasn't. 'I'll take a snap of it on my phone, email it to you,' Daisy said.

We were in the restaurant at the Ginger Pig, coffee going cold in neglected cups in front of us, an expression of hope on my ex-wife's face out of all proportion to the circumstances. A photograph would not return our missing child.

I opened Daisy's email. The shot was a sepia portrait of me aged 30, the bulk of an old-fashioned and unwieldy videocam on my right shoulder, the expression on my face that of a man witnessing something nobody should, the significance of it altogether lost to me. Me in the cellar of the Fischer House. Me filming an event from 1927 I could never have shared with the wider world.

'Who took that?' Samantha asked.

'I don't know.' The truthful answer.

'What does it mean?'

'I shot a film at a derelict mansion on the Isle of Wight. A place reputedly haunted. It was my big breakthrough. If I remember right, your dad posted it to you.'

'That's right. I had to switch it off.'

'I saw something there from the past I've never spoken about. A ritual murder. I saw something from the past and they saw something from the future. They must have done. One of them photographed me.'

'Did they try to communicate with you? Stop you filming them killing someone?'

'They were drugged. The place had the stink of an opium den. I think they thought I was some kind of hallucination, drug induced. I knew they were ghosts.'

'You sure you've never spoken about it?'

'Only to Daisy and only very recently. And I'm certain she has told no one else.'

'That photo was sent to you by someone from the present, Tom. A descendant of the men you saw?'

'They belonged to a cult. I think its dynastic. And still in existence, still influential. This is their way of telling me they're got our daughter.'

'They want their film back. Give it to them. Give them back their film.'

Samantha was pawing at me with her hands, pleading with me, the shrillness of hysteria in her rising voice. Her eyes wide with incomprehension.

'I will,' I said. But I knew it couldn't be that simple. If the film was all they wanted, why had they waited years to plot its recovery? Why run the risk of exposure for a day longer than necessary? Maybe they wanted me to think it was only the film they were after. That would make sense. But there had to be something more.

Pragmatic, I knew, to let Samantha believe what she believed, to let her hang onto that hope. I knew her well enough to know that she was close to collapse. Better for her if she could avoid breaking down completely. I gripped her tightly by her upper arms and looked her full in the face.

'Are you capable of driving?'

'Yes. No. I don't know. Why?'

'I want you to go back to Richmond. What's the name of your Mr Right?'

'Richard. Richard Purcell.'

'Does he know what's happened?'

He's phoned a few times. I haven't picked up his calls.'

'Will he take care of you, Samantha?'

'Yes. He's kind. But I need to be here with you.'

I said, 'I'm not staying in Hove. The film they want is in a Hatton Garden strongbox. I'll get Daisy to courier it to me here. Then I'll make contact with them and do what they want me to do to get our daughter back. It won't be here, Samantha. Not with the police here on the hunt for whoever took Claire.'

She nodded and rose and went outside, where she would get a stronger signal on her phone. I stared at the sepia image of me, stranded briefly in the pre-war past, thinking there's more than one kind of ghost, knowing that my confrontation with the Jericho Society had been inevitable ever since hearing Edward Swarbrick's cruel bark of mirthless laughter as a child. I knew the what, without remotely knowing the why. I was at a dangerous disadvantage. Perhaps if I could locate the man who had claimed his name was James Balfour, I could beat the information out of him. But I knew that if I started to do that, I would never stop.

Samantha eventually returned. She didn't sit back down, so I stood. She smiled, unconvincingly. She said, 'Richard is taking an immediate leave of absence from his academic work. Easier to do out of term time. He runs some of Kingston's summer school courses, but a substitute tutor can fill in. Architecture is one of their best staffed departments.'

'That's good,' I said.

'He's a good man.'

'I don't doubt it.'

'So are you,' she said. 'Promise me you'll find her, Tom.'

'I'll find her,' I said.

We hugged one another. I remembered her driving ban. 'How will you get back?'

'The same way I got here,' she said. 'By taxi.'

'The train might be quicker.'

A breath shuddered out of her. 'Couldn't be that public,' she said. 'Do you understand?'

'Yes,' I said. 'I do,'

I called Daisy and asked her to courier me the films. Both films; the one I'd shot and the one Al Hodge had shot at the Birkdale Palace Hotel and bequeathed me. She asked me, concern in her voice, about Samantha. So I told her what was happening with that. Then I called the company I rented my strongbox from and told them to expect a woman named Polly Chain who would identify herself using her drivers' license. She would be there later that afternoon and was to be given full access. Then I settled Samantha's bill.

My phone rang and I recognised Julia Pettifer's number.

'I've remembered the name of that contradictory bay,' she said. 'It was Freshwater.'

I closed my eyes. Contradictory indeed, because the sea is salt. And Freshwater Bay was on the island I seemed incapable of escaping.

I was in for a further surprise on that long day. It occurred when my courier arrived in the lovely shape of Daisy Chain. Seeing her made me realise how little I had been looking forward to a solitary evening. We embraced, me gratefully.

'I had to come,' she said. 'You sounded so desolate earlier, on the phone. You were better before Samantha left, but by then I think she had gone. You might not think you need company tonight, Tom. But you do.'

'I think I know where to find him,' I told her over a drink in the Ginger Pig's bar. 'I think I know where he lives, or at least where he's from. He's from Freshwater Bay. It will be crowded now, at the height of the holiday season, with people still so reluctant to travel abroad. But I know what he looks like, how he sounds, the gait of his walk. Even the wristwatch he wears. He's very easily recognisable.'

She was staring at me. She said, 'Have you told the police?'

I shook my head. 'The people who have Claire are people without pity. Totally ruthless, completely unscrupulous. I suspect he's no more than a foot-soldier, but if the police arrest him, I think they'll kill her.'

'Your first instinct was to go to the police.'

'As much to try to comfort Samantha as anything,' I said. 'And I'd love them to gather the evidence to convict him once Claire is safely back. But until then I think I'm wisest trying to handle this myself.'

'Well,' she said, 'you have a proven talent for vigilantism.'

'Thanks. I'm sure that's intended as a compliment.'

'I'm sorry. I can't begin to imagine what you're going through. You and Samantha both. She loses her daughter for years, reconnects and then loses her again.'

For good, she was thinking. I could hear that in the finality of her tone. But Daisy was wrong. Samantha hadn't let Claire languish without her mother's attention for the five years our daughter had been resident at the Retreat. For the first four of those years, she had visited faithfully. And often. But the visits took their emotional toll because there seemed to be no change and therefore no hope.

I thought Samantha might break down in Hove because she had broken down a year earlier. I hadn't witnessed it. Mutual friends told me, as tactfully as they were able to. And obliquely, I was informed about it by Julia Pettifer. That was when Samantha's visits to Claire had stopped. About twelve months before she found the strength and resolution to resume them. She had never stopped writing, or feeling, or wishing. It wasn't that she didn't care. It was that she had cared too much eventually to endure those encounters with her daughter, believing Claire's condition to be incurable. Hope, was the thing Samantha had lost.

I told Daisy this, explained it to her. My former wife did not need a character reference from me. But she was a good, kind, compassionate woman and she deserved to be regarded as such.

'Part of you is still in love with Samantha,' Daisy said, when I had finished speaking.

I wasn't going to argue with that. Instead, I said, 'If anything happens to Claire, I don't think she will survive it.'

'And neither will you,' Daisy said, quietly. 'I think it would kill both of you.'

After a dinner I barely touched, we went for a walk at dusk along the seafront. The sunset was tendrils of pink and orange cloud against the darkening blue of the sky. Sometimes the indifference of the physical world to your own feelings seems like a sort of mockery, your surroundings merely set dressing. Waves slapped and hissed on the shingle. People slipped by, oblivious, their faces still strangely naked seeming after everything everyone had been through.

'Did you lose anyone?' Daisy asked, with her knack for reading my thoughts. Though she was not as disconcertingly good at that as my missing daughter was.

'A couple of acquaintances got sick. Nobody died. You?'

'An uncle I didn't really know. I've one very clean-living friend who doesn't believe she will ever have the breath to run again.'

'That's sad, Daisy.'

She stopped walking. She said, 'What are you going to do?'

I said, 'I'm flattered that you think I have a plan.'

She punched me in the chest. She said, 'Of course you have a bloody plan. That was why you wanted those films couriered here. What are you going to do?'

'In the morning, I'll hire a car. Then I'll drive to Portsmouth and take the Wight ferry. I'm going to the island. And I'll take the films.'

'But you won't take me.'

'No, Daisy. I won't take you.'

'Because of what I saw at the orphanage. Because you're not just going to the island. You're going to the Fischer House.' Her voice cracked, 'God help you, Tom.'

It was their domain. I was struggling not to picture my daughter tied to a chair in one of its derelict rooms, now, as darkness approached, and the night encroached on her delicate mind. I had to go. There wasn't a choice. I supposed freedom of choice was the first consideration you lost when obliged to deal with them. They were long practiced at manipulation, expert at compromising people. And nonchalant about making them disappear.

Saying my farewell, the following morning to Daisy, was difficult. She was so bright she was almost febrile over breakfast, but the painted-on smile didn't reach her alert, pained eyes. And when she took her teacup from its saucer to lift it to her lips, her trembling fingers shook tea in a trail of brown droplets over the linen tablecloth.

'Whoops.'

I had my bag in my hand on the pavement. She was gripping the keys to her car in her fist. She nodded at the bag. 'You're remembered the films?'

'For what they're worth. Who has VHS players these days?'

'Not really the point.'

'No. How do you feel?'

She breathed out, a breath that shuddered. 'I feel rather like I felt peering over the edge of that cliff in Ireland with the sea boiling hundreds of feet below us. Like I could lose my balance and pitch into the void and die.' She began to sob. 'I think I will never see you again. Like this is the end of us.'

I held her, inhaled the scent of her with my eyes closed, her loose hair on my cheek, her breath light and precious on my skin.

'I love you,' I said. 'I will always come back to you.'

'Be careful, Tom,' she said.

'I'm always careful.'

Then I turned and walked away from her, only because I had to.

I generally stayed at the Hambrough. But it was high season now and the Hambrough was fully booked out and so I got a room at the Sea View Hotel. Where the views out over the harbour and sea are magnificent. And where I was completely oblivious to anything going on through the window. And where the man who had called himself James Balfour called me before I had been allowed the time to unpack my solitary bag. He had my number. He'd been willingly given it when I still thought him the holy grail of hypnotism come to liberate my daughter.

'You know where to come,' he said.

'When?'

'At the time of your choosing. Just so long as it's after dark,'

'Naturally. Because you are of the night.'

He was silent. Then he said, 'Where did you hear that phrase?'

'In ancient Greek, in Hebrew,' I said. 'Jericho is a word that means moon.'

'Very good.'

'I don't require praise from a piece of shit like you.'

'You shouldn't have hurt me. It was a mistake.'

'My only mistake was not hurting you more.'

'Hubris, Mr Carter. We'll soon shake that out of you.' And he broke the connection.

It was then just after three o'clock in the afternoon. It was July 22 and sunset not going to occur until 9.03pm. My hire car was a VW Golf GTI. After unpacking my bag, I drove around the island for a couple of hours, aimlessly really, but forced to concentrate on something other than the present condition and future fate of my only child. I cannot remember much about the drive. I do recall, at one point, kind of coming to, parked outside what had once been Helena Donovan's cottage. I was weeping when my senses returned to me. On getting back to the hotel just after 5.pm, I went for a run that occupied another interminable hour of time. Then I showered and drank a diet coke and forced down an egg salad seated outside a seafront café.

At 7.pm I got back into the car and drove slowly to the edge of Brighstone Forest, where I sat listening to the radio play a series of songs I could, despite their random nature, link to people and places from my own eventful past. And it occurred to me of course that I might not have a future. That tonight might be the end of me. Though I was curiously unfearful for myself. There was no space left inside me for concern about anything other than Claire's welfare. I wasn't brave or even desensitised. I think I was just as close as I'd ever come to being genuinely possessed. Occupied completely only by the need to save her.

Eventually, the sky began to darken. Light leached out of the day. I saw the ground get gloomier as the shadows of the trees to my right lengthened. The sun was finally in descent, slowly sinking. I got out of the car and locked it behind me and began to walk towards my destination over the loamy earth. The two films they coveted were in a small canvas rucksack I held in my hand. One originally filmed on VHS, the other converted to the format. They should have felt more substantial, given their drear content. But the two cassettes were flimsy things, no burden at all.

Full-dark was approaching by the time I got to where the trees abruptly cleared and the steel encirclement isolating the Fischer House came into view. I had been incurious about how I would breach that bristling tribute to pain and disfigurement. Now I saw that I would not have to. A path had been torn through it, a gap the width of a full-grown man. And beyond, dark windows did not stare blankly back at me. There was light behind some of the panes. It seemed to be the uncertain illumination of candles, feeble, yellow and flickering.

The forest at my back was no longer still. It seemed to seethe suddenly with nocturnal life. Avian flutterings, the whisper of limbs stealing lightly over the ground. The brush of ferns and shiver of branches. And the noises of beasts. A feral grunt, a bark, a melancholy howl that lingered on the air as I studied the façade before me and waited for the last vestiges of light to bleed out of the day before going on.

I saw a pale cluster of children's faces. At one of the upper windows. They appeared to be watching me. They were from a black and white world and their complexions through the weather-furred panes were grey and lifeless. Peter Morgan. Arabella Pankhurst, I was sure. Others whose names time had forgotten, a blood-drained litany of sacrifice. My daughter's face, thank God, I did not recognise among them.

I walked through the gap, breaching the high, dense ring of metal barbs. The thin gravel on the ground was patched in places with moss and slippery under my feet, but my progress was sure, the great door yawing open as I ascended the stone steps to reach it, the man I had briefly known as James Balfour behind it, ushering me into the vestibule with a grin I thought triumphant. He led and I followed to the grand hall I remembered filming in as a young man, before risking the cellar and slipping through the decades and seeing their ritual performed.

Pete Davidson sat on a chair that was more of a throne, high, gold painted wood with carved embellishments, behind a baronial table, formally attired in a three-piece suit and tie. Both black, the colour of mourning. For me or for Claire or for both of us. What looked at first like a mayoral chain of office glimmered in a generous gold loop against his chest.

But closer study banished that comparison. The links were scrolled with a runic character and a blood coloured ruby weighted the chain, the size of a sparrow egg, resting on his sternum. He was lit by a candelabra, dripping wax onto polished wood. Flames burnishing the black cluster of grapes heaped in a crystal bowl in front of him. He lifted his eyes to meet mine and managed a rueful smile. Then he plucked a grape and burst it between his molars and swallowed with a look of satisfaction.

'This is a surprise,' I said. The man who had shown me in had taken a position behind me.

Pete said, 'What can I say, Tom? I am obliged to resort to cliché. Somehow, you always cajole me into doing that. So I'll quote the one about keeping your friends close and your enemies closer.'

'You're a member of the Jericho Society?'

'I'm a member of a number of associations. I'm a clubbable man.'

'Where's my daughter?'

'Safe, for the present. I should tell you that our mutual friend James is armed. There is a Beretta pistol trained on your back. I know you were a bit tasty in your younger days. And I have always suspected a temper lurks. Chichester confirmed that. The gun is there to deter you from attempting anything rash.'

'Who took my photograph?'

He spread his hands. 'There's a paradox. Does it matter? Actually, it was Young Mr Breene, of Vogel and Breene, one of our brethren in that line of work. When he was indeed young. He had a Kodak vest camera with him that night. You were too busy looking at what Klaus Fischer was doing to notice him. But he noticed you. And bingo.' He mimed a shutter click.

'Why wait until now to act against me?'

'We've never known the whereabouts of the film you shot. Or what you planned for it posthumously in the event we arranged a fatal accident.'

I said, 'The film is ancient history.'

'It compromises us,' he said. 'Klaus Fischer has descendants still living. It's exposure where we prefer confidentiality. It might threaten our existence.'

'Daisy Chain knows I'm here,' I said. 'She could be calling the police as we speak.'

'Except she won't be,' he said. 'Because compromise works both ways.'

I said, 'You worked with me only to keep a close eye on what I was doing?'

He shrugged. He said, 'Hype apart, you really are the best at what you do. Ours has been a mutually lucrative association. We've been to one another's benefit. But what that old flame of yours said to me on this very island recently is true. You are ambitious and you are not really to be trusted. Eventually, that film would have come to light. And then where would we have been?'

'That boy's murder would never have been broadcast.'

'Grow up, Tom. You can download the ritual decapitation of a Mexican woman by a cocaine cartel member with a lock-knife. Grisly and laborious. Graphic and real and in full colour. With the executioner's running commentary. Right up to the moment he places her severed head in her lap. Nothing is censored anymore.'

'Who would believe an atrocity carried out more than ninety years ago could be filmed, in colour, in the 1990s?'

'You're being far too modest, Tom. You had more credibility than any of your rivals even before The Italian Job and Chicago. But now? You've got a substantial global audience eating out of your hand. Your name at the top of the credits brings an army of viewers willing to be convinced. More than that, already convinced. Predisposed to believe the ghostly gospel according to Tom Carter. And like any media demigod, you fucking know it.'

'Why kidnap my daughter?'

'Jeff Potts brought matters to a head. A reminder you're in an unusually hazardous line of work. And we still didn't have the film. Claire was the brainwave of the man pointing his gun between your shoulder blades. Call it leverage. Told me you loved your daughter more than your life. And you know what? He was bang on the money. You standing there is the proof.' He shrugged again, 'Two birds with one stone.'

And I knew then with certainty what they intended to do with her.

'I take it the film is in the rucksack?'

I tossed it onto the table. Its contents clattered. 'Two films,' I said. 'Both shot in nineteen-twenty-seven, in a manner of speaking. I've given you the footage of the Jericho Ball.'

'Two for one,' Pete said 'Typically generous, Tom. And now I'm sure you'd like to be reunited with your little girl.'

I thought of the cluster of grey faces at that upper floor window. Wondered whether the rotten staircase would betray their phantom tread if they tried to come down. Wondered would my daughter soon be joining them up there. Felt a hard stab of steel against my spine as the gunman gave me my prompt to get moving.

Claire was bound to a chair in the cellar snooker room. She was wearing only her knickers and bra. She was only feet away from the green baize on which I'd seen Peter Morgan slaughtered. Blood is organic matter and that happened long before my birth. But the fabric was still stained by the manner of his death. The manacles screwed into the table's four corners, I had last seen binding the Welsh boy's hands and feet. They were rusted and dull looking but still looked substantial and strong.

The man Pete Davidson had called James dragged over another chair from a dim corner with a squeal of studded feet on stone. It was straight backed and made I thought from some heavy hardwood, maybe mahogany. He performed the work one-handed, with the gun still trained on me. Then he watched as Pete tied me to the chair with a length of nylon washing line.

I glanced at my daughter, but her face was impassive. She was not gagged. Neither was she blindfolded. I thought I saw a flash of anger as the bonds were tightened on my wrists, but she swiftly suppressed it and replaced it with her bland mask of indifference. I thought, she is going to die, bloodily, while I watch them kill her. She must know that, surely, by now?

They left us. And Claire spoke, quietly. 'Where have they gone?'

'To dress,' I said. 'They costume themselves for the ritual.' I was struggling, trying desperately to free myself. I had already broken the skin on my wrists. The nylon rope was slick with blood, but the knots were securely tied. There was no slack at all in them.

'Don't struggle, Daddy,' Claire said. 'You need all your energy. I would not be able to stop them without your strength. With you beside me, I can do certain things.'

'I have to get free,' I said. Despite myself, I was weeping.

'Don't cry, Daddy,' she said. 'Do you remember what I did with the typewriter? When Piano Man was coming?'

I nodded. I could hardly make her out in the gloom. My vision was blurred by tears.

'That was easy, so I could do it from a distance. This is much harder. I need you with me here.'

'To do what?'

'That made you tired,' she said. 'This will hurt you. Probably a lot. I am sorry for that, but it can't be helped. I mean, it just can't be done without it hurting.'

They came back into the room. They did so both wearing cloaks with runic symbols stitched upon the fabric. One white cloak and the other black. Velvet, with silver, jewel encrusted clasps at the throat. Tarnished silver, antique garments used I supposed by their predecessors in the past. They valued their traditions. Pete Davidson dragged in with him a fat candle in an engraved ceremonial holder, the whole weighty assemblage the same height he was.

The man I had known as James Balfour was now doubly armed. He had transferred the pistol to his left hand. In his right, he held a long dagger with an ornately scrolled blade. I groaned. I had seen it used before. They were both breathing heavily, now, like a pair of panting, predatory beasts. It was excitement, bloodlust. I made another effort to struggle free and felt the cord binding me scrape against the exposed bone of my wrist. Davidson struck a match and lit the candle wick with shaking fingers and a look of something close to rapture on his face. There was a bloom of sulphurous scent. The flame took and steadied.

'We have an audience, Daddy,' Claire said. I looked up. They were arraigned against the far wall. The brickwork was dankly visible through them, but they seemed to be gaining in solidity. I smelled cigar smoke and brilliantine and some antique cologne. I recognised Fischer and Harry Spalding. The grinning, gloating visage of Edward Swarbrick. All three of them in their immaculately tailored prime. There was a look of anticipatory glee gaining focus on Spalding's faded, phantom face. His eyes blued as his features clarified and his body gathered substance and a remembered, sinewy strength.

'Forgive me, Daddy, for what's about to happen,' my daughter said. I felt myself descending into numbness and thought the need to preserve sanity might be lulling me into a state of shock.

Pete Davidson approached Claire and began to untie the bonds securing her to the chair. She kicked out at his crotch and he backhanded her across the face with a blow as sharp sounding as a rifle shot.

She gasped and said, 'You'll pay for that,'

He just laughed at her. Then he gathered phlegm with a cough and spat it into her face.

Her limbs freed, he picked her up and dumped her with a dull thump onto the stained baize of the snooker table and manacled her with what looked like skilled, practised hands. The work was swiftly accomplished. I had never really noticed quite how powerfully built Pete was. All that heavy metal he lifted in his daily gym sessions. I noticed it now.

Claire strained against the chains. 'Soon, Daddy,' she said. Then her body seemed to become limp and her breathing suddenly the deep, swoony sound of someone dreaming.

The man I had known as Balfour stooped with his mouth close to my ear. He said, 'Familiar with the expression, pistol-whipped, Tom?'

I did not respond. He clubbed me twice, heavy, deliberate blows to the back of the head that ground against the bone of my skull and caused me briefly to see a black universe lit by anaemic stars. But I did not lose consciousness or even really have to fight to retain it. I was damned into alertness by what they were doing to Claire.

I could smell something pungent and sweetish. Davidson had an incense burner and was swinging it over the snooker table and muttering some incantation as smoke from the burner billowed palely above where my daughter was chained. Behind me, I heard Balfour put the gun on the floor. Then he emerged from behind me and strode over to the table and with the dagger between both hands, joined in with Davidson's recitation, spreading his feet, raising the dagger, standing with it poised and ready high above his head, the blade long and baleful, gleaming through scented smoke.

'Bravo,' said a voice. I looked at the three phantoms solid, now, corporeal, fully formed against the far wall. It was Swarbrick who had spoken. Each of the trio was clapping, smiling. An erection he did nothing to conceal, bulged in Spalding's groin.

The descent of the blade was sudden and swift and aimed at my daughter's chest, intended to cleave her heart. And arrested with a jolt and a gasp from Balfour and a juddering of physical shock in his arms an inch above her precious flesh.

And something exploded in my head and my ears popped and began to trickle blood and my nose to gush with it from my bowed head through my seated legs to the floor where it puddled, darkly crimson.

Balfour seemed to be in the grip of some kind of physical struggle to bring the dagger further down from the point at which it was poised. It shook in his fists. His upper limbs wracked convulsively. I could hear the teeth grind in his clenched jaw and heard an audible crack as one of them broke. He gasped, perhaps in pain from the exposed nerve of his broken tooth.

'Get on with it, chaps,' said a droll, Bostonian drawl from their audience. Spalding. It was Harry Spalding, who said that.

I was in some pain of my own. Assaulting, reeling pain. I was nauseous and felt as though a large icicle was being hammered into my head. But I did not want that to stop. It was the consequence of what Claire was willing. And I would die in willing agony if that was what it would take to save her.

They were not done. Pete Davidson put down the incense burner and plucked the dagger from his companion's sweating grasp. He wheeled to face Claire wielding it, high in a double grip. He brought it down in a swift, savage arc and this time she seemed able only to deflect rather than arrest the blow. The end of the blade veered at the last point of its trajectory and punctured her upper arm. It went right through. I heard the tip thump against the slate beneath the baize of the table before she gasped and screamed. Davidson worked the blade free of her flesh and raised it again. Blood dripped from it. There were approving murmurs from his dead spectators. He stood there with it poised, a tableau of impending butchery and triumph. Claire emitted a single sob.

Davidson did not move, though. He did not strike with the fatal follow-up blow. He seemed almost to freeze, or petrify, suddenly like a living statue. His eyes stared straight ahead, instead of at their living, breathing subject prostrated on the table. And he looked like he was trying to contort his face into movement somehow denied him.

Beside him, Balfour straightened, almost like someone coming to attention. There was a conflicted expression on his face, as though some deep, internal debate tormented him. He strode over to where he had placed the gun on the floor and picked it up and pointed it at me.

'Better,' said an approving voice from the far wall. 'She has no power, if you only deal with the source.' Wheezy, clogged with nicotine. Heavily accented. Klaus Fischer's voice.

'A bullet through the eye should do the trick,' Spalding.

A snigger from Swarbrick. 'Put an end to the meddler. Then finish the girl.'

Balfour pulled the trigger, but the gun jerked in his grip and I felt the bullet only graze my scalp. It was nothing to the pain I was enduring elsewhere in my body. A scratch, but Fischer was right. With me dead they could perform their sacrifice unhindered. He aimed at me again. Something juddered inside me, like some vital organ wrenched free of its rightful biological berth, and I vomited sourly into the blood congealing between my feet. I raised my eyes to Balfour, swallowing bile. I glanced at Davidson, still standing there, statue-like. Then back to the lethal implement pointed between my eyes.

I noticed that the gun had begun to tremble in Balfour's grip. His facial skin had taken on a tight, queasy translucence. His eyes had a preoccupied look. His mouth flirted with a twitchy smile that looked more troubled than amused. He turned the wrist inward of the hand holding the gun. He seemed to be examining it, like someone looking at an object for the first time, with a bemused curiosity that struck me as almost childlike. As though holding more a toy than a deadly weapon. He emitted a single, self-pitying bark, his chest heaving. He grinned at nothing. Then he raised the barrel of the gun to his right temple and he pulled the trigger, the pistol report a brief, loud boom in the cellar's gloomy confinement.

I reeled in pain, or would have done, unbound. A red-hot poker seared my gut and I breathed only through the vice in which my chest felt tightly secured.

Over by the snooker table, Pete Davidson dropped the dagger with a clang to the floor.

'Bother,' Swarbrick said.

'Game might be up, chaps,' Spalding said.

Claire said, 'Free me.'

'No,' Pete Davidson said.

'Free me.'

With an agility I had never known him possess, he dipped and recovered the dagger and slashed at her with it one handed, steel raking her thigh and opening a wide, deep wound. She bled blackly and he raised the dagger again. Maybe his grip was uncertain with sweat. Perhaps it was her interfering mind, but the third blow she endured only glanced against her right side.

She gasped. Then, 'Cut yourself,' she said. 'Do it.'

He was breathing shrilly now. His features formed an expression I had never seen him wear before that I recognised as fear. And perhaps also apprehension. He reversed the dagger in his grip and paused and then ran the length of its blade along his own cheek opening it up from just below his ear to the corner of his mouth. The weapon clattered once more to the floor.

'Free me.'

Davidson's voice broke with a heaving, self-pitying lurch. He rocked on his heels. His ruined face bled 'Will the pain stop if I do?'

'If you do not, I'll make it worse. Much worse.'

He reached for his pocket and I assumed, the key to the manacles. But his right fist emerged wrapped in a brass knuckle duster and he pulled it back to deliver the punch to her skull that would cave it in and kill my daughter. I had taught Claire to box from the age of four and she knew how to avoid a blow and she slipped the punch, which crashed against baize covered slate, only an inch from her face. He gripped her jaw in his free hand before winding up to deliver a second blow. Then he yelped and shook the weapon free and cradled his right hand in his left.

'You burned me,' he said. 'How did you do that?'

'I only burned your hand. Free me.'

I looked at the discarded knuckle duster, still glowing on the ground with heat.

Claire climbed off the table freed and kicked away the dagger. Pete Davidson's legs seemed to betray his weight, then, he fell heavily to the floor and sat gasping on his backside. The jagged edges of the icicle flayed my brain as it was hammered further into my skull with pounding mallet blows. And my spine felt welded into a barbed column of white-hot bone. I knew I was very close to blacking out.

A pool of gore had leaked out of Balfour's head where the bullet had entered it. His body was prone and still on the flagstones.

'Untie me, Claire.'

'No, Daddy. Not yet.'

'Untie me.'

'No. If I do that now, you'll kill the man sitting on the floor. And then you will go to prison. And I won't even be able to visit you because I'm too young. I'd have to wait two years which is too long and anyway, I don't want you in a prison cell. I know what that's like.'

Through my own pain, I studied Pete Davidson. A part of me couldn't understand why he wasn't fighting back, scrambling his dead companion's gun off the floor. He had a slumped, defeated posture. He looked pathetic, costumed in his now rumpled cloak. Blood and brain matter from his dead companion soiled its hem. His right cheek was a mutilation that would never properly heal. I thought my daughter's will the force confining him there. I looked up and saw that our audience had deserted the venue. Not the performance, after all, they had summoned themselves to enjoy.

Claire turned her head to face the candle and blinked once and its flame went out. I saw that there wasn't even the hint of a wound where the dagger had skewered her arm. Her wounded thigh was unblemished. There was no trace of a nick on her side. She had evidently healed herself. All of this was a revelation. None of it really a surprise.

Davidson climbed to his feet. He did so slowly, clumsily, invisibly weighted. He stood there like someone for whom balancing on two legs was a new skill still not yet properly mastered. He uttered one wheedling word, which was, 'Please.'

'No,' Claire said, curtly.

I winced from an unseen blow and heard and felt the clean snap of my left collarbone as Pete Davidson first unfastened the cloak he had on and then as it fell to the floor behind him, shambled out of the room.

'No more pain, Daddy. I'm really sorry for it all,' my daughter said. And a moment later she began to untie me, and I knew that the bleeding from my nose and ears had stopped.

'How long have you known you could do this stuff?'

'I think I've always known. It was always the problem, I think. I was never reconciled. I punished myself for having gifts I did not want. It's easier to live with, now I'm quite grown up.'

'It unbalanced you.'

'It would unbalance anyone,' she said. 'Knowing things. Not knowing where the borders should be. Nobody wants to think they're a witch.'

Borders. What her psychiatrist would call boundaries. 'Doctor Pettifer knows,' I said. 'What I mean is, when I showed her the note you somehow typed with your mind, she didn't seem all that surprised.'

'I won't do any of it again, Daddy. It costs too much. I mean, look at you, you're in a state.'

My breathing was easing. The burning poker had been plucked from my innards. But I had a headache like the worst hangover ever self-inflicted and my broken collarbone was a deep, dull throb and would need to be reset at a hospital.

'Where did you send him?'

'For a walk,' she said, brightly. 'He is going to walk through the forest and cross the road at the other side of it and then carry on all the way to the shore. He's going to walk into the sea.'

I nodded. Two straightforward suicides. I could hardly be implicated by them in those. But I would retrieve my films before leaving the Fischer House. One of the two was my insurance policy.

'What did they do to you?'

'Nothing much. Dry bread to eat, water to drink, not enough of either. Tied up down here. Untied now and then for a walk around the hall upstairs when I complained to one of them about pins and needles. Not them being nice, just worried I might die accidentally from a blood clot.

'Lots of boring questions again I didn't know the answers to about you. I told them you were retiring and the posh one laughed and said retirement is not an option in your line of work. They treated me okay. But they were going to kill me. They were always going to kill me. I could tell that from the expressions on their faces. When you look at someone intent on murdering you, something dies in their eyes.'

'You didn't explore their minds?'

Claire pulled a face. 'Like I would paddle through a sewer,' she said.

I nodded at the body on the floor. 'Did he try to touch you again?'

She shook her head. She said, 'He was a nasty man. Now he's just an icky mess. We should get out of this place. It's full of ghosts. I don't think they can hurt us. But they are not nice to be around.'

I was free. I hugged my daughter with the arm I could still raise, and she wrapped both of her arms around me and squeezed hard, without any hint of hesitation or reluctance.

The blood from my nose had splashed between my legs to pool around my feet, where it was still congealing. What had tricked from my ears would not show, really, against the black cotton fabric of the sweater I had on. Some had crusted on either side of my neck, but I could scrape those trails away with my fingernails. We retrieved Claire's clothes from the pile they had been left in and she put them on.

We walked through the night forest. It wasn't yet ten o'clock in the evening. I would drive back to the hotel and cajole them into opening the kitchen. There might even still be time, I thought, to order Claire something to eat at the Spyglass Inn. If she could stomach food after what she had just witnessed. And what she had accomplished.

'Are you able to forget things?'

'I'm able to put things away,' she said, 'out of sight.' She nodded back the way we had come. 'Like all the stuff that went on in there.'

'All of it?'

'Everything.'

'Good.'

She stopped walking, abruptly.

'Will it stop me coming home?'

'No,' I said. 'You are home, darling, as of now. You're not going back to the Retreat. You're never going back. Not even to pick up your things. We'll have them posted on to us.'

'Do you think I could stay sometimes with mum?'

'I think that would make her happier than anything.'

I fed my daughter in the Spyglass, where she wolfed down a huge plate of macaroni cheese. While she ate, I spoke on the phone outside, first to her mother and then to Daisy Chain. I was light on detail, saying only that Claire was safe and well and with me. I thought about locking her into my room and letting her sleep while I drove to A&E in Newport. But I couldn't countenance leaving her on her own and dozed uncomfortably on a sofa while she slept in the bed until morning and daylight. Then the hospital. Then the ferry with my collarbone reset and the ache of it dulled by prescription painkillers.

It stopped seeming real after that until seeing Pete Davidson's obituary in The Guardian. Three solid columns of media accomplishments, mostly in broadcast. There was some doubt about whether his death had been accidental. His boat had been moored in the harbour at Cowes. On the facing page, the tributes from his many industry friends were fulsome. He had been after all, as he had said himself, a clubbable man. Perhaps they had tried to contact me, but I was spared the requirement to say a few hypocritical words. By then I had changed my phone number and had a new email address for the clean break from that world I so desired and quickly realised had long needed.

There was vague reference in the reports I read to a mutilation that wasn't specifically identified. I still assume the cheek sliced open from the edge of his mouth to his ear. And one further odd detail; his stomach contained two pounds of small shingle pebbles he could only have swallowed himself. The opposite of ballast, a detail probably not lost on a yachting man in the final, irrevocable moments of his mortal life. Did my daughter compel that parting, stony snack? I don't know and care even less, frankly.

It was Daisy, ever alert, who sourced the story a few weeks later about the Freshwater man whose body was found badly decomposed at a derelict mansion by workmen repairing the security fence around it. The stench noticeable through a broken ground-floor window led them to it. They thought they would find a dead animal. Instead, they discovered a corpse. The coroner said it was a straightforward case of suicide. The victim was a single man of 28 named Jimmy Barrett who I thought had chosen an alias close to his own name simply to avoid any blundering.

He had worked since his late teens as a fairground hypnotist and magician. He was said to have been a skilled illusionist. Good at sleight of hand. He had criminal convictions though for fraud and burglary with artifice; which meant he'd been a conman too. He had been quite good at that. He had fooled me. He had fooled Julia Pettifer, who was probably a shrewder judge. The expensive wristwatch and designer threads and smartly appointed business address had been nothing more than convincing props, paid for I assumed by Pete Davidson. Though Barrett had not really fooled Claire. Or not for long.

I did wonder whether Davidson had been right in telling Claire that retirement wasn't an option in my particular line of work. The more I thought about it, the more I thought fate had shaped my path from being a frightened 11-year-old in reluctant possession of a murderer's top hat, to a mature media figure investigating an alleged haunting at a building once owned by Al Capone.

There had been guidance, hadn't there, along the way? From Joey Delancey, a long-dead journalist with an unlikely taste for the soft rock of America's West Coast. From Tony Causley, concierge of an apartment block he would flee when the hours of darkness approached. From Al Hodge, once head bar steward at a grand hotel which could never successfully shake its ghoulish reputation. From Jack Dooley, Samantha's father, a pub landlord party to at least one grim secret. From Helena Donovan, whose fragile-seeming beauty masked enormous inner strength. From poor Phillipe Suarez, a tortured soul I never got to meet.

A long and convoluted journey, eventful and sometimes bumpy, I had needed all their helping hands in making. But I now felt myself to be at the end of it. And despite being familiar with the hoary cliché concerning old dogs and new tricks, I thought that conviction finally worth putting to a personal test.

Epilogue

I duly wrote my novel. It was a ghost story, of course. I felt I had been researching the subject all my working life. Even before my working life began. Back when I was Bamber, or Bookworm, or Clever Clogs. Some of that material seemed to lend itself quite fittingly to fiction. The book sold well enough, and the film rights were optioned. It wasn't a bad beginning, and I enjoyed the challenge more of using my imagination than I did searching for proof of the paranormal in hazardous places in life. I thought the process might revive traumatic memories, but actually found it to be therapeutic. I felt my phantoms did succeed in rising from the page. But in doing so, they didn't gate crash their way into my day-to-day existence.

Claire divided her time equally between her mother and father's homes until it was time for her to go to university. It was helpful that she took immediately both to Daisy Chain and to Richard Purcell, the Mr Right who became Samantha's husband two years ago. Richard, no mean draughtsman himself, encouraged her drawing and was instrumental in getting her the first exhibition she staged, in Kingston. By then, Claire had extended her range well beyond charcoal sketches.

She dotes on the baby half-brother she now has. And her academic work is brilliant. But then her chosen field of study is Psychology. Not surprising, given the insights she has into other peoples' minds. Claire is in every other regard a typical 18-year-old, something I never thought I would be able to say. She loves drama, cinema and reading fiction. Daisy coached her at tennis before she left for college and she is good enough to play on the university team. I think she is happy. Though she is not and never will be a naïve person about anything. Not with her life experience. She was denied innocence, my daughter, from the moment she became cognitive. I believe that was what provoked the problems she has successfully put behind her.

She has a boyfriend. He seems nice, courteous, steady and straightforward. He's also a good-looking lad. Though I'm sure he has not the remotest notion of what it is he has taken on. Then again, I'm not sure about how serious they are. Not the kind of thing a father asks.

My brother sprung a surprise on everyone when he announced he was getting married. I had always thought Andy a bachelor of the crusty variety unsuited to concepts such as sharing and compromise, intimacy and trust. I knew he was serious, though, when he said he had hung up his climbing boots and put the microlight and hang-glider up for sale on Ebay. Even the scuba diving gear was surrendered.

His choice of bride was an even bigger surprise, until I thought about it. He married the widow of Phillipe Suarez. They became close after he told her about what her husband had endured at the Dolomites orphanage. If his devotion to his niece is any measure, he will make a lovely stepfather to those two young boys. And he asked me to be best man at their wedding, an invitation I was honoured to accept. And so I met Marianne, a wonderful woman who seemed to liberate in him all of the good in my brother he had managed to keep hidden from the world. Claire was bridesmaid. Marianne was someone else she quickly and fiercely became fond of.

The reverberations from the Sacred Heart Orphanage and Chicago series rumbled on as the worldwide audience grew and speculation continued about whether what we had shot and recorded was genuine or just cleverly faked. Attempts were made to demolish the former building using explosives. But after the fourth firm of contractors pulled out of the job, the Italian authorities conceded defeat and it remains, an occasional attraction for those with a morbid interest in such places. An interest I do not mind admitting I feel ambivalent at best about having done so much to encourage.

Daisy is very much the dedicated mum. She made the decision to stop researching and donate herself a healthy chunk of maternity leave, until an interesting development occurred. The East Sussex D.I. heading the hunt for my missing daughter had seen the orphanage series. He called me about three months ago. How he got my changed number, I do not know. I suppose the police have their ways. He wanted to know, were the series revelations all the work of the woman to whom I was now married? I told him truthfully that they were.

He had been headhunted by this point. And promoted. He had been transferred to the Met and was calling from New Scotland Yard. As a courtesy, he told me. Because he wanted to speak to Daisy about a career opportunity.

She talked to him for an hour over coffee at a Costa branch and presumably, prior to that, they must have checked her out. She has been asked to work for them in a civilian capacity. Civilian but investigative, on missing persons cases. Specifically, missing children. And she is going to do it. Maybe doing it will help her get over what happened to the lost children from the Dolomites orphanage. I know she still dreams about them.

Samantha too seems both contented and more fulfilled. There's Claire, obviously. But her Mr Right is a practitioner as well as a theorist. Richard doesn't just lecture on architecture. He takes on those select commissions that interest him. He asked her to attempt some decorative work to embellish his designs. Friezes, reliefs, murals, sometimes sculptural projects. She is doing it and the results have so far earned her a positive reaction both from Richard's clients and the public. Some creatives thrive on collaboration and she has discovered herself to be one of those.

Is a part of me still in love with my former wife? Probably. I won't deceive myself on that score. But I think her father was right when he said in the Old Ship in Southport all those years ago, that I met his daughter too young. We're friends now, which we weren't before. It's something. And it means something significant I know to Claire. I still smile, recalling the way she ordered us off in Hove to reach some kind of settlement together.

I have thought a lot about the timing of what Pete Davidson attempted to do. I think I first came up on the radar of the cult to which he belonged at the age of 16, taking the interest I did in the plot of land upon which the house belonging to the child killer Edward Swarbrick had stood. And I think that the person who warned them about my curiosity was the Kelmscott Court concierge, Tony Causley. He did not wish to be there after darkness fell. He did not want to be confronted by the ghost of

Arabella Pankhurst. He had left his teaching job under a cloud, the consequence of some hushed-up scandal that suggested he was a man of dubious character.

He had described that battle going on between the forces of good and evil over the years in the very road in which he worked when I met him. He had not told me which side of that conflict he was on. And during that curious conversation at my ice-cream kiosk a couple of years after our first encounter, he had named Arabella and mentioned her age in a remark I never understood. I mean, I never understood its truer significance. Though I do now. As terrible as it is to say, I think he was bragging.

They wanted to know what I had found out about them all those years ago. They wanted to know too, how I had found it out. Their obsession with secrecy motivated them. They thought they could get their answers from Claire because Pete Davidson knew enough about me to know that my daughter was the person in my life to whom I had become closest.

I don't think Claire's abduction was part of their original plan. That had been only to pump my daughter for the information they wanted about me and how much I knew about them.

I could be wrong about that. Peter Morgan's sacrifice in 1927 gained potency in their eyes because of his intellect and potential. The man calling himself Balfour at the time could have become aware that my daughter was singularly gifted in a way that made her sacrifice potentially significant. But I honestly think that had they been aware of Claire's talent for havoc, they would not have provoked it in the cruel and callous way they did. They would have steered clear of my daughter altogether. I think the power of her mind to effect events came as a complete and completely unwelcome surprise to them.

Ironically, Pete Davidson was instrumental in bringing matters to what he considered a crisis point. The series based on the Dolomites orphanage had cemented my reputation at home. The Chicago brothel series had made my name in America. Was I going to follow all that with something anticlimactic, shot on the cheap on the Scottish coast or in the depths of rural Ireland? Or was I going to shock the world with something cruelly sensational. Pete thought he knew the answer to that question at least, and it panicked him into action.

Just a theory.

I have been left alone since those two men met their unexpected deaths. The film is back in its Hatton Garden strongbox. Maybe it protects me and maybe I only delude myself into thinking it does, but I would rather have it there than not. I did not know the identity of their sacrificial when I filmed his death, but I later learned it. And murder seems an even graver crime when its victim ceases to be anonymous. The passage of time makes it no less shocking, something the Orphanage of the Sacred Heart taught me in Italy.

Last year, a one-time rival of mine investigated the alleged County Clare haunting. It was a thorough probe into the legend that discovered no singing phantoms or even mysterious lights burning at night. What it did unearth was corpses, twelve of them, well-preserved by the peat they had been buried under. All shot in the back of the head, execution style, by what a ballistics expert identified as a large calibre British Army service revolver. A Webley manufactured during the Great War. An item maybe pried itself in that war's Irish aftermath from the dead fingers of a Black and Tan.

Ten of the victims were identified and re-interred in solemn ceremony. Daisy, having sensed their presence on our own visit, had said they were only at rest. Now, I hoped they were finally at peace.

Recently, over the Christmas break from university, I was the beneficiary of a precious hour alone with Claire. Those used to be frequent. They are rarer, now she is completely well and so popular a person. Someone compensating for the solitary life she was forced for so long to lead. On a whim, I asked her, what was the best advice she had ever received?

'You gave it to me, Daddy,' she said.

'Really?'

'Absolutely. You were the one who told me that sometimes, the monsters are real.'

I am not unaware of what some of you will think of as the elephant in the room. My daughter was responsible for the deaths of two people, deliberately inflicted, so by any definition, murders. Except that had she spared either, they would only have returned better equipped for the task to which they were by then grimly committed. Which was to put an end to both of us. Mine, pragmatic. Hers a ritual sacrifice. What she did to them, or compelled them to do, was no more really than self-defence. She was a 16-year-old seeing the world with the black and white certainty of someone immature but in possession of enormous power summoned and used only in desperate extremity.

Claire had never flaunted her abilities. She had saved me and my companions from that blighted Riverdale building. And she subsequently ended the lives of a pair of determined killers. Was she even given a choice? I know my own answer to that question, with which I have made my peace. You are fully entitled to make up your own minds. Your objectivity being a luxury I will never possess.

My daughter has the capacity to put such matters behind her. I can witness that, from the serenity that now characterises her. A happy knack I do not personally share. But I can live with myself and continue to love her. And to cherish Daisy. And get on with whatever is left of the rest of my life without enduring the torment of looking back too often.

Printed in Great Britain
by Amazon